TWEEN FICTION R

NEVERLORE

NEVERLORE

H. S. Ramsby

First Page Publications

First Page Publications
12103 Merriman Road
Livonia, MI 48150
Phone: 1-800-343-3043
Fax: 734-525-4420
www.firstpagepublications.com

Printed in the United States of America

Ramsby, Henry, 1951–
Summary: Fast-paced fantasy/self-empowerment adventure about a wheelchair-bound twelve-year-old boy who accidentally stumbles into a magical land.

ISBN # 1-928623-64-6
I. Ramsby, Henry. II. Title
Library of Congress Control Number: 2005905720

To my son Tyler, who has helped me realize all the joys of fatherhood.

To my wife Lonna and daughter Hannah, for tolerating the time away from them while writing *Neverlore*.

To all my close friends, who have offered me encouragement through this journey, and to Alex for his invaluable juvenile insight.

To Sarah, for her patience and for holding her tongue during my quirky moods, and for helping me bring it all together.

To my mother, may she rest in peace.

And to Jackie V., for bringing *Neverlore* to life.

The Past . . .

Preface

Today, the boy ventured higher in the tree than he'd ever been before. Up here the sun felt warmer, the sky seemed bluer, and off in the distance he could see the town water tower shimmering in the haze. A slight breeze was blowing and the leaves rustled, calling to him, coaxing him on.

Ever since he had been old enough to walk he had been climbing on things—the back of the sofa, the dining room chairs, his father's work-bench in the garage ("Get down from there boy. There're tools up there that will bite you!" And then his dad would laugh and haul him back down to safety).

But the biggest tree in the backyard was his favorite challenge. It was a huge oak with many large climbing branches that spread out over a good portion of the yard. It was a magnificent tree—it provided cool shade in the summer and plenty of acorns for sling-shot ammo in the fall. The boy spent a good part of his time clambering around among its branches. "Don't go too high! And be careful!" his mom always said. But in her voice, he heard how proud she was of him.

Now, with warm sun on his shoulders and the breeze at his back, he loosened his grip on the trunk and slid slowly out on the limb, pretending he was in the circus on a tight-rope, high above center ring. The branch swayed slightly. "Whoa, easy does it," he said to himself softly, dipping to maintain his balance. His father had taught him to keep his balance in fishing boats by looking at a distant point on the horizon. The boy did this now, concentrating. It worked. He spread his arms out like the wings of a plane and inched forward, placing one foot carefully in front of the other. The branch tilted under his weight.

"I'm doing it! I'm a tight-rope walker!" he cried gleefully, and imagined the crowd below, cheering him on. He smiled at the thought and stepped smartly forward. At that moment, he was master of his universe.

Then, something happened. Maybe it was an extra puff of breeze that drew his attention. Maybe it was an unexpected rustle, or a glint of sun flashing off a car windshield many blocks away. Out of the corner of his eye, the boy glanced down. The ground was farther away than he'd imagined. His stomach knotted. *Maybe this is far enough,* he thought. He wanted to remain calm, confident. *I'm going to go backward. I'm going to be okay.* But even as he thought this, and his hand reached behind him searching for the safety of the trunk, the horizon seemed to wobble.

His back foot slipped and inside, his heart went cold because he knew he had made a mistake. All around him was open air, nothing to hold. It happened so fast he didn't have time to scream. He had a brief sensation of weightlessness. Then the ground rushed up at him like a speeding train.

The Present . . .

Chapter 1

In a small town called Norwood, at the edge of Whispering Valley, lived a boy named Jamie Nichols. Jamie, who was almost thirteen, was an inquisitive boy with a quick smile and an even quicker imagination. He had brown eyes, and his brown hair had just enough curl in it to make him crazy when he tried to comb it. He was neither tall nor short for his age, and was slender and wiry. Jamie favored T-shirts, tennis shoes, and cargo pants. He liked having extra pockets to carry unique stones, oddly shaped pieces of wood, or any other treasure an inquisitive boy might be drawn to.

Jamie liked building model airplanes, listening to music, and mastering his e-Cubix video game. He enjoyed watching action videos and movies about the exploits of mythical heroes. Jamie also loved the outdoors and had subscribed to several wilderness adventure magazines. He'd eagerly watch the mailbox, and when each one came, Jamie would read it from cover to cover. His mother appreciated and encouraged this, as Jamie quickly became bored if he didn't have something to occupy his time with.

Jamie's mother, whose name was Carolyn, was a pretty woman with the same brown eyes and curly brown hair as her son. She had an easy smile, but it often showed a hint of worry, especially when it involved Jamie. She had good reason to be concerned, though, for in a single moment a few years prior, an event had occurred that had changed her son's life forever.

At the age of seven, Jamie had fallen out of a tree in his backyard. The accident had left him paralyzed from the waist down, and since that time, he had been confined to a wheelchair. The abrupt change in his life was profound and overwhelming. It had taken Jamie quite a while to adjust and cope with his disability. A long time passed before he had attempted to venture outside his house, and even so, anything he did was usually under his mother's watchful and worried eye.

Time passed, and Jamie began to realize he couldn't stay inside forever and hide from his disability. He reluctantly accepted the fact that living in a wheelchair was what life had come to for him. He learned new ways to do the things he liked to do, and in spite of not being able to walk, he became fairly mobile. This new experience of getting around was often frustrating, but he managed to persevere in spite of the challenges presented to him.

Jamie started reading adventure books, and, in his daydreams, he often became the main character of these novels. At times he'd push his wheelchair around his yard and imagine he was a fighter-jet pilot, or a racecar driver, or the engineer of a fast freight train. At other times, he'd pretend he was a great explorer or a brave warrior. As he got older and his desire for adventure grew, Jamie ventured further away from the safety of his backyard and his mother's or brother's help.

Jamie's brother was named Andrew, and was almost two years older. He was tall, blond, and lanky, and the star of their school soccer team. Andrew was good-looking and had discovered girls.

Actually, as their father liked to brag, they had discovered him. ("Family trait, son, no keeping them away!" his father would laugh. He was proud of Andrew.) Andrew and Jamie had been close friends when they were younger. But after the accident, other things became more important to Andrew than playing with his brother. Andrew tried not to show it, but Jamie's wheelchair had become a bother and slowed him down. As time passed, he began spending less of it with Jamie and more with his other friends.

Jamie did very well in school and excelled in math and language arts. He was an honor student and was well liked by his teachers. His classmates, however, mostly ignored him because they resented the fact that a boy with a handicap was smarter than they were. Because of his wheelchair, Jamie had to sit at the back of the classroom by himself. This made it even harder to interact with his fellow students.

Since his accident, Jamie had been forced to give up soccer with his brother and volleyball with his (former) friends. He still liked girls, but any he was interested in were more interested in the *cool* guys. He had a friend named Hannah and she pushed him around school sometimes. But Jamie had the feeling she did it more out of pity than anything else. Jamie had tried to have several conversations with his dad about girls, but his father never seemed to have the time.

Jamie's father owned a successful consulting business and traveled a lot. He and his staff flew all over the country and sometimes abroad, giving seminars on "economic trends in emerging third-world nations," as he explained it. Jamie's dad was a busy man and was away from home for weeks at a time. Jamie sometimes felt like his disability might have something to do with it. He had tried to talk to his mother about it on many occasions, but she was always distant and evasive about the situation. Jamie had finally quit asking her when his father would be home because it only seemed to upset her more.

Other than his mother and Hannah, Jamie didn't have many friends. Most of the time he felt his disability prevented him from meeting any new ones and subsequently, he spent most of his time alone. Jamie became good at entertaining himself, a vivid and colorful imagination his closest companion.

Jamie lived near the end of a long, winding street on the side of town closest to Whispering Valley. His house had a paved drive, a nice lawn, and a fenced-in backyard with plenty of shade trees. Because he liked being outdoors as much as possible, Jamie kept a well-equipped backpack under the seat of his wheelchair. It contained a flashlight, hatchet, rope, and a pair of binoculars. To be safe, in case (hopefully) he became stranded somewhere away from his house, Jamie had also included a canteen, matches, and a mess kit he still had from his time in the scouts. And for extra measure, he had put in his slingshot and a water gun. Jamie was ready for any adventure an almost-thirteen-year-old boy could dream up. He would camp out in his backyard, explore the large field at the end of his block, or visit his neighbor's house up the street. Jamie never stayed in one place long enough to become bored. He knew that if he got bored, he'd start dwelling on his physical limitations, and that always felt horrible.

His neighbor's house was the only other house on Jamie's street. It belonged to an old widow named M. Emily Duncan. She lived alone with an orange tabby cat named Helix. Jamie enjoyed the widow's company and visited her often. He'd asked her what the M. stood for but she'd only given him a quick smile and replied that she couldn't remember. He'd often call her M. and

Em, and they'd both laugh at his joke. The widow Duncan was full of secrets that inflamed Jamie's imagination.

During spring and summer, she spent most of her time working in the flower garden in her front yard. The brightly colored roses and flowering crabs always smelled so good that Jamie would sometimes sit for several moments, his eyes closed, breathing in their fresh fragrance. The widow Duncan wore large, colorful hats, long summer dresses, and always smelled of patchouli. The feature that always captivated Jamie the most was her piercing blue eyes. She had a wizened look that made Jamie think that she must be Mother Nature herself. He felt quite at ease when he visited Mrs. Duncan, and would often confide in her his hopes, fears, and dreams.

The widow Duncan was also full of wonderful stories, and often she told him about her childhood. She maintained that, as a young girl, she worked with her uncle on a boat on the treacherous Dursey River. She would tell Jamie about searching for treasure on sunken ships, or climbing mountains near the coast, or exploring castle ruins. The widow Duncan also told Jamie stories about a legendary land called Neverlore.

"Neverlore," she'd say, "is a place of imagination and mystery. Legend has it that strange and wonderful creatures live there. Animals talk, trees walk, and magical goings-on occur. Trolls, sorcerers, dragons, and shape-shifters are said to inhabit the land." She'd point at the distant horizon to the north. "Legend has it that Neverlore exists somewhere at the furthermost reaches of Whispering Valley."

When she told her stories, the widow Duncan would sit on the swinging lawn chair under her flowering crab. She'd gently sway back and forth, and a faraway look would pass over her face as she spoke of the mystical land. Her stories seemed so real that sometimes Jamie would put his chin in his hands and daydream he was there. The legend would equally intrigue and frighten him at the same time.

It was one of those days when Jamie felt especially lonely. It was late morning and he decided to pay a visit to the widow. Her stories always seemed to cheer him up when he was feeling blue. Jamie said goodbye to his mother, wheeled down the front ramp, and set off down the sidewalk. As he neared her house, he saw her working in her garden as usual.

"Hi, Mrs. Duncan," he waved cheerily. Already he could feel his spirits begin to rise. The widow waved back.

"Hi Jamie," she called. She waved him into her yard. "It's hot out and I was just about to take a break. Come and have a nice cold drink with me."

"Thanks, don't mind if I do," he said happily, as he wheeled up the walk. Jamie joined her in the shade of her crab tree and accepted a glass of lemonade. The glass felt cool and wet in his hand and the ice tinkled merrily as he took a long drink. "Mmmm, this is good," he proclaimed. "Better'n what you get at the store."

The widow Duncan snorted good naturedly. "It'd better be. I just squeezed the lemons an hour ago. Only way to make *real* lemonade. So, what brings you out today, my boy?"

"Oh, I'm just bored, I guess," Jamie replied. *And I need some cheering up too,* he thought. They traded pleasantries and made small talk for a while before Jamie got around to the real reason for his visit.

"I don't suppose I could get you to tell me some more about the 'legend,' could I, Mrs. Duncan?" he asked tentatively. "I mean, how does one visit Neverlore?" No matter how many other stories she told, he always ended up asking her to tell him about the mysterious land.

The widow laughed merrily and replied, "Somehow, I didn't think you came over just to make small talk." She set her glass down. "I'll be happy to tell you more about the land. But you must remember, Jamie, Neverlore really is only a legend that exists in the imagination of a good storyteller."

"I don't care if it's only imaginary," he lamented. "I love your stories! They make me feel . . . well . . . happy."

The widow Duncan looked into Jamie's eyes and saw the sadness they contained. She felt a quick pang of sympathy and obliged by continuing her ongoing tale about the mystical place.

"I've been told that if a person is good, and has a sincere wish for change, and happens to be in the right place at the right time, he or she could enter Neverlore," she explained.

"Really? How cool!" Jamie exclaimed. "Sometimes it's so boring in this chair I want to scream. Neverlore sounds like a real adventure!"

"Yes, but it might not be as *cool* as you think," the widow continued. "You see, sometimes wishes, no matter how sincere, don't turn out as we plan. And remember, Neverlore exists only in the imagination."

"I know, you've said that many times already. But what do you mean, wishes don't turn out?" Jamie asked.

The widow Duncan went on. "Because sometimes, when you yearn for something badly enough, you can forget or lose touch with what is genuine. There's the chance that you could end up with something entirely different than what you originally wished for."

"I don't care, I'd still take my chances," Jamie said. "I sometimes think I'm to blame for all the problems my family has. This stupid wheelchair is just a bother to everyone, including me. If only I could walk again, everything would be better."

Jamie surprised himself with this admission. He'd been carrying these thoughts around for some time now, and it felt strange to finally put them into words. "If I wished hard enough, maybe *I* could go to Neverlore. What could be any worse than this?" Jamie asked, staring forlornly down at his useless legs.

"Is it really that bad?" the widow Duncan asked. "A man who has no arms or legs couldn't do any of the things you're able to do in your wheelchair. If given the choice, living in a wheelchair would certainly be most preferable to him."

Jamie thought for another moment. "I suppose. But if that's supposed to make me feel better, it doesn't," he said touchily. "Nobody understands. They all say they do, but they really don't." Jamie was beginning to think that even the widow didn't realize how frustrating his wheelchair was for him.

"How do you know so much about this Neverlore anyway?" he asked. "It sounds like you've been there. But how could you? You said Neverlore is just a story."

"Of course it's only a story," the widow Duncan replied, a strange glint in her blue eyes. "In all my years, I've experienced so many things that even I have a hard time remembering what's real and what's not." She laughed lightly. "Neverlore only exists in my imagination, as it only should in yours."

She bent over and whispered confidingly, "You and I have the same problem, Jamie. We're both blessed and cursed with the same quest for adventure. It's risky for either one of us to think of Neverlore too much. We must both be content with our thoughts and nothing more."

She let out a long sigh and abruptly changed the subject. "It's time for me to get back to work," she said. With surprising grace, the widow stood up from her lawn chair and straightened her apron. She took a pair of clippers from the pocket and busied herself pruning the roses.

"One more story, please," Jamie pleaded. "It's too early to go home, and my imagination's just getting going."

"We've had enough imagination for one day. Some stories are best left for other times," she said. "My flowers need pruning and watering. They're all starting to wilt."

"Your flowers are doing fine. They look beautiful," Jamie replied. "Just one more story? How about one from when you were a little girl."

"I think we need to give storytime a rest for a few days," the widow Duncan said with a mischievous smile. "Remember, too much sugar can spoil the cake. Now run along so I can get some work done."

"Okay, okay, I get the hint. I know when I'm not wanted anymore. I'll go find something else to do," Jamie said with mock anger. He backed his wheelchair out of the garden.

"Now, you know that's not true. You are welcome here anytime," the widow replied kindly.

"I know. I was only kidding. See you later," Jamie said. He wheeled back to the sidewalk, turned, and pushed his way toward home. Sarah, a girl from up the street, waved at Jamie as she rode by on her bicycle. He half-heartedly waved back. It only reminded him more of his disability. His blue mood returned.

"Even though they're good, they're really only stories," he muttered as he pushed himself along. "That's silly—I mean, how can someone *wish* themselves into another land?" Jamie wheeled back to his house, up the drive, and around to his backyard. He sat with his chin in his hands once more, and stared out over the Whispering Valley.

"I don't care what Mrs. Duncan says. I *still* wish I wasn't paralyzed," he said to no one in particular. "I know if I could walk, things would be a lot better. I could play soccer, or ride my bike again, or go on a real adventure. I wouldn't have to wish for some dumb thing that only exists in my imagination."

While Jamie pondered these thoughts, his mother called him for lunch. With one last glance over his shoulder, he turned and pushed himself back to the house.

* * *

School had been out for a week now, and Jamie was once again playing by himself in the vacant lot down the street. Andrew was at soccer camp, his mother was in bed with one of her migraine headaches, and his father was out of town, as usual. However, the day itself was promising. It was sunny and warm, and summer was close at hand. A strong breeze blew up from some distant place in the south. Giant, white, puffy clouds whisked across the sky as if pushed by some huge invisible hand. It was a glorious day, one that was ripe for fun and adventure.

Jamie was up to the task and was trying out a new hobby. He'd recently discovered he could fly a kite fairly easily from his wheelchair. After saving up his allowance for a month, he'd bought a new one. He had chosen the most intriguing kite, one that looked like it would be the most challenging to fly. This one was shaped like a bird with bright blue feathers, a long green tail, and a green crest on top of its head. It measured more than four feet from wing tip to wing tip.

Because of the strong breeze, Jamie decided to try out a new method of kiting. Without his brother's permission (sibling rivalry and all), Jamie borrowed one of Andrew's fishing poles and tied the kite to the line. He sat in his wheelchair, reeled out fishing line, and watched the kite climb toward the clouds.

Jamie pretended he was fishing in the ocean and had just hooked a giant flying fish. The higher the kite climbed, the harder it pulled. The harder the kite pulled, the more Jamie had to tug on the pole to keep it under control. The kite was definitely living up to the challenge. It seemed to Jamie like it was almost trying to free itself. Soon, the force was too much for him to manage easily. Jamie tried to reel the line in, but found it almost impossible to do. The force dragged his wheelchair around the yard and he struggled to stay upright. It became more and more difficult to hang on to the pole and the wheels of his chair at the same time.

"Back off," he yelled up at his kite. "If you keep this up, you're going to pull me right out of my chair." Suddenly, the kite did a giant loop and gave a tremendous jerk on the pole. Snap! The line broke and the kite sailed off. The pole flew back and hit Jamie in the nose so hard his eyes watered and he saw stars.

"Yeouch!" he cried, dropping the pole. He rubbed his nose tenderly and looked up at the kite. It sailed round and round for quite some time, then slowly drifted down from the sky west of the lot. His kite finally came to rest in the trees at the nearest edge of Whispering Valley.

"I don't believe it!" Jamie fumed. "I've only been flying you for ten minutes, and just like that, you're gone! Stupid kite! There goes a whole month's allowance, wasted. I should have bought baseball cards or comics or something else instead of you," he sneered in the direction of the kite.

Jamie sat and stared sullenly at the distant trees. Then he had an idea. *Maybe there's enough line hanging down for me to reach, and I can pull my kite out of the trees.* Reaching under his seat, he pulled the binoculars from his backpack and trained them on the spot where it had gone down. Jamie focused on the tree where it had landed and found the kite entangled in the branches toward the top. Sure enough, just as he had hoped, he caught a glint of fishing line in the sun. It trailed out over the limbs and down toward the ground.

Jamie refocused the binoculars and studied the field between where he sat and the edge of the forest. There was a fence with a gate at the back of the lot and a path that led to the forest from the gate. The lane was long and winding, but it looked to Jamie like he could make it by himself.

"Well, it's worth a try," he said. With that, Jamie wheeled across the lot to the gate. He pulled it open and wheeled through. Once on the other side, he paused for a moment and glanced over his left shoulder at his house. It now looked far away, and Jamie suddenly realized he had never ventured this far from home without his mom or brother. He sat there a moment longer, uncertain if he should go on. For some reason, the story the widow Duncan had told of a close call with a mountain lion on one of her backpacking trips came to mind. As Jamie stared out over the vast forest, a shiver ran down his spine.

Should I or shouldn't I? he thought. He knew his mother would be mad at him if he went alone. She became upset at the littlest things sometimes. But his sense of adventure nagged at him. *I'm brave enough and big enough now to do this*, he thought reassuringly. Jamie weighed the consequences of going down the lane. His mom or his kite . . . his mom or his kite.

Finally Jamie made up his mind. If he wanted the kite back, he was going to have to do it himself. No one else was going to get it back for him. Jamie grabbed the wheels and started pushing his wheelchair down the path.

"I know I can do this," he said to himself. "I don't care what anyone thinks. Wheelchair or no wheelchair, I'm not a little kid anymore."

He hadn't gone thirty feet when a strong gust blew the gate closed behind him with a loud *clang!* Jamie jumped, but didn't look back. Once his mind was made up, there was no turning around.

As he wheeled down the rutted path, he surveyed his surroundings. On either side of the path, the grass rippled in the wind as if swaying to unheard music. Ahead, in the trees, shadows danced amongst stirring branches, and somewhere deep in the forest a raven called, its raspy croak echoing through the valley.

Jamie gritted his teeth and pushed harder. He thought of all the times he'd been left behind because his wheelchair was a bother or he couldn't keep up. If nothing else, he was going to prove to himself that he could make it.

Getting down the lane was harder than Jamie had first thought. He had to wheel around a lot of rocks and push through ruts and loose gravel. When he finally reached the woods, his arms were tired and he was sweating. At the edge of the forest he paused to rest. Looking up into the trees, he located his kite farther ahead. The tail was wrapped around a branch of a tall beech tree, and its wings flapped in the breeze, as if it were trying to free itself and fly away.

Jamie took a deep breath and pushed into the forest. Years of fallen leaves had made the ground smooth and fairly easy to wheel across. Rays of sunlight filtered through the branches and made warm, sunny spots amongst the cool shadows. As Jamie pushed across the forest's floor, he had a sudden premonition that something was different about his surroundings. The hair on his head stood up slightly, as if charged by some unknown force. He glanced around and, unable to pinpoint the cause of his concern, shrugged it off and pushed on.

The beech tree wasn't located very deep in the forest, and in a few moments Jamie reached a small clearing where the tree stood. After circling the edge of the clearing, he stopped to size up the tree and catch his breath. The trunk was huge! Upon further examination, Jamie estimated it was more than twice as wide as he could stretch his arms. The bark was wrinkled, weathered, and gray, and it looked as if it were a thousand years old. There was an old burnt lightning scar in the trunk that started near the top and curled around to the other side of the tree. He wondered if the crack went all the way to the ground at the back of the massive trunk. Jamie felt a twinge of excitement. This was not an ordinary tree, he could feel it.

As he studied the scar, he noticed the fishing line out of the corner of his eye. It dangled down from the branches at the edge of the tree. "Ha! I knew I could do this myself," he exclaimed loudly. Normally, Jamie didn't talk to himself that much, but there was something reassuring about the sound of his own voice.

Except for his voice and the wind rustling through the branches, the forest was very quiet.

Jamie pushed his wheelchair over and grabbed the end of the line. "Okay, kite, come down from there!" he cried, giving the fishing line a good tug. Nothing happened. The kite didn't move.

Frustrated, he wheeled around to where he could get a better angle on the line. "Kite, don't let me have made this trip for nothing," he said, giving the line a harder jerk. It moved a little, but still didn't break free. "That's it! You get one more chance. If you don't come down out of this tree right now, you can stay there for good!" he said in exasperation. Jamie wrapped the line around both hands and gave a mighty tug. When he did, the branch suddenly snapped and down came the kite. *Whoosh!* It swooped by so fast Jamie barely had time to move. It sailed past his head, wings flapping wildly. "Geez!" he cried, ducking. "Kite, you are crazy!"

Jamie watched the kite settle on the other side of the beech tree. It lay on its side, one blank eye staring back into Jamie's, one wing rippling in the breeze. The movement made the kite almost seem alive. Jamie blinked and averted his gaze from it. At the same time, he felt a chill go up his spine. "This forest is weird," he whispered and started maneuvering toward his kite. "If I didn't know better, kite, I'd say you have a mind of your own," he said as he picked it up and laid it in his lap.

Jamie wrapped the line around its beak, and for good measure, he did a couple of wraps around the wings also. "Just in case you feel like flying some more." When he was done, he pushed himself around toward the back of the tree, curious to inspect the lightning scar from that side.

"Wow!" he exclaimed. Not only did the scar reach all the way to the ground, but it had split a wide fissure in the trunk. From this vantage point, the tree appeared to be hollow. With the kite secure on his lap, Jamie inspected the route between himself and the crack. Large roots radiated across the ground in several directions from the bottom of the tree. Each one stuck up out of the leaves like the back of a sea serpent arching up out of water. Jamie cautiously wheeled around several "serpents" and over to the crack. He peered cautiously inside.

It was dim and musty inside and smelled like an old leather shoe or some long-forgotten duffel bag. Jamie stretched forward and looked around inside the trunk. It was indeed hollow, and the insides of the great tree arched high above his head. About fifteen feet or so up, a ray of light shone through a hole and splashed a bright circle on the opposite side of the trunk's interior.

"Hello, hellooooo," Jamie called inside, his voice more nervous than he'd expected. His voice was muffled by the soft rot of the inside of the trunk. Jamie reached down into his backpack and pulled out his mini-mag flashlight. He snapped it on and shined it into the tree trunk, playing the light around. The wood was burned, blackened, and gnarly, as if it had been ravaged by some great fire. The ground was covered with black sawdust and wood chips from the many critters that had chewed at the trunk somewhere further up inside the old tree. Jamie looked up and shivered involuntarily, his imagination beginning to get the better of him. Was anything living up in the darkness, just out of the beam of his flashlight? Was some monster going to drop down out of the gloom and swallow him up? He quickly glanced down and aimed his light around the deep recesses of a hollow at the other side of the tree. It was then that he noticed something extremely peculiar.

"Whoa, what's up with this?" he asked incredulously. Jamie stared at what appeared to be a small, arch-topped door in the scarred wood at the back of the tree.

"What's this? A door?" he exclaimed. "Trees don't *have* doors! Trees are *made into* doors!" Jamie rubbed his eyes and looked in again. Sure enough, there definitely appeared to be a small door in the back of the trunk. And it had a doorknob on the right side, about two feet up from the ground. "Well, if there's a doorknob, then I guess there *must* be a door," he said uncertainly.

"But how can this be?" He leaned back and studied the outside of the beech tree. Except for the lightning scar and its tremendous size, it looked like any other tree in the forest. Jamie looked back into the crack. He was still looking at a door. "This is *way* too crazy!" he said. The uneasy feeling he'd felt earlier came back again, only much stronger now.

As if drawn by some unseen magnet, Jamie moved closer and examined the crack. In spite of the strange feeling he had, his curiosity drew him on. He realized that if he wiggled back and forth a little, he was able to slide his wheelchair into the opening. He grabbed the edges on either side of the crack and slowly pulled himself forward. In spite of its rough looks, the wood was smooth and worn. The bark felt warm to the touch.

"I've got to check this out," Jamie said. "This *is* bizarre." With some trepidation and a couple of good grunts, Jamie pulled his wheelchair through the opening.

Once inside, he shined his light all around to make sure he was alone. An odd sensation of being watched still dogged him, but curiosity prevailed in the end. Satisfied there was nothing lurking anywhere in the shadows, Jamie cautiously wheeled over to the door.

"No one will ever believe me," he said to the kite, still staring up at Jamie from his lap. "I k*now* there was no door on the outside of this tree. Am I having some kind of strange dream?" He reached out uneasily, grabbed the doorknob, and slowly turned it.

It too was warm to his touch.

Click. The lock released. He wheeled back a little, pulled the door toward him, and peered carefully around the edge. Jamie gasped in astonishment. "I don't believe it!" he cried. "This is *very* bizarre!"

Jamie opened the door the rest of the way to get a better look. His jaw dropped, and he found himself gazing at a remarkable scene. He was staring into what looked like another world! Jamie closed his eyes tightly and rubbed them again. When he opened them, the unbelievable sight was still there. "This can't be happening! There's got to be an explanation for all this," he said, wheeling forward to the edge of the door. The harder he thought about it though, the harder it was for him to come up with a plausible answer.

Jamie wheeled into the doorway and balanced his wheelchair on the threshold. He gawked in wonder. A narrow path led down and away from the doorway. After about thirty or forty feet, the path turned to the left. It disappeared through thick alders that grew alongside a clear green pool. To the right, a small stream bubbled merrily through a flowered meadow, over a waterfall, and into the pool. Jamie shaded his eyes against the bright sunlight and looked further. A great forest continued for a long way from the other side of the stream. Off in the distance, Jamie saw a majestic mountain range stretching up into a robin-egg-blue sky.

"*Awesome!*" he cried. In the jumble of confused thoughts that followed, a few of the widow Duncan's tales crossed Jamie's mind. But even her best story was nothing compared to this. As Jamie sat there, undecided as to what to do, a sudden gust of wind blew in through the tree trunk behind him. It caught the door and slammed it into the back of his wheelchair. The sudden jolt knocked his chair the rest of the way over the threshold and onto the path. With the kite still in his lap, Jamie suddenly found himself speeding down the path toward the pool.

"Whoa-aaaah!" he cried, trying to slow his descent. It was no use. He was rolling too fast to stop. Suddenly, the right wheel hit a rock, and Jamie and the kite were airborne. End over end went Jamie, the wheelchair, and his kite. After two or three rolls, both Jamie and his kite flew out of the chair. Jamie ended up on his back in the middle of the path. The kite landed farther down in the grass. Dazed, Jamie stared blankly back up the path. As his eyes focused, he saw his wheelchair lying on its side, one wheel still spinning crazily. Beyond that, he could see the tree and the outline of the door in its trunk.

Slowly, Jamie sat up, wondering if he had broken anything. Aside from being dusty and disheveled, fortunately he wasn't hurt. Just a few scrapes and bumps and a throbbing elbow. *Wow, that was lucky!* he thought. *I could have broken my neck!* He leaned back on the palms of his hands and looked around. He saw the sky above, heard the waterfall behind, and tasted the dirt in his mouth. But the path he had wheeled into the forest on was no longer there. In its place was a grassy mound surrounded by brush and rocks. It was like the path had never existed at all.

What just happened? Where am I? Jamie thought anxiously. The thought of being thrust from the safety of his neighborhood into some unknown place gave him an awful fright. His heart quickened. Jamie had always wished for an adventure, but this was not what he'd expected. (He wasn't sure *what* he'd ever expected.)

"Where am I?" he asked tentatively. "How can there be a place that you get to through a tree? How is it that mountains appear out of nowhere? This can't be real! This has to . . . wait a minute, did I knock myself out or something?"

"Nope, I don't think so," a raspy voice suddenly said.

Jamie jumped at the sound. "Wh-who said that?" he asked, looking around in bewilderment. There was no one else in sight. The voice seemed to be coming from his kite, which lay in a heap in the grass. He studied it more closely now. The fishing line was still tangled around its body, but had come unraveled from its beak. Somehow, though, the kite looked different. It looked rounder, bigger, more colorful. Did he see the kite just move?

"*I did*, silly!" the voice said again. Jamie stared. The voice *was* coming from his kite! "Don't just sit there, dummy, help me out of this mess!" The kite rolled around, trying to free itself.

"You *talk?*" Jamie gasped. "This can't be happening. Since when do kites talk?" Jamie was still disorientated and extremely apprehensive. An alarming thought came to mind. Maybe he had fallen through some kind of time warp. He remembered reading about them at school. Some scientists believed the Earth traveled through space on one of many parallel time waves and one could get to a different time by crossing over celestial channels.

"Wow! Maybe I accidentally changed cosmic channels and that explains what's happening here." He laughed nervously. "Or maybe I'm having some kind of weird, out-of-body dream!" *But that doesn't explain why my kite could talk*, he pondered.

No, that can't be right either, Jamie thought rapidly. *I must have hit my head and am now in some kind of coma.* "Oh, that's just great," he said aloud. "First I'm paralyzed and now I'm brain damaged. What next?"

Somehow that rationalization didn't work either. It all felt a lot more real than any dream he'd ever had, and since he could still talk, he knew he wasn't in a coma. The dust in his hair, the gurgling stream, and the voice from his kite seemed all too real.

The kite spoke again. "If you'd get me loose instead of whining so much, I could bite you to prove you're not dreaming." He snapped his sharp beak to prove his point.

Jamie rubbed his elbow. The pain was indeed real. He eyed his wheelchair up the path and the door beyond. "Dream or no dream, I can't get to you without my wheels. And besides, you're way too rude. You need to get better manners if you want anyone to help you." Jamie still couldn't believe he was actually talking to his kite. He started dragging himself back to his wheelchair. "This all started with that stupid kite and the door in the tree," he muttered to himself. "If I can get back through the door, this will all go away . . . maybe . . . hopefully."

The kite replied in a more kindly voice, "I'm sorry for snapping at you. That *was* rude of me. It's just that all my life I've longed to be free, to fly like a real bird. Only I've been trapped in a plastic body, destined to be hooked to a line all the time. Look at me now. I'm finally alive in some strange and wonderful place, but I'm *still* trapped by this line. I'm the one who should really be complaining."

Jamie stopped dragging himself along. "Strange and wonderful place? Th . . . that's what Mrs. Duncan always says about Neverlore. Could it really be—" The kite interrupted him. "I don't know what you're talking about, but—*sshhhh!*" The kite interrupted itself. "Did you hear that?"

"Hear what?" Jamie asked. "I don't hear anything."

The kite whispered, "*Sshhhh!* Keep your voice down! There it is again!"

Jamie strained to hear. Suddenly he heard a splashing sound that was definitely different from the gurgling waterfall. Something was coming rapidly up the stream.

Splish-sploosh-splash. The noise was getting louder. *Splash, splash.* A deep and gruff voice called out, "I've got you now, my slippery, slimy little friends. You won't get away from ole Barly *this* time."

That sounds too big and deep to be human, Jamie thought fearfully. He looked around anxiously for a place to hide. His wheelchair was too far away and the door in the tree was even farther. The only thing close by was a boulder on the side of the path. He dragged himself toward it as quickly as possible, glancing back at the kite. It had rolled into some taller grass and peeped out from between the blades. The boulder was barely big enough to conceal him, and Jamie had just gotten behind it when a loud *kersplash* came from just down the stream. He peered around the edge.

"*Aarrggh!* Where'd you go now?" the deep voice boomed. Suddenly, fiery red eyes, a flash of green, and something like scaly wings flew out from behind the alders. Jamie caught sight of some bizarre-looking fish sailing through the air. Whatever they were, they landed in the pool and continued on. Right behind them, a second or two later, lunged a huge bear!

The bear hesitated, swinging his head left to right, then dove into the pool after them with a splash. *Kersploosh!* Water rained down everywhere. A few drops landed on Jamie's head. He swallowed hard and ducked, holding his breath. Then, except for the noise of the waterfall, all was quiet. A few brief seconds passed, and Jamie's curiosity got the better of him. Exhaling slowly, he cautiously peered out from behind the rock again.

Suddenly, the bear began floundering around underwater and the bizarre-looking fish exploded out of the further side of the pool. They flew over the waterfall and quickly disappeared upstream. Jamie shook his head in bewilderment.

"A talking kite, a talking bear, and winged monster fish? This is *not* happening!" he said under his breath. He glanced up at the door again, calculating the distance. *I've got to get out of here! I've got to get away from this craziness!* his mind screamed. But his limbs wouldn't respond and he remained frozen where he lay.

The bear came to the surface and stood up, blowing out a mouthful of water.

"Drats, missed again! Now, what's ole Barly going to do for lunch?" He stood there in the pool and scratched one ear, deep in thought. The huge bruin waded to the edge, hopped out, and waddled over to a nearby stump. He sat down with a wet plop. As he stared forlornly into the pool, a puddle of water began to form on the ground all around him. While the bear was facing away from him, Jamie propped himself up to get a better look. In spite of the apparent danger, he had to suppress an urge to laugh.

Barly was a strange sight to behold. He was half black and half white. His sides, back, and legs were black, while his belly, paws, and ears were white. His tail was black with a little fluff of white on the end. Dripping all over the ground, he looked to Jamie like a big sack of wet laundry. Before Jamie could stop it, a giggle escaped.

At the sound, Barly turned and looked up the hill. "Whoa, what do we have here? Laughing rocks?" He stood up and started toward them. "Let's have Barly take a look-see."

Jamie ducked down behind the boulder. He bit his lip to keep from crying out.

What had he done now? He'd never even seen, let alone been this close to, a bear before! And now he'd given his hiding spot away. Jamie looked around frantically for a way to escape. *Maybe if I could reach my chair in time, I could wheel back up the hill to safety,* he thought. But his chair was at least twenty feet away. *I'll never make it in time! I'm trapped! Why did I ever go after that dumb kite in the first place?*

Barly, meanwhile, stopped when he saw the kite. "Huh? What's this?" he asked. "Now, isn't this peculiar? A pretty bird all wrapped up for ole Barly." He picked up the kite and held it at eye level. "I wonder where you came from. You weren't here yesterday."

"Keep your paws off me, you soggy bearskin rug!" the kite screamed. With that, he bit Barly squarely on the end of his nose.

"Eyooww!" the bear cried. He threw the kite down and grabbed his nose. "Ow, ow, oowww!"

At the sound of the bear's frightful howl, Jamie's heart leapt into his throat, he yelled, and he sprang to his feet! Jamie, who hadn't walked since he was seven, turned and sprinted up the path toward his wheelchair! The commotion startled Barly so that he snorted loudly, turned, and darted the other way.

In his haste, he tripped over the kite and went rolling down the path. *Kersplash!* Back into the pool he went, head first, his behind and tail sticking up out of the water.

"You clumsy oaf, watch where you're going!" the kite yammered, flapping around in the dirt.

Jamie reached his wheelchair, flipped it upright, and quickly sat down. It was then that he realized what had just happened.

"Oh my gosh, I . . . I just walked!" he cried, completely befuddled. "No, I just *ran*! Did you see me, kite? I ran! How can that be? I'm par—I mean, I'm supposed to be paralyzed. I can't walk or run or do anything with my legs. What's going on? *What is going on?*"

The kite flapped and rolled around even more madly. The fishing line had become entangled around its beak again. It mumbled, "Mmmpphhh . . . mmmpphhh," its eyes wide open in fright.

At the same time, Barly righted himself and stood up. He knocked water out of one ear and glared up at both of them.

"That's a fine way to greet a person, sneaking up and scaring the wits out of him. You both ought to be ashamed of yourselves!" he yelled out. "Who are you and what are you doing around my pool?"

By now, Jamie had seen and heard enough. He held up his hands and shouted, "STOP! Stop it right now! I can't take it anymore! A little while ago, I was flying my kite near my house, and now we are both here, wherever *that* is. I have absolutely no idea what has happened. Have I gone crazy? My kite is a now bird or something and I've got a talking bear in front of me. Can someone tell me what's going on *here*?" He pointed both thumbs to the ground for emphasis.

The big bruin stared at Jamie for a moment, his mood softened, and he chuckled. "Whoa, boy, slow down! Don't go and get yourself all riled up. It's obvious you're not from around here." Barly waded over to the edge of the pool and climbed out. "Tell me what happened and I may be able to explain it to you."

Jamie eyed the bear warily. "Whoa! Don't come any closer," he ordered, holding out his hand. He still couldn't believe he was talking to a real bear.

The big bear put his paws up in front of him and replied, "It's okay, son. I know I look gruff on the outside, but that's all it is, just looks. I won't hurt you, I promise. If you tell me where you came from, maybe I can help you to understand." The big bear's easy manner calmed Jamie down somewhat.

"O . . . okay, then," Jamie said. "But please, just stay where you are, at least for the moment. I don't have a clue as to what just happened. I just fell through that tree behind me and ended up . . .

well, I'm not sure *where* I ended up."

"I'll stay right here until you feel safe enough," the bear continued. "I'm not going to attack and eat you, if that's what you're worried about. Shucks, where I come from, your kind doesn't even taste good to us."

"That's a comfort, I guess," Jamie said. He looked around warily. Satisfied the immediate peril had passed, he said, "Well, I'm definitely not at the end of my street anymore, or anywhere even close, from the looks of things."

"Where *do* you come from?" the bear queried.

"I live in a town called Norwood. It's . . . in a land called America which . . . is . . . part of a planet called Earth," Jamie began. "Wow, it sounds weird to talk about home like that." He briefly told about flying the kite from his wheelchair, his solo trip down the lane to rescue it from the woods, and the magical tree. "I don't believe I just confided in a complete stranger, and a talking bear no less," he finished. "Hey, what's your name, anyway?"

"My, my, where are my manners?" the bear answered. "Allow me to introduce myself. My name is Thaddeus Barly. I can't stand Thaddeus, so you can just call me plain ole Barly. And by the way, you're a complete stranger to me also, if you think about it. You could be some deranged bearskin hunter for all I know."

"I hardly think so." Jamie laughed. The bear's friendly manner helped ease his concern even more.

The bear named Barly wiped the water out of his eyes and pointed at the wheelchair Jamie still occupied. "Back where you come from, you have to be in that to get around?"

"I'm afraid so," Jamie replied. "At least, I had to before I got here. Now I'm not so sure." Jamie gingerly pushed himself up from his chair and took a few tentative steps. He was somewhat wobbly, but to his complete surprise, he found he was indeed able to get around without his wheelchair. "I *can* walk!" he cried. "This is unbelievable! My dreams have come true." Jamie was delirious with joy. He tested his new legs, alternating between striding, hopping, and shuffling up and down the path. "Look at me, I'm doing it! I'm walking! I'm no longer paralyzed!"

Barly laughed. "From your actions, and the sound of your story, it's as I suspected. Just like *I* did many seasons ago, you and your kite have stumbled through a portal into the land of Neverlore. Apparently you got here like a lot of folks. Quite by accident, quite by purpose."

"No *way!*" Jamie cried in amazement. "For real? I know about Neverlore—it's a favorite story of mine. But it's a legend, only a story, something you imagine. The widow Duncan told me about Neverlore, but I never knew whether to really believe her or not. How can it be that we're here?"

Barly ambled over to a nearby log and sat down. "Because I'm here, that's why," he answered.

Jamie examined himself, still standing. By now, his state of mind was somewhere between euphoria and total confusion. But, once again, Jamie's inquisitive nature took over. He waved his hand at his new surroundings. "Could you please tell me about all this, before I lose my mind, Mr. Barly?"

"Barly, call me Barly," the bear reminded him.

"Okay, Barly it is. Tell me the things about Neverlore the widow Duncan never would," Jamie said matter-of-factly. He put his hands on his hips and cocked his head. "Tell me I'm not going crazy."

Barly smiled. The big bear looked less scary when he did this. "I'd be happy to, but first, what's your name, lad? And who's this Mrs. Duncan person you keep referring to?"

"My name's Jamie. Jamie Nichols," Jamie answered. "And Mrs. Duncan is one of the few friends I've got back home. She tells me bits and pieces about Neverlore, but I can never get the whole story from her. She always acts so . . . so . . . secretive about the whole thing."

"Well, Jamie Nichols." Barly chuckled again. "I don't know if I can tell you the whole story, but I'll be happy to tell you a little of what I've learned so far." He picked up a leaf, blew his nose loudly, and continued. "It seems this land exists somewhere at the far end of a place called Whispering Valley. I don't completely understand it, but if you happen to pass through one of these doors, or portals, somehow you end up here, in Neverlore."

"It's just as I've been told," Jamie said. *There's no way*, he thought. But when he looked down, Jamie saw that he could indeed move his legs and feet. Part of him was beginning to believe the big bear.

"Believe it," Barly went on, as if reading Jamie's mind. "At first I didn't either, but things kept happening that proved I had ended up somewhere very different from my own home, Adelwilde. The inhabitants were different. The plant life had changed. Animals were peculiar and yet wonderful."

By now, the kite had shaken the fishing line off its beak for good. "This is a really nice story, but it still doesn't get me untangled," it said. "I don't suppose either of you could stop talking long enough to help me, could you?"

Barly walked over to the kite. "You, my impatient friend, should learn some manners," he said, picking it up. With a quick flick of his wrist, he threw the kite into the air and unraveled it like a big yo-yo. Free of the fishing line at last, the kite flew wobbly up to the nearest tree. It perched on a limb and glared down at

Barly. Giving a loud "humph!" it said no more and proceeded to straighten its feathers.

Jamie laughed at the sight. "This kite has been acting like it's got a mind of its own all morning. And now it can fly all by itself! I have the feeling this is the start of something very unusual."

Barly turned back to Jamie and went on. "I agree, it's almost not plausible. So far, however, everything's been so real I've begun to accept it. And since I've managed to keep a full belly most of the time, I'm happy." He shook the rest of the water from his coat and sat back down on the log. "It looks like you both *did* get here like me and a lot of others. I'll tell you the rest of what I know if you care to listen."

"Okay, but go slow. I've always dreamed of something like this, but like I said, this is all still pretty hard to swallow," Jamie replied. "Remember, just a little while ago I was flying a kite in my own world." He crossed his legs and eyed the bear. Barly really did look like a big teddy bear instead of some savage beast. And Jamie's curiosity and adventurous nature were beginning to get charged.

"That's fine. I know what you mean," the big bear said. He scratched his left ear and proceeded to tell Jamie his story.

Chapter 2

So far, I've learned Neverlore is a place where people and beings just . . . well, just . . . mysteriously arrive," Barly began. "It seems that if one is at the right place at the right time, he or she can pass through one of those doors and end up here." He waved a paw vaguely in the direction of the tree through which Jamie had passed and went on. "Apparently, certain things, like a special wish or a dream, somehow become real in Neverlore. Your kite became a genuine bird, you can walk again, and we can talk to each other. There's a kind of magic on this side of the doors that accounts for it all. It sounds far-fetched, I know, but it's what I've gathered so far."

Jamie whistled. "This *is* the same story the widow Duncan told me, but she has always insisted it's just legend. If it's really true, like you both say, I guess it does explain what happened. But where did you come from and how did you get here?" he asked.

"I come from a land on the other side of one of the portals called Adelwilde. My father was a polar bear and my mother was a black bear from the lowlands. Consequently, I was born looking like this. From the time I was little, my parents argued over me because I had both colors. I didn't fit in with the black bear cubs, and I didn't associate with the white bear cubs. I didn't have many friends, and therefore, not much fun as a youngster. It was pretty depressing."

"I know the feeling," Jamie agreed sadly. "I mean, I'm not a bear and I'm from a different planet than you, but my life is pretty similar. It looks like we have something in common." Something inside told Jamie he could trust the big bear.

"It would seem so," Barly continued. "Anyway, more than anything, I wanted to be accepted for who I was inside, not what I looked like outside. But no one did. Finally, when I got old enough, I ran away. One day, quite some time ago, I wandered into a cave in the mountains. I wasn't paying close enough attention to where I was walking and I fell through a crack in the rock. Before I could climb out, the crack sealed up and I ended up here, in Neverlore."

"But how did you find out where you were?" Jamie asked, edging a little closer to the big bear. He was still giddy from being able to walk and his curiosity was rapidly overcoming his fear.

"I didn't at first," Barly said. "You can imagine how scared I was. One minute I was minding my own business, and the next I'd disappeared from my world completely, just like you did. It was very distressing. I stayed near the rock, hoping it would open up, but it never did. After waiting several days and getting hungrier by the day, I left in search of food. Nuts, berries, and fish were plentiful, so that problem was soon resolved. I wandered around for some time, and although the land was beautiful, it was unfamiliar to me. It was then I began to accept the fact that I'd probably never see my homeland again. But in a way, it was good. Food was more plentiful and I didn't have to fight the other cubs to get it. The weather was nicer, so I didn't have to find a cave every time I wanted to sleep. And nobody made fun of me for my colors. I found myself beginning to like my new surroundings.

"One day while I was fishing, I met my first acquaintance, a lady named Joria. She had lived in Neverlore for some time, so she was able to tell me a little more about the land. Joria was a high witch, a priestess from a world called Yulionn. She had been evicted from her coven for casting good spells and helping people. One night, while flying on her broom board, she accidentally flew into a huge thunderstorm. A bolt of lightning knocked her out of the sky, and when she fell through the clouds, like you and me, she found herself here in Neverlore. Her story seemed to support most of what I'd been able to figure out already on my own." He furrowed his brow and scratched his head. "Even so, I guess I'd still like to get a few more answers."

By this time, Jamie was pretty sure he wasn't in any risk of dying. He took a few steps, ran down to the edge of the pool, then turned and skipped back up the path. "You don't know how long I've wished I could do that," he said with a big smile. While he was facing that direction, Jamie glanced at the tree trunk. It was then that he noticed the door had disappeared.

"Oh, no! Barly, look there! The door's gone, like your crack in the rock! Does that . . . does that mean there's no way out of here for me either?"

Barly glanced at the tree. "I don't know, it could very well be. But I don't think it matters. In the time I've been here, I've not heard of anyone leaving Neverlore. I know I don't want to leave anymore."

"What? Y-you mean I'm trapped? Stuck here in Neverlore?" Jamie asked anxiously.

"If that's how you choose to look at it," Barly answered. He held up his paws and shrugged his shoulders. "But why would you feel like you were trapped? And even if you could, why would you want to go back? You'd most likely be like you were before, unable to walk."

"I couldn't walk?" Jamie asked incredulously. He was even more confused, but after he thought about it for a moment, he said, "You're probably right, Barly. The magic of Neverlore is on *this* side of the tree. I *would* have to go back to living in my wheelchair again, wouldn't I?"

"I expect so," the big bear continued. "When you think about it, it's obvious there *is* some kind of magic here, otherwise how do you explain what's happened? I'm sure you being able to walk, and you and I and the kite being able to talk in the same language, only exists in Neverlore. I know whatever magic's occurred here definitely doesn't exist where I came from. That's why I quit looking for a way out and am still here. I don't want to leave and have to go back to my old life again."

Jamie's face brightened and he rubbed his chin in thought. "You know, you *are* right, Barly," he said presently, looking around him. "This might not be all that bad. I mean, look at the potential adventure I've just stumbled into. From where I stand," he laughed at his pun, "this land definitely needs some investigation."

Jamie did a little jig for emphasis. "I haven't been able to use these for a long, long time," he said, pointing down at his legs. "They need some exercise. You know, I don't think I want to leave after all. At least not before I've had the chance to explore some."

The kite, listening intently, now spoke up. "I can see what you mean. I know I never want to go back to being a kite. I always dreamed of life as a real bird, swooping and diving and flying about. Before, my wings were too stiff and I was always held by a kite string. I feel so free now." To prove his point, he spread his wings and flapped them around. "See what I mean? I'm alive now."

But Jamie was only half listening. He suddenly felt guilty for not wanting to get right back home, and suddenly wasn't sure what to think. To walk and to run had been his utmost dream for a long time. Now that his dream had come true, the possibility of being confined to his wheelchair again was indeed a dismal prospect. *Besides being a major pain for me, this wheelchair really is a bother to everyone else,* he tried to rationalize in his mind. *I probably would be better off staying here, like Barly says.*

Jamie thought of his mother and felt another pang of guilt. In spite of his handicap, he knew his family loved him, or at least his mom did. He also knew she would start to worry if he was out of her sight for very long. *Maybe she's already looking for me,* he thought. *And with Dad being gone most of the time, this won't help.* Jamie could imagine his mother looking all over for him. Jamie realized he hadn't really told her where he was going when he had set off to fly his kite.

"What am I going to do?" he asked, looking up at Barly, a frown on his face. "More than anything I want to be able to walk, but I can't disappear from home just like that. As it is, my mom's going to be upset that I've been gone for over an hour already." He pointed to his watch. "Especially since I didn't tell her where I was going."

Barly walked over and patted Jamie on the arm. Jamie didn't jump or even flinch. "It's not as bad as you think," Barly said. "First of all, time in Neverlore is . . . well . . . different from other places. Among other things, Joria shared with me the fact that time passes much slower in other worlds than it does here. Because of this difference, you could be away from your earth for several hours, maybe even days, before you were even missed."

"Really? No kidding? That's great—I suppose. But . . . but even so, how am I going to get back home?" Jamie asked. "There's no door, no way out. I can't just disappear for good. My mom will be worried sick. She'll think I'm dead or something. What am I supposed to do about that, Barly?"

"I don't know. Since it appears you can't go back the way you came in, I'm not sure what you should do." He scratched his head. "The only answer that comes to mind is Mistemere."

"What's a mistemere?" Jamie asked.

"Mistemere isn't an object, it's a place. It's also known as the Castle in the Clouds, below the snow line at the top of the mountains," Barly said. He pointed a paw at the distant peaks. "That's the Barrier Range, almost three days' journey to the west. Mistemere is near the top of the tallest mountain. Neverlore is supposedly ruled by a sorcerer who lives in the castle. He's called Araflore or Irindore or something like that. Even if you could get there, I don't know if he'd help you or not. I've never met this sorcerer and know nothing about him."

Jamie took a few steps back, then took a few forward. He had a confused look on his face. Jamie kicked a stone and sent it flying into the pool. "Oh great, now I have a wizard to deal with? This isn't exactly what I wished for," he said. "If I stay in Neverlore, I may never get to see my home or family again, but I'll be *able* to walk. That's good. If I manage to find a way home, I'll most likely end up like before, *not* being able to walk. That's not good. It's crazy! What kind of choices are those?"

"I don't know, Jamie, but that appears to be the way it is. Even if you *had* the option to choose, this is a decision only you can make," Barly said. He laid his paw on Jamie's shoulder. "Life isn't always fair, and the choices we have to make aren't always easy, I know." Jamie said nothing. He sat and pondered for a good long time, watching the ripples from his stone as they spread over the pool.

"Well, I suppose I should do *something*," Jamie said at last. "I don't want to pass up the ability to walk and I don't want to permanently leave my family either. So I'll do what's best for both. Since there's no door left here, I *obviously* have no choice but to explore more of Neverlore." Jamie didn't sound too disappointed. "Let's check things out, Barly. I may never get the chance for an adventure like this again. Let's go see if we can find that wizard! Maybe, when I decide to, he can help me get back home."

Jamie then wrinkled his nose. "Except I don't know anything about this land. I don't suppose you'd be willing show me around, would you, Barly?"

Barly mused. "Hmmm. Explore a little, you say? I don't know. This land can be both friendly and unfriendly at times."

"I suppose, but like you said, I don't have many choices. Anyway, with you along, no one would bother us. You're pretty big and look like you could be awfully scary if you needed to be," Jamie said.

Barly chuckled. "Oh, I don't know about *that*." He rubbed his chin, thinking it over. "I guess it wouldn't hurt to help you out, at least for a while. I don't have anything really pressing to do, except look for food. I suppose I could be your guide for a few days. Might find some new places to get a good meal."

Jamie flexed his legs. "Let's do it then. I'm willing to risk a little trouble at home for a few days of being able to walk here. And who knows? Maybe we *will* end up at the Castle in the Clouds and I'll have fun in the process. If this sorcerer can't help me and I'm stuck in Neverlore, at least I'll have tried. And that counts for something, doesn't it?"

"It does, indeed," Barly agreed. "I can't promise you it'll be all fun along the way," he added. "But you know, lad, we'll never know unless we try."

"I'll take my chances," Jamie replied. "What do I have to lose? My ability to walk? I've already had that happen, and as much as I hated it, it didn't kill me."

The kite, meantime, flew back down and landed on a rock. "What about me?" he asked. "I don't want to go back and become a kite again, but I don't want to hang around here either. Can I go with you, or at least part way?"

Barly laughed and said, "I see no reason why you can't go with us, kite. You can be our lookout. By the way, what's your name, anyway? We don't even know who you are."

"My name? You know, I don't believe I have one," the kite answered, looking puzzled.

"Then we'll have to give you a name. What would you like to be called?" Barly asked.

"Hmmm . . ." the kite said, scratching his head with one wing. "What would be a good name for me?"

"How about Kip?" Jamie suggested. "I had a pet parakeet when I was younger, and I called him Kip. He got out of his cage one day and flew away. I was sad because I never found him. You can take his place, since you're real now."

"Kip. Hmmm . . . Kip. I like it," the kite said after pondering the name for a moment. "I like it a lot. And since I have a name and I *am* a real bird now, will you please quit referring to me as *your kite?*"

"Okay, Kip the bird it is," Jamie said. "And a free bird at that. Now, what's the *longest* way to the mountains, Barly?" He hopped on one foot back to his wheelchair and took his backpack from under the seat. He slipped it on and tightened the straps.

Barly looked at him for a moment, then said, "You know, Jamie, I've never met anyone like you before. There's an enthusiasm about you that's catching. Danger or not, I think this adventure of ours is going to be fun, like you say."

"I know, Barly. I've wished for an adventure like this for a long time," Jamie said. "I have to try. If I don't, I'll never know if I could have succeeded. As you can see, there's no sense waiting around here. It could be a long time before this door opens up again."

"You're right about that. So we might as well get started right away," Barly replied, waving his paw toward the path alongside the river. "We have a lot of ground to cover yet today. We'll want to stay on the other side of the river tonight. Tomorrow or the next day we'll make our way to a place called Robinwood. From there, you can decide where you want to go exploring. South will take us to the plains and west to the mountains."

"Cool," Jamie said. "Finally I'll be able to do something on my own without someone telling me how to do it. Thanks, Barly."

"Think nothing of it," the bear answered. "If the castle is your choice, we'll travel west through the Forest of Whispers. Barring any unforeseen circumstances, we'll be at the mountains shortly afterward. From there, if we decide to split up, I can point you in the right direction to Mistemere."

That said, Barly stood up and headed down the path. "If you're all set, follow me," he called over his shoulder.

Jamie looked at his wheelchair. "Guess I won't be needing you anymore, or at least, not for some time," he said to the chair. He ran and caught up with the large bruin. Kip flew overhead in front of them.

"What's the Forest of Whiskers?" Jamie asked.

"Whispers, Forest of Whispers," Barly corrected him. "I've only been through there once or twice. It's an unusual place, just beyond Robinwood. I'll tell you about it along the way."

Jamie fell in step alongside Barly. He wondered if anyone would believe him back home. *If I ever get back home,* he thought. Part of him accepted what was happening, but part of him still couldn't. He thought of his mother, the widow Duncan, his house, and his general problems before. They now seemed surreal, like they were all on the other side of some high, impenetrable wall.

I don't have a clue what to expect from here on out, he thought. However, as Jamie glanced down at himself walking, the sight eased his concern. He made up his mind that the outcome was going to be worth the risk.

Chapter 3

The odd band made its way along the path beside the water. It was narrow and grass-covered in places. "This path connects to one of the few roadways through Neverlore," Barly offered. "To my knowledge, it's little used, as this area is sparsely populated. Most of the inhabitants of Neverlore seem to get around by other means. This is the farthest east I've ever traveled from Robinwood. I don't know who or what lurks over here and would feel a lot better on the other side of the river."

Jamie experienced another twinge of excitement at Barly's hint of danger. "Well, I'm glad you happened to be here when my kite—I mean Kip—and I came through that tree," Jamie said. "I— we would have really been lost without your help."

The stream began to widen, and the farther they traveled, the faster and deeper it flowed. Jamie skipped down the path, every once in a while kicking a root or a stone just because he could. They were wonderful sensations. He breathed in deeply. The air next to the stream smelled of wet earth, leafy green vegetation, and fragrant flowers. The smell was invigorating. Barly ambled along beside him and continued his story.

"As I indicated, it will take us a good day, maybe more, to reach Robinwood," he said. "When we get there, we'll spend the night. If you want to continue on, we can travel through the Forest of Whispers the following day. That is, if they're there."

"Why is this forest different than any other?" Jamie asked, looking up at Barly.

"This forest is an oddity, a peculiarity of plant life. Treesers, they are called, a very old stand of birch. They are almost ghostly in appearance," Barly continued. "The Forest of Whispers is a place where the trees are . . . well . . . alive, so to speak. They can whisper amongst themselves in their own language, hence the name. And at night, they sometimes uproot and move about."

"No kidding. Walking, talking trees!" Jamie exclaimed. "Wow, they could rake their own leaves in the fall." He snickered at the thought.

"Come on now, be serious," Barly scolded. "The Treesers are a strange bunch, and if you do something to provoke them, they can become menacing. They won't bother us in Robinwood, though. That's why it's best to get there before dark."

"Talking kites and bears, and now walking, talking trees. I can hardly wait to see what's next," Jamie said.

Kip squawked down from up above, "Hey, I'm no talking kite anymore. I'm a real bird now!"

"Sorry," Jamie called up to him. "I'll try to remember." He then turned to Barly. "You know, it kind of makes sense that there's a Forest of Whispers in Whispering Valley. Especially if the trees are alive. It seems to fit in with what I've been told so far about Neverlore. Do you think they're here by coincidence or by purpose?"

"I don't know. Never gave it much thought," Barly replied. "I wouldn't get too concerned, though. The Treesers might not even be in Robinwood. They move around a lot."

"Well, I hope they are. They sound cool and spooky," Jamie speculated. The thought of walking, whispering trees sent a shiver of anticipation through his body. *This adventure is going to be great*, he thought.

By early afternoon, the stream they had been following turned into a dark gray river. Huge, willow-like trees with spiky blue-green leaves lined the banks on either side. Their long branches dipped down into the water and made little swirls in the current. Colorful birds flew from one side of the river to the other, and tall cattails and wispy grasses grew everywhere.

Kip circled overhead, occasionally calling down things that might be of interest. At one point he told them, "I see a thin line of smoke far off in the distance. What do you suppose it is?"

"Sounds like someone has a campfire," Jamie said, recalling his camping experiences in the scouts. In fact, the area they were traveling through then reminded him of the time he and his troop had camped out beside a river. As Jamie thought back to that particular time, he felt a bit funny that he was reliving one of his favorite times in another land all together.

Kip had just finished telling them about a flock of purple birds with extremely long necks when he cried out, "Quick, get off the path!" Barly and Jamie barely had time to dive out of the way when a large, elk-like creature with gigantic antlers came running through the alders. His head was lowered and he snorted loudly at them as he sped past.

"Whew, that was a close one," Jamie exclaimed. He stared at the receding animal, then picked a couple of thorns out of his finger. He glanced up at Kip, cupped his hands, and yelled, "Thanks a lot! You saved us from becoming pin cushions."

"I'll say," chuckled Barly. "Better those thorns than those horns. I wonder what spooked him?"

"I wonder what he was!" Jamie cried. "I've never seen an animal like that before. Did you see him, Barly? He was huge and such a golden brown color!"

Barly chuckled again. "I did. This is Neverlore, remember? You're not at home anymore. You might as well get prepared for a lot of unexpected things to happen. For all we know, that stag could turn around and come right back at us."

"Well, let's not stick around and find out," Jamie said as they scrambled back onto the path. He called up to Kip again. "Keep your eyes open for anything else that may be of concern to us."

"I will," the bird answered back. "Right now, I don't see anything other than a flock of crows behind us, and a few rain clouds way off beyond the mountains."

With that, they continued on their way. It was mid-afternoon when they came around a curve and found their path led to a bridge over the river. Although the bridge looked solid, it appeared to be very old. It was made out of huge, moss-covered blue and gray stones. Halfway across stood a tall, stone wall with a gate of iron bars. As they approached, Jamie could see that the gate was locked with a big padlock. "What kind of bridge has a gate with a lock on it?" he asked, walking up and giving one of the bars a tug.

"It's a troll bridge," Barly replied.

"Don't you mean a toll bridge?" Jamie asked. He stepped up on the bottom bar and tried to squeeze through, but couldn't fit.

"No, it's a troll bridge," Barly said again. "A troll owns this bridge. I've crossed it a couple of times before and there's only one way to open this gate and get across the bridge. You'll soon find out, if he's here. Be careful what you say, though. It's not smart to get a troll mad at you. They're ornery enough when they're in a good mood, let alone a bad one."

At that very moment, a door appeared in the rock next to the gate. It opened quickly, and out stepped a frightful sight. Jamie jumped off the gate and quickly retreated behind Barly. "Yeow!" he cried. "What are you?"

The troll was about four feet tall, with large, pointed ears, a pointed chin, and scraggly gray hair. Large gold hoops hung from each ear, causing his earlobes to droop almost to his shoulders. His skin was warty and greenish, and he had hair on top of his feet. He wore a grimy leather tunic, and stuck in the belt around his waist was a long, wicked-looking dagger. Worst of all, he stunk like dead, rotten fish.

"Stop where you are!" the creature commanded in a harsh voice. "Who are you, and what do you want?"

Jamie wrinkled his nose in disgust. "Pheeww," he said, backing away even further. He waved his hand in front of his face as the troll glared at them with bloodshot eyes.

"Who we are is our concern," Barly said calmly. "What we want is to cross your bridge."

"Oh yes? Well, everyone wants to cross my bridge sooner or later. But it's not that easy," the troll cackled. "Only those who guess my riddles are allowed to pass." Slowly, his cracked lips stretched into a leer. Several of his teeth were missing and the few that remained were rotted and yellow.

"Come now. Must everyone play this foolish game every time they want to cross the river?" Barly asked. He took a step forward.

The troll dropped one grubby hand to his dagger and snarled, "I am Axl, keeper of the bridge. It's my bridge and my rules. If you want to pass, you have to guess the riddle. Now, if you come any closer, I'll cut you." Barly stopped where he was and eyed the troll warily.

"What does he mean Barly, *keeper of the bridge*?" Jamie asked in a low voice.

"I've been told Axl got this bridge as payment for some foul deed he did a long time ago," Barly replied, glancing over his shoulder. "Since a troll has little use for money, he gets his reward by making life miserable for others. If we want to pass, I guess we'll have to play his little game and guess the riddle."

"You could always swim," Axl added with another evil cackle, pointing at the swift current passing under the bridge.

"Okay, okay, if we must." Barly sounded exasperated, but he turned to Jamie and winked. "Axl is old and forgetful, and his riddles have become easy. We won't have any problem guessing the answer," he whispered.

"Easy!" Axl snorted. "Old and forgetful? For that you will have to guess my hardest riddle."

"Ask away," Barly sneered, crossing his arms. "We don't have all day for this foolishness."

"Listen up then, for I will only ask it once," he said. The troll wrinkled up his face, put a forefinger on his temple, and closed one eye. He then proceeded: "A big elf and a little elf were out hunting one day. The little elf was the big elf's son, but the big elf wasn't the little elf's father. Ha, ha, ha! Who was the big elf?" Axl then pulled a watch from his pocket and peered at it. "You have exactly one minute to answer."

Jamie looked at Barly, then back at Axl. "Say what? You went way too fast. Repeat that for us."

"Ha, ha! You don't listen very well, do you, boy. I said no repeats." Axl looked at his watch again. "Now you only have forty-five seconds left to answer," he said.

Jamie had a puzzled look on his face. "Boy, Barly, I don't know what the answer is. I can't even remember half the riddle."

"Me neither," Barly replied. "Let's see. A big elf and a little elf . . . The little elf and the big elf were related but, hmmm, I guess we'll have to . . ."

Just then, in a great show of flapping wings, Kip flew down and landed on the rail of the bridge. "That's easy," he laughed. "The big elf was the little elf's mother. Anybody could figure that out!" Kip poked his beak at the troll and stuck out his tongue. "Now open the gate so my friends can pass across your stupid bridge."

Axl stomped up and down and howled, "Foul fowl! You can't answer for them! You don't even need the bridge to get across, you can fly over. Your answer doesn't count."

"Well, I say it does. Since I'm with them, my answer *does* count," Kip replied. He snapped his sharp beak at Axl several times.

"He's right," Barly agreed. "Since he's with us, his answer does count. Now open the gate and let us pass." He stepped menacingly toward the troll.

"And what if I don't?" Axl sneered. He pulled his dagger out and pointed it toward them.

"Then I guess I'll have to pry the gate open with your head!" Barly growled. He let out a fearsome roar and leapt forward.

"Eeyikes!" Axl yelled. Quickly deciding he was no match for an angry bruin, he sprang backward through the doorway. The door closed with a bang, and then immediately disappeared. It now looked like there had never been a door in the rock at all.

"He's gone!" Jamie cried in amazement, stepping forward and running his hand over the stone. "And look, the lock's gone too."

He walked over and pushed on the gate. It swung open with

a loud creak. "Come on," he said, jumping through. Barly followed quickly. He was no sooner through when the gate slammed shut behind him with a loud *clang!*

"Whew, that was another close one!" Jamie exclaimed. "That Axl sure is crabby."

"Just like I warned you," Barly replied. "And like the stag, this is just the beginning. From here on out, there's no telling what we'll get ourselves into."

"If it's no worse than this, I can handle it," Jamie said with a certain amount of glee. He flexed his legs again, did a little hop, and elbowed Barly in the side. "Big softy, eh," he said. "You looked pretty scary back there."

"I am a big softy, really," Barly said, a mock scowl on his face. "However, I won't let someone push me around when I know I'm right."

"Well, I'm glad of that," Jamie said. "Axl sure didn't want to mess with you after you growled at him."

"I suppose you're right. Being scary-looking could come in handy, I guess," the big bear said with a bemused look.

They continued over the bridge to the other side of the river. Kip flew down and landed in a bush beside the path. Jamie sat down on a log beside Kip and eyed the bridge behind them. "I sure hope we don't have to come back this way," he said. "We may not have the answer to his next riddle."

Barly sat down next to Jamie and said, "I'll say. It's a good thing Kip knew the answer. I couldn't even remember half of the riddle. How did you figure out the answer so quickly, anyway, Kip?"

"You know, I'm not really sure. Birdbrain logic, I guess," Kip answered.

"Well, however you did it, you sure saved us a cold swim," Jamie laughed. "Now that that's behind us, I'm hungry, Barly. Where can we get something to eat? I've got a few snacks in my backpack, but not enough to last all of us several days."

Barly got up, laughing. "Good idea. I'm hungry too. I missed lunch, no thanks to you two." The big bear then scratched one ear as if deep in thought. "I've only been through here a few times, so I'm not . . . ah-ha, I remember a place. There's an old garden not too far from here. It hasn't been tended to in years, but some crops still grow wild there. We should be able to find something to eat."

With that, they set off down the path again. Jamie picked a blade of grass, stuck it between his teeth, and looked around. He still wasn't sure what to make of his surroundings, but he knew he didn't want to leave quite yet. The land reminded Jamie of many of the photos contained in his adventure magazines. The mountains off in the distance, the river behind them, and the miles of woods and rolling plains all around looked wild and tame at the same time. While they walked along, he asked Barly questions about Neverlore. Barly told him as much as he knew about the mystical land while Kip soared overhead as their lookout.

"Except for the rain clouds I mentioned a little while ago, all is clear, especially the sky. Just look at it," he called down.

Jamie scanned the entire vista. Kip was right; it was indeed beautiful. The sky started out blue-green on the horizon and gradually melted into the deep, robin-egg blue he had seen earlier. As he looked up, Jamie could see thin, white, wispy clouds stretching as far as the eye could see in either direction. They had tinges of peach and gold at their edges. Straight overhead, the sky fused into a deep, cobalt blue.

The afternoon sun shone brightly on their faces as they headed in its direction. The mountains seemed closer now, and Jamie felt he'd never seen anything as majestic before. It wasn't hard to imagine that he had become an explorer or frontiersman from one of his favorite adventure novels. For a brief moment, Jamie again thought he might be having some kind of extraordinary dream. But he quickly pushed the thought from his head as he gazed at the splendor before him. Whatever it was he was experiencing, he was going to enjoy it as long as possible. *The consequences of my wish have turned out pretty good after all*, he thought. To be on the safe side, though, he reached down and pinched his thigh. Sure enough, he felt the pain.

Jamie smiled and did another little hop. It had been a long time since his legs had felt anything. He started humming a happy tune and tried to imagine what his journey held in store for him next.

Chapter 4

By mid-afternoon, the ground had begun to rise. The air was warm and filled with the sounds of flying insects and chirping birds. A huge dragonfly flew across the path in front of them.

"Wow! Did you see the size of that?" Jamie asked excitedly. "That dragonfly must have been at least a foot long!"

"Yes, I saw it," Barly replied. "From what I've seen so far, it's not that unusual. Neverlore seems to be inhabited by the ordinary and the extraordinary. Like I said earlier, bugs can be bigger, the plant life can be more bizarre, and, as we saw earlier, animals—and trolls—can be very different from what is normal. I don't know about your Earth, but a lot of species here are dissimilar from what I know. Some are harmless and some are dangerous. It behooves us to be careful. We don't want to run into a dire-wolf, or a saber cat, or one of the heat perceptors that live in Neverlore."

"Whoa—what's a heat perceptor?" Jamie asked.

"Oh, a creature like a tombat, or a wisil," Barly replied. "They sense the body heat of their prey. But don't worry too much. The tombat usually doesn't hunt anything bigger than rodents and other small animals. And the wisil lives mostly on the other side of the mountains. There are others, but they live far to the north."

Jamie was silent for a moment. "Others, huh? It seems Neverlore might not be as peaceful and friendly as it appears," he said. "Promise me you'll stay close by and warn me of anything bad, Barly. I didn't expect an adventure that would be *really* dangerous." He slipped a hand into his pocket and felt for his jackknife. *It's not much, but at least it's something*, he thought.

"You'll be alright. Do as I say, however, and don't go wandering off or touching anything without first telling me," Barly replied. Jamie readily agreed and they continued on.

After a while, they came to where another path crossed the one they were traveling on. As Barly had indicated, a garden, or the remains of a garden, grew close by the intersection. Jamie scanned a sad looking sight. The garden looked like no one had cared for it in a long time. There were weeds everywhere, and a few carrots, onions, and stalks of corn were all that grew in it now. To the rear of the garden was an old, scraggly apple tree and a walnut tree. An empty grapevine and a few isolated sunflowers completed the forlorn scene.

Barly motioned for Jamie to follow as he turned off the path and walked down what was left of the rows. "We should be able to find enough here for lunch," he said.

Jamie stepped into the garden gingerly. Looks were deceiving, though. Surprisingly, what was still growing was firm and fresh. "Boy, this could have fooled me," Jamie said as he pulled a big carrot from the earth, wiped it, and took a bite. "This is sweet and crisp and tasty."

Barly chuckled. "This garden is most unusual. The few times I've been here the crop is always fresh and good to eat. Neverlore must really have a long harvest season, as the crop is ripe most of the year. And everything always seems to grow back so quickly after being picked."

"Maybe it's magic," Jamie said.

"Probably is. If so, lucky for us," Barly replied. For a while, he and Jamie busied themselves gathering apples, nuts, and vegetables. There was more than enough and Jamie stuffed as much in his backpack as room would allow. "I help my mom in the kitchen a lot," he said. "I could use these to make us soup some time."

When they were done, they sat in the shade of the old apple tree and ate lunch. Kip flew down and landed on a branch above them.

"What are you doing?" he asked.

"We're having a late lunch," Jamie replied.

"What's lunch?" the bird asked.

"It's eating. A midday meal, food," Jamie said. Then he laughed. "I guess since you were a kite before, you wouldn't know what that was. Eating is when one takes food and puts it in his mouth, chews it up, and swallows it. Well, at least we chew—birds don't. Food gives your body energy, keeps you alive. One generally eats three times a day, if food is available. Try a walnut and see what we mean. The nut's inside the husk inside the shell."

Kip flew over to the walnut tree and did as he was instructed. He pulled off a nut, pecked through the husk and shell, and began picking at the meat inside. "Mmmm. It's good. So, this is eating? I like it. What else do I need to learn?"

"Hah!" Barly laughed. "When we get to water the next time, you put that in your mouth and swallow it, too. Keeps you from drying out. Then at night, you rest and sleep. It will all come to you eventually, I think."

"This being alive stuff sounds like it requires a lot of work," Kip grumbled. Jamie and Barly laughed again. Jamie took a granola bar and some raisins from his backpack and shared them with Barly.

In between bites, Barly told Jamie more about himself. "Part of the problem I had when I was younger, besides being different in color, was that I was big for my age. Consequently, a lot of the bears thought I was a bully or something. I wasn't, but I didn't have a lot of friends because of that."

"I know what you mean," Jamie agreed.

"No friends equals no fun," Barly said. "I think if we're going to—"

"Look, somebody's coming," Jamie interrupted in a low voice. Jamie interrupted. He sat straight up, and pointed down the path. After Barly's previous warnings, he wasn't overly anxious to meet new strangers. He reached into his backpack, pulled out his binoculars, and trained them on the advancing figure. "It looks like a girl, carrying a bag of some kind. And she has an odd-looking animal riding on her shoulder!" he exclaimed. Jamie held the binoculars so Barly could look through them. Barly pulled back when Jamie held them up to his eyes.

"What are those things?" he asked warily.

"Don't worry, they won't hurt you. These are binoculars. They make things look closer than they are," Jamie answered.

He adjusted them to fit the big bruin's face, and Barly gingerly put his eyes up to the lenses. "This is fascinating," he said after a moment. "Everything *is* close up. And you're right. She is a girl and does have a creature on her shoulder. I've never seen either before, but they both look harmless enough. Let's find out who she is."

"How can you be so sure?" Jamie asked. "She could be a . . . well . . . some mass murderer for all we know," he finished lamely. He looked through the eyepiece again and studied the approaching figure carefully. The girl appeared to be close to Jamie's height and was slender with shoulder-length, reddish-brown hair and very tanned skin. "She's got pointy ears!" he exclaimed. Jamie adjusted the focus a little. Sure enough, he could just see the tops of her ears sticking out of her hair. They were indeed pointed.

"Pointed ears are not that uncommon in Neverlore. I've heard that some people here are descendents of an early race called the Elvenkind. They still bear some of the old features," Barly said. "If this girl is one of them, then she's definitely not dangerous. The Elvenkind are said to be a trusting, gentle race, elfish in origin."

By now, the girl was close enough that Jamie could see her clearly without his binoculars. She wore a sleeveless leather tunic over a brown shirt, and green pants that were cut off just below the knee. On her feet were leather moccasins laced up calf high. Around her waist was a green belt, and hanging on one side was a small sheath with a knife. Jamie was intrigued by the sight. She looked like she had just stepped out of one of his books about Robin Hood's Nottingham Forest, except she had no bow or arrows.

"I'll fly up and take a look to see if there is anyone else behind her," Kip said from the tree above them. He took off, flew around behind the walnut tree, and made a wide circle in the direction the girl had come from.

When she was only ten or fifteen feet away, Jamie and Barly stood up.

"Hello," Jamie called out. "My name is Jamie and this is my friend Barly. What's your name and what is that strange-looking animal on your shoulder?" He rushed through his words, but tried to sound friendly.

The girl was obviously startled. She whirled toward them, crouched into a fighting stance, and whipped out her knife. The creature gave a big jump off the girl's shoulder and disappeared in the tall grass alongside the path. It made a jingling sound when it landed.

"Whoa, whoa now!" Barly said quickly. "We're unarmed and mean you no harm. We're just surprised to see a girl out walking in the middle of nowhere, that's all. What's your name, lass?"

The girl stayed in her crouch, her knife pointed toward them. Kip, meanwhile, flew back down and landed in a bush nearby. He nodded in her direction and said, "She appears to be alone. I didn't see anyone or anything following her."

"Of course I'm alone. Koki and I travel by ourselves a lot," the girl said, straightening up somewhat. She glanced warily between Kip, Barly, and Jamie. "Who are you? What are a huge bear, a bird, and a boy doing out here all by themselves? We don't get many travelers around these parts, at least none that bring goodwill. And I know of no friendly bears in Neverlore."

Barly chuckled. "Like the boy said, he's Jamie, I'm Barly, and this is Kip. And contrary to what you think, we *are* friendly. We were just having some lunch and resting from our journey. What's your name, girl?" Barly asked again.

"How do I know you mean us no harm?" she asked.

"If we meant to hurt you, which we don't, we would have done so already," Barly said. He pointed to her knife. "You can put that away. That little thing would only be a pinprick in my side anyway."

The girl stared at them hard for several moments without saying anything. She scrutinized Barly's friendly face, narrowed her eyes at Kip, and looked so long and searchingly at Jamie that he felt a little uncomfortable. She lowered her knife and straightened up. "I am called Deena," she said at last. "And this is my faral, Koki." She made a low chortling noise in her throat, and the bushes rustled near the path. As Barly and Jamie looked on, the creature stuck its head out of the grass. It jingled again, like the sound of tiny sleigh bells.

"Wow! He ... she ... it's really neat," Jamie exclaimed. "What is it?" The creature was indeed cute. It had long, furry ears that stuck straight up from its head. Its face looked like that of a large mouse, with long whiskers and big black eyes with green pupils. The creature hopped out of the grass and sat up on its hind legs. It was tawny colored, had a pouch under its belly, and stood a little over a foot tall. Around its neck was a tightly wrapped leather collar, attached to which were small brass bells.

"It looks a lot like a miniature kangaroo," Jamie said. "What's a faral, anyway? And why does it have a collar with bells on it?"

Jamie's sincere interest seemed to dispel the girl's suspicions. She sensed the trio meant her no harm. Deena sheathed her knife and motioned to the creature. It jumped off the ground and scurried up her back to her shoulder. Jamie could now see a braided leather band under her bangs, tied around her head. The animal grasped the braid and made the same chortle the girl had before.

"A faral is a gatherer," she began. "Koki is female and she collects the seeds and kernels of plants for me. The collar is so she won't swallow them, and the bells are so I can locate her in the tall grasses and bushes. I am L'masse, a harvester, just like the rest of my tribe. My grandfather's grandfather's grandfather was Elvenkind. We have lived here since this land was very young. We are essence masters, in charge of the herbs, flowers, and berries that grow in Neverlore. But enough. Now that I have told you of myself, you must do the same for me."

Jamie looked at her skeptically. "Well, I'm not sure if you're going to believe this, because I'm having a hard time believing it myself," he began. "Kip and I have only been here a few hours, Neverlore-time, that is. Barly's been here longer." Briefly he told Deena the story of how he and his kite had come to Neverlore through the tree, of how he could walk, and how his kite had come to life. Jamie explained that the door had disappeared and told how they had met Barly. He described his plan to explore Neverlore and possibly travel to the Castle in the Clouds. Jamie finished with how they happened to be in the garden.

Deena was taken aback. "You came through a door in a tree? You're outlanders?"

Barly glanced at Jamie and Kip, then back at the girl. "I guess you could call us that. We're not from Neverlore if that's what you mean."

Jamie went on. "Yep, the door completely vanished in the tree trunk. That's kinda the reason for my exploring. Looking for a way out of here."

"The door disappeared, you say? That's very odd . . ." Her voice trailed off, and then she changed the subject. "Was the garden to your liking? Did you find enough food?"

"Yes, we did," Jamie said. "We had a great lunch here."

"I've wondered about this garden," Barly said. "It's in pretty sad condition and in terrible need of tending. Who planted it, anyway?"

"It is sad," Deena said. "However, it wasn't always this way. Long ago, a settlement of farmers and sheepherders lived around here. They were friends of the Elvenkind, and worked the land for many generations. The Irthken, as they were called, planted this garden for the travelers who passed through this area. At one time, before Axl took over the bridge, this spot was the intersection of the two main roads through Neverlore. In its prime, this garden was beautiful to behold. There were rows and rows of almost every vegetable imaginable and many different fruit trees were planted around the perimeter. Many a traveler was fed from this garden."

"What happened to the Irthken, and the garden?" Jamie asked.

"It is a long story." She then leaned forward and whispered, "One that is best told elsewhere."

"Why do you say that?" Jamie asked. This sounded like something he wasn't sure he wanted to hear.

"Trust me, it is as I say," she answered. "You are on your way to the Castle Mistemere? For what purpose?"

"I said *maybe* we'll travel there," Jamie corrected her, suddenly not sure if he trusted her or not. He eyed her narrowly. "*If* we end up at the castle, I may meet with this sorcerer, Araflore. He seems to be the only one able to answer some questions I've got. We're in no big hurry, though, because I don't know if I want to leave this place just yet." He waved his hand around for emphasis. "Besides, if I do leave, Barly says I'll probably end up like I was before, not being able to walk," Jamie continued. "So you can see, I've got some difficult decisions ahead of me."

"I see. That is quite an endeavor you're attempting," Deena said. "Leaving could prove more of a challenge than you think. And by the way, the sorcerer's name is Erenor, not Araflore."

"Whatever," Jamie replied. "Hey, what do you mean, 'more of a challenge'? I've already heard that several times today."

"I can't tell you here," Deena whispered. "And we shouldn't be saying his name out loud so much."

Jamie made a face. "What's this 'I can't tell you here' business? Can't you give me a direct answer?" he replied testily. "The more you can tell me about this sorcerer guy, the more helpful it would be. To walk again has always been my biggest wish. Now that I'm in Neverlore, to stay or to go is not an easy decision, believe me. But it's my decision and no one else's."

"The choice may not be yours to make," Deena replied.

"What makes you think you know so much, anyway?" Jamie said in exasperation. Her evasiveness was beginning to irritate him.

"I live here, remember? You don't," she answered, pointing a finger at his chest. "Therefore, I know a lot more about Neverlore than you do."

"Well, if it's all the same to you, I'd appreciate it if you'd keep your opinions to yourself," Jamie responded contritely. "All I want to do is explore, and see and do the things that I'm not able to back home. I don't need some girl to help me, no matter how much she thinks she knows."

"Hey, hey! Easy now," Barly interrupted. "You two remind me of the bickering bear cubs I left back home. Jamie, if you give Deena a chance, I think she's trying to tell us something."

"Barly's right. In spite of what you think, you do need my help. There are many things you may want to know about Neverlore before you continue on this journey. And you really don't want to be out here after nightfall," Deena said.

"Why, what's wrong?" Jamie asked.

"My father says Neverlore's not the same as when he was young. He informs me the land is changing and maybe not for the better. You'd best choose a protected place when you go to sleep at night," Deena responded.

Jamie felt a twinge of anxiety in his stomach. "I thought the dangerous creatures lived on the other side of the mountains," he said, gesturing over her shoulder.

Kip, who had been listening quietly, cocked his head to one

side. "Remember what Barly said, Jamie? I think I'd trust those who have been here longer."

Jamie considered the earnest warning, but said nothing. As he thought about it, his frustration slowly changed to concern. Maybe this new acquaintance was right. Maybe he'd been too quick to judge her, and, like Kip suggested, he should listen to the girl. After all, he had only been in Neverlore for a few hours, and the only things he knew about the land were what Barly and the widow Duncan had told him. Neverlore appeared to be the place where his dreams could come true, but it also appeared to be quite unpredictable. Reluctantly, he decided to defer to Deena's judgment, at least for the moment. "What do you suggest?" he asked.

"That you all come with me and be my guests at our hamlet," Deena replied. "You'll be safe there for the night. And, if Father's of the right mind, he'll tell you some of the history of Neverlore. It may help you."

"How can a story change my mind?" Jamie asked. "And what makes you so sure that I—I mean we—can't travel on our own?"

"Well, to begin with, you may want to know about the dragon that lives somewhere in the mountains," Deena said, cocking her head and pointing to the Barrier Range.

"You've got to be kidding! A *dragon*?" Jamie cried. "I don't believe it. There's no such thing as dragons."

"Then it's *not* a myth," Barly responded in a low voice. "I've heard rumors, but they were always very hush-hush. No one ever talked about it openly. If Deena says there's a dragon, I don't think I'd doubt her. She lives here, we don't. Remember?"

"Barly's right. I don't say it in jest," Deena went on. She shrugged and Koki shifted her weight to keep her place on the girl's shoulder. "But if you want to go on by yourselves, the choice is up to you."

Jamie wrinkled his nose and frowned. "But a dragon, how can that be?" he asked disbelievingly. "I mean, dragons only exist in fairytales."

Kip spoke up again. "I think you answered your own question, Jamie. Back home, everything about this land is legend, a fairytale. But it's pretty obvious, now that we're here, that everything is about as real as your imagination wants it to be."

"Kip's right," Deena said. "The dragon, whose name is Alizar, is as genuine as Kip is a bird and you are able to walk. However, you needn't worry. Alizar has not been seen or heard from for a long, long time."

"Why's that? You said he lives in the mountains. What's not to say today or tomorrow is the day he decides to reappear and toast us all?" Jamie asked.

"Because he is under an enchantment and has been asleep for over a hundred years," Deena replied. "The chances of you finding a way out of Neverlore are probably better than him awakening and terrorizing us. The spell is very powerful."

Jamie's head was beginning to whirl. He held up his hand. "Okay, okay, enough! Treesers, tombats, wisils, and other creatures I've never heard of. And now a dragon? You win, Deena. I don't know about Kip and Barly, but I accept your invitation. I've had almost all the adventure I can take for one day."

"I think you choose wisely," Kip said. "Safe is better than sorry. I'll go too."

"Kip's birdbrain logic is right again," Barly agreed. "And as long as there's a good meal to be had in your village, I'm all for it."

Deena laughed lightly. "We don't very often have guests, especially outlanders. I think Father will be very interested in hearing your stories. And yes, we have plenty of food. We are L'masse, gatherers. Remember?"

"You did mention that, didn't you?" Barly grinned.

Jamie shrugged. "I wished for an adventure, and it looks like I've got one. Lead the way, Deena. It looks like we'll stay the night in your village."

"Good," said Deena, and she smiled for the first time, warm and sincere.

With that, the even more odd-looking group headed south from the intersection. Kip flew back into the clear blue sky and took up his position as lookout. Jamie put his backpack on, and he and Barly fell in step with Deena. The faral proved to be quite friendly, and Deena let Koki ride on Jamie's shoulder as they walked along. The afternoon was warm and inviting and a light breeze blew in their faces. Every once in a while, Jamie caught a fragrance on the wind.

"Where's that sweet smell coming from?" he asked, looking around. "It reminds me of orange blossoms, but it can't be. I don't see orange trees anywhere." The aroma reminded him of the time his family had spent Christmas in Florida. He remembered it because it was the year before his accident.

"I've been wondering that myself. The smell is making me hungry," Barly said.

"Why is it everything revolves around food" Jamie sniggered. "You just ate a few hours ago and you're hungry again?"

"I don't know. Big bear, big stomach, I guess," Barly said. They all hooted.

"It's from the yota bush. But it's not food of any kind," Deena replied. "When the petals are boiled down in water, the liquid is drained off and used as insect repellent. If you put a drop behind each ear, the biting ones won't bother you all day."

"Cool. It sure smells better than the bug spray my mom used to put on me when we went camping," Jamie said. At the mention of his mother, Jamie briefly thought about his family. *I wonder if they miss me yet. Nah, I've only been gone a short while.* He felt that his dad and Andrew barely noticed him anyway. The thought saddened him and right then he was having too much fun to have any sad thoughts. Jamie quickly pushed that thought from his mind.

The rest of the day passed by without incident. Insects buzzed and hummed all around and birds called out to one another. They saw several more of the giant butterflies Jamie had seen by the bridge. Kip circled high overhead, drifting lazily around on the shifting wind currents. Every now and then, Jamie closed his eyes for a few moments, then opened them to see if everything was gone. Every time he reopened them though, the beautiful land was still all around. His spirit of adventure was peaked. Whatever dangers spoken of earlier now only made him more excited.

As they walked along the path, Deena told Jamie about herself and some of the history of the L'masse. Her father was *pere-or,* or head of their tribe, and she was an only child. Her stories were intriguing and Jamie found himself warming up to her, so he in turn told Deena about his life before Neverlore. Barly listened, but for the most part but didn't say too much. He was more interested in the wild berries that grew on either side of the path. Occasionally he wandered off to pluck some from their bushes and pop them in his mouth.

As they made their way south, the surrounding trees, shrubs, and flowers gradually disappeared. The vegetation gave way to hillocks of tall grasses, thickets of bushes and rolling plains. Some of the plant life was familiar and some Jamie didn't recognize.

Here and there, like a lone sentinel at watch over the land, a tall tree stood out against its surroundings.

The sun eventually dropped to the horizon and wisps of mist spread out over the cooling, grassy plains. It was twilight when, at last, they came to Deena's village.

Chapter 5

To call it a village was an overstatement, Jamie decided. From a small rise, he surveyed the small grouping of huts before him. Hamlet was probably a better word for it, as Deena had previously indicated. Spread out in an area slightly smaller than a football field were no more than a dozen tent-like structures. Each was about the size of a large SUV, and resembled a big, upside-down bread pan.

The hamlet was located at the edge of a small stream which was bordered on either side by a row of boulders. The huts were situated in groups of two and three under several unusual trees growing alongside the stream. If he hadn't known where they were, Jamie could have easily overlooked the huts. Their color was the same as the grasses and shrubs, and from a distance, they blended in with their background perfectly. He could see several figures moving about with his binoculars, and as he looked closer, he spied a faral on a leash by the door of some of the huts.

"What weird-looking trees!" Jamie said. They were no more than twenty feet tall and resembled large umbrellas, except wider and more flat on top.

"Those are somebreno trees," Deena answered. "They are quite unique in that their leaves and branches are so tightly interwoven that they keep our obacs safe from the elements. They also provide exceptional shade in the heat of the summer."

As they got closer, Jamie could see that the huts were made of thatched reeds of some kind. Each one had a flap on one side which, he assumed, served as a door. Small slits at eye height, about three feet apart around each hut, appeared to be the only windows. "These obacs, as you call them, what are they made of?" he asked.

"They are constructed by weaving willow saplings and obac grass together, hence the name. The L'masse, besides being seed harvesters, are also accomplished weavers. Obacs, when constructed properly, will last several seasons without repair," Deena explained. "Our obac is the larger one closest to the stream. It's where we'll spend the night."

"These things remind me of the igloos I used to see when I visited my mother's family," Barly said. "They have a similar shape."

"Yes, but I'll bet they're a lot warmer inside than an igloo," Jamie said.

As they made their way toward Deena's hut, they soon found themselves surrounded by a noisy throng of youngsters. Almost all resembled Deena, with reddish-brown hair, deeply tanned skin, and pointed ears. Several adults approached cautiously and stared and pointed at the group. They too looked the same as Deena, except that the adults' hair was dark red with no brown mixed in. Some of the elders leaned on staffs, and their hair was pure white. Man, woman, and child dressed in similar fashion, and they reminded Jamie of some of the Indian tribes he had read about in social studies.

"I hope they aren't dangerous," Barly whispered to Jamie.

"They're probably saying the same thing about us," Jamie whispered back.

Kip, meantime, flew around above their heads, eyeing the situation. He wasn't sure if he wanted to land in the middle of anything yet.

When they reached Deena's obac, she put Koki down and attached her to her leash. She bent over and called inside. "Father, Mother, we have visitors. Come out and see." A few seconds later, the flap was pulled aside, and Deena's parents stepped out. They were both taller versions of Deena, except her father's hair was grayer in color. They were taken aback by the sight.

"Deena, what have you done now?" her father said. "Who are these beings? You know we have to be extremely careful of strangers."

"It's no problem, they're quite safe," Deena said as she introduced them to the trio. "Jamie, Barly, this is my father, Selth, and my mother, Arlann. There is another, Father, a bird, but he's flying around overhead right now. I met them at the garden. They tell me they are outlanders." A hush fell over the crowd and some started to back away.

The next several minutes were filled with confusion and questions, especially because of Barly. It was obvious that none of the L'masse had been that close to a bear before. For the moment, most of the parents and children kept a respectful distance, chattering back and forth amongst themselves.

"Don't worry, they won't harm us," Deena said. "They are traveling across Neverlore and I invited them to spend the night."

"How do you know they're not one of the . . . others?" Deena's mother asked skeptically. "How do you know we'll be safe around them?"

"Because I do. I've gotten to know them and I feel secure. Remember, I've got that seventh sense that helps me tell good from bad." Deena smiled and Jamie couldn't tell if she was joking or not.

Selth rubbed his chin as he appraised the group. "The girl's right, you know, Arlann," he said at last. "She's always had that gift. None of the animals or friends she's ever brought home caused us any problem, remember? She always seems to know."

"Yes, but she never brought home a friend *that* big," Arlann said, pointing at Barly.

Jamie spoke up. "Barly may look scary, but he's really only a big softy, harmless. He really wouldn't hurt anyone, I'm sure of it. He doesn't act mean unless he's trying to protect himself or one of his friends."

Some of the younger children had overcome their fear and crept closer to the group. A few of the braver ones started to rub and pet Barly. "Ooh, that tickles," he said, laughing. One of the bravest, a little boy with red freckles, reached out and scratched behind Barly's ears when Barly lowered his head. "Now that feels good!" he exclaimed. "Hey, who wants to go for a ride?"

Several raised their hands and said, "I do! I do!" So Barly obliged and allowed two at a time to scramble up onto his back. With a "hold on tight," he ambled off around the hamlet. Soon the sounds of their squeals and laughter filled the evening air.

"There, doesn't that prove that I'm right?" Deena asked, pointing. "He's as harmless as Jamie says."

"It doesn't prove anything," her mother said. "If anything happens, it'll be on your shoulders." She turned and went back inside.

"Nothing's going to happen, trust me," Deena called after her.

The sun had set and it was beginning to get dark. Kip flew down and landed on top of the obac. Deena introduced him to her father.

"So you three are outlanders. I would be extremely interested in hearing your stories," Selth said. "Since Deena is determined that you be our guests, I suppose you should join us. You can tell us about yourselves over our evening meal."

"Thank you, Father, you won't be sorry," Deena said, reaching up and giving him a kiss on the cheek.

"Yes, thank you very much," Jamie said. "This really *was* Deena's doing. She persuaded us to join her. We won't be a bother, I promise."

"Yes, she said we'd be safe staying here for the night," Kip said. "However, if you don't mind, I'd rather stay outside. No offense, but small places make me uncomfortable. I prefer the outdoors now."

"As you wish, Kip," Selth said. "One obac is going to be pretty much the same as the next, so outside probably would be best for you. In the meantime, Jamie and Barly, feel free to look around. Arlann will call when it's time to come in. You'll find we are a simple folk with simple needs and tastes." He pulled Deena aside. "I trust your instinct for the moment, but keep watch over them. We can't be too careful," he said in a low voice.

"I will, Father, but you're beginning to sound like Mother," she whispered back. "Don't worry so much!"

By now the crowd had dispersed. The parents went back to their huts and began preparing for their evening meals. Fires were lit outside some of the obacs to ward off the evening chill. Only two or three children were left waiting for a ride on Barly, and Kip had flown off in search of dinner.

Jamie walked down to the stream with Deena. She led him to a large rock in a small clearing next to the stream. The rock was about five feet long and had a natural seat on the side nearest the water. The stream gurgled before them, on its way to some distant destination. They sat down and Jamie stared off to the west at some low hills. Where land met sky, the last rays of the sunset painted the horizon brilliant yellow, orange, and rose colors. Lines of purple clouds radiated up from the earth like giant fingers reaching toward the heavens. All around, the air was fresh and cool and smelled of mysterious and enticing things.

"It's beautiful!" he exclaimed. He couldn't remember the last time he'd seen a sunset like this.

Deena said, "It is indeed. That is where I will travel tomorrow to gather gula berries." She pointed. "You are welcome to join me, if you like. We will be gone all day and you could see a part of Neverlore you might not see otherwise."

"I'll think about it, thank you," he said. "What's a gula berry?"

"Well, it's called a berry, but it's really the small fruit of the gula bush," Deena said. "We dry them and mix them with certain grains and nuts. They provide great energy and a little will last a long time."

"Sounds like trail mix," Jamie said.

"What is that?" Deena asked.

Jamie explained what trail mix was as best as he could, and they ended up comparing the different foods and drinks of their respective lands. Jamie showed her the mess kit he carried in his backpack. Deena marveled at its structure. She was just telling Jamie how they only cooked with earthen pots when her mother called them for dinner.

"Mother is irritable tonight," she said. "For what reason I don't know. We'd best not keep her waiting." They jumped down from the rock and hastened toward the obac, meeting Barly on the way back.

"I've never had that much fun with little ones," he said happily. "I never got to play like that when I was younger because I looked so different."

"How sad. Children of the L'masse are taught at a young age to be considerate of others, no matter how they look or act," Deena said.

"We could use a lot more of that where I come from," Jamie said. Barly readily agreed.

They reached the obac and Deena pulled the flap aside and motioned Jamie to enter. She ducked in behind him and motioned for Barly to follow. It was then that they discovered the big bear was too big to squeeze through the opening. He had to be content with squatting at the doorway with only his head and front paws poking through. He looked quite comical, especially when viewed through one of the window slits. Only his behind and tail could be seen sticking out of the obac. The sight made Arlann laugh and seemed to put Deena's parents more at ease with both Barly and Jamie.

Jamie looked around, marveling at the interior of the obac. Inside, it was much more spacious than it appeared from the outside. In the center was a pole that supported the domed roof of the structure. The pole was actually a tree with many branches still attached to it. They had been trimmed back, and on each hung a pot or cup, or some other cooking utensil. All were made of clay or carved from wood.

Attached to the saplings at one end of the obac hung three hammocks woven from the same grass as the hut. Next to them were several wicker chests and around the room were scattered various baskets of many sizes and shapes.

"This is different," Jamie said. *This is better than the Discovery Channel*, he thought. Next to the pole in the center was a low brick oven, inside of which a small fire burned. But the oven had no chimney, and as Jamie inspected it, he could see the fire gave off hardly any smoke at all.

"How is it your fire doesn't smoke?" he asked.

"We burn wood from the charo tree," Selth answered. "When it burns, it gives off an even heat and entirely consumes itself in the process. Consequently, very little smoke. There is only the need for a small hole in the ceiling above it." Jamie's eyes followed the pole up to where it intersected the roof. Sure enough, a hole about the size of a tennis ball was all that he could see.

"That is very interesting," he said. "Wood that hardly smokes when it burns."

Deena's father motioned them to sit down around a low table to the left of the pole. Around the table were placed cushions made of soft animal fur. They smelled nice and fresh, as if filled with aromatic grass. Jamie took a seat next to Deena as Arlann served dinner.

Their meal consisted of a stew-like mixture of nuts and herbs and other items Jamie couldn't identify. As Arlann placed a steaming bowl in front of Jamie, the smell wafted up to his nose. *This smells delicious,* he thought. *Like the stew Mom and I make, only with nutmeg and allspice added for flavor.* However, after a few bites, Jamie discovered there was no meat in the mixture. It was then that he learned that the L'masse were vegetarians.

"We don't believe in killing animals for food," Deena said between mouthfuls. "We eat fish but only when the stream provides an excess. And the fur and skins we use comes from the yaxx. They shed their outer skin once a year and we gather it to make clothing and such.

"Interesting," Barly said, eyeing the stew. "It's good to know none of my relatives were used to prepare this meal." Everyone chuckled at this.

A coarse-grained bread and a sweet, honey-flavored drink completed the meal. Arlann prepared a big bowl for Barly, who thanked her profusely. Jamie found he was famished and ate with gusto. He had two bowls before he was full. "That was excellent," he said, wiping the last bit from the corner of his mouth with a leaf the L'masse used like napkins.

"Very good indeed," Barly agreed, having eaten a total of four bowls himself.

After the meal was finished, Deena and her mother cleared the table. Deena started a torch from the fire and they both left to clean the dishes at the stream. Barly backed out of the entry to let them pass and went with them to get a drink. Selth took down a long, intricately carved wooden pipe from a shelf and filled it from a leather pouch attached to his belt. He pulled a coal from the fire and placed it in the pipe. After a few puffs to get it lit, he sat down cross-legged at the head of the table. Like the oven fire, his pipe produced little smoke. What he exhaled dissipated almost right away. Jamie sniffed the air. There was only a faint odor of anything burning at all. It smelled vaguely of damp leaves smoldering, neither agreeable nor disagreeable.

"Let me guess," Jamie said. "You're smoking charo tree leaves. That's why it doesn't smoke very much."

"It's charo bark, actually," Selth said with approval. Maybe he had been too quick to judge the strangers. The boy was perceptive. "So, you three crossed through into Neverlore. We very seldom encounter outlanders anymore, for, to my knowledge, very few doors remain open. I thought most, if not all, had been sealed long ago."

"What do you mean, sealed?" Jamie asked, leaning forward eagerly.

"Closed up permanently. In the beginning, outlanders passed through regularly. But over time, events changed this," Selth went on. At that moment, Deena and her mother returned from washing dishes and Barly stuck his head back in the doorway.

"Kip's asleep in the tree above our heads. Did I miss anything?" he asked.

Jamie answered. "Deena's father was just beginning to explain about the doors between here and other lands. Please go on," he said politely, turning back to Selth. "What do you mean, some things have changed?" he asked. "What was Neverlore like before these changes happened?"

Selth drew on his pipe. "Tell me your tales first. If you speak the truth, I may be able to clarify many of your questions," he answered.

"Tell the truth? We have no reason *not* to tell the truth," Jamie said indignantly.

"The boy's right," Barly added. "Why would we lie about how we got here? It would serve no purpose."

"Like I said before, we have to be extremely careful of outlanders. The portals didn't always admit welcome guests," Selth said ominously. "How you came here and why you came here could be entirely different from each other. There could be some devious purpose to your arrival, honestly."

Jamie frowned and looked at Barly. "Devious purpose? I have nothing to hide, and I don't think Barly does either. This is all becoming very confusing. We both got here entirely by accident."

"Tell us your stories and we will be the judge of that," Selth said. "I'm particularly interested in the doors you and the bear passed through."

Jamie looked at Selth, then at Deena, then back at Selth. He shrugged his shoulders. "Suit yourself. I'll tell you what I know." Jamie went on to tell a brief story of his life at home, how he and Kip had come to the land of Neverlore, and the events leading up to that point. All three interjected with questions and seemed very interested in his story. It occurred to Jamie to tell them about the widow Duncan and how familiar she was with the so-called legend of Neverlore.

"I still don't understand how she knows so much about this land, though. I'm beginning to think maybe she has been here somehow," he said after describing her. Selth and Arlann listened intently and exchanged long looks with each other while Jamie talked, but said nothing.

When Jamie was finished, Barly took his turn and told his story. Afterward, in the silence, Selth held up his hand and turned to Deena. "Very intriguing tales. What do you sense, daughter?"

"My intuition tells me they do not know," she replied. "I feel they speak the truth, Father."

"Know what? We *are* telling the truth," Barly and Jamie said in unison.

Selth stared at Jamie and Barly solemnly. "Very well, then," he said at last. "I will explain many things to you. But to do so, I must first tell you the history of Neverlore." Selth drew on his pipe, exhaled, and began.

"The story begins almost fifteen hundred years ago when our ancestors, the Elvenkind, were the first stewards of the land. Neverlore was beautiful and serene then, and no discord or strife existed. But as it often happens, men and beasts left to their own policies become discontented with one another and power struggles inevitably develop. As history progressed, violence, thievery, and lawlessness increased throughout the land. Different groups tried to dominate the weaker ones. The stronger tried to rule, and anarchy began to spread."

"But Neverlore seems like paradise," Jamie said ruefully. "I thought it was a place where wishes always come true."

"No, sorry to say, it is not always so," Selth said. "With no one to manage it, even a land so bountiful and beautiful as this one can go awry. Fortunately though, chaos and disorder was subdued. The first successful rule in Neverlore was in the form of a sorcerer and sorceress named Barador and Valletha. They established the Order of Lowring, and after great struggle and resolve, restored calm to the land. Out of gratitude, the Elvenkind fashioned a crown of gold from the mines of Arcada. They weaved spells of elfin magic into the band, and from that time on, only the pure of heart could wear it upon their heads and rule. It became a potent vestige, a powerful heirloom passed down from one monarch to the next. He or she who wore the crown had abilities a hundred times more powerful than before.

"Barador and Valletha governed over Neverlore for many, many years, and in turn, passed the rule and crown on to their only son, Baradon. He married and the Lowring regime passed from generation to generation for well over a thousand years. Near the end of the reign of Lowring, a great plague swept across the land, wiping out almost every living thing that breathed. It was then that Xiticus, the twelfth sorcerer of Neverlore, came to power. He quickly recognized that life in Neverlore risked extinction because people were dying faster than they were being born. After great thought, he devised a plan. Xiticus rationalized that certain deserving or 'special' outlanders, such as yourselves, might welcome the opportunity to enter and live here. This might help repopulate the land, and since the common tongue was spoken here, everyone could understand one another.

"But therein a problem existed. To get others to Neverlore was not going to be an easy task. You see, this land is an island completely surrounded by three vast oceans: the Normic, the Avalin, and the

Celtic. Neverlore is also unusual in that it is literally an island in time, a time only parallel to that of other worlds. Subsequently, Neverlore is unreachable by conventional means of travel."

"So it's true?" Jamie interrupted. "Parallel time *does* exist?"

"Yes, in some ways," Selth replied. "Our land is not unlike a netherworld, but that's another story altogether. It became apparent to Xiticus that the only way to reach Neverlore was to cross time itself. Therefore, utilizing special magic, he created portals, or doors, from other worlds parallel to Neverlore through which beings could pass. And it was rumored he also created a few doors that worked both ways. That is, so someone could *leave* Neverlore if or when circumstances dictated. I almost believe this. Otherwise, how else would we know of the time differences between Neverlore and different lands? Or how would Xiticus have sent certain outlanders who didn't fully qualify back to their previous worlds?"

Jamie's ears perked up. "So there *may* be a way out of here," he stated.

"We don't know. To my knowledge, no one after Xiticus ever found one. Remember, it's only speculated that an exit from Neverlore ever existed in the first place," Selth said. "At this point, I can't say for certain."

"Then I may be trapped here after all," Jamie said matter-of-factly. He had the same feeling he'd felt several years before when he had gone into a haunted house on Halloween. Jamie had been both excited and apprehensive to enter, but was safe with the thought that there was a door at the end of the maze through which he could leave. Only now he wasn't sure that a door existed.

"How many doors did Xiticus create?" Barly asked. "Including Joria's, Jamie's and mine, I know of three. But they all closed up afterward."

"We never knew," Selth continued. "Sorcerers are very secretive and mysterious. We do know, though, that the doors were the most important part of his plan. Xiticus figured only those with high-quality skills and abilities could be screened and allowed to enter. This would ensure that a good mix of inhabitants ended up here.

"As a precaution, he required four qualifications be met before anyone could enter through any of the portals. The being had to be virtuous in nature, have a legacy to pass on, be sincere in his or her desire to better themselves, and have needs that couldn't be fulfilled in his or her own land. Those requirements would ensure only appropriate life forces entered, and at the same time safeguard Neverlore against any undesirable beings coming through. Xiticus felt any qualified individual who entered would find this land a better place than his or her previous one, and therefore live a life of harmony."

"Life force. I've never been referred to as *that* before," Jamie mused.

"Was his plan successful?" Barly asked.

"Yes and no," Selth went on. "A lot of good creatures and beings settled here like he planned, but there was an unanticipated problem. Every few hundred years, this land gets restless and we experience earthshakes. The ground literally moves and shifts beneath your feet."

"Earthshakes?" Barly interrupted. "No one told me anything about them!"

Jamie echoed his concern. "We have them in my world also. We call them earthquakes. That's swell. A dragon, and now earthquakes?"

Selth continued. "Fortunately, they don't happen very often."

"But you can't predict when it will happen next, can you?" Jamie said dourly.

"No, but we don't worry about it," Deena said. "It's like any other thing we have no control over. We put it to the back of our minds and don't think about."

"Well, that's a comfort," Jamie said contritely.

"We live with it," Selth said. "The story doesn't end here, however. Xiticus created one of his portals on the other side of the Barrier Range, and that's where the problem arose. During the last earthshake, or earthquake, that particular portal was damaged."

"I thought they were magic. How is magic damaged?" Barly asked.

"Sometimes even magic can't withstand certain powers of nature. Because the portal was damaged, the safeguards were lost," Selth said.

"I don't think I'm going to like what happened next," Jamie said grimly.

"Unfortunately, it's part of the story," Selth went on. "By the time Xiticus discovered there was no protection on the portal, it was too late. A legion of mercenaries had passed through undetected. They were led by one called Druin of Medea. He was a necromancer and a warlock with an unquenchable thirst for power. In a surprise midnight attack, he and his evil force stormed Mistemere and slayed Xiticus. During the battle, the Crown of Arcada was lost. Druin proclaimed himself sovereign lord, and at that time the reign of Lowring came to an end. The Age of Shadows had begun. Druin was cruel and ruthless, and he ruled for almost two centuries."

"Okay, a lot of the bits and pieces I've heard about Neverlore are starting to make sense now," Barly offered. "This is a frightening story."

Jamie asked, "How long do sorcerers live?"

"A sorcerer can live five hundred years or more," Deena answered. "A warlock much longer."

"Pheww!" Jamie whistled. "And I thought the widow Duncan was old."

"Druin was a master of the dark arts," Selth continued. "In addition to using black magic to rule, he brought a monstrous army with him. And to make sure all of Neverlore obeyed his army, he exploited a dragon named Alizar."

"Deena told us of him," Barly said. "Up until today, though, I thought a dragon was only myth in Neverlore."

Deena spoke at this time. "They exist. Druin discovered Alizar when he was just a baby and beguiled him. Dragons are quite susceptible when they are young. Druin cast a spell on him, causing him to breathe fire. As Alizar grew, he forced the dragon keep watch over all of Neverlore. Alizar was powerless to resist and carried out Druin's evil commands. He burned down houses, destroyed crops, and drove people into the hills. Even Druin's army feared him."

"From here on out the story gets somewhat better," Selth said, continuing the tale. "Unbeknownst to Druin, Xiticus had a young son, and just before Druin slew the sorcerer, Xiticus was able to send his son to safety. He placed the boy in the protection of a trusted chambermaid, and during the battle, they both escaped from Mistemere. The chambermaid took the young boy north into the mountains, far away from the sight and influence of Druin. After making sure he was safe, she mysteriously disappeared, never to be heard from again. She was thought to have passed through one of the doors into another land.

"Erenor, as he was called, was raised in the Order of Valory and taught by shamans the secret magic of the old masters. Time passed, and about a hundred years ago, the young and now powerful sorcerer was ready to avenge his father's death. He waited patiently until the warlock's attention was diverted from the north, and without warning, swept down on Mistemere. With an elite band of loyal guardsmen recruited from the mountains, he defeated Druin and freed Neverlore. Erenor transformed Druin's army into inhabitants of the deep and cast them underwater, where they have been imprisoned ever since. He broke Druin's evil spell on Alizar, banished him to his cave, and cast his own spell on the dragon. Erenor could only cause Alizar to fall into a long, deep sleep, for even a powerful sorcerer has great difficulty destroying a dragon. However, Erenor transformed Druin into a statue of hematite. And to this day, he keeps constant watch over the warlock. If the spell is ever broken or even diminished, Druin would emerge with a vengeance and a great tragedy would befall Neverlore."

"Is Druin still alive?" Jamie asked tenuously.

"You are observant," Selth said. "Yes, Druin is alive but to what extent, we don't know. Animate suspension may be a better term. None of the L'masse has ever seen him firsthand, and therefore, we haven't been able to verify or monitor his condition." Now Selth leaned forward and looked earnestly at his wife, his daughter, and then at Jamie. "Strange things have been happening lately. We have seen an increased gathering of wolves, and there are new creatures roaming the land I haven't been able to identify. There are other instances also, but I would rather not speak of them now."

The uneasy feeling Jamie had felt earlier was back again. "Does this story get any better?" he asked. "I mean, I thought Neverlore was supposed to be a good place to come to."

"Neverlore itself *is* very good. It's the outlanders that arrived with Druin that are very bad," Deena said.

"And it appears that Druin and his outlanders might be preparing for something," Selth added. "Your arrival may be fore-shadowing certain events that can't be ignored anymore."

Jamie still wasn't satisfied. "You said before there were hardly any doors left open in Neverlore. If Xiticus created them for good beings to enter and settle in Neverlore, why did he turn around and seal them?"

"He didn't. Druin sealed them, including the door he came through. He wanted to ensure none more powerful than he could enter and threaten his rule," Selth answered.

"I've known bruins like that," Barly said. "No matter how big and mean and tough the bullies were, they always worried that someone bigger and meaner would take their place."

"This is definitely different than the stories I've been told," Jamie said. "Where does it all end?"

"I was just coming to that," Selth continued. "You see, even though Erenor was a powerful sorcerer with many weapons and spells, the fight with Druin was brutal and long. In the heat of the battle, just as Erenor turned Druin to stone, Druin managed to project fiery mind rays at him. These rays scorched and shriveled Erenor's flesh. He was sapped of a great amount of magic power, and left sightless. The battle wounded him deeply in both body and soul. In some ways, the sorcerer lost as much as he'd won.

"Because of his appearance and condition, Erenor became very reclusive and seldom ventured from Mistemere. It's said he's partial-ly recovered and keeps control with the powers he has remaining. To our knowledge, he still controls the land, or at least the southern plains area where we live. For many years, entrance to Mistemere has been restricted, and news from the castle is infrequent. Because the L'masse are plainsmen, we don't feel secure in high places, and therefore don't travel in or through the mountains. I can't say what it's like to the north or on the other side because we don't travel there either. But, on occasion, we get travelers through here and their news contains rumors of happenings at the castle. It's never specific, however, and since we aren't directly affected, we pay little heed.

"We are a peaceful race and keep to ourselves. We find if we associate little with outsiders, we don't invite confrontation. Ours, and the Mithrin tribe to the west, are the only L'masse left in Neverlore. We never fully recovered from the plague and our time here grows uncertain. It behooves us to spend our remaining years living in harmony with the plants and animals of the land."

Selth paused and looked into the smoldering embers. In the stillness, Jamie became aware of the cacophony of night sounds outside the obac. The chorus was similar to cricket and frog sounds, but wilder, louder. At last Selth spoke again.

"But if indeed what I suspect is true, there are signs that our tranquility is being disrupted. Evil once again is stalking the land. Each and every subsequent stranger is a potential threat to the balance of our accord. More than ever now we must be diligent in our observations. We are the L'masse; it is our job.

"And so ends our tale. Now that you've heard the story of Neverlore, you know why we are so skeptical of outlanders. We had to be sure of where you three came from, and what your intentions were."

"That finally answers most of the questions that have been bothering me," Barly said quietly. "I now understand things about Neverlore that I didn't before and was never able to ask anyone about."

Jamie let out a low whistle. "I understand a lot better also, especially when I think of what the widow Duncan was trying to tell me. Everything isn't always what it seems. There *can* be a dark side to something good. Now that I've heard all this, I'm wondering if a journey to Mistemere *would* be worth the effort. From the sound of things, Erenor may not be able to help. My options seem to be dwindling."

By this time, the fire in the oven had burned down to nearly nothing and its dying flames sent shadows dancing about the inside of the obac. Jamie stared into the embers, as if looking for answers. Arlann spoke. Her mood had softened. "You seem like a bright and sensitive young lad, Jamie. I sense that you are true of heart and mind, but because of your past affliction, you are not sure of direction. If I had a son, I would accept him no matter what he was like or what his limitations were. A mother's love knows no boundaries, and I suspect your mother's is no different than mine. Let your inner conscience guide you, for it will be true."

"This is a lot to comprehend right now. I'm afraid I'm getting so tired that it doesn't make much sense anymore," Jamie said. He stifled a yawn.

Arlann continued. "You are right. It's getting late and we have filled both your heads with quite a bit for one evening. You and your friend Barly are welcome to sleep with us tonight. Tomorrow is a new day and another adventure. Maybe then you can decide where your journey will take you."

"She speaks well," Selth said. "The horizon is almost always brighter at dawn. The *real* Neverlore is much better than the dark picture I've painted. You just have to see the good through your own eyes, that's all."

Jamie couldn't stop it this time and yawned. The events of the afternoon, the good meal, and the story he had just been told were indeed taking their toll. "I hope you're right. It's hard to believe that a few hours ago, I was flying my kite in my own neighborhood, and now I'm here. I thank you for your hospitality, but I'm worn out."

With that, Deena led him to the other side of the obac and showed him to his bed. It was a mat on the floor filled with sweet-smelling straw and covered with soft pelts. "This is where you'll sleep. In the morning I'll leave early to gather nettle-leaf and gula berries. Like I said earlier, you and Barly and Kip are welcome to join me if you want. Koki and I will rise shortly before dawn and set out."

Jamie yawned again. "I'll see how I feel in the morning, Deena. What about you, Barly?" he said over his shoulder. "Where are you going to sleep?"

The big bear chuckled. "Well, I certainly can't come inside, so I'll just go out and sleep next to the somebreno tree. It'll be warm enough, and besides, I'm a bear. I'm used to sleeping outdoors."

"I'd almost forgotten," Jamie said. "I'm a bit out of it. Good night. I'll see you all in the morning." He laid his backpack down, crawled onto the mat, and pulled the pelt blanket up to his waist.

Barly said goodnight and pulled back out of the hut. Selth, Deena, and Arlann climbed into their hammocks, saying their goodnights in return.

In spite of his exhaustion, Jamie lay on his back with his hands behind his head. He stared up at the dome of the hut. Images of his first day's adventure flashed through his head. He also saw his mother's worried face, the widow Duncan telling him of

Neverlore, and his wheelchair where he had left it. He saw a beautiful sunset, the purple and misty mountains, and a foot-long butterfly. He glanced down and wiggled his toes. *Still working,* he thought. Then his imagination began to wander and other images came to mind. A fire-breathing dragon and creatures with strange faces and long claws he'd never seen but could now picture lurked in the shadows at the top of the obac. *What have I wished for? What will I get?* he thought dreamily.

It was some time before Jamie slept. Somewhere outside, off in the distance, an animal howled a long, mournful wail. Jamie cringed involuntarily and pulled the pelt blanket up to his chin. The eerie sound was the last thing he remembered before he finally drifted off into a fitful sleep.

Chapter 6

Time to set out," a voice whispered in Jamie's ear. "We have a long way to travel before we get to where we need to be."

Jamie stirred from his slumber. He felt as though he had just barely fallen asleep. "Oh man. Can't I sleep a little longer, Mom?" he grunted.

"I'm *not* your mother," the voice replied. "I'm Deena and it's time for us to set out for the day."

Jamie sat straight up on his cot. Memories of the previous day flashed across his mind. "Wow, this isn't a dream!" he exclaimed groggily. "It did happen. I really am in Neverlore aren't I?"

"Shhhh!" Deena whispered tersely. "Yes, you are, and I really must leave. I have to pick the nettle-leaf before the dew is dry for it to be any good. Are you coming with me or not?"

Jamie leaned back on his palms and shook his head to clear the cobwebs. "Okay, okay, take it easy." He rose unsteadily to his feet and picked up his backpack. Deena helped him get the straps over his shoulders and took his arm. She guided him to the door in the obac and motioned for him to stoop down. As Jamie stepped outside, he glanced over his shoulder at her parents. They were still asleep in their hammocks with their backs toward the door. "They're not going with us?" he asked.

"No, Father is the head of our tribe, so he stays and manages things. Mother prepares the various essences and compounds from the leaves, berries, and roots I bring back. The young gather and the elders make provisions. It's the way of the L'masse and has been from the beginning."

Jamie yawned and said, "Seems fair enough. But I'm hungry, and thirsty too. When do we eat?"

"I have gula bars to eat on the way. They will fill you and keep your stomach still for quite some time. And here, drink from this," Deena said, handing Jamie a leather flask.

"What is it?" he asked.

"It's aldirberry juice, honey, and water. Quite healthy and thirst-quenching," she replied. Jamie took the flask, pulled out the stick cork, and took a drink.

"It's delicious," he said. "And good for me, too? I find that hard to believe. At home, anything good for me usually doesn't taste this great." Mentioning home made him pause for a moment and think of what his family might be doing. His dad would be at work as usual. His brother was probably off chasing girls. He wondered what his mother was doing. Was she worrying about him? Was she calling around because he had been gone so long? He felt Deena shake his arm. "Are you still with me? You look pale. Are you alright, Jamie?"

Jamie realized he had come to a complete stop and was staring off into space. "I was just thinking about my family," he replied softly. "I'm afraid my mother's in a panic by now because I've been gone all night without her knowing where I am."

"Hey, not to worry. Time is much slower where you're from, remember?" a familiar voice said. Barly walked around from behind the obac.

Jamie's face brightened up at the sound of his voice. "Hey yourself! You're right, I had forgotten. How *does* time work in Neverlore, Deena?"

"It is different than where you are from, I'm sure," Deena answered. "Though we think certain entities may have passed back and forth and discovered this during Xiticus's reign, time is one thing no one has ever been able to reconcile in Neverlore. From what we've gathered, for the most part, an hour here is only a minute in most other worlds. A day here is less than a half an hour there. Our time is quite disproportionate to other times."

Jamie did some quick mental arithmetic. "If your time estimates really are true, I may have only been gone a half an hour or less," he calculated. "That works!"

"It is as I say. But we *must* go." She turned to the bear. "Jamie and I are heading out to gather this morning. Do you wish to join us, Barly?"

Barly rubbed his chin with a white paw. "Hmmm," he said. "If it's alright with you, I'll pass. I'd rather stay here and play with the youngsters. They didn't all get rides last night."

Deena laughed warmly. "Who are you kidding? I believe all you really want to do is make up for the time when you were a cub and didn't get to play."

"Is it that obvious?" the big bruin asked sheepishly.

"That's quite okay," Jamie said, walking over and patting his big head. "You don't have to be ashamed. I, of all people, understand what you mean."

"Thanks, Jamie. I'm glad you do," Barly said.

"Think nothing of it. I guess it's just you and me, then," he said, turning to Deena.

"I'll go with you, if you don't mind." This time it was Kip who spoke. He was perched on top of the obac.

"That will be good," Deena said. "You might be of help to us. Now, since we have this settled, follow me." She unsnapped Koki from her leash and chortled to her. The faral responded with the same sound and scampered up to her usual position on Deena's shoulder. Deena turned and began walking back the way they had come from the day before. At the edge of the ridge overlooking the hamlet, she went left off the main path and headed west. Jamie followed and Kip flew overhead.

The sun climbed slowly up behind them as they set out. The warmth of its rays began to warm Jamie's back and he felt his spirits begin to rise. Guiltily, he realized he wasn't as worried about getting home as he felt he should be. *I guess I'll worry about that when the time comes*, he thought.

Deena gave him a gula bar, which he gladly accepted. As he munched on the nutty, honey-flavored mixture, the horizon brightened around him. *Maybe Selth is right. Maybe the answers do lie somewhere out there*, he thought. *Maybe there is more good than bad to be discovered in Neverlore.* Part of Jamie could imagine staying there forever. *I wonder if I'll ever get home, if I'll ever need to.*

* * *

It was mid-morning when the path they were following began to disappear into the field grass that surrounded them. Deena motioned for them to stop. To their right were several small knolls protruding up above the grass. Clustered on top of each were smallish trees with gray trunks and branches and blue leaves.

"This is the nettle tree. Hopefully the leaves on the side away from the sun still have dew on them," Deena said. She stepped off the path and made her way through the waist-high grass to the first knoll.

Jamie followed through the swath her legs had made as she pushed her way around to the shaded side of the trees. Kip flew on ahead, looking for his breakfast.

"We are in luck. There is still dampness on some of the leaves on this side," Deena called to Jamie. She motioned Koki to the tree and made the faral's sound. Koki jumped off Deena's shoulder and scrambled up the tree. The tree rustled as the picking began.

Jamie followed Deena around as she chose and plucked the nettle-leaves off the lower limbs. He watched in fascination as the faral delicately plucked the upper leaves and tucked them in her pouch. When it was full, she jumped down next to Deena. Deena removed the leaves from Koki's pouch and wound each one tightly around her finger. She then slid the leaf spool off and placed it in a leather pouch she had slung over her shoulder. Deena and Koki moved from knoll to knoll, carefully selecting and harvesting the leaves that were still damp. After about an hour, she announced that she was done. "They are starting to get too dry, so we might as well continue on and find some gula berries."

She called to the faral and Koki climbed back to her shoulder. Jamie walked over and scratched her ears. "Does she always wear the collar so tight?" he asked.

"She doesn't care for nettle-leaves too much, but when it comes to the gula berries, she'd eat her weight in them if she could, and get really sick. I loosen the collar at night so she doesn't choke, and I feed her then."

The two of them made their way back to the end of the path they had arrived on. "Why do you need to pick them while they are still damp?" Jamie asked.

"The sap of the tree is most concentrated in the leaves when the dew is upon them. And the more sap in the leaves, the better the balm that's made from them," she answered.

"What do you use the balm for?" Jamie asked.

"My, aren't you full of questions this morning," she replied with a mischievous smile. "If you must know, when a mother is with child, the balm made from nettle-leaf sap is rubbed on her abdomen and private areas. This assures a birth with no complications. The sap also has healing properties. Are you satisfied or do you want to hear more?"

Jamie blushed and stammered, "I . . . I guess so. Hey, you invited me along. I didn't invite myself. I'm an outlander, remember? I know nothing about the ways and customs of your land, so give me a break."

Deena laughed. "I was only teasing you to get your reaction. You can ask all the questions you want of me. I'm actually flattered that you think well enough of me to ask anything at all. In our tribe, only the elders get asked questions, as they alone are supposed to be the ones with knowledge."

"I think you know a lot," Jamie responded. "You can handle a knife, you know all about the history of Neverlore, you've trained Koki, and you're not afraid to travel alone in a strange land. Well, strange to me at least. You're not like any of the girls that hang around my brother. You're . . . well . . . you seem to be more adventurous . . . a lot like me."

"Why, thank you, Jamie. Your and Barly's compliments are quite appreciated," Deena said, genuinely pleased. She put her hand up over her eyes, shading them from the sun, and scanned the surrounding countryside.

"There is where we want to go to find the gula bush." She pointed off to the southwest. "See that stand of trees over there in that dip in the plains? In the middle of them will be a spring, and that's where the bush will grow."

Jamie looked where she pointed. He could just barely see where she was referring to way off in the distance. "You sure must have good eyes. I can hardly see anything, it's so far away."

"The L'masse have excellent vision. It's the healthy food we eat," Deena said. She glanced up at the sun's position. "It will take us well over an hour to get there," she indicated. "The grass is tall and will try to slow us down. By the time we're there and pick the berries, it will be well after the sun's zenith. We should hurry. We'll want to be on our way back before it gets dark. Come, we'll take turns leading the way so as not to get too tired. But before, eat one more of these. One is good, two are better." She handed him another one of the gula bars and shared her flask with him again. With that, she struck out into the grass. Jamie followed close behind, munching on the tasty treat.

While they pushed their way along through the vast field, the long blades of grasse made *shhhhinnng* sounds as they rubbed against their legs. Insects of many sizes and shapes fluttered and jumped out of the way at their passing. Jamie caught a purple and white bug in midair as it flew up in front of him. He held it by the wings and inspected it. Its body shape and wings looked like those of a moth, but its face had pinchers instead of a proboscis. As he peered at the creature, he was astonished to see the insect change color right before his eyes. In a matter of seconds, it was the same color as the flesh on his hand. "Wow! Did you see that?" he cried.

"That's a camolon," Deena laughed. "They can change color or pattern in no time at all to camouflage themselves. They do it for protection as well as to hunt. Don't put him too close to your face, though. They can spit their saliva up to four feet. It won't paralyze you like it does the ants and crickets it feeds on, but it's quite sticky and is hard to get off your skin."

Jamie held the insect out at arm's length and rolled it around to get a better view. It stared back at him with big, orange eyes. On a whim, he held it down near a clump of yellow flowers with red spots. Sure enough, in a matter of seconds, the camolon had turned the same color and pattern as the flowers. "That is very cool," he said. He threw his hand up into the air and released it. As the moth flew away, he could see it return to its original purple and white colors.

"This place is never going to cease to amaze me," he said, shaking his head.

"It is that different than your land?" Deena asked curiously. "I can't imagine living in a place that was any less wonderful than this."

"I know what you mean. I'm beginning to think the same thing," Jamie said.

When it was Jamie's turn to lead through the grass, Deena showed him how to make better time with less effort. She instructed him to sway at his hips slightly and turn to the left and right with each step. They made good time and Deena's prediction was accurate. In about an hour and a half they arrived at the small forest. From a distance, the size and height of the trees had been deceiving. The stand was a mixture of spruce, aspen, and a few species Jamie didn't recognize. The larger trees had thick trunks and limbs, were all of eighty feet tall, and grew close together in some places. He and Deena started circling around the island of trees, looking for the best way to enter the underbrush that grew at the edge.

"This is awfully thick," Jamie said, bending down to get a better look. "I don't suppose there are any critters living in here that I should know about, are there?"

Deena laughed. "Not unless you're worried about dormice or rabbits or squirrels. That's all I've ever seen in there. And they only attack when there is a full moon," she teased.

"Just thought I'd ask." Jamie laughed somewhat nervously. "Barly warned me not to get into anything I wasn't sure of."

* * *

High overhead a pair of sharp eyes stared down at the three figures below. They had been intently watching ever since Jamie, Deena, and Koki had left the nettle trees. The taller two appeared not to pose much harm to the observer.

While Jamie and Deena were occupied with trying to get through the underbrush, they failed to see a sleek shape drop down out of the clouds above them. Straight as an arrow the figure plummeted from the sky, and when it was just above treetop level, it let out a piercing cry.

The unexpected sound startled Jamie. He twisted around, glancing wildly about. His foot caught a knotted root and he fell to the ground with a thud. He lay there, momentarily stunned.

Deena recognized the sound immediately. "A condor-hawk!" she screamed.

She tried to duck, but it was too late. In the space of a heartbeat, the great bird had swooped down and was upon her. In the blink of an eye, with talons extended, the condor-hawk snatched the faral from her shoulder and headed back up into the sky. Its left wing struck Deena in the head in passing and knocked her to the ground.

"Nooooooo! Kokiiiiiiiiii!" But it was too late. In a matter of seconds, her pet had been jerked from its perch and was gone. The episode happened so quickly that neither she nor Jamie had time to react. All they could do was lie where they fell and watch Koki as she disappeared into the atmosphere, crying and chortling as she dangled from the hawk's tight grip.

Deena began to cry hysterically. Jamie, regaining his senses somewhat, crawled over to her, and put his arms around her. "I don't believe that just happened! I didn't see it coming. I'm so sorry, Deena. If I had, I might have been able to do something. That was a condor-hawk? It's huge, bigger than an eagle!"

"Yes, condor . . . hawk. I couldn't . . . should . . . have known . . . more careful," she stammered between sobs. "Koki's gone. What . . . am . . . I to do? We bond to our farals at birth and they stay with us throughout their whole lives. I'll never get another."

Jamie didn't know what he could do or say to comfort her. "Barly warned me, but he didn't tell me anything about them. What's a condor-hawk?"

"They . . . are . . . giant birds that came to Neverlore through . . . one of the doors years and years . . . ago," she said between sobs. "I've seen them . . . off in the distance, but I've never known them . . . to come so close and attack like that."

"Came through one of the doors?" he asked. He thought, *Condor-hawk, great condor? Condor what!* Jamie racked his brain. *I've read something about some kind of condor. But they're supposed to be extinct. I wonder if . . .*

At that instant, his thoughts were interrupted by another piercing cry up in the sky. Jamie looked up, and to his astonishment, saw Kip dropping like a bullet down from the same cloud the condor-hawk had dived from. "Look, it's Kip! He's come back!" Jamie pointed at the plummeting figure.

Deena stared up through watery eyes and they both watched speechlessly as Kip dove down straight at the hawk's back. They held their breath as Kip struck the hawk a glancing blow. Again and again he struck the huge bird. From above, the side, wherever he could, always just keeping out of range of the hawk's sharp, curved beak.

Both birds circled high above the small forest, diving and snapping at each other, screeching and crying. Jamie and Deena could hear Koki screaming in agony as the hawk's talons cut into her flesh. The battle went on for several seconds when all of a sudden, the condor-hawk released its grip on the faral, turned, and went after Kip. They climbed and dove, slashing at each other with sharp claws and beaks. Their cries and screams receded as their battle took them off into the distance, neither one giving up.

When the condor-hawk released Koki, she immediately plummeted back toward earth. Luck was on her side, for she was directly over the small forest when she was pitched from the hawk's grasp. She spiraled around and down and fell into the trees. The soft upper boughs broke her fall and she came to rest in a mat of needles toward the top of the tallest fir tree. She grasped a branch with her good front paw to keep from falling any farther and proceeded to whimper loudly.

Jamie regained his senses. He pushed himself upright and pulled Deena up after him. "I can hear her up at the top of one of the trees. She's alive!" Deena cried with joy. "Jamie, we have to res-

cue her. We'll . . . you'll have to climb the tree and get her down."
Deena was frantic, clinging to his arm.

At the mention of climbing the tree, Jamie looked up at the
limbs and froze. "I'll have to? Why me?" He had put climbing out
of his mind a long time ago. Climbing didn't exist to him anymore. Climbing equaled falling, equaled being paralyzed.
Climbing had put an end to his normal, everyday life.

"I . . . I . . . can't climb the tree," he stuttered. "I can't! I'll fall. I'll
be paralyzed again. I'll . . . you'll have to do it, Deena. I just can't."

The girl started crying once more. "I am L'masse. We are flat-
landers. We don't climb anything higher than our heads, remember? We lose our equilibrium and fall. Koki's going to die unless
one of us does something, and I can't do it."

Jamie continued to stare up into the boughs and limbs. The sound
of the faral's plaintive cries could be heard somewhere overhead. They
were growing weaker by the moment. Jamie knew something had to
be done, but try as he might, he couldn't get his muscles to move.

Deena walked around and put her face directly in front of his.
She clasped her hands on either side and looked at him with teary
eyes. "Jamie, *please*. Climb the tree and save Koki, for me," she
implored. Deena then did something Jamie had never experienced
before. She leaned forward and kissed him directly on the lips.
"Please, you *can* do it. You *can* climb the tree," she whispered.

It felt like a hot jolt of lightning had shot through Jamie's head.
His lips tingled and his senses jumped. "I . . . I've never been kissed
. . . by a girl before. I've never even kissed a girl, either. Ever."

Deena leaned forward and kissed him again. "You have now,
twice. Do it for me, for Koki," she pleaded.

Jamie felt a strange warmth surge through his body. His
adrenalin began to pump and his muscles tightened up. "Yes, I

think I can," he said at last. "I can do it!" The fear that had held him captive for all those years suddenly melted away. He straightened his back and stared up at the highest limbs. "I *can* do it. I *can* climb that tree." With that, he pulled the coil of rope he always carried out of his backpack. He fashioned a sling at one end, slid the coil up his arm, and hung it on his shoulder. "I'll climb up and put her in this sling. Stand under the tree and I'll lower her down to you," he said.

They ran forward and pushed their way through the undergrowth. Every few seconds, they would stop and listen for Koki's cries. "Over this way!" Deena cried, turning and ducking under a limb. Jamie followed, and soon they were standing under the fir tree that held the faral. Without stopping to think what he was about to do, Jamie dropped his backpack, reached up, and grasped the lowest bough. He swung himself onto it and began to climb. "Move out a little way from the trunk, because she'll probably slide down the outside of this tree's boughs."

Up and up he climbed. He was surprised to find that he could still easily do it.

Just like riding a bike, he thought. In a matter of moments, Jamie had reached the highest point where he still felt safe. The limbs got thinner as he went, and they began to bend under his weight. He could hear Koki's whimpers plainly now. Jamie wrapped his left leg around the trunk and reached out with his right hand. He parted the boughs and could now see the faral. He gasped when he saw her. She had three puncture wounds near her spine and a big gash in the side nearest him. Blood was dripping from the wound and running down over the needles.

"I've found her, but she's in pretty bad shape. She's got a pretty deep cut and is bleeding quite a bit," he called down to Deena.

"Just get her down to me. I have something to dress her wounds," Deena called back.

Jamie carefully slipped the rope off his shoulder and laid it over a branch. He spread the boughs again and gingerly reached for the faral. She cried out and tried to back away. "It's okay, girl. I'm here to help," he said soothingly. Koki looked at him with her big black eyes. They were wide open with fright. She floundered around on the branch and Jamie could see she was losing her grip. It would be only a matter of seconds before she'd fall. Jamie stretched further out toward her. She cried louder and kicked with her one good hind leg, trying to move farther out on the limb.

"She's frightened to death," he called down to Deena. "Every time I try to reach her, she backs away. She can't hold on much longer."

"Listen to me," Deena cried. "Listen to the sound I make. Use your throat and kind of gargle." Deena made the chortling sound that Jamie had heard her do many times. "Try it."

Jamie tried to duplicate the sound, but it came out all wrong.

"Go deeper in your chest and wobble the back of your tongue," Deena said.

Jamie tried again. This time it sounded closer to hers. He tried two or three more times and suddenly Koki chortled weakly back. "I did it, she's responding!" Jamie cried. He made the sound again and the faral responded. "It's working, we're talking to each other. I don't know what we're saying, but we're talking," he exclaimed.

"Keep doing it as you reach for her. She knows you are a friend and she'll come to you," Deena yelled up.

Jamie shifted his grip and reached out as far as he could. His other hand felt wet and clammy as he gripped his anchor branch. For a moment he pictured himself slipping, but a voice from deep inside him said, *No, you can do this.*

He kept making the sound. At last, Koki pulled herself slowly toward him, chortling back. He stretched his fingers out and was finally able to grasp Koki's collar and pull her toward him. As soon as she was safely in his arms he slipped the sling under her front legs. Careful not to touch her wounds, he pulled the rope up around her shoulders and tightened the knot as much as he dared. Koki squealed and tried to pull away. "It's okay, girl. This is for your own safety," he said softly, chortling again. As if sensing that he was there to help, the faral relaxed.

"Alright, I've got her and I'm going to let her down," he said loudly. Jamie gingerly started feeding out line, careful not to let it bounce or drop. As he lowered her slowly, Koki cried loudly. "It's okay, girl. You're going to be safe on the ground in a few seconds." After a few moments, he felt the line go slack.

"I've got her," Deena cried out. "She's hurt badly! Come down as quick as you can. We have to get her back home so she can be tended to properly."

"I'll be right there," he said. "I want to check for Kip first." He glanced around from his high perch. The plains grasses rolled off toward the horizon in every direction. Under different circumstances, he could have imagined he was the lookout in the crow's nest of some tall-masted sailing ship. The blowing, weaving grass was like the ocean as it swelled and rolled all around. The small oblong forest far below was the deck of his ship. He squinted and scanned the surrounding area, but there was no sign of the bird anywhere. *I wish I had my binoculars up here with me,* he thought.

"Poor, poor Kip. The hawk must have gotten him. That was so brave. I just can't believe this is happening!" he said forlornly. The euphoric feeling he'd experienced a short time before was beginning to wear off, and suddenly he was aware again of how high he was from the ground.

"Okay, I just have to make it down safely," Jamie said aloud to reassure himself. He dropped the line and started down slowly. He hadn't gone down more than a few feet when—*craaaack*—a branch he stepped on broke. He was suspended in mid-air for a split second before he dropped like a rock.

"Ayeeee!" he cried, flailing his arms around. Terrifying, painful memories from his first fall, years ago, from the oak tree rushed into his mind. Jamie truly saw his life flash before his eyes. Just as he thought the end had really come, he stopped with a jerk. Slowly opening his eyes, he saw that his belt had caught on a jagged end of another broken branch several feet down the tree.

"Holy crap! I'm still alive!" he cried as he bounced and swayed. Jamie reached over to the trunk and grabbed it tightly to stabilize himself. He unhooked his belt from the broken limb, and with his heart beating wildly, started back down again. He didn't waste any time now, dropping from one branch to the next. Soon he was close enough to the ground that he could jump the last few feet. He hit the grass, rolled twice, and lay there, breathing heavily. Deena rushed over to him with Koki in her arms. She had wrapped a makeshift bandage around her from a piece of cloth ripped from her undershirt. She knelt down beside him and laid the faral in the grass.

"Don't . . . ever ask me . . . to do anything like that again. I think I messed my pants," he panted. Jamie stared up at her while she stared back. There was a moment of tense silence as they looked into each other's eyes. A smile crept over her face and they both began to laugh hysterically. Deena reached down and gave him a huge hug. "That was the bravest thing you could ever do, Jamie Nichols from the outland. You did it. You conquered your fear and saved my Koki! From here on out, your second name shall be Treemaster."

"I really did it, didn't I," Jamie said, getting up, his knees still shaking. He looked up to the top of the tree and a huge grin crept across his face. "I don't think I'll want to do that every day, but after this, I think I could climb again if I had to."

"I believe you could. Now we have to leave and make haste back to my obac. I've treated her wounds with nettle-leaf sap, but it's only a temporary fix. She needs Charmac the Healer to clean the wounds with wortwood salve and stitch them up." She gathered Koki in her arms, stood up, and started back out to the edge of the trees. "Hurry," she said, motioning to him.

Jamie picked his rope up, quickly wound it, and stuffed it back in his pack. Slinging the backpack on his shoulders, he once again fell in behind her. When they reached the plains grass again, Deena paused and motioned Jamie forward.

"Can you go ahead and break the trail?" Deena asked. "I don't want the grass to slap against Koki."

"I'd be glad to," Jamie replied. "I'm pretty good with directions, and if we cut an angle back to the path home, we'll save some time." Before Deena could thank him, Jamie jumped in front of her and started swaying and pushing his way forward. Deena followed as closely as she could. They hadn't walked for more than three or four minutes when Jamie held up his hand.

"Whoa, there's something up ahead under that bush, moving around in the grass," Jamie whispered.

Not taking any chances, he reached in his pocket and took out his knife. "Stay here and I'll go see what it is." Jamie stooped low and began to creep toward the movement ahead. As he got closer, he could hear a loud wheeze. It sounded like something in pain.

Is it an injured animal? he thought. Jamie got down on his hands and knees and crept forward as quietly as possible. When he was close enough, he stretched up and peered over the top of the grass.

"Omigosh, it's Kip!" he cried. "He's alive!" Jamie stood up and rushed to where the bird had beaten the grass down. Kip looked up at him and said in a croaking voice, "I think I got the better of him, but I took a beating in the process."

"Deena, come quick!" he called behind him. "It's Kip and he's hurt pretty badly too."

Deena rushed up, laid Koki down, and knelt beside the wounded bird. Kip was indeed battered badly. He had several gashes about his head and body, and one wing was bent under his body at an odd angle. "You poor thing. Along with your other wounds, your wing is broken," Deena said. Fortunately her under-shirt was long enough for her to rip more cloth from it. She then reached into her pouch. Taking out several of the nettle-leaves, she unrolled them and proceeded to squeeze each from one end to the other. "Hold out your hand." Jamie did as he was instructed.

Deena squeezed a clear blue liquid from each nettle-leaf into his palm. When she had an amount the size of a half-dollar, she dipped two fingers into the salve and rubbed it into Kip's wounds. She then pulled his wing out from under him and tied it to his body. The bird flinched as she applied the first aid. "It's a good thing I found lunch when I did. If I hadn't, I might not have gotten back in time to check on you two," Kip said in a hoarse whisper.

"You are as brave as Treemaster here," she said kindly. "If it wasn't for both of you saviors, Koki would be in that condor-hawk's stomach by now. Here, Jamie, you take Kip and I'll carry Koki." She tenderly picked Kip up and put him in Jamie's out-stretched arms. She then gathered Koki. "Let's keep going. We have two wounded animals to tend to now." They set off at a quick pace through the grass. When they reached the path, they sprinted as fast as they could toward the village and safety. Fortunately, nothing hampered their flight back.

* * *

It was dusk on Jamie's second night in Neverlore when they reached the hamlet. They ran down the path to Deena's obac. "Father, Father, come quick! Koki and Kip have been badly hurt!"

At the sound of Deena's desperate voice, both her parents rushed out of the hut. Barly heard her call also. He stopped the story he was telling the children and hurried over to the small group that was now forming around Jamie and Deena.

Like the previous night, there were several moments of confusion as questions were asked and the returning travelers tried to tell their story. Finally, Selth held up his hand.

"Take Koki and Kip to Charmac's obac and have her tend to them," he commanded. "Then come back and tell your mother and me what happened."

Deena and Jamie did as they were told. At the far eastern edge of the hamlet was a small obac. Unlike the others, however, this one was weathered and gray and was comprised more of tree bark than grass and reeds. Deena called out as they approached. An old, wrinkled, and wizened woman came out at the sound of Deena's voice. She wore a long, brown, hooded robe with small bones and teeth woven into the leather stitching. Around her neck hung a braided grass necklace with a black, tear-shaped stone dangling at the end of it. Unlike the rest, instead of knee-high moccasins, she had a well-worn pair of leather sandals on her feet.

The old woman moved stiffly, hunched over a walking stick. She appraised the assembled group quietly. As Jamie looked under the hood at her face, he was shocked to see she had one blue eye and one green eye. He bit his tongue and said nothing, though. He felt an intense aura about her and sensed he was standing in the presence of a powerful medicine woman.

Deena quickly explained what had happened. The old woman quietly motioned them inside with her cane. Jamie and Deena ducked inside with the two injured animals. Koki had now lost consciousness and Kip wasn't far behind.

"Leave them," the old woman said in a raspy voice. "This is not something you can help with. Let Charmac the Healer use her potions and magic to see if these two can be saved. This first night will tell. If they make it through, they will have a good chance." She motioned them over to a small table covered with soft reeds and flowers. "Lay them there." She pointed.

As Jamie gingerly lowered Kip, the bird grimaced and opened one eye. "My first full day as a bird didn't end so well," he said in a whisper and tried to smile.

"Shhhh. Be quiet and rest. You are safe now. Charmac will take care of you," Deena said soothingly.

"If she says she can save you, then I believe her," Jamie said. "Good luck, friend. We'll check on you in the morning."

Jamie and Deena left the obac and headed back to Deena's hut. Barly was waiting for them outside. "What did she say?" he asked anxiously.

"We won't know until the morning," Deena said, glancing sadly at the empty leash outside her doorway. Her eyes welled with tears. She took Jamie's hand and they ducked inside. Barly bent down and pushed his head in behind them.

A low fire was burning in the oven again and cedar-bark-scented incense was wafting smoke toward the ceiling. The atmosphere had an immediately calming effect on the two.

"I've prepared dinner for you. Sit and eat before you tell us what happened," Arlann indicated. Jamie and Deena sat down at the table, and her mother set plates of steaming herbs and vegetables in front of them. She poured them both tall glasses of cool honey water. "This will make you feel better inside," she added. She then gave a huge bowl to Barly, who thanked her profusely again. He had only eaten a few berries during the day, having been too polite and shy to ask for lunch.

The smell of dinner made Jamie's stomach churn. He hadn't eaten anything since the late-morning gula bar Deena had given him. He dug in with relish, and true to Arlann's prediction, felt considerably better when he was finished. Arlann cleaned the dishes away, Selth lit his pipe up again, and both adults looked at Jamie and Deena expectantly.

"Tell us what happened today, and don't leave any details out," Selth said.

Deena and Jamie then took turns recounting the day's events while Barly listened in.

"I guess I should have gone with you after all," he offered regretfully. "Jamie, I'm so sorry about Kip. And Koki too, Deena."

"That's alright," Deena replied. "It's doubtful you could have done anything. That bird just dropped out of the sky with no warning."

"Just the same, I feel awful I wasn't there," Barly said.

Selth laid his pipe down. He put his hands together in his lap, and bowed his head, deep in thought. At last he spoke. "Xiticus ruled Neverlore for shortly over a hundred years, and many outlanders passed through during that time. Except for Druin of Medea, most were good and lived peaceably here. As stewards of the land, the L'masse watched over all living creatures as well as the plants and flowers. This included the outlanders. However, many were of a solitary nature and kept to themselves, like the condor-hawks. They almost always keep to the mountains and aren't aggressive to our kind at all. To my knowledge, there has never before been an incident like this during the stewardship of the L'masse. Are you sure neither of you did anything to provoke it?"

"No, I'm sure of it. We never even knew the bird was there until it was too late. It came at us without any warning, like it had been tracking us or something," Jamie said. "If it wasn't for Kip, we all may have been attacked. That thing had a wingspan of eight feet or more!"

"They are very big and powerful birds," Selth said.

"Is this condor-hawk native to Neverlore?" Barly asked.

"No," Selth answered. "However, the reason they entered Neverlore was justified. They controlled the wisil population that exploded after the plague. It concerns me greatly that a condor-hawk would now act like that."

"But this doesn't make much sense," Barly said. "If most or all of the doors or portals were sealed, how is it we made it through?"

"I've wondered that since you first arrived," Selth said. "Since I thought there were no portals left, I don't know the answer. It could be that Xiticus created a few very secret doors that only he knew about. Erenor might know the answers, but sorcerers are very secretive and not prone to giving information freely."

Deena had been quiet up to that point. She was still saddened by what had happened and disturbed by her close brush with death. She spoke up. "Maybe there is a purpose for Jamie and his friends being here, but their destination is unknown to us, or them."

Selth stared at his daughter. "That is a deep and insightful thought," he said quietly.

"It's that seventh sense of hers," Arlann said.

"Very possibly," Selth replied. "Her sense has prophesized before."

"I'm not sure what this all means," Jamie said. "More than anything I wished to walk, and I ended up here. I didn't have a purpose for doing so, it just happened. I do know that I'm going to continue this journey to wherever it takes me—alone, if I have to. It may be Mistemere, or it may be someplace else."

The harrowing events of his second day were beginning to take their toll on him. Jamie's mind was a jumble and he was beginning to get tired. He found it harder and harder to keep his eyes open. After some more small talk, he finally excused himself, walked wearily to his bed, and lay down on the mat. "I've had enough for one day, if you don't mind." He yawned mightily. "I need to sleep and give my brain a rest. We'll figure it all out in the morning."

Arlann spoke quietly. "The boy's right. It's getting late and we should all get to sleep soon."

"I'll go check on Koki and Kip," Deena said.

"I'll go with you," Barly said, withdrawing from the entryway.

After they left, Arlann came over and knelt down next to Jamie. She stared deeply into his eyes. It was at that moment Jamie realized that, just like his mother, she had *the* look. It was the look of love and understanding that only a mother can have for her offspring. But, as Jamie stared back into her eyes, he saw something else. It was a look of ageless wisdom. She smiled down at him and he smiled dreamily back.

"I feel you must continue on to Mistemere like you originally planned, but sooner than you think," she said softly. "Only when you have completed your journey will the true reasons for your being in Neverlore be revealed."

Jamie yawned and closed his eyes. "I guess you're right, Mom," he whispered as he drifted off. "See you in the morning. Sweet dreams. I love you." Jamie then fell into an exhausted sleep.

Arlann pulled the pelt blanket up to his chest and gently brushed a lock of hair from his face. She looked wistfully down at the boy for a moment or two.

The door flap opened, letting in a gust of cool night air and interrupting her thoughts. "Charmac has done all that is in her power to do," Deena said sadly. "If Koki and Kip make it through the night, they might have a chance. Their lives are in the hands of our ancestors' spirits now." Arlann rose from her knees and embraced her daughter. She handed Deena a cup.

"Drink. This will help you rest and cleanse your soul of sadness." Deena did as she was told. She put on a sleeping gown, climbed into her hammock, and like Jamie, soon fell into an exhausted sleep.

Barly had retired to his place under the somebreno tree, and soon just Deena's parents were left awake. Arlann came over and sat next to her husband. She leaned her head against his shoulder. "The future is difficult to predict sometimes. There is something here that I can't grasp."

Selth said nothing. He picked up his pipe again and lit it. He gazed at Jamie sleeping quietly with a thoughtful look on his face. *Arlann and Deena are right. As much as I don't want to hear of it, there is trouble stirring in Neverlore*, he thought. He looked up into the shadows of the obac's ceiling. A thin ray of moonlight shone down on them through the hole at the top. He pulled deeply on his pipe and a small ring of smoke wafted out. It drifted lazily up toward the shadows.

Arlann watched in detached interest as it circled and danced around the moonbeam. *This could be a sign*, she thought. But of what she couldn't tell.

"It's time for us to retire too," she said, kissing Selth's cheek. He agreed and laid his pipe back in its container. They washed their mouths with mint water, donned their sleeping gowns, and retired to their hammocks.

Outside, a three-quarter moon bathed the landscape in soft white light. To the northwest, however, deep shadows in the hills defied the light and swallowed it up. From a secluded ridge, several forms crept from the darkness and looked down over the village. Their eyes glowed iridescent green in the moonlight, and as they panted, steam blew from their mouths into the cool evening air. The largest let out a doleful wail. The rest followed suit, and soon the night air was filled with the uncanny sound.

Inside the obac, Jamie tossed about restlessly. He was having fitful dreams again. In his dreams, he saw stairs to the Castle in the Clouds, but he found they didn't have an end to them. No matter how high he climbed, he never reached the top.

Jamie also saw creatures with glowing eyes all around him. Barly and Kip were gone and he faced the eyes by himself, his slingshot his only defense. His back was against the tree that had brought him here. He was facing Neverlore alone.

Chapter 7

Jamie awoke the next morning and indeed found himself alone. Early morning sunlight streamed in through the slits in the walls, lighting up the interior of the obac. He stretched and checked his watch. It read 2:10 PM. *That can't be right,* he thought. *I didn't sleep that late.* He got up and peered out of the closest slit. He could see it was still early in the morning. Then a thought occurred to him. *Maybe time is faster here than it is back home. If so, I haven't been gone an hour yet, my time. Mom won't be that worried after all.*

He paused and thought about home. So much had happened already that it seemed like he'd been gone from home for over a week. His own house and backyard seemed so far away now it almost didn't exist. But he knew it did. And he knew they didn't have condor-hawks, trolls, dragons, or any of the other creatures he had heard about or come in contact with so far. The widow Duncan's warning came to mind. *Be careful what you wish for.* Jamie shook his head. As he walked over to get his backpack, he had a speculative thought. *Maybe Arlann and Deena are right. Maybe I do need to go to the Castle in the Clouds sooner than I planned.*

With his pack in hand, he ducked through the opening to the outside. Looking around, he spied Barly and Deena talking down by the stream. He stretched as he donned his backpack. A low mist was burning off the surrounding plains in the bright morning sun. Drops of dew reflected the light and sparkled on a cobweb like little diamonds. The air smelled crisp and clean, and the visage helped clear his mind and focus his thoughts. Deena saw him and came running up. Barly followed.

"Good morning," he said. "How are Kip and Koki doing? Did they make it through the night?"

"The news is good!" she said excitedly. "They are both going to live! Charmac's magic was powerful enough to help them through. It will take time, but their wounds will heal."

"That's great news," Jamie exclaimed. "After all this, I wish you *would* have been with us yesterday, Barly. I doubt if that condor-hawk would have attacked if you had been around."

"Probably not," Barly agreed. "But, you know, the longer I'm in Neverlore, the more I'm convinced that certain events happen for a reason, even the not-so-good events."

After some thought, Jamie said, "You may be right, Barly. That hawk attack and Kip and Koki getting hurt are suggesting to me that I should go to Mistemere sooner than I thought. After Selth's story, this whole Neverlore fantasy is starting to make me have some not-so-fun questions. Walking is great, but I'm beginning to wonder. It's . . . it's . . . well, it's not my neighborhood or my own backyard. It's pretty scary sometimes, like you said."

Barly gave him a wizened look. "Deena and I were just speculating about that very thing. She sensed you might be feeling a need to move on."

"Don't get me wrong, Deena, I really like your village and you letting us stay with you and all. It's just, I kind of miss my family, and I'd like to know if I *can* get back home," Jamie went on. "In case I want to leave a little sooner than I'd planned," he hastily added.

"I see," Deena said. "I have no arguments with that." She winked at Barly. "So, to help you along the way, I made you a travel pack." She handed Jamie a small leather pouch similar to the one she carried when she was gathering. "This will aid you in your journey."

"What's in it?" Jamie asked, opening the flap and peering inside.

"Oh, a few gula bars and nettle-leaf balm," Deena answered. "For scratches and cuts only," she quickly added. "Remember, it works well on minor wounds also." They both laughed. "I'm also sending yota for insect repellent and powdered borok. You can add the powder to almost anything you could eat or drink and it will make it safe to consume."

"Gee, you didn't have to do that," Jamie said.

"I know I didn't have to," Deena answered, "but I wanted to. It's the least I can do after you climbed that tree and rescued Koki. Actually, though, it was mostly Mother's idea. She wanted to assist you on your journey. I filled your flask with aldirberry honey water and packed the gula bars. She did the rest."

Jamie laughed. "It seems like everyone else knew I was going to go to the Castle in the Clouds before I did. What is it with everybody in Neverlore? Are they all mind readers or something?"

Barly laughed. "I don't think it's mind reading. Some things are just easy to predict, that's all. Like next, you're going to ask me if I'll come with you to the castle."

"Well, you're wrong, Barly. I was going to ask Deena if I could see Kip and Koki. *Then* I was going to ask if you'd go with me." He grinned.

"Very funny," Barly grunted.

"That you can do, Jamie. However, we will have to make it a short visit, as they are still very weak and need to rest," Deena said. "Come with me." She took Jamie by the hand and led him and Barly through the village toward Charmac's hut.

By now, everyone in the tribe had heard about the hawk attack. Several of the children and adults came up and asked questions. Jamie and Deena had to repeat their story many times to inquisitive ears. Barly became tired of hearing it, so he played with several of the younger children to pass the time. It was mid-morning when they were finally able to satisfy everyone's curiosity and continue on to the healing obac. They entered and Barly stuck his head in behind them.

Inside, it was dimly lit and the smell of sweet incense filled the air. It took a moment for Jamie's eyes to adjust. Charmac sat in a low chair off to one side.

"Burning charo leaves provides a soothing, smoke-free atmosphere," the old lady whispered. "So as not to intrude on their healing, you have only a short time to see them. I must get water to boil to add moisture to the air. When I get back from the stream, you will have to leave." Barly grunted, squeezed his big frame over, and she ducked outside.

Jamie walked across the hut to where Kip was perched on a limb that had been planted in the dirt floor. The bird was leaning against an upright branch. He had patches of mud packed in his various wounds, and his broken wing was wrapped with cloth. He appeared to be sleeping.

"Hey, buddy, it's Jamie. How do you feel?" he asked quietly.

Kip turned his head and opened one eye. The other eye had a patch over it. "Oh, hi, Jamie," he wheezed. "I guess I'm not doing so well. I hurt all over and this healing mud the old lady packed in my wounds really itches. If I knew being alive could be so uncomfortable, I might have stayed a kite." He laughed and it sounded like a croak.

Jamie reached out and stroked his head. He was saddened at the sight and sound of the bird. "I must admit, I'm having some second thoughts about this land myself. It's been a bit more than I thought it would be. I guess walking isn't the only important thing out there, is it? It'd be nice not to have to fear for our lives at every new bend in the road. I wish I could stay and help you get well, but I think maybe I should go to Mistemere sooner than I planned."

"I'm going with you, like I promised," Barly added.

"Thank you, Barly. Anyway, as I was saying, I've got to find out if there *is* a way out of Neverlore," Jamie continued. "I guess when I think about it, I can't just vanish from my backyard and never return. This land is beautiful and there is a lot to explore, but I'm beginning to wonder if it's too much for me. I was hoping you could come with us, but you're in no condition to travel. At least not for a good while."

"I *would* like to go with you, but I'd be more burden than help. I wouldn't be much good as a lookout, not being able to fly. And I wouldn't want you to have to carry me all the way," he said hoarsely. "So I guess I'll have to stay with Koki until I heal. It's not so bad, though. I'm looking forward to Deena taking me gathering with her and Koki when I'm better. I can be her lookout for condor-hawks and such." He laughed another croaking laugh at his own joke.

"Charmac the Healer and I will nurse him back to good health again, I promise," Deena said. "You will soar with eagles like you wanted to, Kip."

"It's good to see you haven't quit hoping or lost your sense of humor," Barly said. "That will get you farther than anything."

"He's right," Jamie said. "I'm so glad you made it so I could thank you for saving Koki's life and, very possibly, our lives. I don't know what would have happened if you hadn't come back when you did. How did you know we were in trouble?"

"At the time, I was seeing how high I could fly. When I looked down, I saw this huge bird following you overhead," Kip said in an unsteady voice. He coughed. "It looked like he was up to something, so I started following him from above. It wasn't two or three minutes later that he suddenly dove down and snatched Koki off Deena's shoulder. I knew I had to act quickly, so I did the only thing I could think of. It was practically suicide, now that I think about it. I attacked a bird that was twice as big as me. I don't know what possessed me to do a crazy thing like that."

"It's that birdbrain logic of yours again," Barly said. "Your instinct told you what to do without you ever seeing other birds do it. Small birds do the same to larger birds, like crows or falcons, when they get too close to the small birds' nests. I wouldn't worry about going back and becoming a kite again. You'll do very well as a bird in Neverlore."

"Thanks, Barly. That's kind of you to say," Kip replied.

Jamie looked with affection at the battered bird. "I can see you're exhausted, so I'll say goodbye, friend. I'm truly sorry I didn't get to know you better and share more of this adventure with you. I'll miss you, Kip." He softly patted the wounded bird's head one last time.

"Goodbye, Jamie. I'm going to miss you, too. You're the one who helped bring me to life and I will miss getting to know you, also. Good luck, and may the wind always be at your back." He closed his one good eye and his head nodded.

Jamie wiped a watery eye, and he and Deena moved over to where Koki lay. She was swathed in bandages and resting in a soft, fragrant bed of cedar shavings.

"Can I touch her?" Jamie asked. Deena nodded. He reached out and petted her softly on the only place he dared, between her ears, chortling to her softly. As he did so, Koki chortled back and struggled to get up. "Now, now, girl. You lie there and rest. I've just come to say goodbye to you and Kip. You've been through a terrible ordeal and you need time to heal. I know Deena and old Charmac will take good care of you, and before you know it, you'll be up and gathering again." Koki responded by licking Jamie's outstretched hand.

"I've never seen her do that to anyone but me!" Deena exclaimed. "She must really like you, Jamie Nichols."

Jamie sadly gave Koki one last rub on her long ears and turned away. Just then, Charmac's voice announced from outside that it was time for them to leave. They thanked the old lady once again for helping the two wounded animals through the night with her healing powers, then made their way back to Deena's hut.

"Where are your mother and father?" he asked Deena.

"Father is quite concerned," she replied. "After our accident, he believes this is one more sign that something unknown *is* happening in Neverlore. He and Mother have gone to confer with the Mithrin. They will be back tomorrow," she whispered, eyes widening in awe. "I'm sort of in charge of our tribe until they return."

"I hope they don't run into that condor-hawk," Barly said.

"Me too. He's probably pretty mad at losing his meal," Jamie agreed. "Did you say you're watching your people? Alone?"

"I am," Deena answered proudly. "It's new for me. Women aren't usually allowed to hold positions of authority in the L'masse."

"That's impressive," Jamie said with admiration. "You *are* different from the other girls I've known."

Deena's dark skin turned a shade darker. "Mother and Father have altered their thoughts about certain things since the hawk attack. Mother never travels with him, but this time, she wanted to go and he took her. And he trusted my instincts about you and your friends. Father never has before, not completely. You've made an impression on both. This is rare."

"I guess that's good, then. My mother or father would never leave me alone in our house for a day, let alone all night and all day," Jamie said. "They always have someone *else* stay and look after me."

"If and when you make it home, I think your mother might have a different opinion of you. Remember, you are Treemaster now," Deena offered. "You must continue on, I know, and I will miss you, Jamie. None of the boys I know are as daring or have the sense of adventure that you do. If you direct those qualities wisely, they will take you far in your search for answers."

"It may have taken me too far already," Jamie replied, a slight note of concern in his voice. "It's hard to determine the right thing to do sometimes." He turned to the bear. "What do you think, Barly?"

Barly grinned. "I think we had better get going before you change your mind."

"I guess this is it, then," Jamie said. He shouldered his backpack and tied the pouch Deena had given him around his waist. "I was never much good at goodbyes. I prefer 'see you later.'" His voice took on a husky tone.

Jamie was surprised at the new feelings he was beginning to experience. Ever since the accident, he hadn't been very emotional about anything except being able to walk again. He cared for his mother, for sure, and his imagination had kept him going, but these newfound feelings were different. In the short time he had known her, Jamie found he had become attracted to Deena. The smile on her face, her truly caring attitude, and her genuine friendliness made him warm inside.

As if sensing his thoughts, Deena reached up and took a leather necklace from around her neck. Before Jamie could object, she clasped it around his neck and tucked it in the front of his shirt.

"What's this?" he asked. "Another gift?"

"It's a sea stone. My great uncle gave it to me before he passed on. It may serve you on your journey," she replied.

Jamie pulled the stone out and examined it. It was circular in shape and about the size of a quarter. The outside was smooth and glistened like mother of pearl. He turned it over and examined the other side. It was slightly concave and looked like the inside of a geode. The crystals there were the deepest blue he had ever seen.

"Hold it up to the sun and look at it closely," Deena instructed. Jamie did as he was told. As the sun's rays touched it, the inside of the stone began to glow. Fiery flecks of gold appeared and danced around within.

"That is totally awesome!" he exclaimed. "What's this thing made of?"

"It's called crystal laurium. It came from the undersea volcano that formed Neverlore. When the volcano erupted, lava spewed into the deep and formed sea stones. Once in a while, at low tide, you can find them on the beach at the Avalin Ocean. Normally, sea stones are bigger and have white laurium crystals inside. This one is a bit of an anomaly."

"But if it's a family heirloom, I can't accept it. You should keep it," Jamie said.

"In our culture, it isn't customary to refuse a gift once it is offered. It is a slight to the giver. Refusal says you don't accept or like me. It's only a stone. I can get another sometime."

"But . . . I . . . I . . . do like you," Jamie stammered. "And I'll miss you, too. You're . . . special."

"Then accept the gift and say no more," Deena replied with authority.

Barly walked over and examined it. "What does it do?" he asked.

"The sea stone stores up any kind of energy it is exposed to," she explained. "If you hold it up to the sun, it will store up light. If you hold it next to a fire, it will store up heat. If you wear it next to your heart, it will keep you warm."

It was Jamie's turn to blush. "Thank you, Deena. I don't know what else to say," he said. "No one has given me a gift like this before." He tucked the necklace back under his shirt.

Deena put her finger to his lips. "You don't have to say anything else. All you have to do is say goodbye," she said. She leaned forward and kissed him on the cheek. "I hope you find the answers you are looking for at the Castle in the Clouds. Be safe in your quest, Jamie," she whispered.

Jamie swallowed hard and something happened that hadn't in a long time. His eyes misted over from bittersweet sorrow instead of tears of self-pity. He reached out and hugged her awkwardly. "Goodbye, Deena. Tell your parents thanks from me. Your father is wise and your mother is kind. I won't forget you or your people, no matter where I end up. And who knows? Maybe our paths will cross again." Then, before she could see his watery eyes, he turned away. Jamie cleared his throat and, afraid to look back, he began to walk rapidly away.

Barly's voice was a little hoarse as he said, "Goodbye, Deena.

This has been good for me. I was able to experience a part of my youth that I never did when I was a cub. Tell the children I'll be back someday to give them more rides."

"Goodbye, Barly. You are always welcome here. I know the youngsters would be thrilled if you were to come back and visit." Deena then put her arms around his neck and gave him a big hug. While she had her hands behind his head, she squeezed a drop of liquid from a gula berry behind his ear. It made a dark red stain the size of a dime. "I've left the mark of the L'masse behind your left ear. Wherever you travel in Neverlore, you will be welcome when you show the mark. It will ensure you safe passage. Take care of Jamie for me. He is a special person."

"I will, I promise," Barly said, turning away.

Barly loped up the path and caught up with Jamie at the crest of the ridge. They stopped and turned to look back at Deena who had been joined by several of the children. They all raised their hands and waved goodbye. Jamie and Barly sadly waved back. They turned and headed north, retracing their steps along the path they had arrived on two days before.

* * *

The two companions walked in silence for some time, each lost in his own thoughts. They made good time, as if a new determination pushed them on. It was well past noon when they came to the crossroads and the garden where they first met Deena. Jamie was the first to break the silence.

"Do you want to stop for lunch, Barly?"

"I guess we have time," he replied. He looked to the west. "Those rain clouds Kip advised us of two days ago are still on the other side of the mountains. It will stay light until late today."

They made their way between the rows, and once again found themselves under the same apple tree where they had eaten their first lunch together. On the way in, Jamie exchanged some of the vegetables he had gathered previously with fresh ones.

The two made small talk while they ate. Both were almost through when Jamie spied movement at the edge of the forest to the west. "Ken yu shee whet's booving ober dere?" he asked with a mouthful of gula bar and apple.

"Wha'd do thay?" Barly said, his mouth full of carrot and corn. They both laughed at each other and Jamie choked. He coughed and swallowed to clear his mouth. "I said, can you see what's moving at the edge of the forest?" he asked, pointing. Barly followed his outstretched finger and looked.

"It's white, whatever it is," he replied. "Let's look through those biniclears or whatever you call them."

"Binoculars. They're called binoculars," Jamie snickered. He pulled them from his backpack and focused on the object. "Oh . . . my . . . gosh!" he exclaimed. He got up on his knees for a better view. "I don't believe my eyes. It's a unicorn! Barly, it's a real, live unicorn!"

"What's a unicorn?" Barly asked.

"Here, look for yourself," Jamie said as he adjusted the binoculars for Barly and held them to his big face. His hands were shaking.

"Steady, I can't see with you wobbling like that." Jamie held the binoculars with both hands and Barly peered through. "Well, I'll be! It looks like a horse with a horn sticking out of its forehead. So, what is this unicorn animal that's got you so excited?" he asked. "I've never seen or heard of one before. We have similar animals in Adelwilde, but they are a lot smaller and are black or brown or gray. The only white animals there are bears. I've never seen an animal with a single horn, though. What is it, a cross between a goat and a mule?"

"You've got to be kidding." Jamie laughed. "A goat and a mule? I don't *think* so. In my land, a unicorn is one of the most beautiful and mystical animals of all! But unicorns are a legend. I thought they only existed in fairytales."

"Jamie, this is Neverlore, remember?" Barly reminded him.

"Uh, I keep forgetting. I guess I still have a hard time believing everything I see. A unicorn is about as special as it gets." He adjusted the binoculars and studied the animal closely.

The magnificent creature was grazing near the edge of the trees. Its glossy white mane shone in the afternoon sun, and when it raised its head, the spiral horn reflected the afternoon rays. It was something to behold.

As Jamie peered intently through the binoculars, he noticed more movement behind the unicorn. He adjusted the magnification. "Barly, this is incredible! There's two more—a mother and a baby!" He held the binoculars so Barly could look again.

"I still say they look like a cross between a goat and a mule. Look at the beard the big one has got," Barly said.

"There's no mule or goat in them. They're more like horses, geez!" Jamie exclaimed.

"To each his own," Barly responded.

The grazing unicorn suddenly raised his head and stuck his nose into the wind. He bobbed his head in agitation, whirled around, and in the blink of an eye, all three disappeared into the forest. Jamie sighed and lowered the glasses. "They're gone."

"They probably caught our scent," Barly said, getting up. "We probably should be moving on also." He pointed to the northwest.

"See that lake way over there? That's Lake Longwater. Robinwood is on the other side."

Jamie looked to where Barly was pointing. Beyond several hills and valleys, he could see water shimmering in the afternoon sun. Lake Longwater stretched to the north as far as his eye could see. "Can we reach Robinwood by nightfall?"

"I think so, if we get going and don't take any more breaks," Barly replied, heading back to the path. With no more said, the two continued on their journey.

Jamie kept close to Barly, lost in thought. The silence gave him time to reflect. The more he tried to answer the questions that had been forming in his mind, the more elusive the answers became. Finally, with a shrug of his shoulders, he gave up.

"I guess you're right, Barly. Sometimes it's easier just to accept things as they are, rather than trying to make them into something they're not. But I feel like I'm playing pin the tail on the donkey and keep getting close, but not close enough to win. Do you know what I mean?"

"I don't know. I've never tried to pin a tail on a donkey before. The ones I came across already had their own tails," Barly said.

"Oh man, you're impossible sometimes!" Jamie laughed.

It was dusk when they finally reached the shore of Lake Longwater. The sun had fallen behind the mountains and the air was starting to cool off. Jamie pulled a hooded sweatshirt from his backpack and put it on. He looked out over the water. A long, grassy valley stretched from the far shore into the foothills. Beyond the foothills, the Barrier Range stood imposingly, silhouetted in purples, reds, and blues.

"That's the Forest of Whispers," Barly said, pointing to the grassy slope below the foothills.

"That's a *forest?*" Jamie asked. "I don't see any trees. All I see is grass, rocks, and a few scrub bushes. Where are these Treesers?"

"Oh, they're around somewhere, probably over the ridge or up the lakeshore," Barly answered. "They're never very far from here. They'll come here if there's a need to."

Shadows reached out over the still water as they walked down to the lake's edge. "I'm really thirsty," Jamie said, kneeling down to get a drink. "That aldirberry honey mixture Deena gave me gets a little too sweet after a while." He cupped his hands and scooped water out of the lake.

"No! Don't drink that!" Barly cried. He lunged at Jamie and pulled him back.

"Why not? What's wrong?" Jamie exclaimed, staring at his cupped hands.

"Lake Longwater is under a magic spell," Barly answered. "Selth told me more about Neverlore the day you and Deena went gathering. This is where Erenor cast the army of Druin when he turned them into creatures of the deep." He reached down, picked up a stone, and threw it into the lake. When it landed, it didn't sink. It bounced to a stop and sat on the top of the water, barely causing a ripple. Then it slowly disappeared below the surface. Jamie stared, quickly opened his hands, and wiped them vigorously on his pants.

"If you drink the water, there is no telling what will happen. I mean, you could lose your voice or all of your hair could fall out. You could shrink to the size of a mouse, or worse. Selth warned me not to drink the water."

Jamie asked in bewilderment, "How can I tell what's safe and what's not, Barly? I mean, this place is supposed to be so wonderful, but every time I turn around, I could get into trouble."

Barly answered, "I don't know, Jamie. Some things are safe and some things aren't. I suggest you don't touch anything or wander off without checking with me first. Neverlore can be full of surprises sometimes."

Jamie mumbled, "I'll be sure to remember that."

Barly led them around the shoreline until they came to a small stream flowing into the lake. Jamie made sure not to step in the water along the way.

At the edge of the stream, Barly turned and made his way upstream along the bank. Both sides were lined with thick brush and the going was difficult. Jamie followed as close as he could without getting slapped in the face from the branches.

Finally, the brush ended and they stepped into a small glen. "Here we are. This is Robinwood," Barly announced. He stepped aside and motioned for Jamie to pass. Jamie walked past Barly and looked around. The glen was a small clearing entirely surrounded by dense firs, tall oaks, and smaller trees that looked like a cross between a juniper bush and a pine tree. Amongst the trees were scattered many colored rocks. Toward the back of the glen was a pool from which the stream flowed rapidly. It passed through the clearing and into a tunnel of dense, prickly undergrowth. Around the clearing, the ground was covered with a thick layer of moss that felt like carpeting under Jamie's feet. He felt a sense of security about the glen.

"This is where we will spend the night," Barly said.

"Wow! This is like some kind of fairytale place!" Jamie said with glee. He bounded across the clearing and peered into the water.

"Robinwood is enchanted," Barly answered, sitting down on a rock. "Oh, by the way, you can drink the water here . . . it's safe."

Jamie knelt at the edge of the pool. The water was clear as glass. At the bottom, he could see bubbles rippling and pushing around the loose sand. Because of an underground spring stirring the sand, the bottom looked like it was alive. Jamie bent over and tasted the water. It was sweet and cool, and he drank until he was satisfied.

By now it was getting dark, and the first stars were beginning to appear. "I'm getting chilly. Can we start a fire, Barly?" Jamie asked. He put his hood up and pulled his sweatshirt a little tighter.

"I don't see why not. As long as we don't burn the place down, it should be alright," Barly replied.

Jamie went about gathering sticks and leaves. Next to the rock Barly was sitting on, he scraped the moss away and made a fire pit. He placed the twigs and leaves in the center, took a box of matches from his backpack, and lit the tinder. As the leaves caught fire and spread to the twigs, Jamie added larger sticks. Soon the little fire was a cheery-crackling blaze.

Jamie took the mess kit out of his backpack. It had a pot and lid, two cups, deep plates, and fold-up spoons with forks at the other end. He spread them out next to the fire. "I'll make us some soup," he said. Barly filled the pot with water while Jamie cut up some of the vegetables he had in his backpack. Jamie put the sliced pieces in the water and hung the pot over the fire on a forked stick he had found. It didn't take long to cook, and soon they were enjoying hot vegetable soup. Jamie took a gula bar from the pouch and split it with Barly.

"Okay. Barly, tell me more about Robinwood," Jamie said. "Why is this place enchanted?"

Barly set his plate down and wiped off his chin. "Well . . . let me see. Erenor defeated Druin's army and cast a spell on them, like Selth explained. Then he had them march down into Lake Longwater, and as they went under, Erenor turned the whole lot into mudpuppies, leeches, and the like. He figured if they were kept in the lake, he would know where they were at all times. To be doubly safe, he cast a spell over the entire surface of Lake Longwater to make sure they could never escape. It turns out that Druin's army was so evil, the lake eventually became poisoned. To ensure the spell held the poison in the water, Erenor gave this spring magical properties. As long as the spring flows into the lake, the spell remains unbroken. So you can see why it's safe to drink the water from the spring and not the lake. I always knew Robinwood was a good place, but Selth's account of things finally explained why."

"Whoa, that's pretty scary," Jamie said. He put his plate down. "What happens if the spring dries up and quits flowing?" He glanced out over the lake. A three-quarter moon was rising, and its beams shone across the water. The reflection caused tiny pinpoints of light to dance on the surface. It seemed like a million winking, blinking eyes were looking up from the water at them. The thought of what was swimming and crawling around under the surface sent a shiver up his spine.

"I'd hate to think what would happen if it did," Barly replied. "However, the chances are slim. And of course, the Treesers are always around to guard over this spring, to make sure its flow is never altered."

"But I thought . . . hey, where are they? What do they look like?" Jamie asked.

"According to Selth," Barly said, "the Treesers watch over this whole area around the lake." He waved his paw. "Especially Robinwood and this spring. They are always on the move, patrolling and guarding.

Treesers go back to the time before Druin and weren't affected by his evil spells. They were a natural choice to guard this beautiful place. However, even though they are protectors, I guess they can be an unreliable bunch if they have a mind to be. Selth said that it's best not to do anything to provoke them. They're old and mighty crotchety. Right now though, we're safe enough. I suggest we get some sleep because it's going to be a long day tomorrow. It feels like it could get pretty cool tonight, so you can sleep between me and the fire if you want to keep warm."

"I've got this also, remember?" Jamie asked, pulling out his necklace. He took it off and held the sea stone next to the fire. After a few moments, it began to glow and give off a dull golden light. Jamie put his hand around it. Warmth radiated up his arm. "This is really neat!" he exclaimed. "It's quite warm, Barly." He tucked the stone back in his shirt.

"I've been here a lot longer than you, Jamie, and things still continue to amaze me," Barly said. He slid off his rock seat. "Come, use ole Barly for a big bear pillow."

Jamie didn't need any further coaxing. He threw more wood on the fire, then moved over and curled up next to Barly. "You're sure we're safe here?" he asked, yawning.

"I'm sure," Barly said, settling back against the mossy rock. "Nothing will bother us here as long as we stay next to the spring. You can sleep easy."

"Mmm, that's good," Jamie said. He could feel the warmth of the sea stone spreading across his chest. "I've had more adventure in the last few days than I've had all my life." As he lay there looking up at the stars, he went on. "This land is the most wonderful place I've ever seen. It's like Neverlore is too real, if that makes any sense."

"I'm not sure what you mean," Barly said. "What can be any more real than what we're doing now?"

Jamie yawned again. "This adventure is huge. I feel like an early frontiersman who just saw mountains or the wild west for the first time." Jamie went on to explain to Barly how his country had been settled, telling of the wagon trains, cowboys and Indians, and wild west towns.

"Interesting story," Barly replied, yawning himself. "Like many have said, one's imagination *can* become real here."

"That's the part I'm not so sure of," Jamie said sleepily. "It's almost scary to think you can do or be almost anything your imagination dreams up in Neverlore."

"Within reason, though. Remember, within reason," Barly said.

"I suppose," Jamie agreed. "I'll guess I'll imagine a little more tomorrow. Goodnight, Barly."

As Jamie slipped into sleep, he thought about his family and home again. The last thought he had was that he would wake up in his own bed and his adventure would have really been some kind of fantastic dream after all.

It took sleep a long time to find Barly. He stared out over the water wondering what manner of ill fortune would befall Neverlore if the spell on the lake was ever broken. If it ever happened, he hoped there would be someone with power great enough to defeat the evil force that was sure to come boiling up out of the water. The bright moon shone high over the lake when he finally dozed off.

Chapter 8

The next morning dawned cool and overcast, the sun barely visible in the low-hanging clouds. Jamie woke up first, opened his eyes, and looked around. The first things he saw were the spring, the ashes from the fire, and the lake in the distance. Barly stirred behind him and let out a loud snore.

"I didn't think it could be a dream. Too much has happened so far," he said, mostly to himself. *And there's more to explore ahead of us,* Jamie thought as he grabbed his backpack and stood up. *I'll miss Kip being our lookout, though.* His mind strayed from Kip, to his trip, to Deena, and he realized he missed her, too. The thought of Deena reminded him of the drink she'd filled his canteen with, and that thought made him thirsty.

He reached down and unhooked the canteen from the side of his backpack. He unsnapped the top and drank the rest of the aldirberry water. *She's right, it does give me energy.* The last vestiges of sleep passed from his body and he was ready for a new day. *I must admit, things almost always look better in the morning than they do at night,* he thought happily.

Jamie reached into the backpack and pulled out his water gun (certain protection from an older brother who would surprise attack now and then). It was a Drencher II model, with a battery operated plunger (perfect for distance defense), large capacity reservoir, and a collapsible stock.

Might as well fill this while I'm at it. No telling when we'll come across water again, he thought. Jamie walked to the pool and knelt next to it. He filled the canteen part way and took a long drink. He then filled it up the rest of the way. Next, Jamie filled his water gun. As he did so, he spotted several smooth, round pebbles the size of marbles lying on the bottom of the spring.

Slingshot ammo. Jamie collected a handful from the water and walked back toward the fire pit, slipping the pebbles in the side pocket of his backpack.

Suddenly there was a loud splash from the pool. Startled, Jamie spun around but could see nothing unusual. "Hello?" he asked, cautiously returning to the water's edge. The only thing he saw were bubbles rising lazily up through the water.

A large form surrounded by a burst of bubbles suddenly came streaking up from the bottom. *Sploosh! Splash!* The calm surface erupted and out leapt a *gigantic* frog. "Ribbit!" the frog croaked. It landed at the edge and hopped a few steps toward him. Jamie was so startled he jumped backward, stumbled over a rock, and fell flat on his back. The wind was knocked out of him and he lay there, staring wide-eyed at the frog.

"What on earth? W-who are you?" he stammered, catching his breath.

The unexpected arrival, an odd sight to behold, hopped closer. The frog wore a blue vest and a gray pair of pants. Perched on his nose was a pair of wire-rimmed spectacles, behind which bright yellow eyes blinked. In his hand he carried a staff. He stopped, pulled himself up on his hind legs, and leaned on it for support. He was at least five feet tall!

"Ribbit! I'm Artimus Prince," he croaked. "I live in this spring. Who might you two be?"

All the commotion roused Barly. "What is going on here? Can't a bear sleep in peace?" he asked, rubbing his eyes. He sat up and surveyed the scene in front of him. "Who's this? Where'd *he* come from?" he grunted in surprise.

"H . . . he just jumped out of the pond and scared the wits out of me," Jamie said.

"Like I said, my name's Artimus Prince," the frog said. "I live here." He blinked again.

Barly eyed the strange figure before him, not sure how to react. He stood up his tallest, just to be sure.

"I'm Barly, and this is Jamie," Barly said, making the introductions. He helped Jamie up. "If he lives in Robinwood, he can't be too bad," he whispered.

"What are you prince of?" Jamie asked, regaining his composure. "Did a witch cast an evil spell on you or something?"

"I beg your pardon, what are you talking about?" the frog asked, adjusting his spectacles. He straightened up to his full height and blinked again.

"You know, when a wicked witch casts a spell on a frog, and only the kiss of a beautiful princess can break it," Jamie answered, feeling a little foolish.

Artimus laughed a croaking laugh. "Oh, I see what you mean. Ha! I wish it were that simple. Prince is my last name, not my title. I am—or was—a shepherd," he added ruefully.

"Well, I don't know much about shepherds, but I *do* know they don't live in ponds," Jamie said matter-of-factly.

"You're telling me?" the big frog said. "It wasn't my choice, that's for sure. My family and I didn't even live near Lake

Longwater or Robinwood. One day, a long time ago, I brought my flock down the side of the mountains to graze and look for water and we ended up here. We had just finished drinking from the lake when suddenly, all my sheep shriveled up like dandelion puffs, and a breeze came along and blew them away. At the same time, a terrible thing happened to me. I turned into a huge, cursed frog! It's been a dismal existence ever since that day. I've been a frog for so long now, I've given up any hope of ever changing back to my normal self."

"Whoa, that's too bad," Jamie said. He glanced out at the lake uneasily, remembering how close he had come to drinking the water.

"I told you if you drank the water, bad things could happen!" Barly said smugly.

"Do you know why?" Artimus croaked eagerly. "All these years I've been wondering. I could never get anyone to talk about it."

Barly obliged him and told an abbreviated story of the rise and fall of Druin, and how Erenor had cast Druin's army into the lake. He explained how Erenor cast spell over it and how the Treesers guarded the area. "There's no such thing as a harmless sip of evil. Lake Longwater should be renamed Lake Deadwater. It's ironic, but as long as the water is dead, Neverlore remains alive."

"Well, that explains a lot to me," Artimus said. "I was very little during the time all that happened I barely remember a dragon or Druin and his army. They were more like scarey tales or something told to us children. Now I know, among other things, why those strange trees would arrive with no warning, and leave the same way."

In spite of Artimus's plight, Jamie started to laugh. "I'm sorry. I'm not laughing at you," he said. "It's just, the longer I'm in

Neverlore, the more unbelievable things become. Half of the time, I think I'm dreaming or hallucinating or something, and the other half, I'm not sure what to think."

"Well, I don't know about that," Artimus croaked. "But I do know I'm sick of eating bugs all the time. Blah! I'd give anything for a good meal."

"Hey, I can help you with that," Jamie exclaimed. He reached in his backpack and pulled out an apple he had taken from the garden. "Here, try this. It's not a meal, but it's better than bugs." He took out his pocket knife and cut the apple into several bite-sized pieces.

"I don't believe it! Thank you, kind sir," Artimus said, accepting Jamie's offering. He took a big bite. "Mmmmm. This is delicious. Where did you get it from?"

So, once again, Jamie and Barly told the story of their events together over the previous two days. "Your tale is similar to mine, Artimus. We've both been transformed," Jamie continued. "The problem is, I'm not sure *what's* right now. If I stay, I can most certainly walk and do most of the things I've wanted to do for a long time. But once I've done them all, where do I go from there?" He showed Artimus the sea stone, then told him about the extinct volcano, Alizar, and the hawk attack. "I've left my home, family, school, and a lot of other things I didn't think I cared about before. And for what? I could be blown up, roasted by a dragon, or possibly turned into who-knows-what by an evil wizard. I need to find some things out, so we're taking this path to Mistemere in hopes of seeing Erenor," he finished.

Artimus swallowed the last of his apple and looked at the unlikely pair of travelers. He rubbed his chin. "I'm not troubled about the volcano, because it's never erupted in our time. And the dragon? I suppose there have been dragons in Neverlore from the very beginning, but there have been none since Alizar. And Druin or no Druin, I've found it does little good to concern myself with events I have no control over. I have no need for worry and stress."

"For a frog, you seem to have a lot of wisdom," Barly said with admiration. "Jamie could learn something from you."

"What's that supposed to mean?" Jamie demanded.

"I wasn't always a frog, remember?" Artimus croaked. "As a shepherd, I spent a lot of time tending my sheep. It was a simple and fulfilling existence, and I had a lot of time to ponder my being. I discovered that if I didn't involve myself in circumstances I couldn't control, situations didn't occur that would affect me negatively."

"Wisely spoken," Barly said, for Jamie's benefit. "You seem like a likeable sort. You are welcome to join us, if you like. If it's possible Erenor can help Jamie, there's a chance he can help you too."

The big frog responded, "Robinwood is a remote place. Very few people travel by here anymore. And any that do have not been able to help me," he said sadly. "Anything has got to be better than living in this cold spring. It is quite kind of you to ask me to join you, and I gladly accept your invitation. Maybe Erenor *can* help me. How long do you think it will take us?"

"It's almost three days from here to Mistemere," Barly said. "The sooner we get going, the sooner we will get there. I suggest we have a quick breakfast, then head up the valley. It looks like it could rain today."

Jamie started to say something, then thought better of it. Instead, he emptied the fruits and nuts from his pack and shared them with Barly and Artimus. He divided two of the gula bars and passed them around.

"This is much better than the bugs and fish I've been eating," Artimus indicated, smacking his frog lips. "Like I said, I didn't venture far from this pool, few people came by, and even fewer shared their food with me. It's been a long time since I've enjoyed the taste of something that didn't fly, swim, or live in the mud."

When they had finished, Barly stood and said, "We'd best get going now. We'll take a way out of Robinwood other than the way we came in. I discovered it a while back. Follow me, and whatever you do, stick together."

Barly led them around the spring to the back of the glen and took a narrow path that was hidden behind a thick clump of alders. Jamie went next, ducking under low branches growing across the path. Artimus followed Jamie, using his staff for support. His step was a cross between walking and hopping. When Jamie looked over his shoulder to see if the big frog was coming, he had to cover his mouth to suppress a chuckle. Surprisingly though, the frog was able to keep up with them easily.

Barly looked up at the sky. "The clouds are pretty thick and black up ahead. It looks like we're in for a storm. And that's not all. You better prepare yourselves for what may be ahead."

Just then, they broke out of the dense undergrowth. As the group rounded the last bend, the path began to climb. Barly stopped and held up his paw. "Ah-ha! I thought they might show up to check on us," he said in a low voice. Jamie peered around him and caught his breath.

"Are those Treesers?" he gasped.

"Yep, those are Treesers," Artimus answered. "I've seen them around Robinwood many times before."

Jamie stared in fascination. The day before, the meadow had been empty all the way to the ridge. It was nothing like what he saw now. Spread out on both sides of the path was a forest of the strangest trees he had ever seen. Their roots were long and crooked and spread out over the ground like octopus arms. The trunks were gnarled and ashen-colored, and sinuous limbs reached out every which way like spindly arms. Scattered amongst the limbs were clumps of lengthy, twisted, white leaves that resembled hair. The Treesers looked like ghostly old women.

In the same low voice, Barly said, "I've never seen this many together at once before. I don't know if it's a good sign or not. Stay behind me in single file and keep as close to the middle of the path as possible. If we are quiet and mind our own business, we shouldn't have any problems."

Jamie and Artimus did as they were told and formed a line behind Barly. As they began walking again, a few chilly raindrops began to fall. Jamie huddled beneath the hood of his sweatshirt. He felt the lump of the sea stone through the fabric. *I wish I would have built a fire this morning and heated this thing up*, he thought.

While they walked, Jamie studied the Treesers. "These things give me the creeps," he decided, shuddering.

"*Sshhhh!*" Barly whispered loudly. "The Treesers don't like being talked about. Don't say or do anything that will upset them."

"Well, just the same, this is a bit spooky," Jamie whispered back tensely.

As they moved further along, the Treesers shifted closer and tighter to the path. The three tried to pretend they didn't notice and made their way along as quietly as possible. The wind picked up and the raindrops started coming down harder. As the wind blew through the Treesers' branches, it made a low whispering sound. It sounded to Jamie like the trees were talking amongst themselves. The farther they walked, the louder the sound got. He shuddered involuntarily.

Here and there, long limbs drooped down over the trail. They began to hang lower and lower. As Barly, Jamie, and Artimus passed underneath, wet, sticky leaves began to brush against their heads. It seemed to Jamie like the roots of the trees were actually trying to trip them as they stumbled along. They had to veer off the path more and more to keep moving forward.

"My goodness, this is becoming most difficult," Artimus said, pushing branches out of the way with his staff. "I dare say, if it gets much worse, we may have to turn back."

"I think it's too late for that," Barly said grimly. He pointed behind them. Jamie and Artimus looked over their shoulders. The path had disappeared! Treesers had closed in behind them. Retreat was now impossible.

"What do we do now?" Jamie asked. The rain fell steadily, and all around them, the branches creaked and groaned in the wind.

"There are Treesers everywhere," Barly growled. "This doesn't make any sense. I have no idea why they are acting so hostile."

"This *definitely* isn't good," Artimus said. "In all the times they've come to Robinwood, I've never seen them act this way and they don't usually move around during the day. This is some storm! We had better start looking for shelter. But first, let's get away from these Treesers."

Jamie and Artimus followed Barly as he forged on, forcing his big body through the dense branches. They scrambled around limbs and over roots until the going was so difficult they had to stop. Artimus squinted ahead into the brush. "If I'm not mistaken, it looks like there's a cave just beyond that last clump of trees!" he cried above the storm. "It appears big enough for all of us to fit in. Follow me." Beating back the limbs with his staff, he pushed forward.

"That's easy for you to say. How are *we* ever going to get

through this tangle of branches?" Jamie yelled. He had to shout to be heard above the wind and rain. Off in the distance, lightning flashed and thunder rumbled. "I don't know about you guys, but I've had enough of these nasty Treesers," he exclaimed. He reached in his backpack and pulled out his hatchet. He tore off the sheath and started hacking at the branches in front of him. Suddenly, as if by magic, the branches lifted away from the path. They could now see the cave, just off the path to their right. The entrance was underneath the limbs of a particularly large and gnarly old Treeser.

"I don't know what you've done, Jamie, but we better run for it before they change their minds!" Barly yelled. "Quick, after me!" He dashed for the cave.

Neither Artimus nor Jamie needed any further coaxing. They sprinted through the low brush and crossed the remaining distance quickly. Barly reached the cave first. He ran inside with Jamie and Artimus close behind.

By now, thunder crashed constantly and lightning flashed everywhere. The clouds opened up and rain came down in sheets. As they peered out into the storm, they could see the frightening trees advancing on the cave entrance. "Well, we'll see about you Treesers! I'll teach you to mess with us!" Jamie yelled. He pulled his hood down tighter and held up his hatchet. Before Barly or Artimus could stop him, he charged toward the approaching trees. Without warning, *swoosh,* a large limb dropped down and covered the cave entrance, blocking his way back.

"What's going on?" Jamie yelped, jumping back. The branches and leaves made a thick barrier across the mouth of the cave. Jamie jumped forward and pushed on them. "I don't believe it," he exclaimed. "These things won't budge!"

He raised his hatchet high above his head. "Take that, you miserable excuse for a tree!" he yelled, bringing the blade down sharply on the largest limb. *Clang!* The hatchet glanced harmlessly off the limb. The shock was so great that it flew out of Jamie's hand.

"Yeoch!" he howled. He shook his hand, trying to ease the sharp pain shooting up his arm. "I nearly broke my wrist!" Jamie was mad now. He shoved his whole body against the branches again and again, but they still wouldn't give. "Stupid, stupid trees! What in Neverlore's going on here?"

Barly stepped forward and felt the branch. "Well, I'll be! This wood is rock-hard and feels like steel. My guess is that it's an Ironwood Treeser. I remember hearing of them, but I've never seen one. They're supposed to be very rare, and only found up north."

"An Ironwood Treeser?" Artimus asked. He hopped up next to them and peered through the leaves.

"I've only seen one since I've been here," said Barly. "The Ironwood Treeser supposedly only appears when there is a grave disturbance in the spring or lake. Something must have prompted it to come here. It looks like it may take more than a hatchet to get us out of here."

They all stared through the branches. "I don't understand it," Barly said. "I've never heard of Treesers bothering harmless travelers before, have you, Artimus?"

"No, can't say that I have," Artimus replied. "I wonder what could have happened to make them act like this."

Jamie walked over to where his hatchet had landed, picked it up, and sheathed it. He put it in his backpack. As he did, a stone fell out of the side pouch. He eyed the pebble in the dirt. A disturbing thought came to him.

"Uh, Barly? Do the Treesers really look after Robinwood that well?" he asked, picking it up.

Barly looked narrowly at Jamie as he answered. "Especially Robinwood. They guard over the spring, remember? Why do you ask?"

Jamie took a few steps backward. "Um . . . well . . . you see, I . . . I took some stones from the spring this morning. I was going to use them for ammunition in my slingshot," he stammered. "I . . . uh . . . also filled my canteen and water gun while we were there."

"You what? How could you?!" Barly cried. "That spring is sacred! It's no wonder an army of Ironwood Treesers is trying to stop us. When did you do a fool thing like that?"

"Whi-while y-you were still asleep. I didn't even think about it at the time," Jamie stammered again, hanging his head. "Can't I give them back and say I'm sorry? I mean, they were only pebbles."

"Not hardly," Artimus answered. "Stealing from the spring is a serious offense to the Treesers. They don't take that lightly."

"I didn't steal anything," Jamie said defensively. "They're just plain stones. What's the big deal?"

"Well, from the way they're acting, I'd say they were more than just plain ol' stones," Barly said. "Since the spring is enchanted, I'd guess the stones are magical in some way."

"Oh great!" Jamie exclaimed. "I pick a few rocks out of the water and this happens! What next? I think I'm beginning not to like Neverlore so much." He plopped down on a nearby log.

Just then Artimus held up his hand. "Wait a minute," he said. He stuck his nose in the air and sniffed. "I think we may have a more serious problem." He walked over to where Jamie sat and sniffed again. He bent down and looked at the log. Either end disappeared in the dirt. "I've smelled this smell before, but it was a long time ago. This doesn't look like a log. It looks more like a big root. If I were you Jamie, I'd—" He stopped when the log started to stir.

"Hey! What's going on?" Jamie cried, jumping up. "My seat just moved!" As they watched in fascination, the root began to twist and turn. Slowly it began pulling itself up out of the cave floor.

Suddenly, Artimus let out a stifled shriek. "Now I remember where I smelled that smell before! We've wandered into the lair of a Snakeroot! We've got to get out of this cave, now!" He jumped toward the entrance of the cave but when a Treeser limb snapped in, searching for him, he spun around and raced instead to the back of the cave. Jamie and Barly followed.

"What's a Snakeroot?" Jamie cried.

"It's a vine serpent," Artimus replied. "They're the most *awful* creatures. When I was a boy, they used to catch the sheep that wandered away from the flock and eat them. They'd lie in the grass and snatch them one by one. I thought the last of the Snakeroots died off a long time ago."

They stared in horror as the Snakeroot pulled its head up out of the dirt. What a hideous-looking thing it was. It had fiery eyes, three curved horns, and feelers twisting about on its chin. The fearsome head sat on a long, thick neck and it swayed around like a great snake looking for prey. The dank smell of musty, rotten leaves filled the cave. The Snakeroot let out a fearsome hiss. It was staring right at them. When it opened its mouth, they could see long, dripping fangs.

"Oh no! What do we do now?" Jamie cried. Their backs were against the wall and there was no place to go.

"We better hope this cave has a back door, or we're going to be his next meal." Barly breathed heavily.

The Snakeroot reared to its full height. Its head brushed the top of the cave as it slithered toward them. "I sees zee Treesers has delivered me a fine deenner," the beast hissed in a raspy, wicked voice. "Frog legs for zee appetizer, a plump bear for zee main course, and a tasty man-boy for deessert. What a feast ziss vill be!"

The Snakeroot was entirely out of the ground now. Jamie gasped at how big it was, at least twenty feet long, and as thick as a bushel basket in the middle. "*Woowww!* How do we fight something like this?" he cried.

Artimus was the first to react. "I'll give you an appetizer!" he yelled. He picked up a rock and heaved it at the Snakeroot. The rock struck the beast on the side of the head, breaking off one of its horns.

The Snakeroot let out such an awful scream they had to cover their ears. It was like the magnified sound of fingernails clawing across a blackboard. All three winced. However, the monster stopped where it was and eyed them carefully, its head swaying back and forth again. Barly picked up a rock and got ready to throw it.

"Come any closer and I'll put this one right between your eyes," he growled in a threatening voice. For the moment, it was a stand off.

While Barly held the Snakeroot's attention, Jamie fumbled for his flashlight and shined it around the back of the cave. He spotted something in the shadows behind a rock and moved closer to inspect. "Ugh! A body!" he cried, stumbling backward. Sprawled out on the floor of the cave was a partially decomposed skeleton. Jamie dropped the light as he caught himself.

"Yessss," hissed the Snakeroot. "Zee remains of my last meal, which, by zee way, vas some time ago. You might as vell give up, no one's gotten away from me yet." The monster opened its mouth and hissed at them again. Poisonous slime dripped from its fangs.

"Here, munch on this!" Barly cried. He heaved the other rock at the creature.

This time the brute was ready and dodged the projectile. It slithered a little closer.

"You think you can stop me with zose leettle rocks? Ha!"

Barly stepped next to Artimus. "You may think we would make a good meal, but I assure you, we won't go down without a fight," he growled. He picked up a large stick and swung it around his head.

While Artimus and Barly held the Snakeroot at bay, Jamie found his flashlight and shined it on the rock again. He noticed a good sized crack in the back wall near the floor. He knelt down and, shining the light through the opening, could see a tunnel. Jamie crawled through the opening, and when he pointed his flashlight ahead, he found it went farther than the light did. He turned and looked back into the cave. Both Barly and Artimus were throwing rocks at the Snakeroot with little success. The monster was almost upon them.

He called to them, "Hey guys, there's a tunnel back here! It looks like it goes a long way. Quick, it's our only chance!"

Barly threw the club and Artimus threw the last rock at the exact same time. Fate must have been with them, for when the Snakeroot ducked to miss the rock, the club hit him right between his eyes. The beast reared back with a mighty roar and, in doing so, smashed its head against the ceiling of the cave. It slumped forward, momentarily dazed. Artimus and Barly seized the opportunity, turned, and dashed toward Jamie's voice. Quickly, they knelt down and squeezed through the crack.

"Let's get out of here fast," Jamie whispered tersely. "If we can get in here, so can the Snakeroot."

He shined the light ahead into the darkness and started down the dark shaft. The tunnel wasn't high enough to stand in, so they had to stoop as they ran. They hadn't gone two hundred yards when they heard a muffled screech in the darkness behind them. The Snakeroot had entered the tunnel and was coming after them!

"Oh my soul, we are in a bad fix," Artimus panted. "I sure hope this tunnel doesn't end before we find a place to hide. That monster is going to keep coming, no matter what."

They ran on as fast as they could. Even so, the Snakeroot appeared to be gaining on them. Blood-curdling sounds came ominously from the darkness behind them.

The three of them pushed on harder. Deeper and deeper into the mountain the tunnel took them, farther and farther from the only way they knew of to get out.

Chapter 9

After a few minutes, the tunnel became tall enough for them to stand up. They were able to make better time then, although Barly kept bumping into Artimus, who, in turn, kept running into Jamie. They were just rounding a corner when Jamie tripped over a rock, and all three of them fell into a tangled heap. The flashlight flew out of Jamie's hand and rolled down the tunnel. The light went out, leaving them in total darkness.

"Why didn't I charge my sea stone up with the flashlight?" Jamie lamented. "We'd have another light."

"Like you had time to do it," Barly said mournfully.

"Get up, hurry!" Jamie cried, floundering around in the dark. The Snakeroot's horrible cries grew closer.

"Somebody get your elbow out of my ear!" Barly cried.

"Somebody get your knee off my stomach!" Artimus cried back.

Artimus pushed himself off Barly, and they all managed to get to their feet. As they rummaged around, frantically trying to find the light, Jamie whispered anxiously, "I can't see a thing. Barly, reach in my backpack. The matches are in the front pouch."

Barly felt his way over to where Jamie stood and pawed around until he found the pouch. He took out the matches and handed them to Jamie. Jamie fumbled with the pack and struck one against a rock. The match flared to life and the flame lit the darkness around them. They discovered that just in front of them was a fork in the tunnel. While they looked down either fork, trying to decide which one to take, the match burned down to Jamie's fingers.

"Ouch!" he cried, blowing out the flame. They were again plunged into darkness.

"Hey! What's that up ahead?" Artimus asked excitedly. It was then they noticed a dim glow ahead, in the left fork of the tunnel.

Barly was the first to regain his wits. "I've got an idea. Light another match, Jamie."

"This is the last one I've got," Jamie said, striking it on the rock wall. "I hope you have a good plan." When it flared to life, they saw the flashlight a few yards down the right fork. Barly ran down and switched it on. Luckily it still worked, so he ran farther down, and set it on a rock.

"That should buy us some extra time," he said as he ran back to them. "When the Snakeroot gets here, he'll see the flashlight and take the right fork. Meanwhile, let's head for the light in the left fork. If we're lucky, maybe it's a way out of this mountain."

"That's our only light," Jamie lamented. "What if there isn't a way out? Then what? How will we find our way?"

"The way I see it, unless you have a better plan, we'll be dinner for the Snakeroot very soon," Barly replied.

Jamie thought about it for a second, then said, "I guess you're right. Let's get out of here."

Barly took off down the left fork. Artimus and Jamie ran after him. The light ahead began to get a little brighter. As soon as they could see well enough, Barly held up his paw. "Listen," he said, catching his breath. They stopped and strained their ears.

They could still hear the sounds of the Snakeroot, but they were now muffled.

"It worked!" Artimus exclaimed, clapping. "We fooled him!"

"Let's keep going," Barly said urgently. "It will only take him a few minutes before he finds out we've tricked him." Sure enough, a few minutes later they heard a blood-curdling shriek.

"He's discovered our trick!" Jamie cried. "We're done for!"

The group ran as fast as they could, careful to avoid stumbling in the dim light. Jamie led the way with Artimus and Barly close behind. They could hear the frightful sounds getting louder as the Snakeroot found the left fork and started after them again.

The light ahead was a soft glow now. All the sudden, the tunnel ended and they dashed out into a large cavern. "Whoa!" Jamie cried, holding up his hand. They all managed to stop just in time to keep from tumbling over the edge of a deep crevasse.

"Wow! Will you look at this!" he exclaimed. He dropped to his knees and crept up to the rim. A few pebbles rolled over as he looked down. "We almost ended up down there! It's so deep you can't even see the bottom!"

A dim glow coming from a shaft near the top of the cavern offered just enough light to make out the other side of the gorge. But, indeed, they couldn't see bottom. As they peered around in the gloom, they found they were perched on a narrow ledge that stretched off into the darkness in either direction.

Artimus crept up next to Jamie. He tossed a rock down into the void. "Let's see what we've got here," Artimus said. They listened intently, but heard nothing.

"I didn't hear it hit!" Barly said nervously.

Jamie muttered, "What'll we do now?" He looked up. In the dim light, he couldn't see the top of the cavern, so getting out that way seemed improbable. "We can't go back, we can't go up or down. We're trapped in here!"

"I wonder where *here* is," Barly said, carefully inching along the shelf of rock.

"Me too," Artimus said. "I wish I were back in my pond now. I may not have been happy, but at least I was safe. I never had to worry about being eaten by an evil Snakeroot or falling into a bottomless pit."

They didn't have long to think about it, for at that moment, a loud shriek came from inside the tunnel. It would only be a matter of seconds before the Snakeroot would be upon them again.

"Oh no! It looks like this is it!" Jamie cried. He pulled out his hatchet. "It's not much, but at least that nasty thing won't get us without a fight!" He turned toward the tunnel and planted his feet determinedly.

Just then, Barly called to them from farther down the ledge. "Hey, I found a bridge over here! Quick, come see!"

Artimus and Jamie turned and looked over their shoulders. They could just barely see Barly motioning to them from the shadows. They hurried over as fast as they dared to where he was standing. Sure enough, a rickety rope structure stretched out over the crevasse in front of them.

"I wonder how this got here," Jamie exclaimed. He walked over and examined the bridge. It had wooden planks and rope siderails. He stepped cautiously onto it. "Do you think it's safe to walk on?" The bridge bounced up and down.

"I don't know about this. It sure feels shaky," he surmised. As Jamie jumped carefully up and down on the planks, the whole thing swayed crazily, but the ropes held.

"Right now, we don't have any other choice but to take the bridge," Barly said. "You two go first. Since I'm the heaviest, I'll go last."

Jamie and Artimus needed no further prompting. The sounds of the Snakeroot were getting louder behind them. Jamie moved farther out and Artimus crept on behind him. They began to inch their way over the rickety planks. The bridge creaked and groaned with each step. Neither one dared to look down.

They were almost to the middle when the Snakeroot burst out of the tunnel with a mighty roar. It spied the narrow ledge ahead and made a frantic effort to stop. It was too late. Before it could halt its forward momentum, the monster toppled off the outcropping of rock into the chasm with a blood-curdling scream. Down into the void the beast fell, its cries receding in the gloom until they could be heard no more. The three travelers gasped in amazement at their turn of fortune.

"Did you see that?" Artimus exclaimed with joy.

"I sure did!" Jamie responded. "It looks like our luck is finally beginning to change for the better. What'll we do now? Should we go forward or head back?" Jamie asked tenuously. "What do you think, Barly?" he called to the bear.

The shaky structure bounced ominously. Barly had started out after them.

Barly's voice came out of the dimness. "There's no sense going back, we can't get by the Treesers. If there's a bridge over this canyon, it must go somewhere. Keep going and see where it ends. I'll be right behind you."

Jamie and Artimus groped their way through the darkness toward the other side. The bridge swayed dangerously back and forth as they reached the middle. They had just started up the other side, when—*crack!*—two of the planks broke under them.

"Aaahhh!" Artimus screamed, plunging down between the broken ends of the boards. Jamie grabbed hold of the ropes to keep from bouncing over the side.

"Artimus!" he shouted. He dropped to his hands and knees and crept back to the broken planks and peeked down. By sheer luck, Artimus's staff had hooked on one of the ropes when he toppled through. He dangled under the bridge, holding on to his staff tightly with both hands.

"Help me!" he cried. His face was contorted with fear.

Jamie lay on his stomach and reached through the broken boards. "Here, Artimus, grab hold! Hurry!" Artimus hesitated, then let go with one hand and reached out. He grabbed Jamie's outstretched hand and Jamie pulled back as hard as he could.

At the time Jamie was pulling Artimus back onto the bridge, Barly reached the spot where they had stopped to watch the Snakeroot fall. "Are you okay up there?" he yelled. "This bridge could give way any minute!"

"Just a minor inconvenience here," Jamie grunted. With one last mighty heave, he pulled Artimus back up onto the planks. They both started for the other side again. It bounced terribly underneath them, slowing their forward progress considerably.

"I sure hope this thing holds!" Artimus exclaimed, fearfully looking over the edge. They managed to make it to the other side, and just as they stepped onto solid ground, Barly reached the spot where Artimus had fallen through. In the dim light, he didn't see the broken planks. His foot slipped between the ropes and he fell, wedging his big body in the opening. "Oh no! I'm caught!" Barly cried. He struggled desperately to get free.

The bridge sagged dangerously under Barly's weight. Jamie and Artimus could see the ropes starting to fray and part.

"Oh, get up, Barly! This bridge isn't going to hold much longer!" Jamie yelled. "I'll try to—" *Snnaaapppp! Crrraaaccckkk!*

He was interrupted by the sound of breaking rope and splintering wood, and suddenly the bridge parted in the middle. For a brief moment, Barly was suspended in mid-air as the bridge fell away from under him. Then with a *"JAAAmmmiiieee . . ."* he plunged into the gorge after the Snakeroot. His cry echoed around inside the cavern and he disappeared into the black void.

"Barly! Baarrrlyyy!" Jamie yelled as the bridge crumbled before his very eyes. He looked helplessly at Artimus. "This can't be happening!" He crawled over to the edge and looked down. The broken bridge swung down against the side of the gorge with a loud bang, and the pieces disappeared into the blackness.

Artimus and Jamie stared in disbelief into the empty space. An eerie silence descended upon the cave, broken only by a creaking sound as the remains of the bridge rocked back and forth against the sides of the chasm.

Jamie screamed, *"Baaaarrrrlllyy!* Can you hear me?" Silence.

Jamie let out a slow, tortured breath. "Now we're really in trouble. First Kip gets attacked, and now poor Barly's dead." He moved gingerly back from the edge.

Except for the sound of his voice echoing back, they heard nothing. He ran along the edge of the crevasse, frantically looking for a way to reach his friend. "There's got to be a way to get down," he cried. "Artimus, help me find a way to save Barly!"

Jamie was in a panic. Artimus ran over and placed his webbed hands on Jamie. He shook him by the shoulders and commanded, "Jamie, look at me! Barly's gone and there's nothing we can do to save him. The canyon is bottomless, remember? Slow down or you might slip and fall in yourself."

Jamie stared into the frog's big, luminescent eyes for a moment. They succeeded in having a calming effect on him. He sank to the ground with his head in his hands. "Where in Neverlore are we? How will we ever get out of here?" he wailed. Jamie was suddenly overcome by a flood of emotions: feelings for the loss of his friend, the enormity of being lost and trapped underground in the dark, and the disappointment of a promising adventure gone awry.

"I don't know if I can go on," he said in a defeated whisper. "Neverlore's getting the best of me."

Artimus didn't reply. Everything had happened so quickly. Finally, he managed to collect his thoughts. "Now, now, let's not give up. I don't think Barly would accept that kind of talk," he said in as soothing a voice as he could muster. However, his voice wasn't too reassuring. "I know it looks bad right now, but surely there must be another way out of this mountain. That bridge wouldn't have been built just to get over the gorge, and then not go anywhere."

Jamie slowly looked up at Artimus. "This happened so fast, I don't know what to think," he said, choking back a sob. "Barly's vanished, we don't have a light, and we don't have a clue which way to go. Oh, why didn't I stay in my backyard?" Jamie felt panic building up inside him again.

"I must admit, it doesn't look good," Artimus said, closing one eye and scrunching up his face. He had a habit of doing this when he was perplexed. He walked over to a nearby pile of rocks, sat down, and laid his staff across his knees. Jamie walked over and sat down beside him. His shoulders drooped and he let out a long, sobbing sigh.

Artimus lamented, "What an awful way to go. If Barly could have just made it a little farther, he'd still be alive."

"I know. I'm really going to miss that big old teddy bear," Jamie agreed dismally. Tears ran down his face.

"But at least that beastly Snakeroot is gone," Artimus went on, trying to be rational. "We're lucky in that respect."

This was little consolation to Jamie. He looked out into the darkness. The surrounding gloom matched his mood completely. He wondered if he would ever see his home again. He wondered if he was even going to get out of the mountain alive. "The Snakeroot might as well have gotten all of us," he said forlornly. "Unless a miracle happens, you and I are doomed, too."

Several minutes went by as the two unfortunate adventurers sat thinking about their friend. Artimus was the first to hear a bizarre sound coming from somewhere in the cavern. He cocked his head.

"What's that strange noise?" he asked, standing up.

"What noise?" Jamie asked, deep in thought. Artimus had startled him.

Clip-clop, clip-clop, clip-clop . . .

Jamie could hear the odd sound now. It was coming out of the darkness off to their left. The sound was getting closer.

"Oh no. What's next?" he exclaimed.

"Ssshhhhhh," Artimus said, putting a webbed finger to his lips.

Jamie put both hands over his mouth to keep from betraying their presence. The sound stopped. Jamie and Artimus both held their breath and stared into the darkness. The sound started up again.

"What do you think that is?" Jamie whispered from between clenched fingers.

"I'm not sure," Artimus replied. "But, whatever it is, it better not find us out here. Quick, behind these rocks!" They both scrambled behind the pile and peeked over the top, straining their eyes to see into the gloom.

The sound grew closer and closer, and soon they could see a low gleam in the darkness ahead. Whatever made the sound appeared to have a light. It seemed to be coming from another tunnel, and shadows began to bounce off the walls. They could see that the biggest shadow had many legs, a tall hump on its back, and long pointy things sticking out of what looked like a head.

"Not again! What kind of monster do we have to deal with now?" Jamie whispered tersely. He reached for his hatchet.

Clip-clop, clip-clop. The monster continued toward them. Jamie and Artimus prepared themselves for the worst. Then, from around the last bend in the tunnel, out walked a most peculiar sight.

"It's a donkey! And it's got someone sitting on its back!" Jamie whispered in shock.

As the donkey got closer, they could see the rider was a small man. "Both of them together aren't much taller than my dad!" Jamie whispered in relief.

His fear vanished in an instant. He was so astonished at the outlandish sight, he had to cover his mouth to keep from laughing hysterically. "This is the monster I was so afraid of? I can't take much more of this craziness!" he whispered through his fingers. He put the hatchet in his backpack and snapped the flap.

They could see that the light came from a lantern which rocked back and forth on a wooden post attached to the saddle.

When the strange pair walked by, Jamie and Artimus saw that other than being small, the donkey appeared quite normal. The man, though, was a sight to behold. He had a big handlebar mustache and long, messy red hair. He had a red bandana around his neck, and a pair of six-guns strapped around his waist. Completing the spectacle was an old, misshapen cowboy hat that was perched on his head. But the strangest thing of all—he was riding the donkey backward!

Jamie couldn't contain himself any longer. He'd never seen anything this comical before. He bit his lip to keep quiet, but a giggle escaped.

At the sound of Jamie's laugh, the donkey stopped and gave a loud "Heehaw!" At the same time, the man jumped out of the saddle and drew his guns. He pointed them both toward where Artimus and Jamie were hiding.

"Whoa, now, Florabel. Looks like there's someone a-spyin' on us from behind them there rocks," he said. The donkey let out another "Heehaw," and they turned in the direction of Jamie and Artimus. The little man walked slowly forward, keeping both guns pointed in their direction. Despite their predicament, Jamie started to giggle uncontrollably.

"All right, come on out from them there rocks whoever ya are, and put yer hands high in the air where's I kin see 'em!" the man commanded. He cocked the hammers on both pistols.

"Don't shoot! We mean you no harm!" Artimus cried. He stood up slowly, his hands over his head. Jamie did the same, except he kept one hand over his mouth to keep his giggles under control.

"Well now, if you two ain't a couple-a dandies! Will ya look at that, Florabel? We done got us a walkin', talkin' frog." The man motioned toward them with his guns. "You two ease round them there rocks nice 'n' slow, 'n' no false moves."

Jamie and Artimus did as they were told. Artimus exclaimed, "Dandies indeed! You haven't got much room to talk. Have you looked at yourself lately? You wouldn't win any prizes looking like *you* do."

"Whoa! I'll do the talkin' round here," the cowboy said. "Who are ya, and what are y'all doin' down here?" His voice had a Western twang.

They stared at each other for a moment. "I'm Artimus Prince and this is Jamie Nichols," Artimus said at last. "We're lost and need help. We just lost our friend to a terrible monster! Can you show us the way out of this mountain, sir?"

"Whoa! I'll do the askin'," the stranger said. He kept his guns pointed at them. "Ah'll ask ya one more time, whach 'ahll doin' here?"

Artimus dropped his hands to his hips, and said exasperatedly, "Come now, you can see we're not armed. Would you please put your guns down before they go off and hurt someone? We've just been through a most frightful ordeal. Besides, if Jamie hadn't laughed and caused you to stop, your donkey would have walked right out onto the bridge, only the bridge is no longer there. You should be thanking us instead of threatening to shoot us. You and your donkey would have fallen into the gorge along with that beastly Snakeroot."

"And poor Barly, too," Jamie added sadly.

"Whoa, slow down. Bridge out, Snakeroot, Barly? What 'n tarnation y'all talkin' about?" the cowboy drawled.

"See for yourself," Jamie said smartly. He was regaining his composure some. "The bridge is gone, Mister, Mister . . . hey, what's your name, anyway?"

The comical little man eyed them dubiously. After a moment, he replied slowly, "Name's Prairie Bill Jackson, or PBJ fer short. This better not be no trick," the cowboy said, backing away from them. He turned and looked into the gorge. "Thunder 'n tarnation, the bridge *is* gone! Florabel, would ya look at that!" PBJ turned back to Jamie and Artimus. "Well, seems y'all well been tellin' the truth," he said.

"Of course it's the truth! We have no reason to lie to you," Jamie said, irritated. "*We are lost!* If you'll listen for a minute, you'll know why."

"Okay, okay," PBJ said, slowly releasing the hammers of his guns. "You, non-frog one, talk."

"Man, this is about the fifth time I've had to do this," Jamie grumbled. He then went on to recite the whole story again of how he ended up in Neverlore, of meeting Barly and Artimus, and of how they had become lost. "So you see, it's kind of important for us to get to the castle Mistemere and ask Erenor for help," he said. "But Barly was the only one who knew the way."

When Jamie ended his story, PBJ shook his head. "Well, ah'll be switched," he said. "Maybe I ain't so loco after all. Me an' Florabel never could figger out where we was er how we got here. Times ah thought ah's goin' crazy 'cause it didn't make no sense." He lowered his guns, but kept his fingers on the triggers.

"You mean, you don't live here?" Jamie asked in surprise.

"Not 'xactly," PBJ replied. "Ah mean, we does now, but it weren't always like this. Some time ago, ah's a cook at a mining camp out west. Always had me a real hankerin' fer prospectin', but ah never got ma chance. All them men said ah was too short ta be any use. Said they needed big, strong men to mine fer gold. So me 'n' Florabel'd sneak off in the mountains lookin' fer gold whenever we had us a chance. Anyway, one day we was a-goin' down this box canyon when, sudden like, there's a rock slide b'hind us. Dadblame thing trapped us in there like rats in a box. We didn't have no choice but ta keep goin' on ahead, 'n' pretty soon that canyon narrowed down ta nothin'. Them walls were too steep fer us ta climb up, so we had ta stop. While I was pondern' how ta get us out, Florabel found us an ol' tunnel b'hind some bushes.

"Anyway, we went inta the tunnel, only when we come out we found arselves in a diff'rent part of the land. It was all mighty confusin', 'specially when the tunnel closed up behind us 'n' disappeared. We waited round a spell fer it ta open, but it never did.

"After that, me 'n' Florabel wandered around fer a long time, and finally ended up in these here mountains. We met a few folks now 'n' then. Fer the most part they was good folks, and paid us no never mind. Told us bout this here land called Neverlore. Some said they was born here and some said they come here close ta what we did. Ah never believed 'em 'cause it sounded too crazy-like. So me 'n' Florabel's been a-livin' in these here mountains ever since. We been doin' a little prospectin' now 'n' then, but it don't appear there's much gold round these parts. Me 'n' the donkey was just fetchin' to get out of these mountains 'n' head somewheres else."

"Well, it was a good thing we were here, or you and your donkey might have ended up at the bottom of the gorge," Artimus said when PBJ ended his story.

"Oh, don't know bout that," PBJ answered. "Florabel here's pretty sharp. She's saved us from more'n one scrape long the way." Florabel let out another "Heehaw!" and everyone laughed.

"Do you always ride on her backward?" Jamie asked. He walked around the front of the donkey and rubbed her nose. Her whiskers tickled his hands as she nuzzled him.

"Well, I'll be switched!" PBJ exclaimed. "Ole Florabel don't take ta strangers so easily. If she likes ya this quick, ya must be okay." He holstered his guns. "Ah ride her back'ard sometimes to make sure nothin' sneaks up behind us. Florabel watches the front 'n' I watch the rear. These here caves 'n' tunnels go a long ways back in the mountains. There's no tellin' what's lurkin' round in the dark back there. Better safe 'n' sorry."

"That's great! Just what I didn't want to hear," Jamie complained. "More creatures hanging around in the dark."

"What do you suggest we do now?" Artimus asked. "With the bridge out, we can't go forward and we can't go back the way we came. Do you know of any other way out of this mountain?"

PBJ scratched his ear and said, "Don't rightly know. Never did try to find another way out. Me 'n' Florabel always just left this way. Only way we was ever sure of."

"Well, we better get out of here soon," Jamie said. He put his backpack on and added, "This place gives me the creeps."

"We could go back ta where me 'n' Florabel camped when we was prospectin'," PBJ said. "Least there we'll be safe from them nasty packratters."

"What's a packratter?" Jamie asked sharply. Rats were his least favorite animal.

PBJ motioned for them to follow as he walked over and climbed on Florabel. Only this time, he sat facing forward. "A packratter's a big black rat bout the size of a small dog. Ugly lookin', rascally devils. They'll take anythin' that ain't tied down, 'n' put somethin' else back instead. Bite yer hand off if'n they get a mind ta, so watch sharp as they're apt to be most anywhere." He gave Florabel a swat on the rump. "Giddy-up," he said, heading back into the tunnel. He called over his shoulder, "You two follow long 'n' keep watch behind us."

"Oh great, we get to bring up the rear," Jamie muttered to Artimus. "As if everything else isn't bad enough, now we have rats as big as dogs to worry about."

Artimus fell in alongside Jamie. "Look on the bright side," he said. "At least we don't have to find out about them on our own, and at least for now we're saved."

"Yeah, but it's a small comfort. It could have been anything else but rats," Jamie said in a disgusted voice. "I hate rats!"

He strained his eyes, looking into the darkness. On either side, he saw nothing but rocks, rocks, and more rocks. He stared into each crack and crevice, his imagination playing tricks on him. Were packratters there staring back at him, with beady red eyes, watching, waiting? He shuddered and moved closer to Artimus. *I wish Barly was still here*, he thought sadly.

Chapter 10

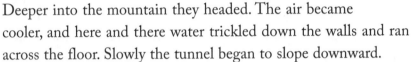

Florabel's hooves echoed through the tunnel as they made their way toward PBJ's camp. Deeper into the mountain they headed. The air became cooler, and here and there water trickled down the walls and ran across the floor. Slowly the tunnel began to slope downward.

They walked for some time, making small talk as they went on. The lantern swayed back and forth to the rhythm of Florabel's hooves, causing their shadows to bob up and down on the tunnel walls. It was an amusing sight, but it did little to relieve Jamie's anxiety. He wondered if miners felt the same way when they went to work deep in the mines.

Occasionally, a cool draft blew across the tunnel from one of the many cracks in the walls. Jamie tensed whenever this happened and imagined some new and terrible creature breathing on them from behind the rock.

"Stay close now, you two," the prospector warned. "Don't want to lose one a ya down some bottomless pit."

"I sure hope PBJ knows where he's going," Jamie whispered to Artimus.

"Me too," Artimus whispered back. "We don't even know who this guy is. For all we know, he could be leading us to our doom.

I sure hope we haven't been saved only to end up in some other terrible mess."

They had walked for about an hour when, once again, they came to a fork in the tunnel. PBJ held up his hand for them to stop. "Yonder, down that left tunnel's where we'll camp," he said, pointing. "That tunnel ta the right is the one we're takin' when we head out tomorrow."

Artimus walked up to him and leaned on his staff. "Do you have any idea where we are?" he asked, looking about. "I'm so turned around I don't hardly know which way is up, let alone the right direction out of here."

"Well, this is what I reckon," PBJ answered. He pointed up the right tunnel. "I'd say that thar tunnel runs roughly northeast. It'll probably be our best way ta findin' a way outta here."

"How do you know it's the right way out?" Artimus asked. He looked up the tunnel doubtfully.

"'Cause that's where we did most ar prospectin'. There's lotsa tunnels 'n' caves up in there. One of 'em has to lead us outta this mountain, 'cause there ain't no tunnels leadin' off 'n any other direction round here, 'cept this un, that is."

"Well, I'd like to know for sure," Jamie said. He reached into the pocket of his sweatshirt and pulled out a compass. PBJ laughed.

"That thing ain't gonna do ya much good down here," he said. "This here mountain's fulla ore. Ya ain't gonna get no good headin' 'cause of it. Makes yer compass go crazy."

Jamie held the compass up to the light. Sure enough, the needle spun around wildly. "You *can't* get a compass heading down here!" he agreed, and put it back in his pocket. "I guess we don't have much choice but to trust you," he said reluctantly.

"Yup, that's bout the size of it," PBJ said. "That's 'less you want to strike out on yer own." Jamie and Artimus looked at each other, then shook their heads vigorously.

"Didn't think so," PBJ laughed. "Follow me, then. We'll camp fer t'night, then head up 'n that other tunnel tomorrow." He turned Florabel toward the left tunnel and prodded her. "Giddy-up," he commanded again.

"How far is camp?" Jamie asked as they set out again. He was getting hungry and wondered if PBJ had any food in his saddle-bags. He knew he didn't have much left: a few carrots and an apple or two in his backpack, and two or three gula bars left in his pouch.

"Ain't too far from here," PBJ answered. As if he'd read Jamie's mind, he added, "When we get to camp I'll rustle us up some grub. Ain't cooked up a good prospector's meal 'n quite a spell."

They walked for a while longer. At last they came to a place where the tunnel widened and ended in a cave. When they entered the cave, Jamie whistled. Scattered in the cave walls were dozens of blue and green crystals. The reflection of the lantern made the rock look like it was on fire. The ceiling of the cave was lost in shadows, but hanging down out of the darkness were sta-lactites formed of clear crystal. These too refracted the lantern's light. "This is spectacular!" Jamie looked around, his mouth agape.

Toward the rear of the cave, water bubbled from between two green crystals and collected in the hollow of a rock. It spilled over the edge and flowed out to the middle of the cave where it disap-peared through a hole in the floor.

"This little spring is really neat," Jamie said, inspecting the hole. "It comes out of the ground and disappears back in the ground a few feet further on."

"Looks good, but don't taste so good," PBJ said over his shoulder. "Tastes like sulfur."

"Hey, I can fix that, I think. Give me something to collect water in," Jamie said.

PBJ produced a deep pot and handed it to Jamie. "Whatcha fixin' ta do?" he asked. Jamie took the pot and filled it with spring water.

"I'm going to try a little magic," he answered. Jamie took out the container of borok powder from his pouch and sprinkled some in the pot. Immediately, the water began to seethe and bubble. After a few seconds, it was calm again. "I hope Deena was right about this stuff," he said. He gingerly scooped some out and tasted it. "There's no bad taste at all," he exclaimed.

"Whatcha talkin' bout, boy? The last time I drank some, it tast'd like skunk water," PBJ exclaimed. He grabbed a tin cup and filled it from the pot. He put it to his nose and sniffed. "Don't smell no smell," he said, surprised. He took a sip. "Well ah'll be switched! The water tastes fine. If this doesn't beat all. Whatcha put in there, boy?" Jamie then told them the story of Deena giving him the pouch and listed its contents.

"Well, I guess that problem's solved," Artimus said. He surveyed the immediate area. Near the center of the cave was the spot where PBJ had previously made camp. Around the remains of a fire were placed several large rocks that looked like seats.

"Looks like you were expecting company," Artimus said, counting the rocks. There were five of them.

"Nah. Just wanted ta be facin' different direction's when I was a-eatin', so's to keep an eye out."

"Keep an eye out for what?" Jamie asked.

"Oh, ya know. Things. Visitors, packratters, whatever," PBJ

answered off-handedly. Jamie involuntarily flinched at the mention of packratters.

"Don't be a-worry'n bout that, though," he said. "Help me ta git a fire goin' so's I can get dinner cookin'. Fire'll help keep them pesky critters away."

Next to one of the stone seats was a pile of twigs and branches. Jamie gathered an armful and placed them in the fire pit.

PBJ shredded some bark off of a dry log, put it in the center of the pile, and arranged the bigger twigs around the bark in a teepee. He reached in his pocket, withdrew a small leather pouch, and took out a short file and a small rock.

Puzzled, Jamie asked, "What are you going to do with those?"

"It's a flint 'n' steel. Don't ya know, boy? I'm gonna make a spark with 'em 'n' get the bark burnin'."

"Why don't you just use a match?" Jamie asked.

"'Cause I'm keepin' them matches to light the lantern 'n' right now I'm down to ma last few," PBJ replied. He chuckled. "Ain't no general store in Neverlore."

Jamie and Artimus watched in fascination as he struck the flint against the steel three or four times. After several sparks flew into the dry bark, it caught fire. He bent over and gently blew on the small flame. As the fire grew, he added more wood. When he had a good-sized blaze, PBJ took off Florabel's saddlebags.

He took out a skillet, a kettle, and a coffeepot. With the last of Jamie's vegetables, some dried beef, and biscuit mix, he soon had cooked a scrumptious meal of stew and biscuits. They sat on the rocks around the fire and ate dinner.

"Mmmmm, this is good," Jamie said between bites. "Other than the soup last night, It's been a long time since I've had food cooked over a campfire." He laughed cheerlessly. "I wish Barly were here to share this meal. That big guy always seemed to be thinking about food."

"And I haven't had a cup of coffee like this in a long, long time," Artimus agreed. He held up his cup in a toast.

Jamie split up an apple and his last granola bar for dessert, and passed them around. After they ate, he and Artimus washed the dishes in the pool and set them aside to dry. PBJ filled the coffee pot with water for breakfast.

Afterward, while they sat around the fire, PBJ pulled out a pipe and lit it up. As he puffed on it, the cave filled with the sweet smell of cherry tobacco. He blew little smoke rings that expanded and rose lazily toward the ceiling. Every once in a while, one would circle one of the stalactites.

Jamie yawned and leaned back, mentally exhausted. It had been an exciting, yet distressing and painful day, and he was glad it had come to an end. Jamie tried not to think of Barly's screams when he fell, and instead, watched as PBJ's smoke rings vanished into the shadows overhead.

"I can see it's time ta get us some shut-eye," PBJ observed. He took his bedroll from the saddle and spread it out on the ground next to the fire. He placed the saddle at one end of the blanket. "This here blanket's big 'nough fer all three of us ta sleep on," he indicated.

Jamie didn't have to be told twice. He laid his backpack at the head of the blanket for a pillow, took off his sweatshirt, and lay down in the middle. He pulled the sweatshirt over himself and curled into a ball. Artimus lay next to him on one side, and PBJ lay down on the other. He used his saddle for a pillow and covered both of them up with his poncho.

"Just like in the old west movies," Jamie said, yawning again. "Who stands watch?" he asked sleepily.

"Don't be a-worrin' bout that. Florabel's a real light sleeper, an if'n anything comes near us, she'll make quite a ruckus," PBJ answered.

"That's good to know," Artimus said, also yawning. He was glad he didn't have to stand watch.

PBJ reached over and turned down the lantern until just a small blue flame was left. It flickered dimly.

When Jamie's eyes got used to the dark, he could see that the crystals in the walls around them gave off a faint glow. "What a great nightlight," he said. "This is way better than my old seashell nightlight back home." He stared at the crystals for a long while before he dozed off.

The doorway in the tree seemed so far away now. Jamie was still happy he could walk, but the scale of his adventure had begun to overshadow that fact. *I wonder where my legs are taking me?* he pondered. *Every step seems to be taking me farther away from my family and home. I wonder if I'll ever see Earth again.* He forced those thoughts from his mind, and when Jamie finally slept, he had fitful dreams about dragons and sorcerers and a sorrowful one about Kip and Barly.

Jamie also dreamt that packratters scurried around camp poking their long, ugly noses into everything. They were nasty creatures with spiky tails and grimy black fur. Jamie's face twitched as he slept. Even in his dreams he hated rats, especially rats as big as dogs.

Chapter 11

PBJ was the first to wake the next morning. He turned up the lantern, stirred the coals, and added some wood to the fire. After a small blaze started, he made coffee. While it brewed, he fed Florabel oats from the saddlebag.

The smell of the coffee woke Artimus. "Mmmmm, that sure smells good," he said, yawning. He did a few hops to loosen up and poured himself a steaming cup. "Before last night, I'd almost forgotten its taste." Artimus smacked his frog lips.

Jamie was the last one to wake up. He sat up and stretched. "I'll pass on the coffee. My mom said it stunts your growth. Oops, I'm sorry!" He covered his mouth and blushed, looking at PBJ's stature.

"That's alright, son," PBJ said. "When ah was a-cookin', they used ta tease me all the time bout havin' drunk too much coffee when ah's a little un. Got so's ah didn't listen to 'em after a while."

Artimus changed the subject. "How do we go about finding our way out of here once we head up the other tunnel, PBJ?"

The prospector explained his plan. "Well, once we get up ta them caverns where me 'n' Florabel was a-prospectin', ah remember now, thir's a tunnel that used ta lead outta this mountain. Once er twice, me 'n' Florabel went that way ta git out. It caved in some time ago, but the tunnel might still git us close 'nough ta the outside though. We can mebbe blast our way out." He patted one of his saddlebags and added, "Dynamite."

"Dynamite? Are you kidding?" Jamie exclaimed. His eyes grew big and he backed away from the fire.

"We may need ta use it. Dadblamed roof collapsed in the tunnel. Thar's no tellin' how much rock's in the way now."

"Now, wait a minute," Jamie interrupted. "I'd rather try to dig my way through if we can get close enough to the outside. You could bring this whole mountain down on top of us with that stuff."

"Jamie's right," Artimus added. "Did you give that any thought?"

PBJ picked up the saddle and put it on Florabel, then tied on the saddlebags. "We'll see how much rock y'all dig through 'fore ya decide blastin'll be easier," he said, shrugging his shoulders. "But suit yerselves. Now, quit fussin' 'n' help me break camp."

"Well, if you *have* to take that stuff with us, at least be careful," Jamie muttered. He went to collect the dry dishes from beside the pool. Artimus helped PBJ pack the rest of the gear.

As Jamie stooped to pick the dishes up, he cried out in wonder, "PBJ, will you look at this? Something's wrong here!"

PBJ stopped rolling his bedroll and looked over. "Now what's the probl'm, boy?"

"This! All the dishes have been stolen. No . . . replaced," Jamie exclaimed. "Switched with ones made of . . . of . . . this looks like real gold!" He picked up a bowl and examined it.

"What the . . . ? Switched, ya say? With gold?" PBJ asked in surprise. He and Artimus ran over to the pool, where they found Jamie turning the bowl over in his hands.

"Wouldn't you say this looks like gold?" Jamie asked, handing the bowl to PBJ. Jamie picked up a spoon. "And this looks like silver," he added, examining it closely. "Hey, I thought you told us Florabel was a light sleeper and that nothing could sneak up on us."

"Normally she is. She musta been extra tired last night," PBJ replied. "Looks like the work a them nasty packratters. They musta been so sneaky 'n' quiet, even she didn't hear 'em."

The prospector reached down, picked up a gold cup, and held it up to the lantern. It had tiny blue stones around the middle. "Tarnation. If'n I'm not mistakin', these here are sapphires!" he exclaimed. "This is quite a treasure! Maybe them packratters ain't as nasty as I thought. These dishes gotta be worth a fortune!"

"Obviously, these packratters have no idea of a fair trade," Artimus said, checking out the cup. "I mean, to swap your plain dishes for some as priceless as these?"

PBJ frowned as he picked up the rest of the dishes. "Said they was nasty, not smart," he mumbled.

"Who do you suppose they got these from?" Jamie asked.

"Don't know. It's mighty odd. Bet whoever it was, though, won't be too happy fer the trade," PBJ answered. "Best put these away fer safe keepin'. Don't want no wrong people seein' us with this treasure." He walked over to Florabel and put the dishes deep into the saddlebags. He turned to Jamie and Artimus and shrugged his shoulders. "Ain't no use standin' round scratchin' our heads bout this. What's done's done," he added. "We best finish packin' and get outta here in case them ratters come back. We got us a ways ta go 'fore we're close to gettin' outta here."

PBJ finished rolling up his bedroll while Artimus put out the fire. As Jamie walked by the pool, he caught a glimpse of his reflection in the water. In the reflection, it looked like two beady red eyes were staring down at him from overhead. He jumped back, glancing up quickly. He scanned the darkness above the pool, but saw nothing. Jamie looked back at the pool, but the apparition was gone.

I've been in this mountain too long. My imagination's starting to get the better of me, he thought. He hurried back to the others. "I'm all set," he said, putting his backpack on. He said nothing of what he thought he had seen.

They started walking back the way they had come in. After a short while, they were at the fork in the tunnel again. PBJ got out of the saddle. "Pretty rough goin' from here on," he said. He took the reins and led Florabel into the other tunnel.

"Follow me, but step careful now." PBJ took the lantern from the pole on the saddle and held it in front of him. They started up the tunnel in single file. Jamie brought up the rear, glancing over his shoulder often. He stayed close to the others.

The group carefully picked their way over uneven ground. The tunnel began to rise, and they often slid in loose sand and rocks. At one point, Jamie slipped on the unstable footing and slid toward the edge of a gaping black cleft in the rock.

"Yeoww!" he cried. Artimus turned at the sound and instinctively pushed out his walking stick. Jamie grasped it tightly and the big frog pulled him back up.

"Thanks. Quick thinking Artimus. You probably just saved my life," Jamie said gratefully. He scrambled back to safer footing, visibly shaken from his close call.

"It could have been any one of us," the big frog said, taking his arm and steadying him.

"Ah told ya ta be careful," PBJ said from the gloom ahead. "Now quit dilly-dallying and let's git a-goin'."

Eventually the floor evened out and the going got easier. After a while, the tunnel ended and they found themselves in another large cavern. PBJ held the lantern over his head and motioned for them to stop. He studied the cavern as Jamie walked over.

"How do you know which one to take?" Jamie asked. There were a dozen or more tunnels and small caves heading off from the cavern in all directions. It looked liked they were at the hub of some giant wheel with the tunnels branching off as the spokes.

PBJ pushed his hat back a little and said, "Well, several of 'em Florabel 'n' me 'splored already. Ah cain't remember 'xactly which's the one that the roof caved in, 'cause after a while, they all look like one 'nother. We'll check them others out one by one, but both a ya stay close. Either of yas wanders off 'n the path too far an' ya could fall down some crack like the boy almost did. We'd never find ya."

Jamie and Artimus heeded the advice, both remembering Barly's fate. They stuck close behind Florabel as PBJ led them across the cavern. After shining a light into it, they passed by the first tunnel. It dead-ended into solid rock. They continued on to a small cave and peered in. There was no sign of an exit.

They walked on, struggling over rocks and ruts in the path. As they continued around the cavern checking out various openings, the going got rougher. Even Florabel began to have trouble picking her way along. The ridges of rock and sand became more frequent, and they found themselves next to another crevasse. Loose stones rattled over the edge and disappeared into the shadows.

"Watch your step, guys. We don't want to end up like I almost did," Jamie reminded them.

They only had a few more caves to check out when they came to a rather small one on their right. PBJ dropped the reins, bent over, and shined the lantern inside.

"Here's one that looks more promisin'," he said. He stooped down and clambered through the opening. A short distance inside, the cave was high enough to stand up in. He slowly swung the lantern around and saw that near the back, the cave started to rise. "In here. This'n goes back a ways."

Jamie took the reins and pulled Florabel's head down so he could lead her through. Artimus followed close behind.

"Goes back farther'n the light's a-shinin'," PBJ said, holding the lantern up so they could see. "Look sharp now. No tellin' what we may be a-runnin' into."

He began to pick his way gingerly forward. Something farther up the tunnel caught his eye. "Whataya see up thar?" he asked, pointing. "Think that'd be daylight comin' through the rock?" He turned the lantern down a bit to get a better look.

But at that moment, Artimus was inspecting the floor for fissures and Jamie was checking the shadows for packratters. When the light dimmed, Jamie stopped abruptly and looked up. When he did, Artimus ran into him, poking him in the back with his staff.

"Ouch!" Jamie cried. He stumbled forward and crashed into PBJ.

"Hey, watch where yer a-goin'!" The prospector exclaimed. He fell forward onto his knees, and the lantern flew out of his hand. It sailed through the air and slammed against a rock. For a brief moment, they were bathed in bright light as the lantern shattered and burst into flames. The lantern fuel dripped off the rock burning in a fiery waterfall, but the flames quickly died out. Once again, they were surrounded by darkness.

"Oh no, not again!" Jamie moaned.

"Now look what ya gone 'n' done," PBJ exclaimed angrily as he picked himself up. "Our light's been deestroyed."

"What *we've* done?" Jamie exclaimed. "If you would've let us know you were going to turn the lantern down, we would have been prepared."

"Just the same, it's the only light ah had," PBJ replied in a sour voice. "Ahs beginnin' ta think ah shoulda left yas were ah found ya."

"Well, thanks for nothing, if that's the way you feel about it," Jamie replied in an equally sour voice. "You'd be at the bottom of the mountain if it wasn't for Artimus and me. I don't know about anyone else, but I'm really getting tired of all these caves and tunnels. I'd sure like to see the sun and the sky. Anything but darkness, rock, and more rock."

Artimus picked himself up and looked forward past PBJ. "Quit whining, you two. PBJ's right! It *does* look like there's a light up there. It looks like there could be a hole in the rock!" he cried happily.

"Where do you think it's coming from?" Jamie asked. He moved to get a better view. Just then, a dim light began to radiate from his chest.

Artimus pointed and exclaimed, "Jamie, look! The front of you is glowing!"

Jamie glanced down. "Will you look at this?" he cried. "The sea stone must have been jarred out of my shirt when I bumped into PBJ. When the lantern flared up, it looks like the laurium collected enough light for us to see by." He fumbled for the necklace, unsnapped it, and held it above his head. It gave off a faint glow and they could see well enough to pick their way through the rocks and rubble. Cautiously, they moved forward.

The group inched their way toward the gleam and finally reached the back of the cave. Jamie held the necklace high above his head. They could just make out a large pile of rocks ahead.

Behind one of the boulders, they saw a crack in the wall with a ray of light shining through.

Jamie pulled himself up onto one of the boulders and peered at the crack. "Rats! It's too small to climb through," he said in disappointment, dropping back down. "We're so close! How are we ever going to get out of this cursed mountain?"

"Well, bout the only thing we can do is blast that thar hole bigger 'n' hope it takes us outside," PBJ said.

Jamie and Artimus stood in silence while they mulled over the idea. Jamie was the first to speak. "I was afraid of this. If we use the dynamite, PBJ, how can you be sure it'll be safe?"

"Yes, it won't blow us up too, will it?" asked Artimus.

"Well, ah'll only use a half a stick ta start with," PBJ answered. "The 'splosion won't be so big as to bring the whole mountain down."

"I sure hope you're right," Artimus replied.

"Me too," Jamie echoed. "I'd sure hate to get blown to bits when we're this close. Please be careful, PBJ."

The decision made, the prospector rummaged around in the dark preparing the blast. He carefully removed one stick of dynamite from the saddlebags, broke it in two, and stuck one half behind the boulder. "It's ready," he said after a few seconds. "Ah put a real long fuse on. You two take Florabel 'n' lead her back out inta the last tunnel. Careful, don't be trippin' in the dark. When y'all's clear, let me know."

Artimus and Jamie did as they were told. Artimus walked ahead using his staff to keep them on the path. "Now I know what it's like to be blind," Jamie said. *I think I'd prefer living in a wheelchair to not being able to see though*, he thought. It took some doing, but finally, they were safely out of the cave and in the last tunnel. Jamie yelled to PBJ that they were ready.

"Okay, ah'm a-lightin' the fuse now," PBJ hollered back. They could see a faint glow as he struck a match. Soon he appeared, running out of the tunnel, still holding the burning match.

"Now move on over behind that big ole boulder, 'n' put yer hands over yer ears." Jamie grabbed the reins and led Florabel. The other two followed.

They had just gotten safely behind the boulder when the match burned out.

They all crouched down in the dark and covered their ears. A few seconds later, KABOOOMMMM! The cavern was filled with a deafening explosion. The ground shook and a blast of fire and debris blew out of the cave entrance. The sound of the explosion echoed throughout the mountain, dust and smoke filled the air, and rocks and silt fell everywhere.

"Everybody alright?" PBJ asked, standing up slowly. Luckily, except for ringing ears, Artimus and Jamie were okay. They brushed themselves off, crept back into the cave, and made their way toward the light. Only a small pile of rubble blocked their way now. "Looks like we kin dig ar way through this an' get out in a jiffy," PBJ said. All three attacked the pile with determination.

They cleared the rock and debris from their path in no time, continued forward, and ducked through the opening. A short way ahead, the tunnel ended and the light was much brighter.

"Looks like thar's finally a light at the end a the tunnel. Ha! Light at the end a the tunnel," PBJ laughed. "Git it?" Suddenly, there was a loud rumble, and stone and rubble began to fall from the ceiling behind them.

"Cave-in! Lordy, everybody run fer their lives!" PBJ shouted. He and Artimus sprang forward, pulling Florabel with them. Jamie glanced over his shoulder into the cavern. Rock and dirt rained down. It looked and sounded like the whole mountain was coming down behind him. He sprinted after Artimus and PBJ.

They had all exited the final tunnel and reached the light safely, when the ground shook violently, and a huge blast of dust and dirt blew past them from the cave behind.

"I sure hope we didn't start an earthquake," Jamie shouted. With a thundering crash, the tunnel caved in. They closed their eyes and clung to Florabel and one another.

For the next few terrifying moments, the whole mountain rumbled and shook around them. They all feared the worst.

Gradually, the ground quit shaking and the dirt and rocks stopped falling. The dust settled and everything finally quieted down. Jamie was the first to open his eyes.

"We're still alive! Are we lucky or what? This whole mountain could have squashed us like bugs!" he exclaimed. He brushed dirt out of his hair.

"You can say that again," Artimus agreed. "I wonder where we are now," he mused, wiping dust from his glasses.

They were in another large cavern, but instead of darkness, they could see rays of sunlight streaming in from outside up ahead. "Look, over there!" Jamie said excitedly, pointing at the other side of the cavern. "That must be where the light was coming from when we were in the tunnel."

"Ah'd say we're pretty close ta the outside." PBJ nodded. "Judgin' by the angle a the sun, ah'd say the way out's round them last few rocks. We best be goin' 'fore this mountain starts cavin' in again." He grabbed Florabel's reins and headed for the light.

"I sure hope this isn't another disappointment," Jamie said. He and Artimus caught up with PBJ, and as they rounded the last wall of rock, they caught sight of an opening in the side of the mountain.

"Hooray, we're saved!" Jamie cried. The cavern entrance was covered with vines and leaves, but bright sunbeams filtered through. He took out his hatchet and started toward it. "Come on, I'll take care of these," he said joyfully. "We'll finally be out of this creepy mountain!"

Suddenly, they became aware of a loud hissing noise on the other side of the rocks. Jamie had only taken a few steps when PBJ pointed and cried out, "Whoa boys! Our troubles ain't over quite yet! Whooee, will ya look at that!" Jamie and Artimus stopped and their eyes followed his outstretched arm.

"Now, what's the . . . oh no!" Jamie gasped. "This is bad, very bad." He froze in his tracks and gripped his hatchet so tight his fingers hurt. PBJ's hands slowly dropped to his pistols, the color draining from his face. Artimus's big eyes bulged out and he began to tremble.

Behind a half wall of rock was a low plateau. Scattered about on it was a collection of silver and gold treasure, the likes of which Jamie could never have imagined. This, however, was *nothing* compared to what was lying on top of the treasure. He caught his breath and stared in disbelief. Spread out over the plateau was a dragon! A dragon that was as big as a school bus!

Jamie tried to swallow but found his mouth was too dry. He tried to run but his legs failed him. *My scariest dreams have come true. This is it, we're finally done for*, he thought.

Chapter 12

The group didn't move as they watched the dragon's great sides begin to heave. With each breath, small flames shot from his mouth and smoke rolled from his nostrils. They watched in horror as one of his eyes slowly opened and rolled their way. Artimus's mouth hung open. PBJ clenched his pistols so hard his knuckles turned white. Jamie tried to look away, but couldn't.

"Alizar!" Jamie breathed. The L'masse's story about the dreaded dragon flashed through his mind. Jamie had only half-believed them, but now he was face to face with the monster! He looked around wildly. There was nowhere to run.

The dragon was curled up in a ball, his long tail draped over his snout. His enormous body was covered with sharp green and yellow scales. A row of jagged green armor plates started behind his head and ran the entire length of his body. A pair of giant blue wings were folded against his body. As the dragon stared at them, the tips of his wings began to twitch.

"Who dares disturb the mighty Alizar?" he said in a low rumble. He slowly raised his huge head and turned it their way. A long, black, forked tongue shot from his mouth when he spoke.

The dragon's movement scared Florabel so much that she reared and let out a loud "*Heeeehaawwww!*" PBJ struggled to stay on her back as the donkey bucked and kicked wildly.

"Look out!" he hollered, but lost his grip. PBJ flew out of the saddle backward and landed on his head.

Jamie jumped aside to avoid being hit by Florabel's flying hooves. He tripped into Artimus and they both fell in a heap. Florabel whirled around and headed back the way they had come.

Jamie and Artimus struggled frantically to get away as the mighty dragon stood up. Alizar stretched his huge wings and gave a great yawn. He leaned over toward them and another flame shot from his mouth.

"I asked who you are!" he thundered. His fiery breath stunk like burning garbage. "What are you doing in my cave? Do you know what the penalty is when you disturb a sleeping dragon?"

"He's going to torch us! PBJ, do something quick!" Jamie cried. PBJ didn't answer. He just lay motionless where he fell.

"Oh no! PBJ's dead!" Artimus shrieked. "Jamie, what'll we do?" He covered his head with his webbed hands.

Jamie rolled away from Artimus, his mind racing. *I'm not going to die without a fight.* He didn't know anything about dragons, but he did know the best way to fight fire was with water. With one swift move, Jamie pulled his backpack off and ripped out his water gun.

He rolled on his stomach and faced the huge dragon. "Maybe, just maybe . . ." he said under his breath. "That's a pretty rude way to greet guests. Scaring us like that and causing our friend's death," Jamie shouted in the most courageous voice he could muster. The huge dragon climbed off the treasure pile and lumbered toward them. His tail dragged through the treasure pile, scattering it all around.

Jamie gulped. *He's longer than a school bus!* he thought.

"Guests? The only guests I ever have are dinner guests," Alizar growled.

He then laughed a wicked, raucous laugh. A searing blast of flame and smoke shot from his mouth. "And they usually end up being my dinner! I haven't tasted boy flesh in a long time."

"What are you trying to do, get us roasted like marshmallows?" Artimus hissed.

"Ssshhh!" Jamie whispered back. "No time to explain. I've got to get him nearer." He peered through the sight. "Just a little closer . . ." He quietly counted to himself. "Seventy feet, sixty, fifty . . ." He said a silent prayer.

Alizar looked down at Jamie's prone figure. "Ha, ha, ha! Do you think that puny little weapon is strong enough to stop me?" he sneered. "It will take more than—"

He was interrupted by a blast of water from the pistol. It hit him squarely in the nose. The dragon jerked his head back and roared. "What the . . . ?" Jamie squeezed the trigger again. The second blast sent a stream of water past his forked tongue. Alizar sputtered and coughed and opened his mouth to keep from choking. Jamie snapped the trigger again, sending two more quick shots down his throat. The great dragon reared back and *Aaaachhoooo!* Out spewed a tremendous sneeze of hot air and phlegm. Jamie threw up his hand to protect his face.

"Ugh! Gross!" he cried, wiping his hand in the dirt.

Then, an extraordinary thing happened. As the mighty dragon stood before them, choking and sputtering, steam began rolling out of his nose. The big dragon put his claws over his mouth, and more steam shot out between them.

"Now look what you've done!" He coughed and hacked, his whole body shaking violently. "You've choked me half to death and extinguished my fire! I'm Alizar the Terrible. How can I be a fearful dragon without fire? How will I be able to make people cower just by opening my mouth? How can I . . . ?"

Suddenly, a look of amazement came over the dragon's face. "My fire *out*? Wait a minute, you put out my fire!" he exclaimed. "I can breathe freely again! I can sneeze without scorching everything in front of me. I can talk to anyone I want without setting him or her on fire! The spell's broken!" With that, Alizar started dancing around, flapping his wings.

"I'm freee, I'm freee!" he sang with joy. The ground shook and the cavern echoed.

"Hey, dragon! Take it easy, will you?" Jamie yelled. "You'll bring the rest of this mountain down on top of us." He kept his water gun aimed at the dragon and got warily to his feet.

Just then, PBJ started to move. "Oh ma achin' head," he groaned. "Where am I? What happened?"

"Miracle of miracles, PBJ's alive!" Artimus shouted.

PBJ sat up, groggily rubbing his eyes. "Thunder 'n' tarnation, what's all the ruckus about?" he asked. As his mind began to clear and his eyes focused, he saw the big dragon dancing all about. "Look out! He's gonna attack!" PBJ shouted, reaching for his pistols.

"Don't shoot!" Jamie ordered. "I think something miraculous just happened. I may be wrong, but I think we're looking at a new dragon now."

PBJ pulled his pistols halfway out of their holsters. "What'n the world ya talkin' bout?" he asked. "A dragon's a dragon! How's this one any different?"

Alizar calmed down somewhat. "The boy's right. I am changed! My fire's gone and the spell of Druin is at last broken. I've been transformed back into the good dragon I was long before."

"Fire out? Spell broken?" PBJ asked. "Would someone tell me what's a-goin' on?"

"It looks like Jamie just achieved a miracle," Artimus exclaimed, standing and brushing himself off. "He doused Alizar's fire with his water gun." He turned to Jamie. "That was the bravest act I've ever seen! You saved our lives, Jamie. How in Neverlore did you know that would work? "

"Well, I didn't. It was just a wild hunch," Jamie answered modestly. "It was really the water from Robinwood that did it. Remember? I used the gun to carry extra. You know, in case we had to walk across a desert or something. Anyway, it was the only thing I could think of. I prayed that the spring was magical like Barly told me, and hoped it would work on dragon fire."

"Well, ah can see his fire's out, but how come that dadblame dragon's actin' so weird?" PBJ asked.

"I can answer that," Alizar said. "That is, if you want to hear my story." He sat down on his haunches, folded his great wings against his scaly back, and lowered his big head toward them.

Jamie was still wary, however, and kept his water gun pointed at the dragon. "Go ahead. We might as well hear it."

"Thank you for the opportunity," Alizar began gratefully. "I wasn't always this way . . . I mean, breathing fire and being mean.

You see, I wasn't born a bad dragon, most dragons aren't. When I was very young, I was stolen from my mother by an evil wizard named Druin of Medea."

"Unfortunately, we've heard this story," Jamie said.

Alizar went on. "But you haven't heard my side. When I got old enough to fly, Druin cast a spell on me. It caused me to breathe flame every time I opened my mouth. I couldn't control it. You can't imagine how miserable my life became. Every time I tried to talk to anyone, I burned him or her. Nearly every time I opened my mouth, I caught something on fire. Soon no one would come near me. I became very lonely and depressed. I became mean. This is exactly what Druin had planned on.

"Druin then cast a second spell on me. This one forced me to do his evil bidding . . . collecting taxes, destroying crops, burning people out of their homes, and sometimes worse. I was powerless to stop it, and soon I was hated everywhere I went. This went on for years and years. Then, a little over a hundred years ago, Erenor overthrew Druin and banished me to my cave to sleep forever. I might have been here for eternity, if you hadn't come along and caused me to wake up. You truly saved me." The huge dragon looked at the strange group before him. "Who would you be, kind strangers, and how can I ever repay you?"

Jamie, Artimus, and PBJ looked at one another in amazement. "Well, if that don't beat all. A reformed dragon. No less, a reformed dragon offerin' a reeward," PBJ said. He shoved his pistols back in his holsters and stood up. A peculiar look passed over his face. He rubbed his chin and stared at the treasure.

Jamie made the introductions, and went on to tell Alizar the whole story of how they had all met and ultimately ended up in his cave. "As for repayment, you could help us get out of here. It would also be a big help if you could take us to the Castle of the Clouds. We've lost a lot of time in this mountain," he finished.

"Ah don't care much about Erenor or the castle, but ya could be reewardin' me with that," PBJ said, pointing greedily at the pile of riches. He walked over and picked up a handful of gold coins. "Yes, sir, this is a lot better'n prospectin'. This would suit me *just* fine. Whachya say, dragon? Can this treasure be my reeward?"

"Be my guest," Alizar replied. "It's of little use to me. Druin had me steal all this treasure and guard it here. He knew no one would dare come to a dragon's cave looking for it." He turned to Jamie and continued. "I'm sorry, but I'm afraid I can't be of much help to you and Artimus. Taking you to the Castle of the Clouds wouldn't be such a good idea."

"Why's that?" Artimus asked. "You can fly us there a lot faster than we can walk."

"I could, but can you imagine what everyone would do, if, after a hundred years, a dragon appeared again? They'd panic and try to shoot us down. I know, it's happened to me more times than I care to count. Without my fire, we'd be helpless. I'd never be given the chance to explain, I know. All of Neverlore hates me, even after all this time. I was a very bad dragon back then."

"Alizar's got a good point," Jamie sighed dejectedly. "I guess we have to do it ourselves, Artimus. But how will we ever find our way?"

"Actually, it's not as hard as you think," the dragon answered. "If it weren't for the mountains, you could almost see the castle from outside my cave."

"Well, that's something, I guess," Jamie said. He turned to PBJ. "What about you? Are you going with us, PBJ?"

PBJ looked up from the silver bowl he was examining. "This 'splains where those packratters got them there dishes they put back 'steada mine. 'Member, ah told yous they liked ta 'xchange stuff fer other things. There's a bunch more here just like the ones ah put in ma saddlebag." He added, "Thar's no tellin' where the dishes thay stole from me ended up."

Jamie put his hands on his hips and said sternly, "You didn't even hear me, did you? I don't care about packratters, treasure, or anything else, PBJ! I'm sick of this mountain and tired of being lost. I need to get to Mistemere and see Erenor. Something's not right in Neverlore and I need to find out what. Are you going with us or not?" Jamie surprised everyone, including himself, with his outburst.

"Thunder 'n' tarnation, boy, don't go 'n' get yerself all riled up," PBJ snapped back. "Ya don't need me no more, y'all be just fine. Ole PBJ has been lookin' fer a find like this un fer years. You 'n' Artimus go on ahead without me. Ah gots all ah need right here."

"Fine, suit yourself! You're right! We *don't* need you anymore. We *can* do it by ourselves!" Jamie exclaimed. He put his hatchet and water gun back in his backpack and slipped the straps over his shoulders. "Come on, Artimus, let's go. We're wasting our time here. PBJ's got treasure-brain!"

"You're right. You might as well save your breath," Alizar said. "I've seen what the lure of gold can do to a man. No good, mostly. If you're ready, follow me."

The dragon led them to the entrance of the cave, bent down, and put his shoulder against the brush and vines. He gave a mighty shove and broke through to the outside. He squeezed the rest of his body through, then stood up and looked around in wonderment. "It's been a long, long time since I looked out from my cave. There are more trees and flowers, but it's mostly like I remember. You can come out, it's safe."

Jamie gave one last look over his shoulder. PBJ was so occupied, crawling all over the pile of treasure, that he wasn't even looking at them. Florabel stood nearby and looked after Jamie and Artimus longingly. "This is your last chance. Are you sure you don't want to go with us?" Jamie asked.

"Nope, y'all go on," PBJ answered without looking up. "Ah gots no reason ta go ta no castle."

"Okay, if that's the way you want it. We'll go on by ourselves." Jamie shrugged his shoulders. After the last four days, he felt he was capable of anything. He turned and followed Artimus out into the bright sunshine.

Outside, they found themselves standing on a ledge of rock. They stood there for a moment, blinking their eyes as they got used to the sunlight. Jamie took a deep breath and looked to the sky. "I feel like I've just been freed from a tomb," he said thankfully. "I will *never* take breathing fresh, clean air for granted again. Or being alive, for that matter."

"We're finally free from that awful mountain!" Artimus said joyfully. He looked out over the valley below, finding it hard to believe they really *were* free.

"Yes, this is fantastic," Alizar said, taking a deep breath. "It seems like a lifetime since I've done this." He bent over and sniffed a wildflower growing near the mouth of the cave. "Mmmmm, this smells wonderful. Do you have any idea how long it's been since I've been able to smell a flower without it wilting before my very eyes?"

Artimus shaded his eyes and replied, "Yes. I've got an idea how you feel. To me, it seems like ages since we entered this mountain. For a while, I thought we would never see the light of day again."

"Me neither," Jamie echoed. "I was beginning to think I was never going to continue on my journey." He looked out over the valley and found he could see for miles. "Which way to Mistemere, Alizar?"

The big dragon lumbered over to the edge of the cliff. He pointed down from the ledge. He said, "Go this way down to that gully, and continue on there until you reach the base of the mountain. At the bottom of the mountain, turn left on the road. You can barely see it from here."

Jamie took out his binoculars and focused them where Alizar pointed. He found the road and followed it to the south. Far off in the distance, he caught a glimpse of water shimmering in the sunlight. "Hey, I think I know where we are. I can see Lake Longwater." Jamie shifted the binoculars and looked closer. "Oh my gosh, we made a big semi-circle inside the mountain and this is the far end of the Forest of Whispers! I don't believe it, the Treesers aren't there anymore! They've disappeared! I tell you what, Artimus, that valley sure looks a lot safer now." He could see where the path met the road Alizar indicated.

Alizar continued. "If you take that road straight north, eventually you will come to the River Crystal, just like your friend Barly told you. It's a ways beyond those hills, which are beyond the forest. You see?" He waved a claw to his left. "When you get to the River Crystal, turn left again and go west to the base of the waterfall. From there, climb the stairs up Mt. Andiril. The Castle Mistemere is at the top. All told, it's about a three-day walk from there. Until you have to climb the steps, it's pretty easy."

"Three more days?" Jamie asked. "This is just great! If I ever get home again, I'm going to be grounded for a year! Come on,

Artimus, we'd better get going before something *else* happens to slow us down."

Artimus looked at Alizar. "What are you going to do? I mean, you don't have anywhere to go, or any friends left after all these years." He suddenly felt sorry for the dragon.

"Oh . . . I'll probably hang out around here," replied Alizar. "I didn't have any friends back then either. Maybe I can become friends with PBJ. He doesn't seem that bad, just a little misguided. I'll help him sort through the treasure. Maybe I can convince him to give some of it back to the rightful owners."

"That seems pretty unlikely, judging by the way he was acting," Artimus said.

"Well, I hope everything turns out alright for you," Jamie said. "I'm really glad we were able to help you." He walked over and carefully shook the dragon's claw. "I'd like to stay around and get to know you better, but we have to go."

Artimus went over and patted the dragon's scaly side. "I hope everything turns out too. I'm sure if people give you a chance, they'll see you've changed. Goodbye, and thank you again for helping us get out of the mountain."

"Thank you again for saving me," Alizar said. "I would have gone to my grave as a terrible fire-breathing dragon if it hadn't been for you. For that, I will always be grateful. Goodbye, Jamie and Artimus." The big dragon shed a tear over his change of fortune.

Jamie turned and headed down the mountain. Artimus followed in his peculiar hop-walk, using his staff for support. They didn't look back. As they picked their way down, Artimus said, "He wasn't so bad after all. Hard to believe he was an evil, fire-breathing dragon."

"Yeah, the poor guy," Jamie agreed. "Just think, no family or friends, and nowhere to go. What a lonely life to have. I kind of understand how he feels, being left out and all."

They continued on in silence. The gully was narrow and winding, and they had to pick their way between loose rocks and gravel. It took them well over an hour to reach the valley. However, once there, the going became easier, and by mid-afternoon they had reached the bottom of the mountain.

As they headed north on the road, Jamie was the first to speak. "You know, it's strange how things happen sometimes. I mean, if I hadn't met Deena and gone gathering with her, Kip would still be with us. If I hadn't taken the spring water, and if we hadn't gone in the cave, Barly would still be with us, too. I feel like it's all my fault somehow, and that I should have done things differently. And speaking of Kip, I wonder how he and Koki are doing."

"They're doing well, I would suspect. They were in good hands in old Charmac's care," Artimus replied. "You know, there's no use blaming yourself, Jamie. From the way you've described the events so far, most appeared to have happened the way they did by accident. You really had no control over them, if you think about it."

"Selth said that too. Just the same, I sure wish it would have turned out differently," Jamie said sadly. They walked on, each lost in his own thoughts.

Artimus was happy. He thought about how great it was to be out of his pond. He hoped he never had to go back to living like he had been for those many years. As he hop-walked along, he glanced at his newfound friend. Artimus was a simple being, but even he could see Jamie was combating some inner turmoil. He started to say something to Jamie, but stopped short. He realized he didn't know the boy well enough to be offering opinions. *And besides, what could a frog say that would help*, he thought. Instead, Artimus occupied his time by making a tap-slap rhythm with his webbed feet and staff as they made their way along the road. He started humming a cheerful tune.

Jamie, in turn, pondered his present situation over and over. *My adventure seems to be turning into a series of misadventures,* he thought. *I hope things start to get better soon.*

Eventually, the bright afternoon sunshine improved his thoughts. The land became more pleasant and inviting the farther they went. There were big patches of lacy flowers he didn't recognize growing alongside the path. Giant black-eyed susans dotted the surrounding fields beyond, and huge butterflies fluttered from flower to flower. Jamie wondered if the butterflies had come to Neverlore through the doors, or if they were native to the land.

Here and there spiderwebs were laced to the stems of plants and flowers. Their perfectly spun strands glistened in the sunlight. Jamie marveled at the precision of their construction.

After a while, Jamie remarked, "You know, it's kind of strange that there's no one around here." He waved his hand for emphasis. "The land is so beautiful and it looks like such a nice place to live. Yet it's odd that we haven't met anyone all afternoon."

"Robinwood was the same way. I met few travelers there, too. This suits me just fine, though. If it's all the same to you, the fewer people we meet, the fewer problems we'll have," Artimus replied.

Jamie laughed. "You've got a point there. Just the same, it seems odd."

The rest of the afternoon passed without event, and as the shadows lengthened and evening approached, they finally came to the forest Alizar had pointed to.

"This reminds me a little of the forest behind my house," Jamie said as they walked into the shadows. He glanced around.

The trees grew close together on either side of them, and their branches met high above the road. The thick canopy above almost completely blocked out the rays of the late-day sun.

"We'd better start looking for a safe place to make camp," Jamie said. "For some reason, I don't think we want to stay out in the open here." He remembered Deena's warning about spending the night in an unprotected place.

They walked on until they came to a large tree alongside the road. It was situated at the edge of a clearing and faced the trees on the other side. The roots had grown up over two or three large rocks and formed a protected hollow underneath. "This looks like as good a place as any to spend the night," Jamie said as he bent down and peered under the outer roots. He sniffed the air inside. It smelled like dried leaves and moist earth. Satisfied there were no crawly things living there, he crept in and took off his backpack. Artimus followed behind.

"I hope it doesn't get too cold tonight," Jamie said. "Without matches, we won't be able to light a fire."

He reached into his backpack and took out his last apple, cut it into two pieces, and gave half to Artimus. Jamie took the last gula bar from his pouch and shared it with the big frog. "This is all we've got left to eat. I hope we can find something tomorrow, or we might starve before we get to Mistemere."

"Starving may be the least of our worries," replied Artimus ominously. "I'll tell you what, something feels mighty strange around here. Did you notice anything unusual when we entered the forest?"

"Other than lots of spiderwebs, not really," Jamie said. "Spiders don't bother me like rats do. You just squash a spider, and you're done with it."

"Well, I noticed it was mighty quiet around here," Artimus

said, looking out from their shelter. It was getting dark. Once the sun dropped behind the mountains, night fell rapidly. "There are no birds or squirrels or bugs or anything. You'd think a forest like this would have critters everywhere."

"You know, I'm not sure what to think sometimes," Jamie replied. "This land is so different, I don't know what to expect from one minute to the next. Neverlore seems to be quite different than the widow Duncan described. She said it was a mystical, magical place, but this land also appears to be a bit more perilous now that I've been here a while."

"I couldn't say one way or the other," Artimus said wistfully. "I've spent most of my years in Robinwood and didn't explore the rest of the land. I guess I was hoping I'd change back to my old self and my family would magically reappear there some day. I see what you're talking about, though. The travelers that happened by the spring didn't speak much about the rest of the land." Artimus scrunched up his face. "Maybe they didn't talk about Neverlore because they were afraid to."

"That's what I mean," Jamie continued. "We know Xiticus created several doors and maybe even some secret ones. But like Selth explained, no one knows anything about them anymore. How many are left? Where do they go, and do they always disappear after one passes through? And besides Druin, who and what came through those doors all these years?"

"Those are puzzling questions," Artimus pondered. "It may be coincidence or it may not be. I guess it's even more reason to try and meet with Erenor. Hopefully he can give us some answers."

"Exactly," Jamie agreed. "And here's another scary thought. If there are any doors left, are any of them damaged, and is there anything else evil lurking outside them, waiting to get through?

By themselves, the way that condor-hawk and those Treesers and the Snakeroot acted are just events. But when you put them all together, they seem to signify something bad happening. I wish Barly were still alive. He'd be able to help me figure it all out."

"Maybe, probably. I don't know *what* to think now," Artimus yawned. "All this speculation is a bit too much for me. I do know that I'm tired and would like to get some sleep." He lay back against a tree root and got as comfortable as possible. "We should be safe in here, Jamie. Just to be sure, though, you take first watch. I'll trade off with you in a few hours." With that, he promptly dozed off.

I wish I could fall asleep that quick, Jamie thought. He leaned back against another root and used his backpack for a pillow. The moon rose over the top of the trees. As it climbed up the sky, the woods became bathed in a pale silver glow. The silence of night magnified every little rustle and Jamie moved as far back into the hollow as he could.

He shared Artimus's concern. Something just wasn't right about the woods. He could feel it now. If anything, Neverlore had begun to sharpen his senses. Jamie gazed out into the woods. Were his eyes playing tricks on him, or did he see movement in the shadows? He rubbed his eyes and looked again. Nothing.

This is crazy, he thought. *My imagination really is getting the best of me.* Even so, he remained wide awake and continued to stare across the clearing.

It was past midnight when Artimus woke up and offered to take watch. By that time, Jamie was extremely tired. He curled up in his sweatshirt in a hollow in one of the roots, and before he knew it, he was fast asleep.

That night, Jamie dreamt of the times when he was younger. It was before his accident, and he and Andrew were in the scouts. They always camped out, cooked over an open fire, and slept in a tent. Jamie was working on his third merit badge for knot tying. He loved playing with rope, and always kept a length handy to practice with.

He dreamt of riding his bicycle. Sometimes he beat Andrew in a race to the end of their driveway. Jamie also dreamt of soccer. He particularly liked playing goalie. Nothing was more satisfying than blocking an opponent's kick. Jamie smiled in his sleep and snuggled deeper in his sweatshirt.

Artimus was not so vigilant a watchman. He dozed, dreaming of the time he was a shepherd. He, his wife, and their young son lived in a stone house with a thatched roof. They called their son Artimus Junior, or Arti for short. Arti was a toddler and he loved to run amongst the sheep and bury his face in their soft, curly wool.

"Oooh, it tickles," Arti would cry with glee. It always made Artimus laugh. Life was simple; life was good. That was, until the day he took his flock to Lake Longwater. A frown appeared on his face, his dreams turned to sadness, and Artimus began to toss and turn. The noise attracted attention.

Up in the trees, many sets of eyes appeared, reflecting the moonlight as they studied the two forms under the tree roots. Several large and grotesque shapes detached themselves from the shadows and slithered silently toward Artimus and Jamie as they slept. The leaves rustled ominously as the shapes crept forward.

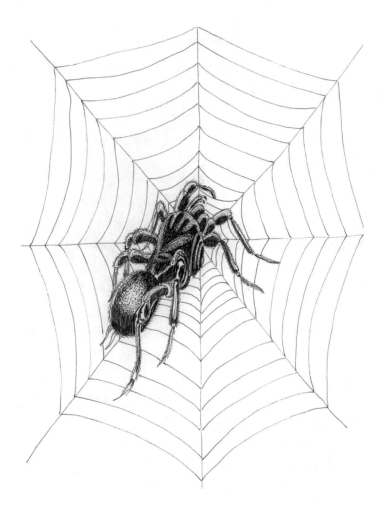

Chapter 13

It was getting light when Jamie woke up. He immediately sensed something was wrong, and when he opened his eyes he found Artimus gone. "Artimus, where are you?" he called, assuming his frog friend had awoken before him. There was no response. He crawled to the entrance of their shelter, stuck his head out, and looked around.

"Artimus, where'd you go?" he called louder. There was still no answer. All around, the woods were quiet.

Jamie immediately noticed Artimus's staff lying on the ground nearby. "That's odd," he said, going over to investigate. With a growing sense of dread, Jamie picked up the walking stick and examined it. There was a black, oozy substance dripping from one end.

"I wonder what this is," Jamie said. He put the staff up to his nose and sniffed. "Yuck, this stuff stinks!" He held the staff at arm's length. A glob of the stuff plopped onto the ground. Jamie scanned the clearing. "This doesn't look good. Artimus never goes anywhere without his staff. Something must have taken him, and it looks like he didn't go without a fight."

He went back to their shelter and grabbed his backpack. He pulled out his slingshot, and then took several pebbles from the side pouch and slipped them into his pants pocket. He held the slingshot and pulled back the sling. Green laser beams appeared on either arm and crisscrossed in between, forming crosshairs. "Watch out! I've got a weapon!" he said loudly, in case anything was listening.

Jamie was very good with his slingshot. It was the latest model and had super-surgical rubber, which gave it twice the striking power. He could knock a can off of his fence from a hundred feet, and if he was using steelies, he could put a hole right through it. Holding his slingshot gave him confidence.

"If these stones are anything like the water from that spring, then whatever's out there is in for an unpleasant surprise," he said in a matter-of-fact voice.

Jamie adjusted the straps on his backpack and wiped Artimus's staff with some leaves. With the staff in one hand and his sling-shot in the other, he set out again. Right away, he found a puddle of the same black ooze in the middle of the road. Just ahead, he found another. *Whatever's got Artimus has got the grossest-looking blood*, he thought, careful not to step in the congealing goo.

Jamie followed the trail of ooze for some time before it finally led off the road and into the brush. Looking through the leaves, he could see another small clearing ahead. Jamie crept through the underbrush, glancing every which way. The puddles of ooze were thicker and closer together now. *Whatever is losing this must be wounded pretty bad*, Jamie thought as he stepped into the clearing. He proceeded very cautiously, for he knew from his adventure books that a wounded animal could be extremely dangerous.

Immediately, the hairs on the back of his neck began to prickle. There was something evil here, he could feel it. Jamie laid the staff down and slipped the slingshot over his wrist. He walked toward the center of the clearing as quietly as he could. He had the uncomfortable feeling that something was watching him. Jamie looked in the brush, but saw nothing. The trail of ooze had disappeared.

"This is really bizarre," he muttered under his breath. Then a sound caught his attention.

"*Mmmmppphhhh,*" the sound went. It came from above his head. Jamie looked up and gasped. Over the clearing, laced halfway up the trunks of several trees, was a spiderweb the size of a swimming pool. Stuck in the center was a huge cocoon. The form in the cocoon was wearing spectacles.

"*Mmmmmppphhh!*"

"Oh no! Artimus, is that you?" Jamie cried.

"*Mmmppphh, mmmppphhh!*" Jamie walked over and stood directly under the cocoon. He could just make out Artimus's face under the fine webbing. His glasses were the only thing that weren't covered. Behind them, his eyes were wide open, staring down at Jamie in terror. He struggled to move but was held fast in place.

Suddenly, the huge web bounced, and Jamie heard an awful hissing noise behind him. He spun around and saw, creeping out onto the web, the ugliest arachnoid he had ever seen. It was as big as a cow!

"Yeeeuck!" Jamie cried, staring in morbid fascination.

The creature had a huge, bloated body that was all hairy like a woolyworm. A fearsome looking head with six eyes was attached to the body by a thick, wrinkled neck. Long, curved fangs extended from its mouth. It had a great hooked tail that arched up over its back, and at the end was a nasty stinger.

"What in heaven's name are you?" he called out. The creature looked like some giant mutated scorpion! Its stinger quivered as it moved, and as the ugly beast crept closer, Jamie spied a wound in its side. From it oozed the same black goo he had found on the road. "Ha! I see Artimus got a good lick in before you hauled him away, you gross looking slug!"

The scorpion hissed fiercely at Jamie. Jamie responded by reaching into his pocket and pulling out one of the pebbles. He slipped it into the pouch of the slingshot and said, "I've got something here that will make you wish you'd never messed with us." Under his breath, he added, "I sure hope this works as well as the water did. Otherwise, we're in big trouble, Artimus."

The beast was almost overhead now. It ripped a hole in the web with its fangs and started to drop through. Jamie knelt down, pulled back on the sling and he took careful aim through the laser crosshairs. "Here, take this, you repulsive monster!" he cried, and let the pebble fly.

THWAACCKK! The stone hit the creature directly in the neck. A look of shock crossed all of its eyes as the ugly beast's thick neck parted and its head blew right off. The head let out a terrible scream and fell to the ground with a sickening *thwop!* Right before Jamie's eyes, the head and then the body started to melt and shrivel up. A few seconds later, all that was left were a few large drops of ooze dripping from the web and a puddle on the ground where the head landed.

"Whoa! Did you see that, Artimus?" Jamie cried. "The stones from your spring *are* magical! That maggot's history!"

"*Ooommppphhh, oommmppphhh,*" was all Artimus could say. Jamie was dancing around over his victory when he caught movement out of the corner of his eye. He glanced up and saw another one of the creatures skittering across the web.

"Looks like you need some of the same medicine as your buddy!" he said loudly. He slipped another pebble into the sling, pulled back, and took aim again.

Whoosh, thwack! This time, the stone hit the scorpion right in the middle of its six eyes. The monster promptly exploded, showering the clearing with smoking black ooze. Before Jamie could get out of the way, a big glob landed on the hand that held the slingshot. Instantly, a white-hot pain shot up his arm.

"Oowww!" he screamed. His arm fell limply to his side and rapidly became numb. His slingshot fell uselessly to the ground. Jamie tried to move his fingers but couldn't get them to budge. He looked down at his lifeless limb in horror. "Oh no, Artimus, my arm's paralyzed!" he cried out in terror.

Just then, GLOP! Another blob landed on the back of his neck. Burning pain shot through his whole body. Jamie tried to scream, but couldn't open his mouth. An icy coldness spread through his body and he sank slowly to the ground. The trees spun above him and everything became hazy.

Oh no, what have I done? he thought wildly. *I can't move at all! I'm more paralyzed than before!* Through blurring eyes he saw another giant arachnoid racing across the web toward him. He watched in detached horror as it slipped through the hole and landed on the ground. It snapped its pincher jaws as it crept toward him. Its stinger tail bobbed up and down with each step.

The beast skittered around him twice before it was satisfied that Jamie posed no more threat. It stuck its terrible face close to

Jamie's and hissed. From the hole that served as a mouth, rotten, putrid breath blew over Jamie's face. He tried to recoil, but couldn't move. The last thing Jamie felt, before everything went black, were jaws wrapping around his body. He tried to cry out, but no sound came from his mouth. Then, there was nothing.

Chapter 14

It was some time before Jamie regained consciousness. When he finally opened his eyes and his vision cleared, blue sky and fluffy white clouds came into view. He lay flat on his back, stuck to the huge web. When he tried to move, Jamie found he was tightly wrapped in spider thread. He could barely wiggle his toes.

Not me, too! I've become a cocoon, just like Artimus! he thought frantically. Jamie lay there in a panic, realizing he and Artimus were in grave trouble. He couldn't even open his mouth to cry for help. *It wouldn't do any good anyway,* Jamie thought dejectedly. *Even if I could, there's no one around.* He struggled to reach into his pocket for his knife, but he couldn't move a muscle.

Why did I ever want out of my wheelchair? he agonized. *Why did I ever leave my back-yard? I want to go home! I want to see my family again!*

While staring sorrowfully at the clouds, Jamie felt movement. He strained to turn his head and saw another one of the ugly beasts making its way toward him. "*Mmmmppphhh!*" he tried to scream. The creature crawled over and stopped, all eyes staring down at him. Jamie tried not to look at the hideous face, but found he couldn't close his eyes or turn his head. As the repulsive thing stared at him, Jamie heard a voice inside his head.

"I can hear what you are thinking," the voice said. What an awful voice it was, shrieking and high-pitched. It sounded like the screeching brakes of a freight train. In spite of his delirium, Jamie forced a smile. He especially liked trains. He wished a big locomotive would appear and squash the ugly monster into oblivion.

The terrible voice in his head let out a wicked laugh. "There's nothing that can save you now. You and the other one will be fine gifts for our queen." The terrible voice hurt more than the worst headache he'd ever had. Hard as he tried, he couldn't keep it out of his head.

"It's no use, you can't block us out," the voice continued. "While you were unconscious, we read your mind. We learned all about you and your frog friend. We know that without your magic stones, you are no longer a threat. You are both alone and there is no one to rescue you. You will make a tasty meal for Yagula."

Oh no! Jamie's mind screamed. *Why is it, almost every time I run into a new creature in this land, it wants to make me its next meal?*

The web bounced as more mutated scorpions approached. Soon, he and Artimus were surrounded by hissing, snapping faces. Jamie felt sick thinking about what was about to happen. He knew scorpions stung their victims with their tails and spiders sucked their prey dry. He was about to feel the pain of both. Jamie thought of all the dried-up flies he used to find on the windowsill of his garage and shuddered to think that this was how he'd be found . . . dried up and brittle like a dead fly.

Jamie watched the hideous faces staring at him and Artimus, unable to close his eyes. A drop of clear venom from the nearest scorpion's fangs dripped off and landed on the net beside Jamie's head. It made a sizzling sound like bacon frying on a hot griddle. Jamie winced and tried to wiggle out of the way as another drop rolled down the other fang.

Goodbye, Mom. I love you! he thought in despair. He tensed his body for the first attack. The closest scorpion raised its tail and prepared to plunge its stinger deep into Jamie's belly. The rest closed in around him.

Suddenly, a shadow fell across the web and Jamie heard a peculiar sound whistling down from the sky. The monstrous creatures stopped their advance and looked up. Jamie strained to turn his head.

"YEEEHAAAAHHH!" a voice bellowed out. "Ah hates scorpions, 'specially big, ugly, hairy uns!" Jamie thought he recognized the voice through the tight thread covering his ears. It sounded like PBJ!

At that moment, Jamie saw the most unbelievable sight he had ever laid eyes upon. A mighty, winged dragon dropped out of the sky with a donkey sitting firmly on his shoulders. And perched on the donkey's back was the most welcome little man Jamie had ever known. *It was PBJ!* He strained furiously at his bonds.

BANG, BANG, BANG! PBJ fired a pistol with one hand and waved his hat around with the other. PBJ's first shot took off the closest scorpion's stinger. His next two dispatched another beast next to Jamie. The scorpions had never been attacked before. This was new to them. They ran around in mass confusion, screeching and running into one another. For the first time, fear now filled *their* eyes.

"RRAARRGGHH!" Alizar roared ferociously as he descended upon them. The great dragon flew straight at the web. The scorpions took one look at the fearsome sight and began to scatter toward the trees, hissing and snapping their jaws together.

They weren't quick enough, though. When Alizar swooped down over them, he smacked several with his long tail and sent them flying. At the other end of the clearing, he wheeled back up and swooped down on the creatures again. He let out another formidable roar and smashed two more as they tried to escape. With the next sweep, the sharp scales on his tail cut into the web. The web fell apart as the rest of the scorpions scurried into hiding.

Jamie and Artimus landed on the ground, rolled across the clearing, and came to a stop against a log. Alizar made one more pass, then landed next to them. Dust and strands of webbing flew everywhere as he flapped his great wings and settled to the ground. PBJ jumped out of his saddle and ran over to Jamie and Artimus.

"Thunder 'n' tarnation! I can't let y'all out of my sight fer a minute," he hollered. He took out his knife and cut open the cocoons. Jamie lay flat on his back, staring groggily into the sky.

PBJ shook him and slapped his face. "Wake up, boy, yer saved!" He stared down anxiously at the inert form in front of him.

A look of recognition flooded across Jamie's face as the poison finally began to wear off. He struggled to sit up.

"Whoa, boy! Not so fast. Let ole PBJ git the rest of this nasty spiderweb off'n ya," the prospector laughed.

"Oh man, oh my gosh, oh wow! Am I ever glad to see you guys!" Jamie cried with joy when his mouth was at last free of webbing. "Another few seconds and we'd have been history! Did Artimus make it?" He turned and was relieved to see the big frog pulling the last of the webbing off of his legs.

"Just a little weak, that's all. You two are miracle workers! We were about to become scorpion chowder!"

Still weak from the poison, Jamie stood up shakily and leaned against PBJ. As he caught his balance, he threw his arms around the little man and said, "You may be small in size to other eyes, but you are giant in mine from now on. Prairie Bill Jackson, you are my hero!"

PBJ beamed and blushed at the same time. He'd never had so fine a compliment bestowed upon him ever before. "Shucks, Jamie, twaren't nothin'," he drawled. "We was just doin' what was right, that's all." Even so, PBJ stood a little bit taller as he helped Jamie walk around to get his bearings.

"Just the same, you truly saved our lives," Jamie returned gratefully.

Artimus said to Alizar, "And don't *ever* let anyone say you haven't changed into a good dragon. As long as I'm alive in Neverlore, I will defend your honor, Alizar. Let no man say a hurtful or wrong word about you, or I will thwack him with my staff. By the way, where *is* my walking stick?"

"Over there, where I dropped it when those monsters attacked me." Jamie pointed.

Artimus hopped over to where his staff had fallen and picked it up. "One of those nasty beasts caught me while I was dozing last night, and I only got in one good swing before it stung me and I blacked out. The next thing I knew, I was here. How did you ever find me, Jamie? You were asleep when it happened."

Jamie told them how he had followed the trail of ooze and ended up in the clearing. "How did *you* know we were here?" he asked, turning to Alizar and PBJ. "You were all wrapped up in the treasure the last time we saw you, PBJ. I thought you'd be staying in that mountain forever."

"Well, ah admit, ah lost my head back thar," the old prospector replied. His face still had a tinge of red. "All that treasure did get ta me fer a while. It were the dragon who saved the day."

Alizar laughed and said, "I don't know about saving the day or not. Saving you two, most likely. None of this would have happened if I had been thinking straight. I guess my brain was still a bit foggy from my long nap. This morning, for some reason, I thought about the Fangling Forest scorpions. It dawned on me that I sent you this way without even warning you. 'What an idiot,' I said to myself. 'They eat just about everything that passes through.'"

"I wondered about all those spiderwebs when we were in the meadow yesterday," Artimus said. "I told you something was amiss, Jamie. But I wasn't prepared for these monsters! A spider-scorpion! How disgusting." He shuddered.

Alizar went on. "I mean, what a way to repay someone who has just done you the biggest favor of your life. I realized I had sent you off to an almost certain death, so we set out to see if we could find you. I was hoping we weren't too late."

"How did you tear PBJ away from all that treasure?" Jamie asked. "He didn't seem to care that we were leaving. He didn't even say goodbye to us when we left."

"Ah kin answer that," PBJ answered. "Ah was rummagin' round through that treasure yesterday, when ah come across this gold crown. It burnt mah hands when ah picked it up." He held up his hands and showed them the marks. "Anyway, ah guess that's what brought me to mah senses. Like the dragon, it was like the fog bein' lifted from mah brain. Tell 'em bout that crown, Alizar."

Alizar continued. "It is called the Crown of Arcada."

"*The Crown of Arcada?*" Jamie exclaimed. "Selth told Barly and me about the crown in his story of Neverlore. But how is that? He said it was lost or destroyed during the battle!"

"It was lost, but only for a while. A short time after the fall of Xiticus, I found the crown and hid it in my cave," Alizar continued. "Unfortunately (or fortunately, it would appear), the crown became buried under all the treasure Druin had me steal and I completely forgot about it. Dragons don't have the best of memories.

"When Erenor overthrew Druin and banished me to my cave, he put me to sleep without ever knowing I'd hidden it there. I've been sleeping on the crown and all that treasure for the last hundred years or so. If events hadn't happened the way they did, I'd still be asleep and PBJ never would have found the crown."

Jamie asked, "What'd you do then, PBJ?"

"When Alizar told me what ah had, we all figgered there's only one, make that two, things we had ta do," PBJ went on. "The first was to rescue you two, if y'all were still alive, 'n' the other was ta get this crown back to where it belongs, and that's on the head of your sorcerer, Erenor."

The realization of what PBJ had explained sank in. Jamie became excited. "You mean, we're going . . . " he began.

"Yes, Jamie, we're going to Mistemere," Alizar interrupted. "PBJ's got the crown safely tucked in his saddlebag. I feel like I'm to blame for this mess. This whole thing started way before any of you came along and got thrown into it. So, I'm going to take my chances after all and try to get you there to see Erenor. I'm going to take all of you with me just to be safe, though."

Jamie's mind whirled. One moment he was all but dead, and the next he was being rescued by a dragon! "You know, this whole adventure is beginning to feel like a wild roller coaster ride that I can't get off of," he said, shaking his head.

"What's a roller coaster?" Alizar and Artimus asked in unison.

"I'll tell you about it on the way," Jamie said.

Artimus had retrieved Jamie's backpack and slingshot from the bushes. He handed them to Jamie and said, "We'd better leave quickly before they start coming back."

Alizar agreed. "I don't think we'd stand a chance if they all attacked at once." He squatted down on his belly. "Here, climb on my back and we'll get out of here."

They did as they were told. PBJ climbed back onto the saddle on Florabel, who gave them all a loud greeting. Jamie and Artimus settled in between the armor plates behind her.

"How do we keep from falling off?" Jamie asked as the huge dragon stood up.

"Don't worry about that." Alizar laughed. "Once you're on a dragon's back, you can't fall off unless he wants you to. You'll be perfectly safe, so brace yourselves." He took a few long strides across the clearing, flapped his wings twice, and, with a jolt, they were airborne.

Jamie felt his stomach sink as they shot up into the sky. He watched in wonder as the ground fell away below them. As if everything wasn't wild enough already, he was flying on the back of a real dragon! How would he ever get anyone to believe him when he got back home? *If I ever make it there*, he thought.

As Alizar flew higher, they could see further and further away. Off in the distance, to the north, the River Crystal came into view.

It wound its way through the meadows and forests like a bright silver ribbon. In front of them, the Barrier Range rose from the plains into great walls of rock. Even though the mountains were still some distance away, to Jamie, it looked like he could reach right out and touch them.

For most of the journey, except for Jamie explaining what a roller coaster was, the group said little. They took in the ride and the beauty of the land below. There was field after field of beautiful flowers, and here and there, they saw deer and elk grazing in the meadows. As they neared the mountains, they spied an occasional waterfall pouring down the sheer face of the cliffs from some high mountain stream. Jamie was once again amazed to think that a land so beautiful could sometimes be so wild and potentially dangerous.

At one point they flew close to the treetops. Unexpectedly, they flew over a small village in a clearing in the trees. People came running out, shouting and pointing, and men shot arrows at them. Alizar swerved and dodged the projectiles as best he could. However, a couple of arrows flew by so closely Jamie could hear them whistle as they went by. He ducked down instinctively and yelled, "Yehaah! This is the greatest ride I've ever been on, Alizar!" The big dragon just laughed and pumped his great wings harder. Soon the village was far behind, and they continued on with no more incidents.

Eventually, the trees, flowers, and meadows began to disappear as the mountains rushed toward them. The meadows and forests gave way to scrub brush and boulders, which in turn gave way to the foothills and peaks. Jamie could see ice and snow on some of the taller ones.

Alizar changed course and began to fly parallel to the mountains. Up ahead, they could see where the River Crystal flowed out of the mountains and dropped in a magnificent waterfall. Walls of sheer granite rose up on either side of the river and disappeared into the clouds.

"We're almost there," Alizar said. "There's Parin's Landing straight ahead. You can see the steps climbing up Mt. Andiril to the castle." He flapped his wings harder and they began to rise alongside the mountain. Into the clouds they climbed, trails of white mist curling and sweeping around them. The air got cooler and the light grew dim. The clouds became so dense that Jamie could hardly see the back of Alizar's head in front of him.

They were only in the clouds for a few moments before they burst from the mist into sunlight so dazzling, Jamie had to shield his eyes to keep from being blinded. He squinted through his fingers until his eyes adjusted to the brightness. "This is outstanding!" he cried out.

All around below them, the crests of the clouds looked like giant cotton balls. They rolled and swelled like huge waves on some great, churning sea. The tops of the tallest mountain peaks poked through the swirl like rocky, deserted islands.

Gradually, the clouds thinned and disappeared, and they found themselves flying over level ground again. A wall of rock appeared on the horizon. As they neared it, Jamie could see that the wall was constructed of huge, stacked blocks of granite. He was amazed by how tall it really was. Evenly spaced along the top of the wall were what appeared to be lookout towers. Jamie suddenly felt uneasy. After his previous experiences, he wondered what new beings were waiting and watching them as they approached.

"This is it. The Castle in the Clouds, Mistemere," Alizar announced. "Let's hope for the best." He then gave a mighty flap of his wings and flew up over the wall.

Jamie gasped in wonder at the scene that unfolded below. It looked like a page out of a storybook. In front of them was a small city made entirely out of stone. Neat rows of houses and shops with blue and white and green tiled roofs lined narrow cobblestone streets. Brightly colored flowering trees were planted along both sides of the streets. Wooden carts pulled by donkeys stood idle in front of several shops. Jamie gazed in awe, but in spite of the picture-perfect setting, he began to realize something was wrong. Aside from the donkeys, the streets were empty. There was no sign of life anywhere.

Jamie had little time to wonder about this, though, for when he turned and looked ahead, the next sight took his breath away. Carved out of Mt. Andiril and rising high into the sky stood the Castle in the Clouds. It looked like it was made of solid quartz!

Round turrets with tall spires stood at every corner, grand colored flags flying from each one. Surrounding the castle was another wall built of massive blocks, and at the base was a moat filled with green water. At the entrance of the castle was a huge drawbridge made of thick, wooden timbers. Standing at attention on either side of the entrance were guards with long, pointed spears. Jamie stared in rapt awe. The whole scene was like every fairytale he had ever been told, rolled into one.

As the dragon swept down on them, the guards dropped their spears and pointed to the sky. They quickly scrambled through a door in the castle wall.

"Well, so much for surprise," Jamie exclaimed. He held his breath as they swooped down over the castle wall.

Chapter 15

Dust swirled as Alizar settled into the courtyard. "Don't do or say anything hasty," he warned them.

The words were no sooner out of his mouth that the doors on both sides of the courtyard burst open and guards ran out. Before they could move, the group was surrounded by rows of spears and swords.

"Don't even twitch!" one of the guards commanded. He stepped warily forward from the ranks, his sword drawn. "Unless you want to feel the thrust of our spears, tell me quick, what are you doing here, foul dragon?"

"We have come to speak with Erenor," Alizar answered in a calm voice.

"What?" the guard asked in surprise. "Are you daft? No dragon in his right mind would fly here unless he meant trouble."

"I repeat, we have business with the great sorcerer," Alizar said again. "*Important* business."

The guard replied gruffly, "Important business, you say? The only one you'll discuss this important business with is me."

"Why is that, might I ask? Who might you be?" asked Alizar.

"I am Grizweld Bonebrake, captain of the guards," the man replied. With a gruff laugh, he added, "I'm afraid Erenor is very ill and not receiving visitors these days. But I am! Now, quit stalling and tell me why a dragon with a boy, an old coot on an ass, and a giant frog would come here." The rest of the guards all laughed raucously.

Grizweld stepped forward, and for emphasis, placed the tip of his sword at Alizar's throat. "Be quick, dragon. My patience is wearing thin!"

While Jamie looked on, a knot formed in his stomach. The captain of the guards was a huge, burly man who looked aptly named. Artimus leaned forward slightly and whispered in Jamie's ear, "I didn't expect a reception like this. I really thought they'd be more friendly around here."

Before Jamie could answer, PBJ broke the silence. "Old coot? Ya callin' me an old coot? Why, ya sorry lookin' varmit! Yer mother shoulda taught ya better manners when ya was a little un!" he cried. He dropped his hands to his pistols.

"They've got muskets!" Grizweld roared. "Seize them all!"

Before PBJ could draw his pistols or Alizar could move, several guards rushed from behind and threw a weighted net over them. As the mesh settled around them, the rest of the guards thrust their spears within inches of their faces. The captives quit struggling.

"I'll teach you to mess with me!" Grizweld thundered. "Take these prisoners to the dungeons!" he commanded the guards. "Take their weapons and gear, and bring it all to me. Stake the dragon out in the courtyard. And bind his mouth so he doesn't burn the place down."

"There's no need for all this!" Jamie cried out from under the mesh. "The dragon can no longer breathe fire, and besides, we mean you no harm. If you'll just take this net off and let us explain, you'll know why we've come."

"Silence!" Grizweld yelled. "A dragon that doesn't breathe fire? Do you think I'm an idiot, boy? There is no such thing!" He turned to one of the guards and said, "Get them out of my sight before I change my mind and throw them in the tar pits. I'll get to the bottom of this one way or another!"

The guards did as they were told. One by one, the travelers were roughly pulled off of Alizar and hauled out from under the net. The guards took PBJ's pistols, knife, and saddlebags. They also took Jamie's backpack and pocket knife and Artimus's staff. Their hands were tied tightly behind their backs and they were led away. The last thing Jamie saw before he was shoved through the courtyard doors was a big black kettle being placed over Alizar's mouth and tied to the back of his head. Florabel was being pushed roughly into a small pen beyond the dragon.

They were led single file along a dark corridor and soon came to a long flight of stairs that led down to the bowels of the castle.

"Down there," one of the guards snarled as he poked PBJ in the back with the butt of his spear.

"Easy thar!" PBJ snapped back. "Ah gots eyes."

The air became cold and clammy as they descended the stairs. Smokey torches, stuck in the stone walls along the way, flickered eerily. Jamie counted over three hundred steps before they finally reached the bottom.

"Keep going," the guard said as he prodded them down another corridor.

Jamie looked around as they walked on in silence. This corridor, like everything else, appeared to be carved out of solid rock. Scattered along the way were puddles of foul-smelling water with black slime around the edges. He wrinkled his nose in disgust and did his best not to step in any of them.

Jamie's mind raced, trying to assess this new turn of events. Just when he thought his adventure was finally coming to a happy end, another twist of fate had intervened. *What good is it to be saved only to have the very people who are supposed to help you make you their prisoner?* he thought. Jamie's hope that he would ever see his home again began to fade once more.

Eventually the guards stopped in front of a wooden door that was set back into the blocks of rock. It had big, iron strap hinges and a small opening with bars set at eye level. The head guard took a rusty key down from a hook on the wall. After fiddling around with the lock, with a forceful tug he opened the door. The door creaked loudly as it slowly swung open.

"In you go," the guard said as he untied them and gave each one a shove. "As you can see, your room has been prepared for you," he said sarcastically. "I hope the furnishings meet with your approval. Just ring the bell if you need anything at all. Oh, I forgot! There's no bell to ring. Ha, ha, ha!" The other guards laughed along in a harsh chorus. Then they turned and left, slamming the door behind them. The prisoners heard the key being inserted and a *click* as it locked. The sound of the guards' footsteps echoed down the corridor, and a moment later, all was silent.

The three looked at one another in the dim light. Artimus was first to break the silence.

"I *can't* believe what just happened. I'm stunned! To think we risked our necks so many times to get here, only to have this happen. Erenor wouldn't treat visitors this way." He added, "At least I hope not."

"Ah should say not. What kinda *good* sorcerer would leave his guests like this?" PBJ agreed. "Specially uns with a 'portant gift like we got."

"*Had*," Jamie corrected him. "Now that Grizweld has the Crown of Arcada, anything could happen. How do you suppose Erenor became ill anyway? I don't know much about sorcerers, but it seems to me he would have all kinds of magic potions and stuff. A sorcerer should *never* get sick."

Jamie went on. "I think you're right, Artimus. Something terrible must be going on around here. When we flew over, I noticed there were very few people anywhere. You'd think a neat-looking village like this would have people everywhere. It's like the place has been deserted."

"Well, whatever is going on, we'll be of no help unless we can figure a way out of here," Artimus said. "Just look at us now. Out of the frying pan, into the fire."

Jamie looked around at their room. Artimus was right. They weren't going to be much help from where they were. The dungeon cell was about ten feet by twelve feet. In this area, the walls and ceiling were built from blocks of stone. Two cots with lumpy straw mattresses were placed end to end along one wall. The opposite wall was bare except for a small hole from which a trickle of water ran down the wall. Jamie walked over and sniffed it.

"Pheeww! I hope this isn't the water we have to drink! It stinks!" he exclaimed.

The wall at the far end of the cell had a window, up near the ceiling. There were no bars over it, and it looked big enough to crawl through.

"Maybe there's a way out," Jamie cried, pointing. "Help me move a cot over, PBJ."

Together, they dragged a cot under the window. Jamie climbed on it and stood on his tiptoes. He was just barely able to peer out. His hopes were quickly dashed, and his face betrayed his discovery as he jumped down and said, "Well, we don't have to worry about escaping that way. It's straight down the side of the mountain. I can't imagine how far down the ground is." He plopped down on the edge of the cot and put his chin in his hands dejectedly.

"What are we going to do now?" Artimus asked ruefully. "This is terrible. Barly dead, your friend Kip wounded, Erenor sick, and the rest of us captured and stuck in this awful place. I now wish I'd never left my pond. I'd be—"

Jamie interrupted him. "Come on, Artimus. It's not the end. It *can't* be. We didn't travel all this way only to have the journey end here. If you think about it, our luck's been too good so far. We'll figure something out, in spite of this setback."

"Jamie's right," PBJ agreed, walking over and laying his hand on Artimus's shoulder. "Shucks, ah been in worse spots than this 'n' made out okay. B'sides, look at it this way. Ev'ry room with a door has a way out, as well's a way in. Sooner or later thet door has ta open, 'n' when it does, we'll figger a way outta this mess."

"Well, that all sounds good," Jamie said. "But what will we do if we manage to escape? Our only hope was the Crown of Arcada and now it's in the hands of that bully Grizweld."

"Ah must admit, thet does pose a bit of a probl'm," PBJ said. "But somethin'll happ'n, it always does."

At that very moment, his prediction came true. They heard a key being inserted into the lock, and the door creaked open. In came Grizweld with another guard. PBJ's saddlebag was slung over the guard's shoulder.

"Your business with Erenor wouldn't have anything to do with what's in this saddlebag, would it?" he asked.

"So what if it does?" Jamie said defiantly. "That belongs to Erenor and Erenor only. Not you or anyone else has the right to keep us from giving it to him."

"I don't know what you see in that!" Grizweld spat. He took the saddlebag off the guard's shoulder and threw it in the corner. "That piece of metal is nothing more than useless junk. Why you traveled here to give that to him is beyond me. Anyway, Erenor isn't so great anymore. He'll soon be dead, and with the help of Druin, I'll take his place as Lord of Neverlore. You all will have rotted away long before anyone finds you. I'll see to that!"

That said, he and the other guard turned and left the cell again, slamming the door behind them. Once again they heard the door being locked and the sound of receding footsteps. They stared at one another with looks of surprise on their faces, then over at the saddlebag lying in the corner.

Jamie was the first to find his tongue. "What was that all about? The crown's useless junk? And Druin's helping Grizweld? I thought he was still a statue. I tell you, something *really* weird is going on in Neverlore." He ran over and picked up the bag. Sitting on a cot, Jamie opened the flap and turned the bag upside-down. He gasped as the crown dropped out onto the bed.

"Thunder 'n' tarnation!" PBJ exclaimed. "How'd *that* happen?"

The Crown of Arcada was as Grizweld had described it . . . nothing more than a worthless piece of rusted tin. Instead of pol-ished gold with precious gems around the rim, they now stared at a dull metal band with plain stones stuck on it.

"This some kinda trick?" PBJ asked. He picked up the crown and examined it. The band barely resembled the crown he had found in the cave. He scratched his head as he stared at the value-less piece of metal. "Ah know ah put a real crown in this here sad-dlebag 'fore we left. Where it went an how this un got in here sure beats me."

"Well, crown or no crown, we've got to figure a way out of this cell," Jamie said. "And while we're at it, I've got to get something to eat soon. I'm starving!"

"Jamie's right. We do have to try and find a way out of here," Artimus agreed. "We'd better get something to eat or we won't have any strength left when we do."

PBJ laid the crown on the cot and picked up the saddlebag. "Can't do much bout the crown, but ah think ah can help y'all with somethin' ta eat," he said, reaching into the leather pouch. "Ah got some 'mergency food in a secr't compartm'nt. This here bag's got a false bottom." To prove his point, he pulled out three packages and passed them out.

"Where did you get these?" Jamie asked. "What are they?"

"Got 'em from the mountin folk," PBJ answered. "Don't look nor taste like much, but they got berries 'n' special herbs, 'n' such mixed in 'em. One a these cakes'll last a body a good long time."

Jamie was pleasantly surprised when he bit into his. He was hungry and ate the whole bar. "That wasn't too bad," he said after he swallowed his last bite.

"And filling, too. I can only eat half of mine," Artimus said. He wrapped up his remaining portion and handed it to back to PBJ, who chuckled and put it back in the bag.

With the immediate need for food out of the way, their thoughts turned back to escaping. "I don't think we can overpower the guards and escape that way," Artimus said. "They're pretty big and mean."

"Maybe we can trick them somehow and get them to leave the keys," Jamie suggested.

"Mebbe we kin jest grow wings 'n' fly," PBJ offered. In spite of their predicament, the three adventurers looked at one another and laughed. Finally, the dimming light through the window let them know it was almost dark. They decided rest would be the better avenue at the moment. They put the two cots together and made one large bed. Jamie crawled into the middle, and PBJ and Artimus lay down on either side. In spite of the dampness, it wasn't that cold.

Jamie wrapped his sweatshirt around him again, and when he got comfortable, he said, "You know, something dreadful has to be happening here. Think about it. First, there were no people around, then we find out Erenor is sick. Then, instead of being treated like guests, we're thrown into this dungeon. *And*, did you hear that slug Bonebrake? With the help of Druin, he'll be the next ruler! We've got to get out of here and find a way to stop whatever it is, or I may *never* find a way out of Neverlore."

PBJ said with a yawn, "If'n we're gonna do anythin' bout it, we'd best get some shut-eye. Somehow ah got the feelin' tomorrow's gonna be one long day."

His friends agreed. Artimus and PBJ got as comfortable as possible and were presently fast asleep. Jamie lay for a while staring up through the window. *Where and how is this all going to end?* he wondered. Many more thoughts followed.

Finally, Jamie could think no more. The answers to his questions were nowhere apparent yet. Exhausted, he began to drift off. The last thing he saw was a star. It was a comforting sight and he made a silent wish upon it. In spite of the lumpy mattress, he slept soundly through the night.

Chapter 16

The day dawned bright and clear. The early morning mist lifted from the moat and floated lazily across the field bordering its edge. Soon it had cleared around the castle, and as the sun rose higher, a ray of sunlight shone down through the cell window. The brightness and warmth on Jamie's face woke him with a start. He was momentarily disorientated and didn't know where he was. However, as he lay on his back looking at the ceiling of their cell, it only took a few moments for reality to set back in.

Artimus sat up next to him. "Well, this is certainly more cheery than when we fell asleep. Maybe today everything will be better." He hopped his frog-walk around the cell, stretching his legs.

PBJ sat up and yawned. "Blazes, did ah have a bad dream or what? Ah dreamt we was a captur'd and . . . " Then he looked around. "Drats, it weren't no dream after all," he mumbled as he got up.

Jamie sat in the middle of the cot, flexing his muscles. He was sore from the lumpy mattress and had a crook in his leg from sleeping on something hard. He reached into his pants pocket and pulled out two round pebbles. It dawned on him what he had in his hand. And he jumped off the cot.

"Hey, you guys, look! I've got pebbles left from the pool in Robinwood," he said excitedly. "Hmm . . . I wonder . . . maybe these are what we need to get out of here."

PBJ looked at Jamie's outstretched hand and asked, "What good y'all think those'll do?"

"I'm not sure, but if they're magical like the ones I used on the scorpions, we should be able to figure something out," Jamie replied. He walked to the door of the cell and checked it over. The hinges were on the outside, so he couldn't do anything with those. The window was too small and the bars were too thick. Then he looked at the lock. It was an iron plate with a ring for a handle and a hole for the key. As Jamie stared at the hole, he had an idea.

"I wonder if this will help to get us out of here," he said, stooping down in front of the lock. The smallest pebble was about the same size as the hole. Jamie put the pebble up to the hole and turned it a little. It slipped right in. He reached up and pulled on the handle. The door didn't budge. He yanked the handle harder. The door still didn't open.

"Rats!" he said disappointedly, and stood up. He gave the door a swift kick. "I thought maybe one of these stones would act like a key, or make the lock disappear or something. I guess that idea's shot."

"Didn't think ya should get yer hopes up too much over them there stones," PBJ agreed. "We're a long way from that pond fer 'em ta be much good."

"I guess you're right," Jamie said gloomily. They started discussing new plans on how to escape. Artimus was in the middle of explaining an idea when he stopped. He pointed over Jamie's shoulder.

"Look, something's happening to the lock!" He pointed.

Jamie and PBJ looked at the door. Smoke curled from the hole in the iron plate. While they stared in fascination, the lock began to glow. A few seconds later, the metal began to hiss and pop. Right before their eyes, the lock melted and the ring handle fell to the floor. All that was left was a hole in the door, and the acrid smell of smoldering wood.

"Blazes, will ya look at that!" PBJ exclaimed.

Jamie opened his hand and looked at the remaining pebble. "These things must have some awesome magic," he said. "Man, I don't know if I want to carry this last one around in my pocket or not." To be safe, he walked over and slipped it into the saddlebag. Artimus and PBJ laughed.

PBJ quickly regained his wits. He took the saddlebag from Jamie and said, "Looks like we jest had 'nother miracle. We'd best make a run fer it 'n' get outta this dungeon 'fore someone comes along 'n' catches us." He walked to the door and pushed on it. It swung open with a loud *creeaaak*. All three stepped into the corridor.

"We best go opposite the way we come in. Don't wanna run into no guards," PBJ suggested, pointing to his right. Artimus and Jamie agreed, so they turned and headed down the corridor.

Smoky torches lit the way as they crept quietly through the dungeon. Here and there, they passed more cells. Jamie peered into the ones with open doors as they crept by. In several cells there were strange contraptions made of wood and steel. They had leather straps and chains connecting to arm and leg bands.

"Probably torture chambers," PBJ whispered. "Pity them poor souls thet was brought down here." The words were no sooner out of his mouth than they passed another cell. In the dim light, they saw chains hooked to the back wall. A skeleton hung from one, the grisly remains of some poor victim.

Jamie shuddered and gasped, "Oh my gosh, I can't believe it. I don't want to end up like that guy did! You've *got* to get us out of here, PBJ!"

"*Sshhh,* keep it down," PBJ said, putting his finger to his lips. "We'll get outta this one way or 'nother. Just stay close 'n' don't go a-wanderin' off."

They continued on, twisting and winding their way through the dungeon. The tunnel abruptly made a sharp turn leading to a set of stairs that led upward. Next to the stairs was a wooden door. PBJ held up his hand for them to stop.

"I wonder if'n this might take us outta here," he stated quietly.

As they stood at the foot of the stairs whispering whether to go up or not, Jamie stood on his tiptoes and peered through the window in the door. It was quite dark inside and hard to see. He gazed around in the gloom. On the far side of the cell was a cot, and on it a large body lay.

Jamie stared at the figure sadly. *Poor fellow, I wonder who he is,* he thought. As his eyes became accustomed to the dim light, the figure began to seem vaguely familiar. Jamie rubbed his eyes and stared harder. He suddenly realized what he was looking at. He gasped and had to cover his mouth to keep from crying out.

Jamie dropped to the floor, his face white as a sheet. Artimus noticed him first. He stopped whispering to PBJ and said, "What's wrong, Jamie? You look like you've just seen a ghost."

Jamie's lips moved, but no words came out. All he could do was point to the door.

"Tarnation, boy, cat got yer tongue?" PBJ whispered. He

walked to the door but, even on his tiptoes, couldn't see through the window. "Artimus, come look in here 'n' tell me what's got him a-goin'. Be careful, though, no tellin' what it is."

Artimus stepped between Jamie and PBJ and peered through the window.

When he looked in the cell, a shocked look came over his face. He caught his breath. "How can this be?" he asked incredulously.

"Not you too," PBJ said, backing away from the door. By now he wasn't sure what was happening. "What on earth's in there that's got y'all so dadblamed scart?"

Jamie finally found his tongue. "Is that wh-who I th-think it is Artimus?" he stuttered.

"It sure looks like it," the big frog replied after a moment. He looked through the window again. "It's hard to tell. The figure has its back to us. I wonder if this is a cruel trick." He glanced down at Jamie.

"I don't know. How can we tell?" Jamie asked.

"Would one of ya tell me what the heck's goin' on?" PBJ asked in exasperation.

"That looks like our friend Barly in there!" Jamie exclaimed. "Remember? We told you about him."

"Ah 'member, but how can thet be? Y'all told me he met his end back in the mountain," he said.

"I don't know. We both saw him go into the gorge," Jamie said. "There's no way he could have survived *that* fall!"

They heard the figure inside stirring and a deep voice suddenly called out, "Is it . . . Jamie, is that you?"

"It *is* Barly!" Jamie cried out. "I'd recognize that voice anywhere!" He jumped up and he and Artimus both pressed their faces against the bars in the door.

"Barly!" Jamie cried with glee. "It's us. Is that really you? But how? I mean, you fell into the gorge. We thought you were dead. How did you get here?"

"Ssshhh!" PBJ whispered loudly. "Y'all'll have all them guards down here if ya don't pipe down!"

Jamie shot PBJ a reproachful look and whispered, "It's Barly! I can't believe it. This is *another* miracle!"

Barly walked slowly to the door. As he did, Jamie noticed he walked with a limp. "Barly, it really is you!" he cried.

"Yes, it's ole Barly" he said. "But how did you two get here? And how'd you get out of that mountain? Did you run into that surly fellow Bonebrake? Did you—"

"It's a long story," Artimus interrupted. "We'd best not waste any more time explaining it right now. What we need to do is get you out of there."

"That's right! And we've got just the ticket!" Jamie exclaimed. He reached into the saddlebag and took out the remaining pebble. At the door, he said, "Stand back, Barly. We'll work a little magic. Watch this!"

Barly stepped back, and Jamie stuck the pebble into the keyhole. He and Artimus jumped back and held their breath.

Just like before, after a moment or two, the lock got red hot and began to hiss and pop. A few seconds later, it melted and fell out of the door. Jamie kicked the hot remains down the hall. He grabbed the door by the window bars and tugged hard. The door swung open with a loud groan, and they found themselves standing face to face with the great black and white bear.

Jamie only hesitated for a second before he threw his arms around Barly. "Oh Barly, it is *indeed* a miracle! We've been through so much since we lost you in the mountains. You don't know how many times I wished you were with us!"

Barly bent over and gave Jamie a gentle bear hug. "You're the last person I expected to see here, Jamie. You and Artimus have saved ole Barly's bearskin. I'm so glad to see both of you."

Jamie eyed Barly up and down. "But how on Earth, I mean, in Neverlore, did you get here?"

Barly limped into the corridor. In the dim light they could see that he had big patches of fur missing, and many scabs and wounds on his body.

"You look like you've been through a war!" Jamie observed.

"Yeah, but it'd take more than a few scrapes and cuts to keep ole Barly down." He looked down the corridor, then looked up the stairs and cocked an ear. "We'd better hide in this storeroom." He pointed behind them. "One of Grisweld's thugs could come along any minute."

PBJ agreed, opened the door to the storeroom, and stepped through. He looked around and, satisfied, motioned them to follow. Inside the room, he put his finger to his lips. "Talk quiet-like," he whispered. He stuck his hand out. "Prairie Bill Jackson's the name. Y'all can call me PBJ fer short if'n ya wants to."

Barly took PBJ's hand and shook it in his big paw. "Good to meet you, PBJ. It looks like you helped my young friend and Artimus here."

"Looks like we're all gettin' a hand in this here savin' business," PBJ chuckled.

Barly went on. "So tell me, how did you three happen to be in this dungeon?"

"No, you first," Jamie said. "How did you get here before us?"

"Okay, okay, me first." Barly laughed quietly. "When I fell from the bridge, I dropped a long way down before I landed. At the bottom of the gorge was a river. I hit the water right next to the Snakeroot."

"It must have really hurt, hitting the water so hard," Jamie said.

"Momentarily knocked me out," Barly replied. "When I came to, it felt like I'd had the wind knocked out of me. I heard a terrible scream, and before I could stop it, the Snakeroot was upon me. Instead of floating, however, we went straight down, twisting and fighting all the way. I came close to drowning. Somehow, though, I managed to break free and make it back to the surface. Once there, I discovered I was alone. The Snakeroot never came back up."

"Wow . . . you were sure lucky," Artimus said in amazement. "That beastly thing was as big as a tree . . . a tree with teeth!"

"Apparently a Snakeroot can't swim," Barly went on. "My guess is, at that point, he was trying to save his own life rather than attack me. He must have sunk to the bottom like a piece of petrified wood.

"Luckily, I bumped into a log that was floating by and grabbed on. I must have passed out and drifted with the current for some time, because when I finally came to, I had floated out of the mountain. I guess I was somewhere near the base of the Castle Mistemere, for I had no sooner made it to shore, when a bunch of guards appeared and took me prisoner. But not without a fight, I might add. They brought me here and threw me in the dungeon. Since then, I've moved from one torture chamber to another."

"Why are they torturing you?" Jamie asked. "You didn't do anything."

Barly continued. "They think I'm a spy or something. Bonebrake and his guards are a nasty lot. They were furious when they couldn't get the information they were looking for. Grizweld himself came and questioned me several times, but I didn't tell him anything. I had nothing *to* tell."

"That's interestin'. They wasn't much interested in what we knew, or at least they wasn't 'fore we 'scaped," PBJ said. "Whooee. Now thet we're outta thet cell, they'll be interested now. We better lookey out!"

"I don't know what he was trying to find out," Barly continued. "At first he beat me, but in the end, said it didn't matter if I talked or not. He said Neverlore would soon have a new ruler, and no one would ever find me anyway."

"Grizweld said the same thing to us, but said he *himself* would be the new ruler of Neverlore," Jamie whispered tensely.

"I don't know what's happening, but whatever it is, it looks like Druin, Grizweld, and their goons are going to take over. I've got a bad feeling about this," Barly said.

"Druin was turned into a statue of stone a long time ago by Erenor. How could his power be coming back?" Artimus asked.

"I'm not quite sure," Barly answered. "From what I've been able to gather, Erenor's power has been gradually fading these last few years. I've learned he's seriously ill and his power is fading very rapidly now. As he grows weaker, Druin's power grows stronger. I think Druin is still a statue, but somehow, he is able to direct his power through Grizweld and some of the guards. They've locked Erenor in his room and won't give him food or medicine. Grizweld hasn't the power to kill Erenor himself, so he's letting nature take its course. When Erenor is finally dead, Grizweld plans to declare himself sovereign lord of Neverlore. Things look pretty grim right now, and most of Erenor's subjects have fled from the castle."

Jamie whistled. "Things certainly *do* look grim. Alizar's been captured, Erenor's almost dead, and we're trapped in this dungeon with a useless crown." He then gave a brief account of the events that had occurred since they had last seen the big bear.

"So Alizar really is alive, just like Deena and Selth said," Barly said incredulously.

"Yes, and he's on our side," Jamie replied. "We were trying to escape and come up with a plan to help Erenor. That is, if we can find him," he added.

"How can we possibly fight Druin when there are so many of them and only four of us?" Artimus asked. "It seems hopeless to me."

"We may still have a chance," Barly said. "I've learned Erenor has a great granddaughter named Alindra. She's being held in her room by the guards. If we can get there and rescue her, she may be able to help."

"Why do ya think that?" PBJ asked. "We needs an army er somethin'. Don't see how only one girl's gonna help us much."

"You'll just have to trust me. I've got a hunch," Barly answered. "Alindra probably knows the way around this castle better than anybody. If she can get us to Erenor's room, we can deliver the crown to him. Remember how Selth and Deena told us that from the time of Barador, the crown only works on the pure of heart? When the Crown of Arcada is on the rightful person, that person's power magnifies a hundredfold. Hopefully, if we can get there in time, it will work and Erenor will be able to stop Druin and Grizweld from taking over Neverlore."

"That all sounds good, but that doesn't solve the mystery of what's happened to the crown," Artimus said. Taking the saddle-bag from PBJ, he opened it and took the band of tin out. "It sure doesn't look like it contains powerful magic to me."

Barly took the crown and looked it over. "Well, if this is indeed the Crown of Arcada, it should shine like it's supposed to when the time is right," he said. "Remember, this crown was made by elves from the purest gold and enchanted with powerful magic. Like I said, it's only a hunch, but it's better than nothing at all."

"Well, ah sure hope yer right," PBJ said. "Just the same, ah wish ah had my pistols back. That'd even out them odds a bit more."

"I think we'd better do as Barly says," Jamie said. "We don't have a lot of time left, and right now this is our only plan."

"Thank you. I know a hunch isn't much, but we stand to lose everything if we don't try something," Barly replied. He opened the door and stuck his head out. "Still clear. Follow me." While Barly stood there, his stomach growled and he hesitated.

"'Fore we start, sounds like you could use some vittles," PBJ said. He took one of the biscuits out of the saddlebag and handed it to Barly. "Here, eat this, it'll help git yer strength back some."

Barly thanked him and quickly ate the cake. "The guards didn't feed me at all while they held me. I'm famished!"

"That helps a lot," the big bear said. "I feel better already."

Barly put a finger to his lips and motioned for everyone to follow him into the corridor. They followed quietly and began to climb the stairs. In hushed whispers, Jamie and Artimus explained to Barly how they had met Prairie Bill and filled him in more fully on what had happened since they last saw one another. Barly, in turn, told them as much as he knew about the castle. They crept quietly up the stairs, wondering with each step what was in store for them at the top.

The bear, prospector, frog, and boy climbed the stairs single file. Jamie, who was right behind Barly, whispered, "How will we know where to find Alindra?"

Barly looked around and answered, "When I was in one of the first cells, I overheard two of the guards talking. They said she's being held in the north tower. I'm hoping it's not far from here."

"How d'ya perpose ta git in that tower? We ain't 'xactly welcome guests round here, you know," PBJ whispered from behind.

"At this point, I'm not sure," Barly whispered back. "I figure when we have to make our move, something will come to us. I know it's not much of an answer, but like I said, we don't have a lot of choices."

At the top of the stairs they came to a wooden door. Barly motioned for quiet, then grabbed the handle. Opening the door a fraction, he peeked out. He was looking into a hallway, and was just about to open the door for a better look when he heard a commotion from down the hall. He quickly pulled the door shut. When the noise had passed, he eased the door open again. They all moved forward and peered through the crack.

They saw a servant pushing a wooden cart with food on a tray. Utensils clattered as the cart's wheels bounced over the uneven stone floor. Burly guards accompanied the servant. They watched as the servant and guards went down the hall and disappeared around the corner.

After they were gone, Barly whispered, "I recognize those guards. Those were the same two I overheard talking. They must be taking food to Alindra. At least now we know which way the north tower is." He opened the door further and looked in both directions. There was no one in sight.

Barly stepped out into the hall with Jamie, Artimus, and PBJ close behind. They set off in the same direction as the guards and servant. When they reached the corner, they peeked around, then quickly ducked back. At the end of the hall was a flight of stairs guarded by the same guards who had accompanied the servant. It appeared that the group had found the tower.

"What'll we do now?" PBJ asked. "Ain't no way we'll ever get past them there guards."

Jamie looked around and whispered, "I've got an idea. What we need is a diversion." Motioning for the rest to follow, he led them back up the hallway to an open window. Looking out, they could see they were at the outer wall of the castle. They could see the north tower to the left, and below, the colored water of the moat.

"Look at the water," Jamie said. "I noticed it when we flew over. It looks *way* too green to be normal. I bet Grizweld polluted or poisoned it for some foul purpose."

He reached into his pants pocket and pulled out the clay vial of borok powder. "Luckily, I put this in my pocket instead of my backpack. A small amount worked on the mountain spring, remember? Hopefully, if we throw it in the moat, something will happen and it'll distract everybody, especially those guards."

"Sounds like a good plan to me," Artimus said

Jamie opened the vial, stuck his arm out of the window as far as he could, and let go. They all crowded around and watched it fall. A few seconds later they could see ripples spread across the surface as the vial hit the water. They didn't have to wait long. After just a moment or two, the calm green water in the moat turned red. Slowly, it started to bubble and boil. Purple steam rose from the surface.

"That's incredible!" Barly exclaimed.

"It's just what I'd hoped would happen," Jamie agreed.

Bright red flames swirled and danced about over the moat. At the same time, somewhere within the castle, an alarm sounded. As they stood there, fixed in awe, they heard the sound of running feet coming toward them.

"Quick, we'd better hide!" Artimus cried. They dashed behind a stack of crates and barrels just as several guards ran around the corner. The guards raced by without even glancing their way.

"Quick, to the tower, before they come back," Barly said. He led the way and they sprinted down the hallway, around the corner, and up the stairs. The stairs spiraled up inside the tower like those in a lighthouse. They bounded up two steps at a time, and at the top, found themselves facing another wooden door.

The door opened and the servant stuck her head out. When she saw Barly, she let out a cry and tried to slam the door, but Barly stuck his foot in the opening. With a grunt, he shoved the door open and entered the room.

The servant cried out, "Don't come any closer," and threw herself over a girl cowering behind a trunk.

"Don't be frightened. We mean you no harm," Jamie said.

Several moments of confusion followed as everyone talked at once. PBJ tried to explain about Alizar and the treasure, Barly told of the L'masse and showed the mark Deena had left behind his ear, and Jamie shouted above the rest, trying to be heard.

The girl finally got up and stepped from behind the trunk. She held up her hand. "Silence! Everyone stop talking! I am Alindra, Princess of Neverlore. If you are who you say, one of you speak to me directly. You have but one minute before I call the guards."

Everyone stopped talking and faced the princess. Having never seen a princess before, Jamie wasn't sure how to act. He stared at her dumbly. He guessed she was about his age, but slightly taller. She had long blonde hair, the bluest eyes he had ever seen, and skin the color of fine china. She wore a long white robe with a gold woven belt around her waist.

"You, the one with his mouth hanging open. Tell me why you have barged into my room uninvited!" she commanded, pointing her finger at Jamie.

"Well, your highness . . . your grace . . . your princessness," Jamie stuttered.

"Call me Alindra," she interrupted.

"Well, Alindra," Jamie went on, "we have come to rescue you."

"Rescue me?" she asked incredulously, eying the strangers before her. "How can a bizarre-looking group like you save me? It will take much more than a bear, a boy, a frog, and a cowboy to save a princess. I've been held in my room by guards for weeks."

"Ya know, if ya'll come down from yer high falutin' horse, ya might learn what the boy's a-talkin' bout," PBJ said sarcastically.

"How do I know you aren't spies for that miserable cur, Bonebrake?" the princess demanded.

"Maybe I can show you something we've brought that will help prove who we are," Jamie said. He took the saddlebag from PBJ, stepped forward, and opened the flap a crack. "This isn't exactly the way it was when we found it. I mean, this was different before it changed. Somewhere along the way it—Would you look at this!" he cried and pulled the flap open so everyone could see. Instead of worthless metal, the crown gleamed like polished gold again and the jewels sparkled brightly. "How can *this* be?"

"What 'n tarnation's goin' on?" PBJ demanded.

"The Crown of Arcada looks brand new!" Artimus exclaimed.

There was a moment of confusion as they all stared at the crown. Alindra was the first to speak. "The Crown of Arcada? How can that be? Where did you . . . how is this possible?" She walked forward slowly and gingerly removed it from the saddlebag. The warmth from the crown coursed up her arms.

"How, no, *where* did you get this? It's been so long since anyone has seen or touched the Crown of Arcada, it's almost become a legend," the princess exclaimed. She turned the crown around and around, examining it from every angle. It glowed brighter in her grasp. "This does appear to be the Crown of Arcada. Apparently, there is some truth in what you say."

They all started talking at once and Alindra had to hold up her hand again. She told Jamie, "You seem to be the spokesman, so tell me how you acquired this crown."

So once again, Jamie found himself telling the story of his travels: how they'd all met, found the crown, and subsequently arrived at the castle.

"The last time we looked, though, the crown was a dull band of tin," Artimus said. "How did it change to worthless metal, then change back to gold again?"

"The crown is protected by magic, like Selth told us," Barly replied. "The Elvenkind were apparently very wise. The spell they put on it must have been a powerful one for the crown to disguise itself like that. Who knows what power it holds and what it can really do?"

"My great-grandfather would," Alindra said. "But I'm afraid it's too late. He's deathly ill, and soon, all will be lost. There's no way the crown will help us now."

"That's mostly why we're here, don't you get it?" Jamie asked. "Maybe this crown *is* what Erenor needs to save Neverlore. We *have* to find a way to take it to him. We didn't come this far and endure so much just to give up now."

"You mean, you risked your lives just to return the crown to Erenor?" Alindra asked. "Not even knowing if he was alive or not?"

"That's the way it's turned out, as we didn't know all of this," Barly replied. "We don't really have much time though. Do you know the way to your great-grandfather's room?"

After thinking for a moment, Alindra answered, "There *is* a secret tunnel that leads from the kitchen to his room. If we can get there without being discovered, it may be possible. But . . . how do I know I can trust you?"

Jamie handed the saddlebag to her. "Here, you take this. If anything happens to us, you get the crown to Erenor," he said.

She only hesitated a moment before she replied, "Okay, I'll trust you for now." She slipped the crown back in and closed the flap. Alinda turned to her servant. "Nedra, stay here and distract the guards. If I don't return by the day's end, you know what to do. Let's go, quickly."

Alindra led them back down the stairs and through several hallways and corridors. Occasionally, along the way, they had to hide as more guards rushed by. Fortunately, they reached the kitchen safely. Alindra took them between several long tables and many brick ovens until they came to a low door.

"This is the storeroom. At the back is a secret doorway to a tunnel that leads right to my great-grandfather's room," she said. She opened the door and went in and the rest followed. Artimus was the last to enter. As he did, he pulled a torch from the kitchen wall, then closed the door behind him.

Alindra led them around large sacks of flour, dried vegetables, and various supplies until they came to the far end of the room. She moved a crate and pressed on a stone. A secret door opened and they looked into a narrow tunnel.

"I'll lead the way, since I've got the torch," Artimus offered. No one argued. With the big frog leading, Jamie, Alindra, Barly, and

PBJ entered the tunnel. The narrow shaft wound its way up and around inside the castle's walls. As they made their way along, the flickering torch caused eerie shadows to dance on the wall. Occasionally, they heard squeals and the sound of scurrying feet.

"Ugh! Not rats again!" Jamie exclaimed.

After a short while, the tunnel ended, and they came to another flight of stairs. When they climbed the stairs, they found themselves face to face with a blank stone wall. It looked like they had come to a dead end.

"This is it," Alindra said.

"This is what?" PBJ complained. "We come all this way only ta . . ."

Jamie held his hand up for silence. On the other side of the wall he could hear voices. Jamie noticed a crack in the stones about waist high. He bent down and peered through the crack. He found he was looking into a bedroom.

The sight startled him. At the other side of the room was a huge canopy bed occupied by a very old man. Jamie could barely see his face, but that was enough to give him a sinking feeling. If the person in the bed was indeed Erenor, they were in grave trouble again. For all the troubles Jamie and his friends had encountered along the way, it now appeared their long journey had been made in vain.

Jamie motioned for Alindra to look through the crack. She handed the saddlebag back to PBJ and knelt down beside him and looked in. "Is that Erenor?" he asked in anguish.

Alindra, shocked by his condition, answered with a sad whisper. "Yes, that's Erenor, my great-grandfather. He looks nothing like he used to, though. That fiend Grizweld isn't letting anyone give him food or medicine. He grows weaker every day and will die very soon if we don't do something."

As they looked on, a guard entered the room. He walked over and shook Erenor. "What's going on outside?" the guard shouted. "The moat is aflame by some unknown magic. What have you done, old man?"

"I don't know what you're talking about," Erenor said in a voice barely above a whisper. "That fool Grizweld has probably fouled up some spell again. He doesn't have the slightest idea what he's doing. You and the rest of those idiots will suffer for his incompetence."

"Ha, ha, ha!" the guard replied wickedly. "You are in no position to be making threats. Every moment you grow weaker, Druin grows stronger. When you are gone, the transformation will be complete. His power will be restored, and together he and Grizweld will rule Neverlore. Why don't you just give up and die? Can't you see—"

He was interrupted by another guard rushing through the door. "The prisoners have escaped!" he exclaimed, out of breath. "Secure this room, then meet us in the Hall of Elders." He whirled around and left as fast as he had come in.

The guard swept his eyes around the room, giving it a quick inspection. When he spotted the crack, he stopped and stared at it for a long time. Jamie and the others shrank back and held their breath. The guard started walking toward the crack when shouts and the sound of running feet outside in the hall distracted him. Changing his mind, he turned and left. He locked the door behind him. The commotion in the hall passed and a deathly silence descended upon the room, broken only by the old man's raspy breathing.

Chapter 17

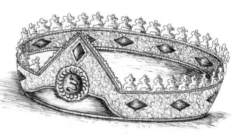

Behind the wall, the group gave a collective sigh of relief. "That was a close one," Artimus said. "What do we do now?"

"Don't know, but we best be a-doin' somethin' quick," PBJ exclaimed. He held the saddlebag at arm's length in front of him. A bright glow shone from under the flap.

"Will you look at that! Something must be happening to the crown!" Artimus exclaimed. As they looked in amazement, the glow under the flap brightened. The whole tunnel was soon bathed in bright light.

Alindra exclaimed, "This *must* be the real Crown of Arcada! It's said the crown stores up power when it's separated from a rightful ruler. When it gets near, it releases that power. We must get the crown to Grandpapa at once! There's no telling what will happen if we don't."

With that, she put her palms against the stone and cried out, "*Abu, bobu, dobu!* Let the rightful ones pass!" Suddenly, a secret door in the wall slid silently open. Alindra grabbed the saddlebag from PBJ and rushed through. She ran to the bed and bent over her great-grandfather. "It's me, Grandpapa, Alindra. We've come to help you." The others slowly entered the room. They shuffled toward the bed, careful to keep a safe distance from the ghostly apparition.

They watched in silence as Alindra removed the crown from the saddlebag. In addition to the light, the jewels around the rim glowed brightly, as if they contained some inner fire.

"Alindra, is that really you?" the old man asked hoarsely. "Come close so I might gaze upon you one last time." He could barely turn his head. Jamie, who was closest to the bed, gasped at the sight.

Erenor's skin was horribly scarred and hung loosely from his frame. His face was drawn and gaunt. A scraggly beard and long, matted, white hair fell down over the pillow. Sunken, bloodshot eyes looked up at them blankly. Jamie stared at the skeleton of a man that seemed more dead then alive.

The two vacant orbs gazed past Alindra and fixed on Jamie. Even in the scorceror's near-death state, Jamie felt the presence of an extreme life-force. He involuntarily shrunk back, feeling as if his very soul had been searched. As he watched, transfixed, Alindra gently raised Erenor's head and placed the Crown of Arcada upon it.

If possible, the crown glowed even brighter than before and began to pulse. Before their eyes, a spectacular transformation started to take place and a drastic change slowly came over Erenor. His wrinkles began to vanish and his long white hair lost its scraggly look. His flesh firmed up and the harsh, skeletal look disappeared. His face regained its ruddiness and the scars vanished almost completely. They now gazed upon a completely different person: a man with the ageless and imperious look of a wizened sorcerer.

PBJ was the first to speak. "Tarnation, would ya look at that! That crown packs a mighty pow'rful punch!"

Jamie regained his composure and found his tongue. "Selth's tale *was* true. It sounded pretty far-fetched at the time and I wasn't sure if I totally believed him."

"Well, it appears those elves knew what they were doing when they made this crown," Barly said.

"That it certainly does! I've never witnessed anything like this before," Artimus agreed. "It looks like the crown has found its rightful owner."

Erenor slowly sat up in bed and put his hands over his face. He gave a loud groan, and when he took his hands away, they all cried out in surprise. Two piercingly blue eyes appeared where the dull, glazed orbs had been.

"We just witnessed one more miracle," Jamie affirmed. "Neverlore is truly a land of magic and mystique! I'll be more believing from now on."

Erenor blinked several times, then looked at the odd crowd standing before him. "It *is* you, Alindra," he cried. "What have you done? Who are these beings?"

It was then that he felt the weight of the crown on his head. The sorcerer reached up and touched the band. "What is this?" he asked, taking it off. When Erenor saw what he held in his hands, an expression of bewilderment crossed his face.

"The Crown of Arcada?" he said, barely above a whisper. "How is this possible? How can it be that the lost crown ends up here at my darkest hour? I've searched for it for over a hundred years to no avail. There must be powerful sorcery involved here . . ." The sorcerer paused. A confused look passed across his face. "But . . . I don't sense any. This is not understandable." He put the crown back on and pointed to the group. "Who can tell me what happened? What manner of magic brought this to me? And who are you strangers?"

Artimus looked at PBJ, who looked at Barly, who looked at Jamie. "I think you are the best one to explain it all," Barly said.

Jamie shrugged his shoulders and replied, "I guess, if you insist." He introduced Barly, PBJ, and Artimus. He told an abbreviated story of how he had entered Neverlore and met his companions, their trip into the mountain, and how they inadvertently awakened Alizar and discovered the Crown of Arcada.

"I traveled to Mistemere to try and find a way back home, but that and the full story will have to wait." Jamie said. "Right now it seems you—we—have got a much bigger problem to deal with. Your castle is under attack!"

There was a moment of silence as Erenor looked them over. "Alizar is still alive, and he is a *good* dragon now?" he asked. "Castle under attack? This is a very strange tale and hard to fathom. How can it be—"

He was interrupted by the door of the bedroom flying open. Before anyone could move, several guards brandishing swords and spears rushed in and surrounded them. Grizweld strolled in after them.

"What's going on here?" he roared. He spied Jamie and his friends. "There you three spies are! How'd you escape? Never mind! Guards, seize them and take them to the tar pits! We'll rid ourselves of these intruders once and for all."

"I told you there was trouble," Jamie warned Erenor.

The sorcerer quickly assessed the situation, and before the guards could carry out their orders, Erenor rose from his bed. By then he had regained much of his strength and now stood majestically before them. He stepped between Jamie and Barly and gave Grizweld a piercing stare.

"How is it that Grizweld Bonebrake is giving orders such as these?" the sorcerer asked. He raised his left hand, palm facing out toward the guards. Immediately their weapons clattered to the floor. Then the guards dropped into a tangled heap and lay without moving.

"What are you doing up? You're supposed to be dead by now!" Grizweld shouted. Then, with a look of shock, he saw the change that had come over the sorcerer. "What the . . . what form of trickery is this?"

He tried to draw his sword, but the sorcerer was quicker. Erenor turned his palm toward the surly man and stopped Grizweld's hand on the hilt. His burly body shook visibly and, too late, Grizweld realized his mistake in challenging the sorcerer. His features began to transform before the group's very eyes. Grizweld's skin turned from flesh color to gray and his uniform lost its texture. The look of shock froze on his face. In a matter of seconds, Grizweld Bonebrake had been turned from the captain of the guards into a statue of stone!

Jamie let out a low whistle. "I don't believe it," he said. "I thought we'd seen everything." They all stared in disbelief. PBJ eased forward and gingerly touched Grizweld's arm. It was as hard as rock.

"That's some mighty pow'rful magic yer packin' there, Er'nore. Ya always git rid of yer enemies like that?" he asked.

"Only the very bad ones," the sorcerer replied with a wry smile.

He pointed both his palms toward the tangled pile of unconscious guards, closed his eyes and concentrated. They began to stir. "Arise and obey. The spell of Druin no longer holds you or your comrades captive." Erenor commanded. "Tell me what evil work Druin is planning. Speak quickly and truthfully or you will suffer

Grizweld's fate!"

The first guard to stand up rubbed his head groggily. "I'm called Raegary. I'm a lieutenant in the palace guard." He stepped forward.

"Raegary, I recognize you. You were one of my most trusted guards. What has happened here?" Erenor asked.

The guard bent to his knee and placed his fist over his heart. He said in a lucid voice, "The fog is lifting from our minds and the spell of Druin is no longer upon us. I repledge myself and my men to your service," he stated. "Your Lordship, as you lay dying, Druin was stealing your power and plotting with Grizweld and his followers. Druin has somehow broken the spell over Lake Longwater and the vermin and monsters imprisoned there have escaped! They have joined with Grizweld's men and organized a formidable army. Under his spell, we were powerless to intervene. As we speak, the hordes are gathering on the glen by the moat. Something must have gone wrong with Druin's plan to eliminate you, though. The moat is now on fire and everything is in disorder."

Erenor continued, "Druin cursed one of my servants and he must have fed me Larcher root. I was fortunate. Only a sorcerer can withstand instant death after ingesting it. But even a sorcerer can't survive this poison for long. Without food or the antidote, I was dying a little more as each day passed. The end was very near." He touched the Crown of Arcada. "This *is* truly a miracle, and my life has been spared. Unfortunately though, my powers are still too weak to fight Druin *and* his army alone. I can utilize the crown's power, but I will need help." He looked at the group standing before him. "We fortunately have the element of surprise to aid us. We must quickly seize the opportunity and prepare. Alindra, do you swear by these soldiers?" Jamie and the others looked at one another in bewilderment.

"Soldiers? I don't know about that. I just came here to see about—"Jamie was interrupted by Alindra.

"They are bearers of the crown, having defeated Alizar to secure it," the princess said. "They risked death to bring it to me and gave it willingly and without malice of heart. And the bear has the mark of the L'masse, which bodes well for them. What little I know of these brave strangers, I swear by."

Erenor gazed intently at each of the companions. "The mark of the L'masse, you say? Show me," he commanded. Barly obliged by moving forward and showing the sorcerer his left ear. "Another mystery in this puzzle of many pieces," he remarked. Apparently satisfied the mark was genuine, Erenor continued, "I don't know how you came by it, but that isn't important at the moment. Only a trusted few are given the mark of the L'masse. As we have little time, we must spend it wisely."

Erenor stretched to his full height. He had a commanding presence and spoke in a solemn voice. "Will you standing before me help defend the Castle Mistemere to secure the future of Neverlore?"

They all looked at one another, then Alindra, then the sorcerer. "Well, ah say it'd be an honor," PBJ said. Barly reluctantly murmured in agreement. Artimus just blinked his big frog eyes behind his glasses.

"You want us to fight a *real* battle? Against an army ten— maybe a hundred—times bigger than *us*?" Jamie blurted out. "I'm not so sure about *that!*" Over the years, his handicap had helped make him strong in many ways, but never in his wildest dreams had he expected it would come to this. *Now what have I gone and gotten myself into?* he thought. *I should have never gone after my kite.*

In spite of his misgivings, however, the sudden turn of events sent his adrenalin racing. He'd planned, fought, and won many simulated battles with his e-Cubix game, and in spite of the danger and the odds stacked against them, the chance to fight a real battle fired his imagination. *I must be crazy!* he thought. But the more Jamie thought about it, the more certain he became that they still had a chance and he could do it.

Barly stepped forward. "How will we fight and what will we use? We'll need more than mortal weapons to win this battle," he pointed out. "Wouldn't it be better to try to escape through some secret passage or something?"

Jamie's mind raced. Concentration showed on his face. "Wait! I have an idea," he commanded, holding up his hand. "We *have* more than mortal weapons. I have Robinwood water in my canteen and water gun. And I have a few more pebbles from the pond in the side pocket of my backpack! I also have one very *good* mortal weapon, my slingshot. I *will* help in this fight, but I need my pack to do so. Can you send someone to find it, Erenor?" His change of heart and confident air heartened the rest.

"And bring me ma pistols 'n' ma other saddlebag. Ah got some s'prises maself," PBJ drawled enthusiastically.

"And my staff makes a pretty good weapon, just ask those scorpions or spiders or whatever they were," Artimus said with conviction.

"Then it is agreed. I hearby swear you to service under the Crown of Arcada," Erenor decreed. "You will fight with honor and dignity." He turned to one of the guards. "Have the station guards raise the drawbridge and secure the outer doors while we still have the chance," he instructed. The sounds coming from outside the castle indicated that their enemy was advancing.

"What's causing all the chaos out there?" Raegary exclaimed. He glanced out of the window. It was late afternoon and dark clouds had rolled in over the mountains. Raegary gasped at the scene below and motioned the others over. They crowded around behind him and looked out. It was then that Jamie told of his diversion with the borok powder.

The fire on the moat had begun to die down, and through the smoke they could see legions of terrible men and beasts gathering in the field beyond. Off in the distance they could hear the sounds of wild creatures crying and the cursing and yelling of many harsh voices.

"What are those disgusting things?" Artimus asked. He pointed at several large, grotesque, blackened forms lying on the bank of the moat.

"Wormongers!" Erenor exclaimed. "From Lake Longwater. This certainly has to be Druin's work. Somehow he's tampered with the spell I cast long ago."

"What's a wormonger?" Jamie asked.

"A bloated, digging parasite!" Alindra hissed. "They can bore right through solid rock with their tusks and slimy, acidic saliva. In a matter of hours, they'll have bored through the outer wall and made a tunnel for the grubbers." She shuddered at the thought. "We're very lucky you had that special powder, Jamie." She said appraisingly.

"We need to act immediately. How many men can you muster, Raegary?" Erenor asked his lieutenant.

"Barely a hundred is all that are left in the castle," Raegary replied. "The rest fled to the mountains. Those who stayed are under the spell of Druin. Grizweld used them to fight your personal guards, the D'nalli. If we count the D'nalli, maybe seventy more."

"Druin no longer controls them," Erenor said. "We will use every man available. They will defend Mistemere or will die by my hand!"

"That's not enough to fight *that* army," Alindra said woefully.

They looked out over the moat. Fires had begun to spring up in the field below and they could hear drums in the distance. Scores of dark figures slithered about the flames and raised their hoarse voices in an unearthly chant.

Jamie pulled out his binoculars and surveyed the scene closely. "There are a lot of large, two-headed black cats with spiked tails out there! There are also bizarre-looking six-legged beasts," he said, sucking in his breath.

"Wormongers, grubbers, and now felions and scaglets. What else has that vile Druin brought against us?" Alindra asked in dismay.

"The spell over Lake Longwater *must* be broken," Erenor replied tensely.

"We need to build a defense," Barly proposed. Just then, the guard ran back in with Jamie's backpack and PBJ's saddlebags.

"Where's ma pistols?" PBJ asked. "Ah needs ma six-guns!"

"And I'd like my staff back," Artimus complained.

"I'm sorry, they are locked away in the armory," the guard said.

"We'll get them as quickly as possible," Jamie said, taking his pack from the guard. He had formulated a plan. "I have an idea. These guys are going to fight like they did in the dark ages . . . no offense to you," he added, turning to Erenor. "It looks like they are going to line up and charge the castle walls. That type of battle plan is ancient. I've played a lot of combat games and know something about modern war strategy. I have a better plan. We need to create another diversion, bigger this time. This is going to be like playing Battalion Men on my *e*-Cubix game."

"What's a *e*-Cubix game?" Raegary asked.

"No time to explain right now," Jamie answered hurriedly. "Since the moat's turned red, it must still be under some kind of spell. We have to act quickly before we lose the chance for surprise. Hopefully the stones will work as well as the borok powder."

With that, Jamie selected two of the largest pebbles from his backpack. He picked up his slingshot, loaded it, and pulled back on the bands. He leaned out the window and sent the first stone flying past the drawbridge to the far end of the moat. Jamie fired the second stone the other way. Fortunately, his hunch worked. Once again, the moat began to flare and boil. This time giant purple and yellow flames shot straight up in the air. Cries of fear could be heard, and the enemy retreated from the edge of the moat. "This should keep them away for a while. Raegary, go gather all the men you can."

"There is more to you than I first believed," Erenor said with approval. "The boy speaks with authority. Raegary, you and your guards muster as many of the others as you can. Give weapons to any who will fight. Those who won't, throw them over the wall into the moat. When you have done this, meet us in the anteroom of the Hall of Elders"

As the guard left, he turned to the rest. "Alindra, take PBJ to the armory for his weapons. There's a key in the guardroom desk. The rest of you, follow me. We must secure the castle by whatever means we have. If we hold them off until dawn, there's a good chance we can prevail. I banished that nasty horde to Longwater once, a long time ago. With your help, I can banish them again!"

He hurried out of the room and started down the hall. Artimus, Barly, and Jamie followed the sorcerer, and Alindra and PBJ departed for the armory. Outside in the distance, they heard the shouts of men and the clash of weapons.

Erenor led the group through several hallways and doors until they entered a room with rough-hewn wooden beams on the walls and ceiling. Jamie outlined his plan as they went.

They approached two massive oak doors. "This is the ante-room. The Hall of Elders is beyond those doors," Erenor said, gesturing toward the doors. An eerie blue light radiated from underneath.

"The statue of Druin is in there. His power is strong, but it appears not strong enough for him to escape his bonds yet. However, to be safe, don't walk through or even near the light."

Erenor led them to a long table in one corner. "This is a map of Neverlore," he said, unrolling a scribed leather manuscript. "And this is Mistemere," he pointed. "The cliffs in the foothills are here to the east. If the plan works, they should stop Druin's army from retreating from the moat any further. To the north is Swamp Bogmire, to the south, River Crystal, another natural barrier.

"Barly, you are the one best suited for this first task. If you can get some water from Robinwood into Dogwood Creek, which flows through Bogmire, the swamp will become impenetrable. Any who enter will never come out again."

"Why do you say I should be the one?" Barly asked, already knowing the answer.

"They won't suspect a bear. You will blend in. I will have one of the D'nalli show you to a secret tunnel out of the castle." He produced a small container with a leather band, and Jamie filled it with water from his canteen. The sorcerer then preformed an incantation over the container.

"You must go swiftly, and most importantly, speak to no one. Druin will have spies everywhere. Follow the stone path all the way to Dogwood Creek. When you get there, pour the whole container in."

Barly hesitated, then took the earthen jug and slipped the band around his neck. "It looks like we must part again, Jamie," he said apprehensively. Jamie walked over and took a paw in his hand.

"This adventure has taken on whole new meanings and directions, Barly. There are now needs more important than our own personal wishes. You, I, we . . . we can do this. For ourselves, and for Neverlore," he said earnestly.

"Sometimes, there is more in each of us than we ever know. It now must be revealed," Erenor added. "Your journey seems to have taken you down many separate paths so far, but your paths are destined to meet again. Believe it."

The sorcerer summoned a D'nalli guard and gave hurried instructions. When he was through, the guard and Barly quickly left through a side door. The big bear looked over his shoulder, waved once, then disappeared into the depths of the castle.

Erenor turned to Jamie and Artimus. "Let us plan our strategy. I then have unfinished business with Druin," he said, looking at the light under the door.

They huddled over the map and spoke quietly. "If my hunch is right, they will challenge us at the drawbridge." Jamie pointed. "That's most always the way these battles start out. If we position men here at the castle perimeter with bows, they can help with the diversion I'm planning." He went on to explain other elements of his strategy as Erenor listened intently.

"This is certainly not a plan I would have thought of," he said approvingly.

"And hopefully, neither would the enemy," Jamie replied. "We *must* initiate the first strike and employ a little modern psychological warfare." As they talked and refined their tactics, Raegary came in. Erenor stood up. "What news do you have?"

"All have pledged to fight. As near as I can count, we have two hundred and twenty men fully armed. This includes the D'nalli and twenty of your best crossbowers. Except for the crossbowers, the rest are stationed and ready to defend the castle," Raegary said.

"Good," Erenor said. "Take Jamie to the crossbowers. He'll show them their part of the battle plan."

"Come with me, young warrior," Raegary said. Jamie shouldered his backpack and followed the guard through another door.

The sorcerer unlocked a cabinet above the table, removed a small leather pouch, and handed it to Artimus. "Take this to Alindra. Help her free the dragon and have him swallow the contents. This will temporarily give him back his fire. Instruct PBJ, Alizar, and Alindra to follow you, and meet me in the courtyard in one hour.

"Time is short and I must attend to Druin immediately. If I'm not there in an hour, I won't be coming. The battle will be lost before it's begun. If I don't make it back, you and everyone in the castle will be on your own to save yourselves by whatever means you can."

Artimus took the pouch from Erenor. His eyes contained a look of fright, and he replied, "Something tells me I *should* have stayed in my pond in Robinwood. At least there I was safe and wasn't battling monsters, evil warlocks, and the like."

"Your pond won't be safe ever again if this evil isn't stopped," Erenor said. "No place in Neverlore will be safe. At least here, you have a fighting chance, which is better than no chance at all."

"If you insist," Artimus muttered. "I just didn't see myself going to battle when I left my pond, that's all." The big frog turned and hop-walked away to find Alindra and the dragon.

"None of us expected that this would be the outcome," the sorcerer said to himself.

After Artimus had gone, Erenor unlocked another cabinet and withdrew a scepter. It was about four feet long. The top looked like a frozen flame, and it was crafted of the purest crystal. He walked over and grasped the iron handle on the oak door. Before opening the door, he raised the rod above his head and shouted in a commanding voice, *"El Domini, Incurin, As Delto!"* The scepter radiated and pulsed as if some internal fire was about to be unleashed. The sorcerer drew himself up, wrenched open the door, and strode into the Hall of Elders.

The Crown of Arcada glowed brightly on Erenor's head. Inside, a heart-stopping wail began. The howl echoed throughout the castle, and as it rose and fell, the blue light flickered even more. As he walked into the radiating light, Erenor commanded, *"Back to stone, you vile creature!* This land had no room for you before, and the same holds true now! Today is a day of reckoning!"

The doors slammed shut behind Erenor and the great room was plunged into a darkness so complete, it extinguished the crown's bright light and reduced the scepter's radiance to an almost imperceptible glow. The battle of good versus evil had begun.

Chapter 18

Jamie donned his backpack and followed Raegary through the castle. They eventually came to a sturdy door at the end of a long corridor. Raegary opened it and ushered him into a good-sized room.

"Wow, will you look at those! This is *awesome!*" Jamie exclaimed, scanning the interior.

Hanging off of wooden pegs on the walls, stacked in rows of three or four each, were countless bows of all shapes and sizes: long bows, short bows, crossbows, and bows he didn't recognize. One of the walls was filled with holes, and these in turn were filled with hundreds and hundreds of arrows of different design, thickness, and length. Each arrow had been fitted with brightly colored feathers. On another wall hung many quivers made of dark leather. The letter M was stitched on each one.

Raegary had previously assembled the bowmen into a group and they were milling around. He introduced Jamie to their captain. "Captain Rorek is prepared to follow your command."

Jamie examined their faces and could see concern for the upcoming battle and doubt that an outlander could be of any help. He responded by extracting a short arrow from one of the holes, walking to a table in the center of the room, and saying in a firm voice, "Men, we don't have much time before we're under attack. I want each one of you to lay your straightest arrow on this table," he said, using his arrow as a pointer. The men did as they were told, some of them grumbling under their breath. Jamie ignored this, took out his water gun, and sprayed each one with Robinwood water. "Take your arrows. Report to your posts." He took out his slingshot. "When I give the signal and shoot this, I want each of you to shoot your arrow at a different point on the advancing edge of Druin's army. If my hunch is right, we'll deliver a shocker, and if PBJ makes it, they'll get an even bigger shock."

The bowmen selected their bows and arrows, filled their quivers, and filed out of the room. Jamie and Raegary followed, giving them last-minute instructions. They climbed a long flight of stairs to a walkway alongside the outlook wall. Every fifty feet or so along the walkway a shooting gap had been left in the stone wall.

"I want two men positioned per opening so you can fire in opposite directions at the same time," Jamie instructed. "When you're outnumbered like we are, you have to go on the offensive before they do. You each have only one treated arrow and only one chance to get the first advantage. Remember, wait for my signal."

He glanced through an opening at the scene below. There were now many large, wheeled towers facing the castle. From their tops, long arms protruded with many ropes dangling from them.

"Breaching platforms," Raegary said. "The grubbers will wheel them to the moat, and the tre-aks will swing themselves across to the walls. Nasty-smelling things they are. Mean as a caged felion. Their feet secrete a sticky fluid and they can climb anything. The rest will follow close behind. I sure hope this plan of yours works, or we are in dire trouble."

* * *

Erenor stood still for a few seconds, letting his eyes get accustomed to the dim light. Up ahead in the darkness, he could see the faint blue outline of Druin's statue. The eerie wail got louder and an ominous voice called out from the gloom. "You are old and have lost your power, Erenor. Prepare to meet thy doom!" The blue light glowed brighter.

"This hall is sacred and no place to battle the scourge of Druin!" the sorcerer shouted back. He raised his scepter into the air and brought it down with a resounding *thwack* on the castle floor. "*Ixapta du furion!*" he yelled.

Immediately, the hall filled with blinding white light and the two figures were instantly transported to an icy cavern in the bowels of Mt. Andiril. The statue of Druin immediately exploded into a thousand pieces, showering the cavern floor with smoking fragments. Almost at once, the shards of stone transformed into screaming, scaly snakes with formidable fangs and whipping tails. They formed a circle around Erenor and slithered toward where he stood, gnashing their teeth and flailing their tails.

The sorcerer responded by sweeping his scepter around his head and pointing the crystal flame at them. A searing bolt of lightning shot out and reduced the worms to shriveled, burnt crisps. Screams of fury filled the cave. Druin's burnt residue smoldered for a moment, then, in a whirling cyclonic wind, massed into a towering, black accumulation of rocks, debris, and ice. The mass morphed into a great armored brute with blood-red eyes, flaming nostrils, and a long, sickle-shaped horn protruding from between its eyes. The monster roared, lowered its head, and lunged forward.

"Neverlore is mine! I will eliminate you like some insignificant insect!" the monster shrieked maniacally.

"Neverlore will *never* be yours," Erenor shouted back at the top of his lungs, catapulting himself to a nearby rock, narrowly missing getting impaled.

The two mortal enemies continued to battle, Druin changing into various beings and hurling himself at the sorcerer, and Erenor, in turn, fending them off and striking back. Back and forth around the icy cavern they charged and retreated. The struggle was intense and eventually began to exact its toll on the sorcerer's strength and powers.

* * *

Preparations in the castle were complete and night was falling. Many fires dotted the landscape on the other side of the moat and macabre figures holding long spears and banners reflected the flames in their armor. Unearthly sounds could be heard in the darkness beyond the reach of the fire's light.

As he gazed at the scene below, a chill went up Jamie's spine. *I've done all I can and there's no turning back now,* he thought. *I have to see my plan through.* Raegary approached and indicated it was time to meet with Erenor and the others and make final preparations. Jamie turned and followed the lieutenant of the guards back down the stairs. They made their way to the courtyard. A few minutes later, they were joined by Alindra, Artimus, and PBJ.

Their shadows bobbed and weaved in the torchlight as they walked to the courtyard. Toward the center sat a granite table surrounded by stone seats. Jamie and the others seated themselves around the table.

In one corner stood Alizar. He coughed and sneezed and small flames shot from his nose.

"Durned dragon can't figger out what ta do now he's got his fire back," PBJ chuckled. "Guess'n we cain't blame 'im though. A good dragon's got no use fer fire."

Jamie got up and walked over to the dragon. "Are you alright, Alizar?" he asked.

"I will be as soon as I stop sneezing," the dragon replied with a fiery sneeze.

Jamie jumped backward. "When you get control, join us." He laughed. "We don't want anything catching fire before it's time."

Jamie returned to the table and looked around. "Where's Erenor?" he asked. "He's supposed to be here by now. We can't do this without him."

* * *

The battle raged on for more than an hour. Druin changed into another horrific monster, and with a howl of rage, he once again flung himself at Erenor. The sorcerer responded by dropping his scepter and putting both hands up, palms outward. He shouted out in as commanding a voice as he could muster,

"I . . . COMMAND . . . THEE . . . TO . . . HALT!"

The charging beast stopped in mid-stride, shuddered, and froze into a huge statue of dirt, rock, and black ice. Breathing hard, Erenor bent down to retrieve his scepter. At the same moment, in a shower of sparks, the statue transformed once again, and became a huge reptile. The loathsome creature had the head of a dagger-toothed viper, the body of a crocodile, and the tail of a serpent. It coiled up in mid-air, shot forward, and whistled so close over Erenor's kneeling body that he could feel the wind of its passing. The snakelike projectile slammed into the opposite wall so hard, it momentarily impaled itself in the ice and rock.

Erenor stood up shakily. He removed the crown from his head, and with as much strength as he could muster, threw it discus-style at the tail of the monster. The sorcerer's aim was true. The crown flew through the air and onto the beast's tail with a definitive *chunk*. The crown glowed and pulsed, causing the beast to writhe in agony. Erenor pointed his scepter at the quivering tail and once again commanded, "Back to stone, you vile creature!" With his remaining energy, he slammed his scepter to the ground, and in another blinding flash of light, they were transported back to the Hall of Elders.

Druin materialized next to the sorcerer's throne as his original statue of hematite. Before the warlock could react, Erenor stumbled forward, grabbed a heavy coverlet, and threw it over the statue. "*El Domini, Incurin, As Delto,*" the sorcerer incanted once more. "Meet your own doom," he added in a hoarse whisper. The figure gave one mighty quiver under the blanket, then ceased to move. Erenor collapsed onto the throne, his energy spent.

* * *

"Something bad has happened. More than an hour has passed and he's not returned from the Hall of Elders," Artimus said, concern evident in his voice. "What if he doesn't return? How will we fight this battle without him?"

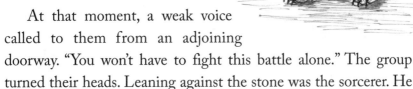

At that moment, a weak voice called to them from an adjoining doorway. "You won't have to fight this battle alone." The group turned their heads. Leaning against the stone was the sorcerer. He stepped forward, swaying as he walked; his skin was ashen in color.

"Great-Grandfather!" Alindra cried. She rushed over, steadied the sorcerer, and helped him to the table. "You look like you just fought the whole battle by yourself!"

"It's okay, Granddaughter, I'll be alright shortly," Erenor said, his voice strengthening. In spite of his age and present condition, the sorcerer was surprisingly resilient. "Are we ready to continue with the war plan?"

"Ah don't know bout the others, but ah'm ready ta git on with it," PBJ said, listening to the sounds outside of the castle. The rest agreed.

"We will proceed, then," Erenor said. The sorcerer looked at them solemnly. Although his voice still had a slight tremor in it, his skin had regained some of its color. "The threat from Druin has been removed."

"Removed?" Jamie asked. "Removed sounds like it's just been relocated." He stared at the sorcerer expectantly.

"Druin's power and influence have been eliminated from this battle," Erenor replied in a stronger voice. "The strength of the enemy has been reduced significantly. Unfortunately, however, it took most of my power to do so. Both the crown and I need to regenerate some before I can face the rest of the battle. Let us go over the plan one last time." His composure was steadily improving.

Alizar had finally stopped sneezing and was able to join them. "I've been held captive until recently, and I have no idea what's going on. What's this plan you speak of? How can I be of help?"

Erenor laid out the map of Neverlore. Jamie used his arrow as a pointer, and together he and Erenor explained Jamie's planned diversion and strategy.

"What if they attack before dawn?" Raegary asked.

"If they do, we must hold out. It should take Barly four or five hours to make it to Dogwood," Jamie said. "Until he gets there, we'll have to defend ourselves as best as possible."

"I hope we can," Artimus said somberly.

PBJ pointed to his second set of saddlebags. "Got a real seep-rise fer them varmits in here," he boasted. "An ah got my six-guns back," he added, patting the holsters at his sides. "We should be able ta hold 'em off fer a while at least."

They talked and planned into the night. When Jamie could see that everyone was getting tired, he took out his canteen and offered them all a drink.

"Ah ain't so sure we should drink that dadblamed water," PBJ exclaimed. "It sure packs a wallop!"

"I can assure you the water is safe for drinking," Artimus said. "It eliminates evil, but does no harm to good. I've been drinking Robinwood spring water for a long time with no problems."

Jamie agreed, and to prove his point, took the first sip. "There is enough for each one of you to have one swallow. It will revive you, I promise." They all stared at the boy. When it became apparent nothing out of the ordinary was going to happen, Raegary took the next drink. He then passed the canteen to the sorcerer, who did the same, and passed it on. They all took a drink, except Alizar.

"No, I have to maintain my fire for the battle. Save the last swig for me, and I'll use it to put out my flame for good." The group laughed. Their laughter helped ease the ominous mood they all felt.

"I think we are—" Artimus began. Jamie interrupted him by holding up his hand.

"Did you hear that?"

"Hear what?" Artimus asked.

Erenor held up his hand. "I hear it too." They all stopped and listened. A rumble could be felt in the stone under their feet, and they could hear a loud creaking sound outside the castle walls.

"The breaching towers!" Alindra cried. "The army is on the move!"

Suddenly, the night air was pierced by banshee screams. A guard from the tower cried out, "The tre-aks have crossed the moat! We're under attack!"

"Not yet! It can't happen yet! Barly hasn't reached Swamp Bogmire!" Jamie yelled, jumping up. At that moment, many enormous, hairy figures could be seen climbing over the walls. They secured rope ladders behind them, turned, and sprang toward the courtyard.

"Ahhhhaaarrgghhh!" they cried together in a loud yowl. Alindra screamed and covered her ears.

"To your stations!" Erenor commanded. "Defend Mistemere!

For Neverlore!" he cried. The group sprang to their feet and rushed in separate directions. Jamie grabbed his backpack and sprinted for the stairs. He pulled out his water gun as he ran.

Several of the D'nalli dashed out from different locations in the castle. They wielded spears, swords, and broadaxes. Erenor and PBJ jumped on Alizar's back. The mighty dragon flapped his wings twice and they were quickly airborne. But the enemy was prepared. Just as Alizar cleared the castle wall, one of the tre-aks launched himself through the air and landed on the dragon's tail.

"No free rides, ya stinkin' varmint!" PBJ yelled. He pulled out one of his guns and fired a perfect shot over his shoulder. The tre-ak let out a fearful yell and let go. They watched it fall into the moat below, where it was immediately incinerated.

"*Good* shot!" Erenor cried. Alizar climbed higher in the sky, and headed toward the top of Mt. Andiril.

The rope ladders had allowed grubbers, wildmen, and howling felions to scale the outer castle walls. They swarmed over the stone edifice, and arrows whistled everywhere as the archers chose their targets. The D'nalli and wildmen were engaged in fierce hand-to-hand combat. Screams of madness and terror filled the night air. The battle was on.

Jamie was fighting his way to the top of the stairs when two grubbers jumped down and charged him. He had just enough time to get off two quick shots from his water gun. His aim was true, and his attackers screamed, fell to the steps, and began to melt before his eyes. Jamie let out a victory yell, and jumped over the dripping mess. He reached the parapet in three steps. The sight before him made his blood run cold.

Several snarling felions blocked his path. A large beast with three arrows stuck in its side spied Jamie. It let out a fearsome roar, whirled, and leapt, its legs and claws extended. Jamie dropped to his knee, quickly aimed, and fired his soaker. The shot caught the felion square in the chest. It gave a great howl and fell into the courtyard below. Below, Artimus raised a sword that he had traded for his staff, and in one swoop, cleaved off both of the fearsome creature's heads.

"I believe they're losing their heads over this battle," the frog croaked. In spite of their dire predicament, Jamie had to laugh. He gave Artimus a thumbs up and turned back to his attackers.

The others stopped their advance and began to circle him. It was a stand off. Jamie had to pass them to get into position, but they blocked his way. He checked his water gun and discovered he didn't have much water left. "I need help up here!" he cried. Out of the corner of his eye, he saw movement.

Alindra bounded up the stairs and stepped behind him. She held a small sword in front of her. "Back, you disgusting beasts!" she cried. The sword began to glow, and a thin purple beam shot out at the nearest felion. The beast screamed and was immediately cleaved in half. Alindra swept the sword around her and Jamie, and she quickly eliminated the rest in the same fashion.

"Keen sword," Jamie yelled over his shoulder, bounding forward. "Thanks for the help." He looked over the castle walls as he ran. The leading vanguard of Druin's army had reached the edge of the moat. Behind them, grubbers pushed a huge battering ram toward the drawbridge. Scaglets followed felions and grubbers up the rope ladders. If his plan failed, the castle would be overrun before dawn.

Jamie laid a pattern of spray from his gun and destroyed many of the enemy as he moved on. Arrows whistled through the air everywhere and near the top, one *whooshed* by so close, it parted his hair. Jamie ducked instinctively.

"Yikes! Watch it, guys!" he shouted and glanced into the courtyard. All around him, the bowmen, archers, and D'nalli were engaged in furious combat. *This will be the only chance I have*, he thought as he reached the center shooting station. "Cover me!" he yelled at the archer there.

Jamie leaned through the opening in the block and emptied his gun on several figures climbing the rope ladder. They fell into the moat, twisting and screaming. Jamie threw his water gun down, pulled a brass whistle from his pocket, and put it in his mouth. He took out his slingshot and hastily loaded it with another stone from Robinwood. He then gave a resounding blast on the whistle. This was the signal the rest had been waiting for.

There was a momentary lull in the battle as the sound echoed over the glen. Jamie pulled back the slingshot and searched for a suitable target. Below, the grubbers pushed a catapult filled with boiling oil toward the moat. As they grunted and strained, a wildman with an axe was poised to cut the ties. At the sound, he paused. All eyes looked to the sound and saw Jamie's figure through the opening in the wall.

* * *

Behind the Castle in the Clouds, standing on a rock outcropping further up Mt. Andiril, Erenor surveyed the spectacle below. Not in his darkest dreams had he imagined it would come to this. Druin's power had grown formidably during the time the sorcerer had lain dying. Lake Longwater had indeed released its vile prisoners, as evidenced by the fearful army assembled outside the castle walls. Unless the strategy of an outlander succeeded, they were most certainly done for.

The encounter in the depths of Mt. Andiril had been a supreme test of will between good and evil. Good had prevailed, but just barely. The duel with the warlock had drained Erenor. Now he only had power enough left for one last feat. The sorcerer watched intently and waited for the signal. Predawn light began to show over the foothills to the east.

PBJ and Alizar sailed high above the clouds of smoke over the battlefield before the castle. After dropping Erenor off on Mt. Andiril, they had flown on toward the foothills. They too were waiting for the signal.

* * *

Back at the castle, Jamie took careful aim on the vat of boiling oil. As the wildman raised his axe to cut the launching rope, Jamie fired. The pebble arched through the air and found its target. It shot into the center of the vat, and several drops splashed up into the wildman's eyes. He screamed and dropped his axe, clutching his face. Immediately the vat of oil exploded, showering him and all those close by with the boiling goo. The grubbers, wildmen, and scaglets screamed and howled and ran in all directions. At the parapets high on the castle wall, the bowmen took aim. Each let loose their arrows. Eighteen of the twenty found their mark. Their targets exploded like the vat of oil, and flames shot everywhere. The flames joined and formed a long wall of fire twenty feet high. The flames danced and twisted, rising higher and higher, never touching the grass beneath. As if alive, the wall of flames advanced toward Druin's army. Those who tried to burst through, using their shields as protection, were quickly consumed by the intense heat. The whole regiment began to retreat in mass disarray, screaming in fright as they ran.

Circling high above, PBJ heard the signal and saw the explosion. "This is it, dragon!" he yelled. "Give 'em yer flame!"

Alizar responded by dropping through the smoke and haze toward the battlefield below. They flew in low over the field and the dragon breathed a tremendous burst of flame as they passed. Man and beast cowered and screamed even louder as the dragon swooped over, just above their heads. The battlefield was in total chaos. Alizar wheeled up sharply and flew toward the cliffs at the far end of the glen at the moat. PBJ reached into his saddlebags. "This oughta do the trick!" he exclaimed, taking out several sticks of dynamite.

When they reached the cliffs, he called to Alizar, "Give me a light!" The dragon turned his head and breathed flame. PBJ reached out and lit the fuses on three sticks. As they swooped up and followed the cliffs, he let them fall one by one, spacing them evenly apart. "Three more!" he cried. They repeated the process.

"Hold on," Alizar called to PBJ. He then flew upward and hovered, flapping his huge wings. "Let's see if this plan of yours is going to work."

They didn't have to wait long. One by one, the dynamite sticks detonated with deafening explosions. Rocks, trees, and dirt blew skyward, and a mighty rumble shook the predawn air. In slow motion, the cliffs crumbled and fell away from the mountain, creating a massive landslide. It rolled down from the hills, gathering speed. The massive wall of crumbling, sliding rock, tree, and dust raced toward the retreating group. The remnants of Druin's army looked over their shoulders at the advancing wall of flame, and then looked ahead in dismay at the collapsing mountain. They had nowhere to go. Pandemonium swept through the horde and many dropped their weapons and fled. Some ran off into Swamp Bogmire and were never heard from again. Others escaped the flame and rock only to tumble over the cliffs into the River Crystal and drown.

High atop Mt. Andiril, Erenor looked on. In spite of his previous misgivings, he was now beginning to take heart. As planned, the army of Druin was in full retreat from the fire and trapped against the landslide. Those who weren't crushed or burned alive raced around the distant field in complete panic. This was the moment they had all planned and hoped for.

Erenor took a deep breath. He closed his eyes and began to concentrate. "*Ixapta fel daedo finis . . . ixapta fel daedo finistral,*" he chanted. The crystal on the front of the Crown of Arcada began to glow. The sorcerer held his scepter firmly with both hands and placed the glass flame in front of the crown's crystal.

The crystal glowed brighter and brighter, and a piercing ray of white light suddenly shot from its depths. Through the scepter's flame, the light coursed. It shined out over the castle below and onto the panicked horde. Their terrified, upturned faces were bathed in an unearthly radiance. The intense light flashed twice, and suddenly several long beams pulsed out and fanned across the whole battlefield. In the space of two or three heartbeats, the light disappeared, and the army disappeared with it! They vanished into thin air, as if they had never been there at all. In the following minutes, the wall of flame was extinguished and the landslide ground to a rest. The smoke and haze slowly cleared and the glen at the moat was empty of any reminder of the malevolence that had trod there moments earlier. Not a blade of grass was burnt, not a flower crushed, not a trace of Druin's army remained. It was deathly quiet, yet strangely serene.

Suddenly, a great cry of victory rose from the castle. Erenor let the scepter drop to the ground and sank to his knees. His power gone, he breathed into the wind. "Neverlore is saved." He bowed down and kissed the ground.

Inside the castle, Jamie rubbed his eyes. The intense ray of light from the sorcerer had momentarily blinded him. When he could see again, he stared around in anticipation. The remaining scaglets, felions, and grubbers attempting to breach the wall screamed and fell into the moat. The ones that made it over the walls were quickly captured or sent to their doom. In less than an hour, Mistemere was back in the control of Raegary, Rorek, and their men.

Jamie gazed numbly upon the scene, rubbing his eyes again.

Had he really just participated in this powerful experience? Had he just fought the mightiest battle he could have imagined and won? Or had his mind's eye invented and acted in it all? His list of questions for Erenor grew longer. His family and home seemed so far away that they almost didn't exist.

Jamie put his slingshot away and started back down the steps. Bodies of men and beasts were everywhere. *No,* he thought. *This really did happen. I just helped fight and win a real-life battle. Even e-Cubix can't compare to this.*

He frowned as he walked back to the courtyard. What had happened to Barly? Had his friend survived?

In the heat of the battle, he had almost forgotten that his friend had been gone for many hours. *Did Barly get to the Dogwood in time? Had he been able to pour the magic water into the stream? Did he survive?* Jamie wondered. Under his breath, he said a little prayer for the bear, and fervently hoped he would see his friend again.

* * *

Calm descended upon Neverlore. Word spread rapidly that the threat of Druin no longer existed. People returned from the mountains, and the village at the castle bustled with activity once more.

After the battle, the bodies were collected and Mistemere was put back in order. The remains of Druin's army were placed in a pile in the glen at the moat and unceremoniously burned. Sixty-three of the bowmen, D'nalli, and castle guards had perished during the battle. They were buried with great honor in the Warrior's Burial Ground. The moat was drained and filled with clean mountain spring water.

Erenor went into seclusion to rest and regain his powers. Jamie slept for almost two days straight, so great was his exhaustion from the whole ordeal. PBJ, Artimus, and Alizar had the run of the castle. People came from far and wide to see the heroes of the battle for Neverlore. They especially came to see the dragon that had turned good. A sense of normalcy slowly returned to the land.

Chapter 19

Sunlight filtered through the bedroom curtains and across Jamie's face. He stirred and awoke with a start. Once again, he was disoriented and his surroundings seemed foreign to him. In that not-fully-awake state, many thoughts whirled around in the semi-awareness of his inner mind. The events of the last day and night came back to him. He sat up and gazed about. *Did all this really happen?* he wondered. *Am I awake or am I dreaming I'm awake?* As the fog in his brain cleared, there was a knock on the door. Alindra walked in.

"You've been sleeping for quite some time, Jamie. I looked in on you now and then to make sure you were alright," she said warmly.

"Thanks," Jamie said. "I was totally worn out. Did it . . . did it really happen?"

Alindra smiled and replied, "Yes, the battle was real, Jamie. You are a hero! It was you who was responsible for saving Neverlore. Great-Grandfather and the rest played their parts, but it was *your* plan that did it. Without your help finding the Crown of Arcada and everything else you did, we wouldn't have won. If you hadn't come to Neverlore in the first place, we would all be prisoners of Druin now, or worse."

Jamie blushed and pulled the covers up a little. He had never been called a hero before. "I don't know if I'm a hero or not," he replied. "Everything just happened the way it did. I didn't plan . . . I mean . . . this is all so confusing. I came to see if Erenor could tell me how to get home. And I had a lot of questions too. But now that I look back, I guess most of them have been answered along the way. I've seen and done more in the past few days than I've ever dreamed of. But I have a real home and family." He added hastily, "Not that I don't like it here. I do. But I've had so many near-death experiences along the way, I feel like a cat that's used up most of its nine lives. Part of me wants to stay, but inside, I know I should go. What do I do, Alindra?"

"Why, Jamie, I'm surprised you are unsure of yourself, those don't seem like the words of a champion or a hero."

"I don't feel like a hero. I mean, I'm very glad things turned out the way they did, but all that doesn't really help me get home," Jamie replied.

"Maybe it does," Alindra said. "Think about it. You've proved to yourself and others that you can do almost anything you set your mind to. The future is *yours* to choose now, not anyone else's. I think you've learned some of life's most valuable lessons."

Jamie looked at the princess thoughtfully. She had on a long, pale pink and green gown with a gold belt around her waist. Her long blonde hair was woven into a braid and wrapped around her head. She wore a crown of red and white flowers and looked as a princess ought to. She spoke with sincerity and there was wisdom in her words.

"Maybe you're right," he said slowly. "Maybe all this *did* happen for a reason." He added thoughtfully, "When I think about it, back home wasn't *that* bad. At least there I didn't risk being eaten by a scorpion-spider or killed by a felion. Maybe there are things *there* that I can save, now that I know how."

"Now *those* are the words of a hero," she said. "Always listen to your heart, for it will tell you the true path to take. And never, ever think that you made the wrong choice once you do. Always remember, everything we do happens for good reason, even though we might not be immediately aware of it.

"But enough of this serious talk. I came to tell you that you have been summoned to the Hall of Elders. Great-Grandfather wishes to see you in conference as soon as you are dressed."

Jamie was fully awake now, and it all came back to him. "What day is it? How long have I slept? What's happened to Barly?" he asked.

Alindra laughed. "One thing at a time. I think all your questions will be answered when you meet with Erenor. But you must dress now and follow me."

With that, she excused herself and waited outside while Jamie got dressed. His clothes had been cleaned, mended, and placed in a neat pile at the end of the bed. On top was a tunic of fine leather with mysterious words and symbols written on the collar and cuffs. When he put it on, he found the tunic fit perfectly. Once dressed, Jamie joined Alindra in the hall. They headed for the Hall of Elders and she took his hand. The warmth of her grip somehow reassured him. As they walked, she told him the history of Neverlore from her viewpoint. Jamie knew it would be very hard to leave.

Once again, he was led through many rooms and corridors. They finally arrived at the massive oak doors leading into the Hall of Elders. Alindra pulled a silken rope hanging next to them, and somewhere inside a bell sounded. One of the huge doors creaked open and they walked through.

Jamie found himself in a vast hall. As his eyes became accustomed to the dim light, he looked around nervously. Tall marble columns lined the hall on each side. High above their heads, crisscrossed oak timbers rested on the columns. The hall was illuminated by light that filtered through stained-glass windows in the ceiling which in turn made colorful patterns on the floor.

"Wow, this is almost spooky," he said in a whisper.

"Shhh . . ." Alindra replied. "There's nothing to be afraid of, just follow me."

She took his hand again and led him toward the end of the hall. At the far end, a ray of sunlight shone through one of the windows onto a raised platform. As it grew brighter, a rainbow began to sparkle and dance in mid-air. In the center of the glow, a throne of solid crystal appeared. On it sat the sorcerer, Erenor. He was dressed in a long, shimmering blue robe. He waved them forward. "Approach, Jamie the Vanquisher," he said in a solemn voice.

Jamie shuffled across the hall toward the throne. He reached the platform and climbed a few steps to the landing in front of the throne. There was a long moment of silence as Erenor looked at Jamie. Jamie fidgeted but said nothing as the sorcerer looked on. Once again he had the sensation that his very soul had been searched.

Erenor began, "I have ruled Neverlore from the day the Age of Shadows came to an end. It has been most difficult to maintain order, as the first battle with Druin left me with diminished powers. I wished fervently for the Crown of Arcada to appear and restore my power, but it was not meant to be. All the years I searched were to no avail. What an irony that the very dragon I banished to free Neverlore kept the crown hidden from me all that time." He reached up and touched the crown. "In my darkest hour, when all seemed lost, out of nowhere a brave group of mortals appeared. And lo, they carried with them my salvation. With the help of you and your friends, Jamie Nichols, and the magic of the Crown of Arcada at my command, we have been able to save our land once more from the devastation of Druin. For this, the people of Neverlore and I owe you a great debt. As repayment, I will grant you any wish that is within my power."

Jamie finally found his tongue. "W-well, your highness, your sorcererness, your majesty . . . What should I call you?"

"Call me friend. Call me Erenor," the sorcerer replied kindly. "And as a friend, I will do all that I can to help you. But to help and properly reward you, I must first learn more about the door through which you passed, and you must tell me fully of your journey to Mistemere. The whereabouts of any of the doors have been unknown to me or anyone else. It was assumed that Druin forced that information from Xiticus before he slay him, and sealed up all the doors long ago."

"Selth and I discussed this when I visited the L'masse," Jamie said. "Like you, he was under the impression all the doors had been sealed. He was very suspicious of outlanders, as he called us, and was worried about who or what else may have come through these doors. Selth was also concerned that some evil disturbance in Neverlore was occurring which caused some of the animals to act the way they did. It sounded pretty strange at the time, but now I see it was all tied in with Druin." Jamie then told Erenor about the condor-hawk and Snakeroot attack, the Treesers' threatening actions, and the fearful howling he'd heard at night.

Erenor raised an eyebrow. "Day by day, unbeknownst to me, the control of Druin grew as I lay dying, my powers fading. By the time I learned of his and Grizweld's alliance, I was too weak to stop the spread of their black influence over the land. Druin's power adversely affected many a man and beast alike. This would explain the actions of the condor-hawk, amongst others."

"That's what Artimus and I talked about on our way here," Jamie said. "The L'masse—Selth and Deena and Arlann, that is— suspected the same thing. They also wondered if my being here might not be accidental like I first thought."

"The L'masse spoke wisely, for apparently your journey through Neverlore had purpose," Erenor continued. "And along the way, all those who were drawn into your journey contributed to this purpose. It would seem, if you hadn't come to our land, met Barly, and undertaken this journey to Mistemere, I most certainly would be dead now and Druin would be in control. There is a magic greater than mine that played into and intertwined all these events."

"That's similar to what Selth and Arlann said," Jamie said. "And Alindra too."

"The L'masse, Selth and Arlann," the sorcerer reflected. "I have not heard those names spoken or seen their kind in a long, long time. They were once close to Mistemere, and I sought their council on many occasions."

"They said the same thing about you, Erenor," Jamie said. "Selth indicated that they had grown distant from the castle, as you never ventured out. During the reign of Druin, the L'masse moved far to the south and stayed to themselves. They felt safer keeping a good distance between Mistemere and their hamlet."

"The L'masse were stewards of Neverlore long before Druin. They go back to the Elvenkind, and their race is almost as old as the land itself. I must reestablish contact with them," the sorcerer mused. "Too many seasons' leaves have fallen from the trees since our friendship with one another lessened."

Jamie frowned. "There's one thing I don't understand about this," he speculated. "Of all those who have entered before, why was I the one who ended up, well, saving Neverlore? I just wanted to walk, that's all. It wasn't my wish to get involved in all this."

"Apparently there is more to you than you know," Erenor replied. "Sometimes, a person's character and inner strengths are stronger and deeper than they recognize. It could have been the magic of Neverlore that identified those strengths in you. Strange as it may seem to you, the battle for Neverlore may have been incidental to the real reason for your coming to our land."

"So you think entering Neverlore and undertaking this journey really might not have been an accident?" Jamie asked uncertainly.

"You are wiser than you give yourself credit for," Erenor said intuitively. "To fully understand your situation and give you council, I must hear about your journey from the very beginning."

So, one last time, in greater detail, Jamie narrated the events that had occurred. He started with flying his kite in his backyard and going through the tree, then he told of meeting Barly, Artimus, and PBJ. He related meeting Barly and staying with the L'masse. He detailed their journey through the mountain, the attack of the scorpion-spiders, their rescue and flight to Mistemere on Alizar. He finished with the occurrences leading up to the moment they entered Erenor's room with the Crown of Arcada.

"This is indeed a fascinating tale," Erenor said when Jamie had finished. "There is certainly much in your tale that needs further study. However, all that will be determined at a later time. First, we must attend to your wishes. How can *I* be of service to you, Jamie Nichols?"

"Before I answer, I have one last question, one that has been bothering me ever since I got here," Jamie replied. "What *is* Neverlore, Erenor? Does it really exist or am I just imagining it?"

The sorcerer gazed at the young boy in front of him. In many ways Jamie reminded him of when he was much, much younger. He replied guardedly, "I can tell you what Neverlore is, but you may not totally understand."

"I'll try," Jamie said.

"Very well," Erenor went on. "Neverlore is the personification of each and every outlander's imagination and longings and day-dreams. It's the embodiment of one's wish. For you, Jamie Nichols, the plants and animals and every nuance of your adventure are what you wanted them to be. Simply put, what you saw in your mind or imagined in your own world became genuine here."

"Boy, you're right. That *is* really deep," Jamie acknowledged. "Maybe I should have just stuck to what my wishes are."

"You can still do so," the sorcerer agreed kindly. "And they would be?"

"Well . . . Erenor . . . before I ask, I would first like to know what happened to my friend Barly," Jamie began. "The last time I saw him, he was headed to Swamp Bogmire. What about PBJ, and Artimus, and Alizar, and—"

Erenor held up his hand, laughing. "Slow down, my boy, your friends are all well and await you in the garden courtyard."

"Even Barly?" Jamie cried with joy.

"Even your friend Barly," the sorcerer answered. "A little worse for wear, but very much alive."

"This is excellent news!" Jamie exclaimed. "When can I see them?" He was so excited, he almost forgot why he had come to see Erenor in the first place. Then reality set in and he said wistfully, "Erenor, I journeyed to Mistemere to ask you to help me get back home, but I'm not certain I want to go. I have my own family and home, but to return to them I have to give up walking. I entered Neverlore on a wish. Do I have to un-wish myself to leave? What should I do? Can you help me sort this out?"

Erenor looked at Jamie solemnly. "Jamie Nichols, have you not listened to what Alindra and I have told you? You are looking the wrong way—look inside, look to yourself," the sorcerer said. "Do not worry, however. In the morning, you will have made your decision," he said matter-of-factly.

"How do you know that?" Jamie asked in surprise.

"Because I am Erenor the Wise, that's why," Erenor answered with a twinkle in his eye. "I'm a sorcerer, remember? It's my business to know these things." He held up his hand. "Now, rest your mind for a while. It's time to see your friends."

"And you can see them now," Alindra said. Until then, she had been silent. Jamie started to say something, but she put her finger to his lips. "Shhh, it can wait. Come with me, Jamie."

She again took his hand and led him down the steps. They went around the throne to get to the courtyard. As Jamie passed by the crystal pedestal, he glanced over his shoulder. Erenor was bent over a figure that had been hidden in the shadows. Jamie caught a glimpse of a blue statue of stone under the lifted edge of a blanket. He shuddered when he looked at the face of the statue. It was a countenance of pure hatred and evil. The black stare of death bore right into him. For a brief moment, it felt like someone had stabbed an ice-cold knife into his heart. Jamie recoiled and shivered noticeably. He tore his eyes away, quickened his pace, and caught up with Alindra.

"Is that Druin?" he asked in a whisper.

"That's Druin," Alindra replied. "Don't ever look into his eyes. Even as a statue of hematite, he still has power over mortals. There's no telling what would happen if you looked at him too long. Grandpapa keeps him covered with a special shroud that keeps Druin under control. Grandpapa has to keep constant guard over him."

Jamie let out a low whistle. "You don't have to tell me twice."

They came to the door and walked into the courtyard. Sunlight filtered through the willows at the end of the garden, and the brightly colored flowers swayed in the breeze. *What a beautiful sight,* Jamie thought. His mood immediately brightened.

Sitting around the stone table were Artimus, PBJ, and sure enough, Barly.

Off to the side stood Alizar and Florabel. She heehawed when she saw Jamie.

"Barly! You made it!" Jamie cried, rushing to him.

"Yes, indeed, I did make it," Barly said. "Once again you had a hand in saving ole Barly."

Jamie gave him a bear hug. "Oh Barly, I'm so glad you didn't die," he said. "What happened? I heard the most awful roars and screams coming from the swamp forest just before the light shot out of the crown."

"Well, I had almost made it to the Dogwood when many scaglets and felions rushed into the swamp. They were obviously terrified and running from something. They had a look of madness in their eyes, and they charged at me."

Jamie stepped back and inspected the bear. Several more pieces of fur were missing, and he had many cuts and bruises on his chest and back. Barly went on. "I managed to fight them off as I ran down the path. It sure made it a lot harder to get there on time. I had just poured the water in when Erenor's light lit up the sky. A large scaglet managed a good blow in passing, and it must have knocked me out. The next thing I remember, Raegary brought me to. He helped me back to the castle and told me the entire story on the way. He said you fought like a warrior."

Once again, Jamie blushed at the compliment. "I don't know about being a hero or warrior, but it was the most exciting and scary thing I've ever done. However, I didn't do it alone. You all helped." Jamie bowed to each one in turn, and they started talking amongst themselves, each reliving his moments of battle.

Almost an hour had passed when Erenor walked in. He held up his hands. "My great-granddaughter, Princess Alindra, wishes to speak," he said.

"Yes, that is so," the princess said. "Jamie, you've explained why you traveled to the Castle in the Clouds, and you are aware that whatever you ultimately decide to do, you will not be able to change your mind. You fully realize that if you leave Neverlore, it's permanent, and Jamie Nichols will go back to being the way he was."

Jamie frowned. With the last few days' blur of events, he had almost forgotten about the paralysis he no longer suffered.

"W-well, Erenor and Alindra," he slowly replied. He wasn't sure where to begin. "Your land is beautiful and wonderful and just about everything a person could hope for. Although, a few friendlier critters would be nice." They all laughed.

"Most of my life, I dreamed of an adventure like this. In my land, I could have never done what I, I mean, what *we* just did," Jamie groaned. "But I admit, I miss my home, my family, and the few friends I've got. I know my mom must be worried sick by now, but I'm having a tough time making up my mind. I can't figure out how to make the decision any easier."

The sorcerer replied in a soft voice, "It is within my power to grant you your wish should you decide to leave, Jamie. However, I can't grant it until you are absolutely sure in your heart of what you want to do. If you are not absolutely sure when you attempt to go back, you could end up in another world altogether. My power extends to the edge of Neverlore, but not beyond. You could end up far worse than being confined to your chair with wheels."

"That's encouraging," Jamie replied. "Don't you think I've agonized a thousand times as to what to do since I've been here?" He paused and scratched his head. "Has anyone else ever left Neverlore?"

"Very few have, Jamie. Except during Druin's rule, no one has really ever wanted to," Alindra answered.

"Yeah, that's what I've been told," Jamie muttered. He was greatly agitated at the prospect of being confined to his wheelchair again. But then he thought of his family, his home, his own bedroom again. *What should I do?* he agonized. *What should I do?*

As if reading his mind, Erenor replied, "Like we said, only you can answer that question, Jamie. If you decide to go back, however, you have to do so by tomorrow night, when the moon is full. A wish to leave Neverlore can only be granted at that time. If you don't do it by then, you will have to wait until the next full moon."

"And that will be *way* too long," Jamie said. "But what about Artimus? He wants to go back to his old self. How is that any different?"

"Artimus's spell is a different situation," Alindra answered. "Also, he doesn't want to leave Neverlore."

"My plight is not much different than yours," Artimus spoke up. "If I don't attempt this journey, I'll remain a frog for the rest of my life. If I attempt the journey and fail, I may die. Not very good choices. At least you know what your outcome will be, and your choice can be made in the next twenty-four hours. Mine can't be made for quite some time. I still have another long journey before me. You don't. I have to travel through the mountains to a place called Blackmoss before I can even think of being changed back to my old self."

"Why's that?" Jamie asked.

"Artimus has to travel to the forest of Blackmoss," Erenor said. "His spell is no ordinary one. Because of this, he has to travel deep into the forest and find the Gumble-limbor tree. He has to bring back four leaves from the highest branches for me to make a potion with."

Alindra went on. "His journey won't be an easy one, and like yours, could be dangerous at times. In order for the potion to work, he has to go alone. His courage getting there and back is part of the magic. So you see, you are not the only one with weighty decisions to make."

"I guess," Jamie said glumly.

"There's one last thing for you to consider, Jamie," Erenor said. "If you leave Neverlore, you will be bound by the Warrior's Oath never to divulge what you have seen or done here. It must remain in your heart and mind, not to be shared with any other outlanders."

"Somehow, I figured it would be something like that," Jamie replied.

PBJ, who had been listening quietly, spoke up. "While you's been decidin' what's good 'n' what's not, ah been a-thinkin'. Don't got much reason to stick round this here castle no more. Me 'n' Florabel gets itchy when we's been in a place fer too long. Need ta get back out 'n' do some more prospectin'. Mebbe fer a little reeward, we could bring that treasure back to the castle for you alls."

"What about you, Barly, what will you do?" Jamie asked.

"I don't know," the big bear replied. "I've got no place in particular to go. Maybe I'll stay around here for a while," he added. "That is, if I'm welcome."

"You are all welcome to stay as long as you wish," Erenor said. "Speaking of welcome, that reminds me. Tell them, Alindra."

"As a small gesture of our appreciation for your help in saving Neverlore, we have ordered a ceremonial dinner prepared in your honor—for all of you," the princess said. "I believe we have talked all the business we need to for a while."

"Now yer talkin'," PBJ said. "What bout Florabel 'n' the dragon? They needs ta eat too."

"I'll have the stable boy take care of them," Alindra said. She excused herself to attend to it.

"Dinner? Did you say dinner?" Barly asked happily at the mention of food. "I'm famished!"

"You're always hungry." Jamie laughed. He decided to take Alindra's advice and give his mind a rest about his decisions. "Now that you mention it, though, I'm starving too. Let's go!"

"If you will please follow me then, I will show you the way to the banquet hall," Erenor said cheerfully.

No one needed a second invitation. None of them had eaten a good meal in several days. They followed the sorcerer, noisily talking and laughing amongst themselves, until they arrived at the banquet hall. Erenor went before them, opened the doors, and ushered them in. "You shall feast until you can feast no more," he said. The sorcerer announced each of them by name as they filed in. Their hearts and eyes filled with wonder at the sight before them.

Chapter 20

The banquet hall was almost as big as the Hall of Elders and had the same massive timbers in the ceiling. At the far end was a giant stone fireplace with a cheerful fire crackling in it. In the center of the room was a long, wooden table surrounded by tall-backed chairs. It was set with fine china dishes, silver uten-

sils, and gold and crystal goblets. Alindra sat to one side of the head chair. A steward stepped from beside the door and proceeded to seat them. Jamie was directed next to her, and she smiled at him as he sat down. "I'm quick," she said in a whisper, reading his mind.

Erenor walked to the end of the table and sat down in the head chair. Alindra clapped her hands, and another steward opened a door and ushered in many others.

Raegary was the first to enter, followed by some of the D'nalli, Rorek, Erenor's governors, and several others of importance. Alindra introduced them all as they were seated. The table was soon full. Another steward walked around and filled their goblets with a clear, yellow, sparkling liquid.

"What is this?" Jamie asked, pointing toward his.

"Nectar of the Distant Hills," Alindra replied. "The vintners there mix the juice of the Summertree grape with a secret spring water only they know of. It's very good."

Erenor raised his goblet and proposed a toast. "The people of Neverlore are forever grateful to you, our honored guests. The Crown of Arcada is back in our possession, and the army of Druin has been vanquished. On behalf of all, I give you our deepest and most sincere thanks." Everyone in the room raised their glasses.

"This tastes fantastic!" Jamie exclaimed as he lowered his goblet. "It's bubbly and tickles my nose!"

Alindra whispered back, "It's Grandpapa's favorite. They send him a little extra each fall when the harvest is done."

Erenor set down his goblet, licked his lips, and said, "Let the feast begin!"

Jamie eyed the food being placed before them. There were steaming platters piled high with roasts, steaks, and chops. There were wild turkeys and sage hens stuffed with raisin and walnut dressing, and huge bowls of fresh fruits and vegetables. The stewards offered each guest baskets of freshly baked breads with wildberry jam and freshly churned butter. They poured chilled goat's milk into the goblets. True to Erenor's promise, Jamie and the others ate until they could eat no more.

When they were finished, the table was cleared and they were entertained by jesters, jugglers, and clowns. They all laughed at the many jokes and skits. Musicians strolled around strumming unfamiliar stringed instruments. Jamie found himself humming to the music even though he didn't know the songs. The celebration lasted well into the night. Throughout the party, Jamie did his best to answer all the questions he was asked about his home.

Eventually, the evening's festivities came to an end. One by one, Erenor's guests thanked them, said their goodnights, and left. Soon it was just Erenor, Alindra, Jamie, Barly, Artimus, and PBJ.

"Well, my friends, this is a fitting end to a long, hard journey. A good night's sleep is in order. After a good rest, one's mind and thoughts tend to be a lot clearer," Erenor announced. He stood up. "Jamie, look into your heart for what you seek. It is there that you will find the real answer."

"Erenor's right," Artimus agreed. "We can all offer advice, but in the end, you are the only one who can make the choice."

"I know, I know," Jamie said, not wanting to be reminded of his difficult task.

"I guess in the back of my mind, I knew this was too good to be true. I figured it couldn't go on forever. It's sad. I just wish there were a different way," he said softly.

They all talked quietly with one another for a few more minutes, then Barly, Artimus, and PBJ excused themselves. A servant led them out of the banquet hall and showed them to their rooms. Alindra offered to take Jamie to his room, so he said goodnight to Erenor and followed her out.

As they walked down the torch-lit halls, Alindra slid her hand into Jamie's. Once again, the warmth of her grip reassured him. They walked along in silence until they came to Jamie's room. Alindra stood and faced him, taking both his hands into hers. She looked into his eyes.

"I want to thank you once again for returning the Crown of Arcada," she said. "You and your friends have helped Grandpapa get back many of the years that were wrongfully taken from him.

He is all the family I have left."

Jamie had a look of surprise as he asked, "He is? What happened to your mother and father, brothers and sisters?"

"I'm afraid that's a story I would rather not speak of now," Alindra said sadly, looking down with a pained expression. "But this is not about me, it's about you." She took a little pouch out of her gown pocket and put it into Jamie's hand. "Take this with water tonight," she said. "This will clear your head and assist you in making your decision."

"But . . ." Jamie started to protest.

"Shhh," Alindra said, putting a finger to his lips. "Don't talk, just do as I say." Then she kissed him. "Remember, your heart will give you the right answer."

Before Jamie could answer, she was gone. He stood looking at the spot where she had been standing, then went into his room. He sat on the edge of his bed and stared at the ceiling. His mother came to mind and he said a silent prayer for her guidance.

Getting undressed, Jamie gave a big yawn. *I guess I'm still worn out from the battle and this whole adventure*, he thought. He poured the pouch into a glass of water and drank it in three swallows. He then climbed into bed and blew out the candle on the nightstand. As he lay in the dark going over the events of the last week, he could feel his lips tingling from Alindra's kiss. Sleep came easily, and the last thing Jamie remembered was the moon outside his window.

Tomorrow night it will be full, he thought before he drifted off to sleep. *By tomorrow I must make my decision.*

While he slept, he dreamt the most wonderful dreams. They were of mystical lands, dragons, and beautiful princesses. He dreamt of magic, sorcerers, and strange, wonderful beasts. Unlike

his previous dreams, though, these had faces and names and meanings. In the early hours of morning, he slipped into a deep sleep. He dreamt of his parents, his brother Andrew, his house, and his backyard. He dreamt of going home. Sometime before dawn, the answer came to him.

* * *

Jamie slept late into the morning. When he finally awoke, he got up and looked out his window. It was a gray and cloudy day. Storm clouds hung low on the distant horizon. In spite of the gloomy weather, his spirits were bright. *Whatever Alindra gave me to sleep last night sure did the trick,* he thought. As he stared into the distance, he thought he could hear muffled voices coming from somewhere outside his room. Jamie walked over to the dresser, cupped his hands, and took a drink from the basin of water. The water was cool to the touch and had a sweet and slightly minty taste. He washed and dried his face. It helped dispel the last few cobwebs from his brain. Jamie felt refreshed, and he finally understood the path before him. As he dressed, there was a knock on the door and a servant entered.

"The others are waiting in the garden courtyard," the servant said, bowing low. "If you will follow me?" Jamie followed the servant from his room, around a corner and down a hall until they came to a door. The servant opened it and said, "Right through here."

Jamie stepped out into the courtyard and walked to the stone table. It was a cool morning and a slight breeze blew up from the glen at the moat. Erenor, Alindra, Artimus, Barly, and PBJ talked with one another. They looked up as Jamie joined them.

"Good morning all," he said cheerfully. "I hope you all slept as well as I did." The group all said good morning to him, then continued talking.

"Well, just the same, ah think someone oughta go with 'em," PBJ said. "He's just as responsible fer returnin' that crown as the rest of us were."

"Yes, and the journey could be dangerous," Alizar said.

"What are you talking about?" Jamie asked, reaching for a slice of melon from a quartz bowl in the center of the stone table.

Erenor looked at him and said, "We are discussing Artimus's journey to the Blackmoss Forest. Like I said yesterday, for the magic to work, he has to make the journey alone. He has to prove his desire to change back to his former self."

"I agree with PBJ," Barly said. "One of us should accompany Artimus, at least part way."

"The potion dictates he go alone!" Erenor said firmly.

Jamie wiped his mouth with his sleeve and caught up with the conversation. "There's got to be a way to get around this," he offered. "What if . . . what if someone just happened to be going the same way as Artimus? Technically, they wouldn't be accompanying him, just traveling the same road at the same time."

"Well, I don't . . ." the sorcerer began. PBJ interrupted him.

"Boy's right. Me 'n' Florabel is gonna be headin' out in a day or two. We could well head the same way as Artimus, 'fore we heads back ta the mountains."

"I still don't think it will work," Erenor said.

Alindra cut in, laughing lightly. "Come, Grandpapa. You made the rules, certainly you can bend them a little."

"I agree with Jamie and PBJ," Barly said.

"I hate to say it, but you are out-voted, sir," Jamie added respectfully.

"Please, Grandpapa," Alindra said. "You said yourself that you have the power to grant almost any wish."

"Okay, okay!" the sorcerer said, holding his hands up. "Unlike Druin, I can see when I'm out numbered. PBJ, you can *accidentally* travel with Artimus as far as the Distant Hills. From there, Artimus is on his own. Is that agreed?"

They both agreed. "Well, that takes care of those two. But what about Kip?" Jamie asked. "Will someone travel to old Charmac's obac and check on his and Koki's recovery? And also say hi and give my sincerest thanks to Deena and her parents? They were most helpful to me and Barly."

"I will see to that," Alindra answered. "I will be the one to journey to the village of the L'masse. We and the people of Mistemere need to reestablish the bonds that were broken so long ago. And on my way, I'll inspect Lake Longwater to make sure there is no longer trouble there."

"That's a good idea. Alindra, when you see Kip, tell him I'm going to get another kite and name it in his honor. After all, if he hadn't known the answer to the troll's riddle, there's no telling how this adventure would have ended up," Jamie said.

He turned to the bear. "Barly, what about you? What will you do? Have you made any plans?"

"That depends," the big bear replied. "It depends on what you are going to do, Jamie."

"What do you mean?" Jamie asked.

"Are you going home or are you going to stay with us in Neverlore?" Alindra asked. "I'm beginning to like you, even if you are an outlander," she teased.

The group looked at him expectantly. "Last night I . . . I had the best dreams I've dreamt in a long, long time," Jamie began hesitatingly. "When I woke up this morning, I finally realized many things that probably have been in front of me all along. I just couldn't see them because other issues kept getting in the way. It may not be perfect at home, but even Neverlore, my biggest fantasy come true, isn't perfect, either. For the first time I can see that my wheelchair isn't the *end* to my life, just a different way of *getting* me there. I think I can enjoy every minute now, no matter what. Does any of this make sense to anyone?" Jamie was having a hard time putting his feelings into words.

"I believe I know what you are trying to say," Erenor answered. "You don't have to explain to us. Like I said, you are the only one you must be true to."

"I've learned so much in Neverlore, but mostly I've learned about myself," Jamie continued. "I may not be able to speak of this place when I'm gone, but I can sure think of the lessons I've learned here. The challenges I previously faced in my wheelchair at home pale in comparison to those that I faced and tackled here. If I can overcome them in Neverlore, I can overcome them at home or school or anywhere else."

"Those are profound and wise words," Artimus said.

"I suppose they are," Jamie replied. "It's still somewhat confusing, but I think the lessons I learned in Neverlore were the *real* purpose of my journey and the battle. I guess a wish *can* contain a much deeper, much better consequence than what one originally wished for.

"And, as you've probably already guessed, I've decided I must leave this wonderful land. My own home is where I belong. With that being said, how will I get home, Erenor? Are you going to cast a spell over me or something?"

"No, actually, it's easier than you think. Between now and midnight, as the moon is in its full phase, all you must do is return to the tree and go back through the door," the sorcerer said. "I've employed some sorcery to make this happen."

"Oh right! How am I going to do that in such a short time? *Fly?*" Jamie said, laughing. "Not counting the time we spent with the L'masse, it took us over three days to get here in the first place."

"That's exactly how you are going to do it," Alizar said. "I'm going to take you there, and Barly's going along with us."

"Wow! We *can* fly! I'd forgotten about that!" Jamie said joyfully. "This will be a fitting end to my adventure."

"Then it's settled," Erenor said. "All you have to do is climb on Alizar when you are ready. I've created a special key for Barly so he can go with you and unlock the door. And now, the oath. Put your right hand over your heart. Do you, Jamie Nichols, an outlander, solemnly swear not to divulge any of what you've seen or learned to any other mortal on your planet as long as you live?"

"I solemnly swear," Jamie promised. His joy quickly vanished as he looked around the table. The time he had been dreading had finally come. They had become close friends and shared so much together. He was going to miss them all, especially Barly. Jamie was glad the big bear was staying with him to the end.

"Well, I guess there's not much sense in waiting any longer," he said. "Can I take my backpack with me, Erenor, or does that have to stay?"

The sorcerer laughed and reached under the table. He pulled out Jamie's pack and slid it across the table. "No, you can take it with you. Hopefully, we won't be fighting any battles for a long time."

Jamie took his backpack and slipped it on. He said nothing. Around him, all fell silent. The only sound was a bee buzzing in a nearby flower. He closed his eyes for a moment. Jamie could see his mother standing in the backyard looking for him. She was extremely worried. He shook his head to clear his thoughts.

"Well then, I guess this is it." He walked over and shook PBJ's hand. "Thank you for helping us," he said. "If you hadn't come along when you did, who knows what would have happened. Give Florabel a hug for me."

"Shucks, boy, I'm the one that should be a-thankin' ya. Who knows, if'n ya 'n' Artimus here hadn't been hidin' 'hind that rock, me 'n' Florabel may-a ended up where Barly did. Coulda just been you 'n' Artimus who done the savin'. You take care of yerself now, ya hear?" The little prospector's voice cracked.

"I will, I promise," Jamie said. He walked over to Artimus. "I wish I could go with you to find the Mumbo-jumbo tree," he said.

"Gumble-limbor," Artimus corrected him, laughing.

"Whatever," Jamie continued. "Anyway, I hope your journey is safe and you can break the spell you're under. I'm sorry I won't be here to see you as your real self. Goodbye, Artimus, I'll miss you." He hugged the big frog.

"Goodbye, Jamie. I'll think of you often," Artimus said. His big frog eyes misted over and he had to blow his nose.

Jamie then walked to Erenor. "Thank you, Erenor, my friend, for everything you've done for all of us. I'll always remember Neverlore, even in my dreams." He took the sorcerer's hand and kissed it.

"Go in peace, young Jamie Nichols. Never think for a moment that you didn't make the right decision. You have a whole life before you with your real family. I have a feeling things will be different with them now." Erenor reached out and squeezed Jamie's shoulder. For an instant, Jamie felt the same warmth from the sorcerer's hand that he'd felt from Alindra's the night before. Jamie turned to Alindra.

"You are a beautiful princess, and I am glad we had time to spend together. Who knows, if things had turned out different . . ." Jamie's voice trailed off. He pulled her to him and kissed her on the cheek. "Please tell Kip that if it wasn't for him, all this wouldn't have been possible. Tell him I hope he flies like an eagle every time he takes to the skies." He hugged her tightly, close to tears.

"Goodbye, Jamie. I think I'm going to miss you, too," Alindra said.

Jamie turned to Alizar. "Let's go before I do something stupid," he said in a hoarse voice. He walked over to the big dragon and climbed on his back. Barly followed and climbed on behind Jamie. "Hurry, dragon! Take off before I change my mind."

"Hold on then," Alizar said. Giving two or three mighty flaps of his great wings, they were airborne. He flapped harder, and they circled the courtyard before heading up over the castle walls.

"Goodbye, everyone! I love you all!" Jamie shouted.

"Goodbye, Jamie, we'll miss you!" They all waved up at him as Alizar cleared the wall. Then they were gone.

The air was cool, and the feel of it rushing past his face helped ease his anguish somewhat. As they flew higher, Jamie stared down at the countryside. He felt regret, but also felt a rush from riding on the dragon's back. *I don't know of anyone back home who can say they have ever done this,* he thought. *But I guess it makes no difference anyway. I took an oath not to tell.*

Jamie was surprised to find that the leather tunic was quite warm in spite of the cool air rushing by them. He adjusted his backpack to keep it from flapping and settled in for the ride. Alizar flew back over the neat stone houses and shops, and over the stone wall surrounding the city. He flew into the gray, misty clouds at the mountain's edge and dropped toward the foothills. Soon they were below the clouds, flying toward the River Crystal. Jamie and Barly spent the time reminiscing over their grand adventure.

They passed over the River Crystal and turned south. Back over the fields of brightly colored flowers, over the Fangling Forest to the meadow of the Treesers. Here Alizar turned to the east and passed over Robinwood, Lake Longwater, and the troll's bridge. At last they came to the pond where Jamie and Barly had first met.

Alizar settled down on the path by the pond. When the dust cleared, Jamie slowly climbed off and looked around. It appeared as if nothing had changed the whole time they had been gone. The fish line from his kite was still lying where Barly had thrown it. His wheelchair was still sitting where he had left it, and the beech tree was still there. Jamie turned to his friends. "Well, this is it, I guess," he said. "Oh Barly, Alizar, this is so hard!"

Barly climbed off and stood next to him. "Yes, I know. I'll truly miss you, Jamie." He laid a paw on Jamie's shoulders. "When you cross the barrier, don't forget about us and the land of Neverlore, because we'll never forget about you."

"How could I ever forget any of you?" Jamie asked. He looked past Barly at the kite string. "I sure hope Kip survived. Will you make sure Alindra sees him? Make sure she says goodbye for me."

"I'll be sure to do that," the big bear replied. "After all, what are friends for?"

"What are friends for," Jamie echoed. "Good. Then I guess everything's settled."

"There is one last thing, I'm sorry to say," Barly said.

"What's that?" Jamie asked.

"You'll have to give me the leather tunic and the sea stone Deena gave you," Barly said. "Remember, nothing from Neverlore but you and your memories can cross over to your side."

"Yeah, I guess you're right," Jamie said reluctantly. He took off his backpack and tucked it under his wheelchair. He took off the tunic, pulled out his necklace, and handed both to Barly. Choking back a sob, he said, "This is really it." He wrapped his arms as far around Barly as he could. "Let's get this over with before I start crying."

Jamie walked over to the dragon and patted him on the side. "Goodbye, Alizar. I didn't get to know you very well, but I appreciate all that you've done for all of us. I hope people really do accept you for who you are now, and don't judge you for what you were in the past. You really *are* a good dragon."

"That's kind of you to say, lad. Take care of yourself also," Alizar said. A big tear rolled down his scaly face and plopped onto the dust.

Jamie walked to his wheelchair, stared at it for a minute, then sat down. It felt strange and unnatural to him now. "I guess I'm as ready as I never wanted to be, Barly. Let's do it."

Barly grabbed the handles and pushed Jamie back up the path to the tree. He removed the skeleton key that had been hanging around his neck and held it against the tree. Suddenly, the door and the lock reappeared. Barly stuck the key in and turned it. The lock gave a *click* and the door opened a crack. Jamie grabbed the doorknob.

"One last thing before I go," Jamie said. "When you get back, what are *you* going to wish for?"

Barly looked at Jamie with a misty twinkle in his eye. "I think I'll save my wish for a rainy day," he answered. "You never know when you're going to need something like that to get you out of a jam."

"Well, I hope it does just that," Jamie said. "Thank everyone once again for me. I'll see you all in my dreams." Jamie's voice shook and tears welled in his eyes.

"Goodbye, Jamie," Barly said. "You helped me more than you'll ever know."

With that, Jamie pushed the door open. Barly gave the wheelchair a shove and sent him over the threshold. *WHOOSH!* A strong gust of wind blew the door shut behind his chair. Then the door vanished as though it had never been there at all.

Jamie was suddenly very dizzy, and everything went black for a moment. He felt like he was rushing through a long, dark tunnel toward a very dim light at the end. As he approached the light, he slipped into a dreamlike state. Everything that had happened over the last several days became a blur, then momentarily disappeared from his mind.

Chapter 21

Jamie woke up and found himself sitting in his wheelchair under the beech tree.

"Wow! I must have fallen asleep," he exclaimed, rubbing his eyes. He looked at the fishing line dangling in front of him. "I wonder where that stupid kite is," he added. He wheeled back toward the edge of the clearing to get a better look.

"Well, it must have blown further into the woods than I thought." Just then, the memories of his adventure in Neverlore flooded back into his mind and he gasped at the recollection. Jamie sat for a few confusing moments recalling his unbelievable adventure. It all now seemed like a dream. He glanced through the crack into the hollow trunk.

longer there.

How will I ever explain this *to anyone?* he asked himself. Then Jamie remembered his promise. "I guess I won't have to worry about

that," he sighed. At that moment, he heard a familiar voice off in the distance.

"*Jaaammiieee!* Where are you? *Jaaammmieee!*" His mother's voice carried on the breeze. Jamie glanced at his watch.

"Oh man! I've been gone for over five hours!" he exclaimed. He turned his wheelchair around and pushed it rapidly.

"Here I am, Mom! Here I am!" he cried. He pushed his wheels harder and headed back through the brush toward the path. Jamie was out of breath when he finally wheeled himself back up the path and through the gate to the vacant lot. His mother glared at him with her arms crossed.

"Where have you been, young man?" she asked, angrily looking down at him. "I was scared to death when you didn't show up for lunch."

"Gosh, I'm sorry, Mom," Jamie said. "The fishing line broke and my kite sailed into the woods, and I thought I could find it. I guess I was so tired after pushing myself down the path that I . . . that I must have fallen asleep. I didn't realize I'd been gone so long."

"Well, I should hope you're sorry. I called your dad and was just about to call the police. I had no idea what happened to you," his mother said.

"Mom, I said I was sorry. I'll let you know next time," Jamie said. "I'm almost thirteen now. I *can* do stuff myself, you know. You can't follow me around forever."

His mother stared at him for a moment, then gave him a big hug. "Okay, as long as you're alright. But don't do something like this again without telling me first, please," she said. "Remember, in spite of what you think, you *can't* do it all."

"Well, if you'd give me more of a chance, you'd be surprised at how much I've learned and what I can do. I'm getting older and there's more to me than you know, Mom," Jamie said, somewhat annoyed. "Can we go get some lunch? I'm really hungry."

His mother laughed. "Okay, okay. There's no need to get huffy. I guess I've been treating you like a little kid for too long. It's just hard for me to accept that you're growing up. I guess I want to protect you as long as possible. But it's a little late for lunch, so I'll make you a snack. That should hold you over until dinner."

"Thanks, Mom. And remember, I want to do more stuff by myself now," Jamie replied. He felt unusually tired, and it was all he could do to wheel back to his house. His mother saw this and began pushing. In spite of his newfound independence, Jamie was glad for her help.

After his snack, Jamie spent the rest of the afternoon in his room napping and reading his outdoor magazines. Dinnertime came, and he listened to Andrew talk about his ball game and his latest girlfriend. His father was out of town as usual.

After playing with his food for a while, Jamie found he wasn't that hungry. His brother's chatter was also beginning to irritate him. Jamie excused himself from the table and wheeled his chair down the hall to his room. His mother followed him to his room and kissed him lightly on the cheek.

"Everything alright?" she asked. "You didn't eat very much at dinner tonight."

Jamie thought for a moment, then answered, "It seems that ever since my accident, no one ever has time to spend with me. Dad's never home and Andrew always has more important things to do than spend time with me. It's not like it used to be. I guess I'm going back to doing some of the things I'd given up after my accident. Like going fishing with Uncle Chuck or . . . or maybe even entering the wheelchair race during the Blueberry Festival. Mom, I'm not afraid anymore."

"I'm glad to hear it," his mother replied, somewhat puzzled at his statements.

Back in his room, Jamie read for a while more, then got ready for bed. He brushed his teeth and was climbing from his wheelchair into bed when his mother came to say good night.

"I had a talk with your brother a little while ago," she said. "You're right, Jamie. It's hard to admit, but we've been letting your handicap get in the way of family time together. Your father doesn't have the time for any of us it seems, but the rest is going to change. That is, if you think you're up to it."

"It's okay. I didn't mean to sound ungrateful, but things *are* starting to change," Jamie said. "I'm growing up, I guess. I may have a handicap, but I'm still my own person. My wheelchair is a way of life for me, and I'm not going to let it keep me from enjoying that life for any reason. When you think of it, the word 'handicap' is just a label, not a barrier." He yawned. "Thanks for caring, Mom. I love you."

"I love you too, Jamie." She kissed him on the forehead, turned off his light, and left his room. She had a look of concern on her face as she walked down the stairs. Her son was acting strangely. All that talk about growing up and being his own person was new to her. She wondered where he got it from. *Maybe he's hanging out with somebody new at school,* she thought. "Maybe he *is* growing up," she sighed.

Jamie could hardly keep his eyes open. The full moon shone through his window and bathed his room in pale light. Even that didn't keep him awake. He rolled over, gave one last yawn, and fell asleep.

Jamie dreamt of many new things that night. He dreamt he rejoined the scouts and started camping again. He had a dream where he went white-water kayaking in the mountains. He also dreamt he contacted the manufacturers of his e-Cubix game with plans for a new battle scene involving a dragon and sorcerer. In all his dreams his paralysis no longer hindered his ability to have fun.

A little while later, Jamie's mother stepped into his room to check on him. She looked at her son wistfully for a minute. In the moonlight, he looked different. Older maybe, more mature, if that was possible.

When she left, she brushed against Jamie's backpack and, as the door closed, it fell over onto the floor. One of the pockets flipped open and two round pebbles dropped out. They rolled through the moonlight and came to rest against the back wall under his bed. In the dark they began to glow a soft, blue light. Jamie stirred slightly and rolled over.

"I promise I'll be back someday, Barly," he called out softly in his sleep, then slipped into a deep, deep dream. The pebbles glowed for a moment or two longer, then their light slowly faded.

Outside, a breeze sprang up. Beyond Jamie's yard, down the hill and into Whispering Valley it blew. The branches of the great trees rustled and murmured at its passing and somewhere off in the distance a lone wolf howled. Unbeknownst to Jamie, his journey hadn't ended, it had just begun.